Rhythm of the Tide

Ruth Saberton

Paperback Edition 1

Ruth Saberton

Copyright

CHAPTER 1

"So what do you think about this property? It's close to the shops and only ten minutes' walk to the station," declared the estate agent. "It's a reasonable rent too."

The Reverend Jules Mathieson knew fibbing was frowned upon, but there was something about this hopeful young man armed with his clipboard and shiny suit that made her loathe to let him down, which was crazy since he was the one showing a property even a self-respecting cockroach would baulk at. Somebody less concerned about protecting the feelings of others would have read him the riot act at least two hovels ago.

"It's certainly bigger than the last one you showed us," Jules ventured. This wasn't strictly a fib. The previous property hadn't room to swing a hamster. As she'd squeezed into the miniscule kitchen, Jules had needed to turn sideways just to fit between the units.

"There's a lovely garden too which has a nice bit of sun in the afternoon. Having outside space in London is a real plus," said the estate agent as he wrestled to open the swollen back door. On the third shove, it gave up the fight and he staggered forward triumphantly. "There! Your own patio! Come and enjoy the fresh air."

A listless city breeze, tainted with the smell of stale fat from the café next door, drifted into the flat with about as much enthusiasm as Jules was feeling. She thought longingly of the sharp gusts of sea-kissed air that blew into her vicarage back home in Cornwall and it felt as though an ice cream scoop was scraping out her insides. Oh dear. It didn't bode well that she was homesick for Polwenna Bay before she'd even moved away.

"Come and have a look," urged the estate agent. "Imagine sitting out here on a lovely summer's day."

Jules was doing her utmost not to imagine this. High above her, aeroplanes instead of seagulls were circling in the blue sky, and rather than

5

hearing waves crashing onto the beach, the backing track here was the rumble of lorries on the main road and the irate tooting of car horns. Litter not valerian bloomed in this garden and the only grass visible was that brave enough to peek out between the cracks in the concrete. A couple of broken bottles glittered in the sunshine as they reposed beside upturned milk crates moonlighting as garden furniture.

I must try to be thankful, Jules thought. This was a little slice of outside living and with a bit of work, and a huge amount of imagination, she was certain she could make the courtyard look nice. Looking on the bright side, maybe that graffiti was a Banksy? It was certainly different. What on earth was a cnut? Some obscure Viking king doing his best to stop the tide of urban sprawl? A fan of peanuts? And why was Keith Davis one? And who was Keith Davis anyway? It would certainly be something to ponder while she sat on a milk crate and sunbathed, and a change from reading the parish newsletter.

"What do you think?" said the estate agent hopefully.

"It's interesting," said Jules's fiancé, Danny Tremaine, who was doing his best not to catch her eye.

Jules could tell Danny knew as well as she did that this flat was not going to be their new London home but, like her, he never liked to let people down or be rude. Even when a previous letting agent mentioned that a ground-floor maisonette was perfect for 'a disabled person like him', Dan had simply smiled politely, and it was Jules who'd wanted to shake the agent until her veneers fell off. Danny was a decorated veteran. How dare anyone patronise him!

Jules had to pray very hard for patience that day. Patience was never her strong point anyway, but when she caught people whispering about or staring at her wonderful, brave, strong fiancé, it was like a match to paper. Dan had been through horrors Jules didn't want to imagine and she would have bet anything that if this tango-tanned blonde had met Danny before he'd been injured, and seen him in all his uniformed glory, she'd have been batting her eyelids and simpering, not talking about handrails and wet rooms.

"You've seen the garden and the sitting room," said today's agent, shepherding Jules and Danny back indoors and locking the door behind them. One mortise lock and two Chubbs, as well as a multitude of window security. Jules had a sinking feeling – after three years in Polwenna, she was out of practice when it came to home security. In the village, most doors were left open and security was down to the likes of Keyhole Kathy or the Pollards, who never missed a trick. It would also be a very fit burglar who'd attempt to rob the houses in Polwenna, most of which you couldn't get a car near and were built high into the hillside. Dan often joked that any aspiring thief would have a heart attack by the time they'd climbed up to his family home and probably end up suing.

It was easy to laugh about such things in a village where the nearest thing to a robbery was seagulls dive-bombing holidaymakers for pasties and ice creams. It wasn't quite so funny when you were back in the city and listening to police sirens.

"There's a good-sized master bedroom," continued the estate agent, ushering them into a dark cave with the smallest of windows and a huge splodge of damp on the wall that wouldn't have looked out of place in a Dickensian slum. Jules gulped.

"It's a little gloomy today, but it could be lovely and bright with some imagination," chirruped the estate agent.

But this was pushing it too far, even for Danny.

"I think even J K Rowling would struggle to imagine this place as anything other than damp and squalid," he said. "It's not for us, I'm afraid."

The agent sighed. "With all due respect, Mr Tremaine, I've shown you every property within your budget. This is a very competitive rental market and you're on a tight and limited budget."

"So you keep telling me," Danny said, and this time he did catch Jules's gaze and she knew he was thinking since when was one thousand pounds a month a tight budget? The answer was, of course, since they would be starting London life living on his army wage while she spoke to the local archdeacons and applied for permission to officiate on a temporary basis. There would be no vicarage to live in and Danny also had a financial commitment to his son, Morgan. At this rate, they'd make the church mice in St Wenn's look loaded.

"Properties like this don't hang around," said the agent.

"I don't doubt it for a minute. They must be lining up to be condemned," Danny replied. "I think we've seen enough. What do you reckon, Jules?"

Jules reckoned she'd be having nightmares for months.

"I don't think it's for us," she said.

The agent nodded. "Fine. What exactly are you looking for?"

"Anything without peeling wallpaper and damp?" Danny suggested wearily. "And maybe a little nearer to the West End?"

"I'm afraid that's simply not possible within the rental margin you've given me," said the agent, who had just about managed not to laugh at this request. "Why don't you go and have a coffee and think about all the places you've viewed today? The one near Acton has potential."

"To be flattened," muttered Danny.

The agent chose to ignore his comment.

"I think the one in Park Royal could be a possibility too. It had all the space you've asked for."

There would certainly be work for her in those areas, Jules thought. She would hand in her notice at St Wenn's and then approach the new diocese. Maybe her bishop back in Cornwall could put in a good word? She knew he was pleased with how the number of worshippers had increased since she'd been the vicar of St Wenn's and, the awkward incident of the Polwenna Bay naked charity calendar aside, Jules thought she'd done a good job. Oh dear. She'd really miss her parish when she left.

A lump tightened in her throat and Jules had to pretend to be fascinated by the limescale build-up on the taps while she fought another tsunami of sadness. This made no sense. She was going to marry the man she loved and they were starting a new life together. It was wonderful and exciting. It was a big adventure.

Even so, Jules would miss Polwenna Bay and the people she'd come to love there. The village and her parishioners had crept into her heart and taken hold there with the same determination and quiet stealth as the ivy which grew over the church porch. Jules was even fond of difficult customers like her bossy verger Sheila Keverne and the Pollards – the wily father and son building duo who caused her no end of grief with their bodged repairs to the church and the vicarage. Yes, Jules was in no doubt about it; she would miss her Cornish life.

She gave herself a mental shake. This was crazy. Polwenna Bay would always be there and she and Dan would be going back to visit regularly. His family lived there and his son too, so there would be lots of trips home. This new army desk job meant the world to Danny, and because Danny meant everything to Jules, she was going to support him each step of the way even if deep, deep down she would rather be staying in Cornwall. Jules had prayed a great deal about their move and she felt sure that if it was meant to be, then everything would work out.

Hmm. Or were all these dreadful flats a very strange answer to her prayers? Was this her Boss's way of saying stay put?

Probably not. This was more likely a case of cold, hard reality saying London life needed them to earn more money. At some point, they'd surely be able to find a home that suited them and Jules knew there were more important matters at stake than where they lived. The main thing was they would start married life together, a much better option than being over two hundred miles apart and having to snatch weekends – not the easiest thing to do if you were a vicar and working on a Sunday was key to your job. She simply had to keep faith and trust that the right house would come to them.

Once the agent had locked up and driven away, Jules and Danny headed for the nearest café where they settled down for a council of war. While Danny spread the estate agent's leaflets onto the sticky table, Jules tipped sugar into her coffee and chose to ignore her diet. Outside, the sun was sulking behind swollen clouds and the entire street, from the gum-speckled pavement to the depressed-looking pigeons, was colour washed in a variation on the theme of grey.

She had the distinct impression it was metaphorical.

Since Danny had proposed, Jules's life had hurtled into fast forward and they had started to make plans for the future. The idea was that Danny would move to London first and commute home at weekends while Jules worked out her notice. Once they were married, she would also move to the city. Their wedding was booked for Christmas and the clock was ticking. London nerves aside, it was all very exciting and Jules couldn't wait to be Mrs Daniel Tremaine. Their marriage was what counted. Surely where they lived was just a minor detail?

"So what do you think?" Danny was asking now. "Anything stand out for you – in a good way, I mean?"

Jules struggled for something positive to say. "The one near Ladbroke Grove wasn't bad."

Dan frowned. "Do you think? I wasn't keen on the thought of you walking through that estate to get to it. It looked rough."

"I'll probably be working there, Dan. There's always a huge need for outreach and pastoral support in deprived areas. Look on it as a short commute."

"I guess I'm just being overprotective. How about the maisonette in Acton?"

"That one was really damp," Jules reminded him and her fiancé sighed.

"Indoor water features aren't all they're cracked up to be, that's for sure. This search isn't going so well, is it?"

"We'll find somewhere that's right for us," Jules said and with far more conviction than she was actually feeling. "We just need to keep looking. The perfect place will come up."

"Do you really think so? Seriously, are you sure you want to do this? I'm asking you to give up so much. Your job. Your friends. Living in Cornwall…"

"I'm not giving anything up because I'm going to be with you!"

"But maybe we should wait until I've found somewhere better for us? Perhaps I'm making a mistake taking this job?"

Danny looked so downcast that Jules knew she had to push her own worries away. This move was something she knew he wanted, needed even, and she had to support him all the way. He'd sacrificed so much and nobody deserved this new opportunity more.

"We've talked about this already and it makes more sense for us to move here together. We need to find a base so that I can look for a new parish. You're not due to start until September and by the time I join you in December, we'll have found the perfect place, I promise."

"You really believe that?"

"Of course I do," she said firmly. This wasn't a fib. They would find somewhere perfect. Jules was praying very hard about it and her Boss never let her down. Sometimes His solutions weren't quite what she expected, but that was all part of trusting and having faith.

Dan smiled at her. "You really want to do this, don't you?"

"Absolutely," said Jules.

And she meant it. If moving to London made Danny happy, then Jules really wanted to move too; it was that simple. She just wished her heart didn't sink quite so much at the thought of it. Fortunately Danny was too busy stuffing the leaflets into his leather satchel to catch the bleak expression on her face.

"I'll give the agent another bell to see what else he can come up with. Maybe we can stretch to another hundred a month? That might help." He glanced at his watch and raised his eyebrows. "We'd better get moving if we're going to meet Zak and still make the last train home."

Danny's musician brother was in London for a big awards ceremony. He lived a glamorous life travelling around the world, recording music and partying hard. 'British Country' was how Dan described his brother's music, a blend of Nashville country and British folk, and now he was solo, it was rumoured that Zak was headed for big things, especially in the States. Dan said that this was Zak's dream come true and that his brother had always lived for music. Jules had met Zak a couple of times when his schedule allowed, and with his sleepy blue eyes, mop of golden curls and fondness for drink, he'd reminded her of a Botticelli angel who'd had a few too many and liked chatting up cherubs. Women found him impossible to resist and Jules could see why. Zak had bad boy appeal in bucket loads.

"I'd cry off," Danny continued once they left the café and were deep in the underground system, "only Granny says he sounded really low when she spoke to him. It's probably jet lag and a hangover, but I know she'll appreciate it if we see him."

The thought of having to socialise when she was tired and grubby wasn't appealing, but Jules knew how much Alice Tremaine worried about her grandchildren. It didn't matter that they were all adults; in fact, Alice often said this made things worse.

"I can't make things better with a plaster or a kiss these days," she would sigh.

Jules loved Alice, and in order to put her mind at rest could put up with a couple of hours in a trendy bar. Besides, Jules reflected as she and Danny stood on the platform and waited for their train, socialising in trendy bars was all part of London life, wasn't it?

It was high time she started getting in practice.

CHAPTER TWO

About seven miles away as the seagull flies, Zak Tremaine was lying on his king-size hotel bed and working his way through the contents of the mini bar. So far he'd had the peanuts, the Baileys and the Smirnoff. He was now contemplating the tiny bottle of champagne, daft really since all he had to do was lift the phone and summon room service to deliver a magnum of the real thing.

The cinema-sized television was playing MTV to itself, the massive spa bath was as yet untried and even the complimentary massage hadn't tempted him. The problem was that after almost eighteen months of trundling from hotel room to hotel room, these things no longer felt like treats. They certainly weren't the novelty they'd once been when, wide-eyed and fresh from Cornwall, he'd first stayed in a plush hotel. That young man, who'd been so excited and who had snapped pictures of everything on his phone to upload them to his Instagram and Facebook page and email to his granny, felt like another person altogether. Life as a professional musician had seemed like such a big adventure back then and the whole world felt like it was there for the taking. Everyone was telling him that it still was, but the sparkle was well and truly gone. These days Zak just felt tired, and one luxurious hotel room was pretty much like another. The same sealed air (windows didn't ever open in these places), the same featureless luxury, the same rush to get to the next venue. Some days he was so close to just walking out the door and catching the train home that it was terrifying.

Home... Zak closed his eyes for a moment and allowed himself the luxury of thinking about Cornwall. Home was where skies were wide and open rather than stuffed between skyscrapers and sooty chimneys. It was where the air was knife sharp with salt and buffeting wind, and where the waves rolled onto the sand in a never-ending rhythm. Home was where he could walk for miles along the cliffs and not see a soul. It was the magical place where he could hear melodies in the calling of the seabirds and catch music in the whispers of the past. Home was where Zak would sit on a bench overlooking the bay while the new harmonies played in his mind, each note as pure and as in tune with the landscape as the elements. When he'd lived in Cornwall, Zak's creativity had been on overload; music and lyrics had poured from him like the waters of the River Wenn through the village, and he'd loved playing in the local pub in return for a couple of pints and a ploughman's. If Zak had ever dared to order champagne in The Ship, the landlord would have laughed at him, and the fishermen, always gathered round the farthest end of the bar, would have taken the mickey out of his pretentiousness for the next couple of decades.

Zak sighed. They'd be right too, but when he was twenty-five, being able to drink champagne and stay in top hotels had been the dream. Nickelback sang about it, didn't they? And now here he was with success at his guitar string-calloused fingertips. Leaving Polwenna Bay and breaking up his original band was the price he had to pay for success because everyone knew that Cornwall, although beautiful, was a career backwater.

For as long as he could remember, being a musician was all Zak Tremaine had wanted. Nothing else mattered. To his grandmother's despair, he'd dropped out of college at seventeen and formed a country-style band called The Tinners. With his friends, Ned and Ollie, Zak had played the pub and working men's club circuit instead of studying for his A levels. It was an education of a very different kind and there wasn't much Zak Tremaine didn't know about dodging flying beer mats, making sure landlords paid up and getting off with the prettiest girls. Yes, especially that. Women loved a lead singer and Zak loved women. It had been as though he was a chocoholic given the keys to Cadbury World and Zak was only too happy to gorge. He was young, handsome and talented, so it seemed ungrateful not to enjoy every minute.

Zak had always known that playing with The Tinners was just the first step on the ladder to fame and fortune, but when he looked back on those early days, he was almost floored by nostalgia. Regrets spiked his conscience almost daily and although he did his best to push them away, Zak knew he'd behaved badly. When had he last heard from his former bandmates? Properly heard, not just gleaned information through the Polwenna grapevine or his sisters? Ned was engaged now and working for a bank, and the last Zak had heard of Ollie, he was a tree surgeon in New Zealand. Neither had pursued a career in music and Zak couldn't blame them. He had let them down.

He gripped the remote control tightly as though trying to crush any regrets. Life was good. Amazing. He was here in London and staying at one of the city's most exclusive hotels. He'd had lunch at The Ivy with his manager and was attending a star-studded awards ceremony tonight. Then he'd party the night away at one of London's trendiest clubs, surrounded by beautiful girls and with vintage champagne on tap. Sex, drugs and rock 'n' roll. This was the dream, right?

But the reality was that no, it wasn't. Meaningless flings were starting to pall, he preferred Pol Brew to bubbles and when it came to drugs, Zak, an all-or-nothing person, was utterly terrified by the mere thought. He wasn't naïve; in his world, they were easily available and Zak knew plenty of people who weren't averse to a line or two of coke. Sometimes when he was so exhausted he needed drumsticks to keep his eyes open, Zak could understand the attraction, but he'd never once been tempted to partake. Thank goodness he always had Granny Alice's disapproving voice ringing in his ears. The telling off she'd given him and his sister Mo when she'd caught them smoking had been bad enough.

He sighed again. Zak hadn't known it then, but those days of being under his grandmother's beady eye, the long nights of gigging until his throat was raw, his arms aching from lugging equipment through narrow streets and up twisty staircases, and the haphazard journeys across the South West in the band's temperamental old VW camper van, would turn out to be some of the happiest times he'd have in the business. He'd been too busy dreaming about success to appreciate just how good it was to be living at home and making music with his friends. Possibilities had stretched before them as golden and as glorious as the long summer days. How ironic that the dream of success had turned out to be sweeter than the real thing. Whoever it was who'd said it was better to travel than to arrive had known what they were talking about.

The Tinners had eventually been scouted, just as Zak had always known they would be. A holidaying A and R man from Alchemist Records, one of the biggest labels, had come across them during the Polwenna Festival. He'd listened to the whole set, bought a round of drinks and swiftly promised they'd be the next Zac Brown Band if they signed with him. Unable to believe their luck, they'd been only too happy to agree and before long had been off to London, bound for fame and fortune.

Unfortunately, this was where the happy rags-to-riches story started to unravel...

Zak screwed up the empty peanut wrapper, lobbed it at the waste paper basket and missed. This felt horribly metaphorical. It was an easy target, he was perfectly placed to hit it and the only thing messing up was him. Here he was with everything he'd ever wanted, only to discover he didn't want it nearly as much as he'd thought. What was the point of all this if you were on your own? And how could you write from the soul when the place that inspired you was out of reach? American country singers wrote about home, dirt roads, blue jeans and fried chicken, and so it only stood to reason that Zak needed to write about winding lanes, muddy wellington boots and pasties. His manager was pushing him to target the US market, but how could Zak write about the States when it was Cornwall that moved him? Anything else wasn't true to him or to his audience.

It was an ongoing row and not one that he could win. Not if he wanted to sign a new contract.

Zak swung his legs over the side of the bed and hauled himself across the suite to an ornate gilt mirror that could have been pinched from Versailles. The reflection peering back at him looked as though it hadn't had a decent night's sleep since the days of Marie Antoinette. His jaw was speckled with stubble and his blonde curls were lank and tangled. Considering he'd left LA just over twenty-four hours ago groomed to perfection and tanned from a month recording in the sunshine, Zak decided jet lag had a lot to answer for.

He'd better sort himself out since he was meant to be meeting his big brother Danny for a drink. Dan was ex-army and always looked neat and groomed, so Zak felt he needed to make an effort. Just to add a little more pressure, Danny was engaged to a vicar, a profession which made a sinner like Zak feel rather antsy. Jules was great, but Zak was convinced that along with the dog collar she also possessed special sin-detecting powers. Would she know that he hadn't texted that pretty brunette back and owed his granny several phone calls? And would she sense his constant guilt at breaking up his band in order to pursue his own success?

Tossing his shirt, jeans and boxers into a heap on the bathroom floor, Zak cranked the shower up to almost scalding and stepped under the steaming jets, but no matter how hard he tried, he knew that just like Lady Macbeth, he couldn't scrub his guilt away. It was with him all the time and it was the reason he was finding it harder and harder to tease lyrics from his soul and sing from his heart.

After a couple of months in London, writing lyrics and laying down tracks, it had soon become clear that the record company didn't have a vision for the band at all and were only interested in Zak. The hastily signed contract gave the record bosses ultimate control regarding the future of The Tinners and when they decided it was a solo act they wanted, there wasn't anything Zak could do; his friends were sent home with their dreams in tatters.

Actually, that was bollocks. Zak could have told Alchemist to stick it where the sun doesn't shine. If there was no contract for his friends, he could have said he wasn't interested either. But Zak hadn't done this. Instead, he'd let his friends down. Doing his utmost to put any guilt aside, Zak had signed a two-year solo contract and channelled all his energy into writing new songs. He'd been teamed with Alex Evans, one of the hottest talents in the industry, as well as some exceptionally talented session musicians, and the result was British Country music he was hugely proud of. So far, he'd heard himself touted as a 'hot Ed Sheeran' and 'the British Keith Urban', and although both labels were hugely flattering, they also left Zak disconcerted because he didn't want to be under the shadow of either of these artists – he wanted to be himself. Zak's own music was a blend of country and rock with a twist of folk thrown in, and it was his and his alone. When he was in the band he'd had creative control, but now he was the record company's property. The latest rumour on the ground was that they didn't think his sound was 'commercial' enough and yesterday his manager had told Zak they wanted him back in the studio to re-record some tracks in a more 'current' style.

What the hell did that mean? Rap? R&B? One bloody Direction?

No way. His music had to have integrity.

Zak scrubbed harder and let the water run over his face and gush over his body, but it didn't help or make him feel any better. He'd let his band down and he should have told the record company that it was all three of them or nothing. The truth of the matter was that going it alone wasn't nearly as much fun. The city was a lonely place when you were on your own.

At the risk of sounding like a spoilt brat, Zak Tremaine was growing exceedingly tired of awards ceremonies, champagne receptions and hotels. He'd had enough of never sleeping in the same place for long and, although he would never have believed it once, there were only so many hours you could pass with beautiful yet vacuous women. It was like eating fast food – great for a short while, but not very satisfying and very bad for you in the long run. Even Alex, who'd become a good friend, had eventually called time on it all, choosing to settle down with his girlfriend, Kat. The last time Zak had spoken to him, Alex and Kat were expecting a baby and house-hunting in Cornwall. Once upon a time, Zak would have pitied his friend for being tied down, but lately he'd started to feel envious and even a little left behind. Like Zak's brothers and sisters, all busy with their own lives and exciting new adventures, Alex was moving on.

Irritated with himself, Zak flicked the shower off and grabbed a fluffy snow-white towel from the huge pile on the washstand. He rubbed his toned body down roughly and blotted his shaggy curls before knotting the towel around his waist and stepping onto heated tiles. Even washing was a world away from the sullen trickle of Seaspray's shower, the threadbare and scratchy towels often full of sand from forays to the beach and the icy lino that forced you to hop all the way back to the bedroom. God knows how Granny Alice had made it to eighty without dying of pneumonia.

I'm moving on too, Zak reminded himself sharply. He was living the dream and needed to be a little less melancholy. Any shrink would tell him that feeling excluded and left behind was a throwback to being a middle child. Growing up, it had always been Danny, Jake and Symon who went off and did things together. Mo and her best friend Summer were a tight duo, while twins Nick and Issie created havoc together. Zak had been adrift. No wonder he'd been wrapped up in music and dreams of fame and fortune. It didn't take the psychoanalytical skills of Freud to see why these things had come to hold such significance.

Zak tossed the damp towel into the bath – part of him feeling guilty because Granny Alice would think this a dreadful waste – and stalked naked across the hotel room to retrieve tonight's outfit from the wardrobe. His stylist had already picked it out for him and nothing more onerous was required than to put it on. That Zak wasn't even choosing his own clothes now was probably just another example of how spoiled he was. He needed to get changed, have a drink with Danny and then haul ass to the awards ceremony. It was hardly a great ask.

So why then, Zak wondered bleakly, did this feel like a huge effort? What on earth was wrong with him?

CHAPTER THREE

When you lived in Polwenna Bay, sunny springtime Saturdays meant trips to the beach, picnics on the cliffs or a lazy hour or two spent in the pub beer garden, unless you were a primary schoolteacher in charge of a class of thirty children. In this case, it meant spending the morning making lesson resources, an exercise which required the creativity of Picasso, the patience of a saint and the ingenuity of a Blue Peter presenter, followed by several temple-pounding and eye-straining hours trying to decipher handwriting in an attempt to grade exercise books. By the time it was half past four and the sunlight had marched right the way across her sitting room, Tess Hamilton's eyes were crossing with exhaustion and her hand was cramped from clutching her green pen.

She needed a break, Tess decided as she shut the latest exercise book. If she stared at squiggly writing for much longer, she'd start to lose the will to live. How many times had she told Lolly Kussell which way round the letter P went? And why had Morgan Tremaine decided to write his entire story in Elvish? Was he still obsessed with Lord of the Rings after reading it with his father over the Easter holiday? Tess pulled off her glasses and ground her knuckles into her eyes until stars danced and flared, erasing the tangled handwriting imprinted across her vision after this latest marking marathon. She was so exhausted she could hardly think straight.

So, all in all, a successful day in the life of a primary schoolteacher.

Outside her small cottage, which was tucked away in a quiet side street at the far end of the village, a couple of holidaymakers were strolling by, hand in hand and chatting away. The woman was petite with long chestnut hair, while her partner, who was smiling down at her adoringly, was a good foot taller and carrying a blonde child on his shoulders. They looked like such a happy family that Tess had to look away quickly. It always took her by surprise how fast and how sharp the grief could still be even after all this time. Focus on putting the resources away, she told herself sternly. Glue. Pens. Mark book. Stickers. Each had their allocated home and everything had its ordered place.

Tess tidied away in her usual methodical manner. Her cottage was neat and tidy with a minimalist look which suited her these days. With plain white walls, stripped floorboards, large blue sofa and big dining table where she worked, there was nothing here to distract her. There were no fussy details or knick-knacks to collect dust. Her sister Chloe had complained that the cottage was bland and empty, but Tess rather liked it this way. Soothing and uncluttered was how she would have described her space and besides, this fisherman's cottage was tiny and there was hardly room to store a pint of milk here, never mind a tonne of belongings. The white goods came with the house, the same for the TV and the furniture, and Tess reckoned that if she had to leave within the next hour, she'd easily be able to fit most of her things into a suitcase. Her violin she could carry, her Mac could go in her rucksack and her books would probably squeeze into a crate. She was totally portable and this thought gave Tess a great deal of comfort. She could always leave if she needed to. Moving on and not being too involved was Tess's preferred survival strategy.

This was the logic behind her minimalistic take on life. It couldn't be more at odds with the family home in Richmond where the Hamilton family had lived for several generations. There, dappled light from the Thames danced across the polished floors and bounced from the many mirrors which reflected the silvery water over and over and over again, sprinkles of light shimmering from the crystal and silver and gilt picture frames. In the Richmond house, each room was crammed with occasional tables and sofas. Standard lamps stood sentinel in shadowy corners and most available surfaces were covered by picture frames and ornaments. Walls were smothered with pictures; David Hamilton looking distinguished as he conducted famous orchestras in Berlin, Paris, Sydney and wherever else his illustrious career had taken him, Miranda Hamilton bowing on the stage at Covent Garden, Uncle Edwin beside his cello, Grandma playing her violin in Prague. There were countless mementoes of Tess's talented musical family all frozen in time and glory for posterity and to intimidate the next generation. Clocks ticked and chimed the years away, always slightly out of synch, while the dust gathered on trophies and awards, wedged in sideboards and hung on the walls. There was hardly room to move in the Richmond house without bumping into some physical reminder of her family's musical heritage.

Tess shook her head. That was her parents' way of living and this was hers. She was her own person here in Polwenna Bay. She was Tess Hamilton, respected teacher and member of the community, rather than David and Miranda Hamilton's daughter and the girl Vassilly Yolov had ditched for a better option...

Time to put her marking pen down, Tess told herself sharply. She must have been indoors far too long if she was starting to think this way. It was time to enjoy the fresh air and the sunshine of this beautiful early summer afternoon. Maybe she'd take a walk up onto the cliffs and stretch her legs for a couple of miles? She could head towards St Wenn's Well and then walk home the long way, just in time to pick up a fish and chip supper from Chris the Cod. Perhaps she'd even eat it on the quayside? That would be a real treat and one she'd earned after working so hard. It also couldn't be further away from the elegant dinner parties her parents liked to hold.

Tess carried her mug into the kitchen where she rinsed it in the tiny sink before drying it carefully and putting it away. Then she returned to the sitting room where she tidied the rest of her work away, neatly putting the books into graded piles, and making certain her pens were lined up in colour order. Once this was done, she glanced outside again and noticed that the little family had stopped by her gate.

This wasn't unusual; people often paused here to snap pictures of the pretty hanging baskets on the house next door, or simply to admire the view over the rooftops and out across the bay. Tess didn't blame them one bit; the living picture postcard of chimney pots, mossy tiles and the deep blue water beyond the harbour wall had been the reason she'd taken this tiny and, truth be told, inconvenient cottage in the first place. What did it matter that you couldn't get a car near the place or that the heating had a mind of its own, when from the attic bedroom you had a constantly changing seascape to admire and at night you could lie in bed and watch the lights of the fishing boats dance across the water as the trawlers chugged home over the inky sea? Tess also liked to think that lugging food shopping and exercise books all the way up from her car parking space might be doing something to counter all the pasties and cream teas she kept eating since she'd moved to Cornwall!

Now that the couple were directly in view, Tess realised the woman was heavily pregnant. She had slumped on the garden wall with her head in her hands. The dark-haired man was frantically fanning her face with some papers, while the little girl looked up at them both with wide eyes. To reach this part of the village was some climb up, and because the street faced south, it enjoyed sunlight all day long. The steep walk up from the harbour in the unexpected heat must have been too much for the expectant mother.

Tess shoved the sash window open.

"Excuse me! Would you like a glass of water?"

The man glanced up. He was very handsome, Tess thought. With his thick dark hair swept back from a chiselled face, a generous mouth and a firm jaw, he reminded her of a classic Hollywood matinee idol.

"That would be really kind, thanks. My wife's feeling a bit faint," he said.

"I'm fine, Alex!" protested his wife. "I'm just getting my breath back."

"You're not fine, Kat. You look as though you're about to pass out."

"Why don't you come inside out of the sun for a minute?" Tess suggested. "It's cooler in here and you can put your feet up for a moment. Honestly, it's no bother."

Kat gave her a wan smile. "I'm fine, honestly."

"Don't be so bloody stubborn, Kat," Alex told her.

"Don't say bloody, Daddy," said the little girl sternly and in a broad American accent.

"Sorry, Emmy," replied her father, "but I'm at the end of my tether with your stepmother. Come on, Kat. Please have a drink and a rest. If not for me, then for the baby."

"You're not going to have the baby now, are you Kat?" asked Emmy, wide-eyed.

Tess hoped not; she'd have no idea what to do. Children arrived at her classroom door when they were fully formed and talking – although not always toilet trained or with any table manners. She guessed if the worst came to the worst, she'd have to run down to the surgery and fetch Richard Penwarren, one of the local doctors. And didn't boiling water come into it too?

"No, sweetie," said Kat to Tess's relief. "I'm just really tired. That hill's steeper than it looks."

"It wears me out every day and I'm not even pregnant," Tess laughed, giving the worried little girl a reassuring smile. To Kat she added, "I'm Tess, by the way. Please come in and have some water and a rest. It's no trouble, honestly, and it'll put my mind at rest. I don't think I could cope with a birth taking place on my doorstep!"

Kat nodded. "In that case, thank you. I could really do with cooling down."

Tess let the family into her cottage and before long, Kat was sitting on the sofa with her feet up on the coffee table while she sipped a glass of water. Gradually her colour began to look slightly less hectic and she closed her eyes and dozed, while Emmy chatted away about her mom in America and how much she liked English ice cream and couldn't wait to have one, preferably with a flake in it.

"Always a great bribe for good behaviour," said her father, ruffling Emmy's hair. "Still, you have been really good all day, Munchkin, so an ice cream is definitely in order."

"Are you having a nice holiday?" Tess asked.

"We're here house-hunting," Kat told her, as she rejoined the conversation. "Not for a second home, though. We're going to live in Polwenna."

While she downed a second glass of water, Kat told Tess how she and Alex had fallen in love with Polwenna Bay a couple of years previously after rekindling their romance in the village. They were currently living in London, but with a new arrival on the way, it felt like the perfect time to relocate to the countryside.

"We've got friends here so it seems to make sense to move to a place where we know people," Alex added. "They're called Tremaine? Do you know them?"

Tess, who knew Nick Tremaine rather better than she wished she did after a daft fling when she'd first arrived in the village, nodded cautiously.

"Everyone knows the Tremaines. I see Tara Tremaine quite a lot and I was good friends with Issie before she moved away."

Alex raised an eyebrow.

"Issie, hey? She certainly knows how to party!"

"She does, but I promise I don't party nearly as hard as her. I couldn't even if I wanted to because I'm the primary schoolteacher here. I have to show some restraint!"

"I'm friends with Zak Tremaine and I don't think restraint is in his vocabulary," said Alex thoughtfully. "I think he pities me giving up a rock and roll lifestyle and settling down."

Kat glanced up. "You can always go back on the road if you miss it, babe."

"Who said I miss it? Long hours. Crap food. Late nights. No thanks. Zak's welcome to it." Alex took his wife's hand. "I've got everything I want right here. Zak can keep the fame and fortune!"

Tess had bumped into Zak Tremaine briefly in the pub one Christmas. He'd been roaring drunk and not registered her at all. As Tess remembered, Zak had the Tremaine good looks magnified tenfold; the same bright blue eyes, killer cheekbones and easy charm as his brothers and a mane of burnished golden curls that he'd tied in a loose ponytail, which had suited him in a wild and piratical kind of way. He'd certainly had a charisma about him that drew admiring gazes wherever he went and which Tess had recognised instantly as star quality. Her parents both had it in bucket loads.

And so had Vassilly. No wonder she'd not been enough for him.

"You're a musician then?" she asked quickly, pushing these memories away.

Alex nodded. "I've been a session musician for over ten years, but I'm going to focus on writing now. You're musical too, I take it?"

He pointed at her violin, placed on a high shelf. Lord. He was sharp-eyed.

"I used to play a bit," Tess said.

This was an understatement, but nobody here needed to know the truth. Tess kept her violin, a one hundred-year-old Giovanni Schwarz which glowed with a century of love and cherishing, because it was precious to her, but she hadn't lifted it from the case in a long time. She hadn't played for years and she didn't know if she ever would again. Some things were just too painful.

"You'll love living here," she said, changing the subject. "It's a great village and really friendly. Have you found anywhere you like?"

Alex looked as though he wanted to ask Tess a little more about her music, but took the hint.

"We've just viewed Sea Thrift. It needs a bit of updating, but I think it could work for us. Do you know it?"

Tess did. Sea Thrift was a beautiful wooden house dating back to the nineteen twenties, with big windows and a steep garden.

"It's just past the church, isn't it? Has beautiful roses in the garden?"

21

"That's it," nodded Alex.

"Dad says I can have a puppy when we live there," piped up Emmy.

"Puppies and ice creams. The two most powerful parental bribes in the book," sighed Alex. "Munchkin, I'll be too busy writing songs to look after a puppy."

"And changing nappies," Kat added. She smiled at Tess, a warm smile that lit her eyes and carved dimples into her cheeks. "I'm a teacher too, Tess, so I'll be picking your brains about schools in the area because I'll be going back to work at some point."

"You don't have to do that, darling," Alex began, but Kat shook her head.

"I'm not ready to give up my career just yet. That was the deal, remember? I work and you write songs?"

There was steel in her voice and Alex grinned. "Someone's feeling better."

"I am," agreed Kat, hauling herself to her feet. "Totally restored and ready to carry on. Thanks for the water and the rest, Tess. I owe you."

"Not at all," Tess said.

"We really do," Alex insisted. "If you've got nothing else planned, how about you let us buy you supper in The Ship tonight as a thank you?"

As if she had anything else planned, thought Tess wryly. Her Saturday nights tended to consist of a quick drink in the pub before the Pollards and Caspar James, Polwenna's self-appointed writer in residence, took root at the bar. Then she usually marked books in front of The X Factor. Tess wasn't quite sure when it was that her social life had come to comprise of people being torn to shreds by Simon Cowell, but it didn't seem like a great step forward.

"There's no need," she said.

"But we'd really love to," insisted Kat. "It's nice to make new friends and you can give us the low-down on the village. Zak exaggerates and Alice Tremaine is far too nice about everyone. What I want is the gossip!"

Tess laughed. "I'm the last person to know that! I'm too busy working. You know how it is with the marking and planning. Sure you want to go back to it?"

"I remember it well," said Kat. "But even so, yes! And anyway, it's Saturday, so you deserve a break. Unless you're busy?"

For a moment Tess considered fibbing and saying that yes, she already had plans, but there was something about this couple that she warmed to and it could be fun to get to know them.

"I'd love to," she said. After all, what did she have to lose?

CHAPTER FOUR

The guest list for her wedding was getting longer and longer, but each time Alice Tremaine attempted to make a cull, she thought of all the people who'd be left off it. It was all very well for Jonny to joke that it should be a very short list because everyone they knew was dead, but he wasn't the one who was trying to organise their big day. And it wasn't Jonny either who would feel dreadful later on when she recalled another forgotten friend or overlooked relative. What about the London Tremaines? Or Jonny's family in America? And did she need to invite the families of her grandchildren's partners?

Oh! It certainly hadn't been this tricky the first time round! Back then, the war hadn't been over for long, rationing was still in place and most people were too busy rebuilding shattered lives and homes to be bothered about places on guest lists or wedding invitations. Alice and Henry had just had a simple service at St Wenn's and a meal in the local hotel with their parents. Even her dress had been made from some leftover curtain fabric and the flowers picked from her mother's cottage garden.

Alice sighed and put the cap on her fountain pen. Her head was aching and she was exhausted. Since when had a quiet wedding, with just family and a few special friends, become something that would give Harry and Meghan's big day stiff competition? She and Jonny were in their eighties. They didn't need all this fuss.

"Simply ridiculous!" Alice said out loud, pushing the paper away and rising to her feet.

"What's ridiculous, my love?"

Alice's fiancé looked up from his chair by the sitting room window where he was puzzling over The Times crossword.

"This wedding," said Alice. "Can't we just run away to Gretna Green?"

"I can hardly walk without my stick these days, Ally. I don't think I'll be running anywhere."

"Oh, you know what I mean," Alice snapped.

She really wasn't in the mood to be teased. The wedding was booked for July and there was far too much to organise to waste time with joking. So far they hadn't even agreed on a first draft of the guest list, and each time she tried to raise the subject of a reception venue they came dangerously close to falling out. Jonny favoured his hotel, which Alice knew made sense with so many guests, but her heart was set on using her own house, Seaspray. With its pretty terrace and views over the bay, it was a beautiful setting and by midsummer the garden and pots would be in full and glorious bloom. Provided their guests could make it up the steep path, Alice thought this would be a perfect spot, although pitching a marquee on the steep lawn might be tricky…

Jonny put his paper aside and regarded Alice thoughtfully over his glasses.

"How many people have we got on that blessed list now?"

"Eighty-six," Alice said in despair. "And before you say a word, I know we agreed on a small wedding and I have tried to whittle the list down, but we simply know far too many people. How can we invite some and not others? It would be very hurtful."

Jonny pulled himself slowly out of the chair to join her at the desk, resting one knotted hand on her shoulder and squeezing it soothingly as he leaned over and studied her pages of notes.

"Darling, you've got half the village on the list."

"I know, and the other half will be really offended if I don't include them. How can I invite the Pollards but not the Kussells? Or Sheila Keverne and not Kathy Polmartin? And what about all the Penhalligans?"

"Ally, there are hundreds of Penhalligans!"

"I know, but they're Summer's family!"

"We don't need the distant cousins and – hold on – why on earth is Silver Starr on the list?"

Silver Starr ran Polwenna's hippy shop and had offered to make table decorations from flowers and recycled fishing net. Alice had really wanted sugared almonds and rose petals, but Silver had been so excited that she couldn't bear to hurt her feelings.

Oh dear. There seemed to be a pattern emerging.

Jonny pushed the papers away and shook his head.

"This is getting out of hand, love. I hate to see you looking so worried. Our wedding's supposed to be a happy occasion."

"It won't be if we leave somebody out," Alice warned. "It will be carnage."

"Hmm. Maybe we should cancel the whole bun fight and enjoy living in sin?"

This made Alice laugh. Living in sin at eighty years old! If only! It was true that Jonny had moved into Seaspray so that they could be together, but he was a total gentleman and had insisted that the downstairs snug was converted into his bedroom.

"To avoid being tempted to get it on with Granny Alice before the wedding?" her grandson Nick had asked cheekily as he'd helped to shift the furniture.

"To avoid climbing the stairs, young man," had been Jonny's swift answer. "Your grandmother's portable! Besides, who says we need a bedroom to enjoy ourselves? Haven't you read her Blackwarren book?"

Nick, who'd read Alice's spicy book when the entire village had been trying to guess the author's identity, looked horrified.

"You didn't think your grandmother made all that sexy stuff up, did you?" Jonny asked, winking at Alice.

For once, Nick had been lost for words and scarpered pretty swiftly. Alice had laughed very hard for a good hour afterwards. Young people! They all thought they'd invented sex and were so prudish when it came to their elders. If Nick knew how badly behaved Jonny had been at his age, or how Alice had sneaked out to meet him, her grandson's blue eyes would pop out of his head and roll down the hill to the harbour. It was one thing for her grandsons to sneak girls home (if Nick and Zak thought Alice didn't know what they got up to, then they were very much mistaken), but the thought of their grandmother doing anything less chaste than holding hands utterly horrified them. In reality, the closest to Fifty Shades of Grey Alice and Jonny came was their hair colour, but she wasn't going to divulge this information – it was far too much fun turning the tables on Nick!

"Come outside and have a break," Jonny was saying now, taking Alice's hand and helping her up from her seat.

"I can't! I'm so behind," she protested.

"The guest list has waited over fifty years for us to marry, Ally, so I think it can wait another five minutes. Come on, it's a beautiful afternoon. Let's sit on the terrace and enjoy the view for a while and do nothing. I think we've earned the right to do that at our age."

Alice found doing nothing very difficult. There was usually a grandchild to sort out or a crisis to avert, but for once her family seemed to all be doing just fine. Her hapless son Jimmy was in the States visiting his daughter, Emerald, and Alice's grandchildren were all on an even keel. Jake was hard at work on the quayside – Alice could hear the whine of a grinder from here – across the bay at Mariners, Mo was probably bickering with her husband Ashley and planning ways to return to three-day eventing, and Danny was in London house-hunting with dear Jules. Then there was Symon busy working on the launch of his new restaurant, Issie away at university and Nick out fishing. The only grandchild who was giving Alice a rather uneasy see-sawing sensation deep in the pit of her stomach was Zak, which was ridiculous because he was living his dream life.

Alice knew she shouldn't have favourites, and she tried very hard not to because she loved each grandchild dearly and in their own way, but dear Zak had always been the most vulnerable of them all, and only Alice knew just how tender-hearted he really was. Old enough to remember his mother, but too young to understand why she had suddenly vanished from his life, he'd clung to Alice desperately for months, his blue eyes filling with distress if she strayed too far or spent too much time with Nick and Issie. Zak felt things deeply, Alice knew, but had learned to bury this side of his personality and protect his heart, skimming across the surface of life like a handsome, blue-eyed pond skater, never staying anywhere long enough to settle or dating a girl long enough to be close to danger. Only in his music and in the words sung in that deep, gravelly voice did Zak open up and reveal a glimpse of his true nature. Alice understood why he needed fame and admiration so badly, but she feared for him, for what would Zak have left if – when – it all ended?

Who would be there for him then? Alice knew she wouldn't be around forever.

"Come on my love, please stop looking so worried. The wedding will sort itself out," said Jonny.

Alice nodded, feeling guilty because at this moment her mind couldn't have been further from their wedding. Reminding herself that Zak was a grown man and more than capable of taking care of himself, she allowed Jonny to take her arm and guide her through the open French doors and out onto the terrace. Worrying wouldn't make a jot of difference and at least Danny was due to see Zak this evening. Fleeting texts and FaceTime calls didn't do much to put Alice's mind at rest.

There was a bench set against the thick stone wall of the house that had been in this exact same spot on the terrace since the day Alice had arrived as a timid young bride. Elizabeth Tremaine, her formidable mother-in-law, had often sat there and it was she who'd planted the plump pink roses that ran riot over the front of the house. Elizabeth was long gone now, but Alice remembered her fondly because she'd been a kind soul, welcoming her son's new wife into the family, even if she must have privately thought he had married somebody far too young and rather beneath his station. It was Elizabeth who had taught Alice the joy of gardening, and as she settled onto the bench, the wood worn and quite crumbly now, Alice was moved by the sight of the garden they'd planted together. In the same way the rose bush was now a woody giant filling the summer garden with a heady scent and unrecognisable from the small plant she'd bedded in all those years ago, so Elizabeth's family had taken root here and thrived. How Alice wished she could see what would happen to them all in the decades that lay ahead.

Just another year, she prayed; just let me see Morgan go to college, Isla start school, and Danny and Jules get married...

Time, which had once seemed endless and something Alice rarely thought about, felt too short and dreadfully precious these days – which was why she had to sort this wedding out. She had to stop faffing about with it all. If they weren't too old and poorly to get travel insurance, Alice would have been tempted to suggest they fly off to the Caribbean and just get married on the beach without any guests at all. Now, that really did appeal, although she probably wouldn't wear a bikini – Jonny did have a dicky heart, after all!

"Didn't I tell you it was glorious out here?" he was saying.

Alice nodded; it was a beautiful afternoon. With warm sunshine, wisps of lazy cloud drifting across a powder blue sky and the golden sand shining, Cornwall was at its best. Polwenna Bay was timeless, the lichen-speckled rooftops and wonky cottages hardly changed since Elizabeth Tremaine had paused here and gazed out over the bay. The sense of continuity was soothing. Alice raised her face to the sunshine and closed her eyes. Life always went on regardless of your inner turmoil and all was generally well in the end.

"You were right, my love," she agreed.

Jonny took her hand. If Alice didn't open her eyes and see the liver spots or feel how the joints were thickened by arthritis, they could have been teenagers once more, sitting on the cliffs and lost in their very own dream world.

"Now, about this wedding, Ally," Jonny said eventually. "I'd marry you anywhere, you know that. It's not about the day. It's about being with you. Bugger the hotel. Have the reception in the bus shelter or the village hall if it makes you happier."

Alice opened her eyes to see Jonny looking at her with such love that all her fretting about guest lists and place settings seemed crazy.

She kissed his whiskery cheek.

"Thank you, love. It's all got a bit out of hand and I'm not sure I'm very good at organising this. I only wanted something fairly small, but special."

"And you shall have it, Ally, I promise. May I suggest something a little different?"

"Gretna Green? You're on!"

"Hmm, not quite! I want you to have a special day, but I hate seeing you so stressed about it all, so I've been thinking, why don't we let somebody else sort it out? Do all the donkey work, pick out the details and let us just turn up?"

This idea was very tempting. The nuptial equivalent of Ocado.

"Sounds good," Alice said cautiously.

"So let's make it happen. Ella was doing a great job planning weddings at the hotel. Why don't we ask her to take care of ours?"

Ella was Jonny's granddaughter and until recently had managed his hotel. Now she was setting up independently with her partner Symon, Alice's chef grandson. They were opening a restaurant based in Polwenna Manor, a picturesque, if crumbling, medieval manor house just outside the village. The opening was planned for the start of the season and, if Alice knew Symon, it was going to be incredible. The only fly in the ointment was that the Manor's owner, Perry Tregarrick, was perpetually broke, which meant Ella and Symon had needed to plough all their savings into the project and, Alice feared, take out massive loans in order to bring the place up to standard. It was certainly a gamble, but as Cornwall was the must go to place lately, with property prices soaring and celebrities popping up all over the county like field mushrooms, Alice was sure they'd do well. The Manor was gorgeous, Sy's food incredible, and Ella St Milton on a mission made The Terminator look easily distracted.

"Would she have time to do it?" Alice asked doubtfully. The young couple had enough on, surely?

"I wouldn't expect her to do it for free. We'd hire her and the venue in a professional capacity," Jonny said.

Alice felt a tingle of excitement. "It's a stunning spot, Jonny. We could have a marquee by the lake for the evening do."

"Only if Perry moves those bloody sheep of his; otherwise we'll be up to our knees in pellets of poo! But yes, that was the sort of thing I had in mind. Plenty of room for the whole village to come and get blotto at our expense – I mean, celebrate with us!"

"This way, we can say that we're only having a small sit-down meal for close friends and family because the restaurant only seats a small number of people!" Alice felt relief wash over her just like the waves washed over the rocks below. Honour was satisfied and feelings were spared!

"And then in the evening we could have a marquee and a party for the rest," Jonny concluded. "I also suspect Symon and Ella will be glad of the funds and since we both know they're too proud to accept any help from us, isn't this the perfect solution?"

Alice took his face in her hands and kissed him gently.

"It really is," she said. "And I love you for coming up with it."

And as he returned her kiss, Alice felt a weight slide from her shoulders that she hadn't even realised had been lodged there. Maybe things were going to work out, after all?

CHAPTER FIVE

Not being a celebrity vicar with her own TV show and regular presenting slot on Songs of Praise, Jules was finding it impossible not to gape at the who's who of famous folk gathered in the exclusive West End bar where she and Danny met Zak. She was doing her very best to concentrate on the conversation but, as fascinating as Alice's upcoming wedding and Symon's new restaurant were, these topics hardly compared to the fact that a real-life pop star had just shimmied past or that the Queen Vic's landlord was chatting to a minor royal by the bar. It was like walking into a live version of Heat! magazine – Jules's guilty pleasure – and although she knew it wasn't cool to stare, she simply couldn't help herself! Jules took a sip of the champagne Zak had ordered and did her best to focus. Hopefully she was doing an okay job of playing it cool.

"Don't worry, it's all right to be a bit overwhelmed by it all," Zak told her.

Oh. Maybe not quite as good a job as she'd thought?

"When I first started coming to these things, I was following people around with my eyes out on stalks," he continued kindly. "Ed Sheeran thought I was a stalker for a while."

"From what I've heard, it won't be long until you're as successful as he is. You'll forget all about us and only hang out with the stars," Dan said, giving his brother a teasing punch on the shoulder.

Zak pulled a face. "Hardly. I'm right at the bottom of the food chain. Practically plankton level, me."

Jules doubted this was true. With his dinner jacket, rakishly undone bow tie and the wild blond curls loose to his shoulders, Zak was the epitome of muso chic. His diamond earring twinkled in the low lighting and his snakeskin cowboy boots struck a rebellious note as they peeped out from beneath his tailored trousers. He must be aware that he drew admiring glances from all the women in the room, waitresses and A listers alike, she thought. Relaxed, at ease with the rich and famous and happily ordering bottles of champagne which cost more than Jules spent on groceries in a fortnight, Zak Tremaine was completely at home here.

He was with his people.

Jules certainly wasn't with hers. These identikit skinny blondes, with their thin worked-out arms and manes of artfully tousled hair, were like creatures from another planet. Their makeup was perfect and, she was willing to bet, didn't come from the sale bin at Boots! They probably didn't colour their own hair either, or wear trainers! No, their high heels had tell-tale red soles and they flitted about like colourful butterflies in their floaty designer dresses with spaghetti straps and dangerously low necklines. Jules had thought she'd made an effort losing half a stone lately and splashing out on a cute red wrap dress, but next to these beautiful people she felt like Nelly the Elephant on day release from the circus. It was just as well God and Danny loved her as she was or else she might start to feel inadequate. One of her thighs wouldn't fit into the entire dress that the blonde on the next table was wearing.

"Trust me, this isn't all it's cracked up to be," Zak was saying. A bleak expression flickered over his face. "I'm only going tonight because my manager thinks it's good to be seen and one of Alchemist's big acts is up for an award. I'm well and truly over these kinds of gatherings."

Danny was puzzled. "I thought this was all you ever wanted?"

Zak shrugged his broad shoulders. "I want to be a musician, Dan. The rest of it is total bollocks."

"The money? The groupies? Recording in LA? Hanging out with the rich and famous? Yeah, must be awful! What's not to like about Playboy bunnies and hot tubs? Where do I sign up?"

Jules swatted her fiancé's arm.

"Enough of that! There's a vicar present!"

"You can join me in a hot tub anytime," Danny said to Jules with an exaggerated wink. "You'd look cute in bunny ears and a pom-pom tail!"

"He's joking!" Jules said quickly when Zak didn't look amused. He wasn't laughing with them. He looked really fed up.

"Take it from me, most of the time it's hotel rooms and long hours. I don't know if the music I've recorded will even be released. It's all up in the air until the new contract's signed."

"What does that mean exactly?" Jules was confused. She'd thought Zak was about to become the next big thing. It was what Alice was always telling everyone.

"It means they own all the songs I've been working on for the last two years," Zak said bleakly.

"All your work? And those tracks you co-wrote with Alex Evans?" Danny was horrified.

"Yep. The whole lot. Basically, if I don't go along with what they want, I'm screwed. Two years and the band all down the toilet for nothing. They don't like the sound and my manager says they want to try another avenue, whatever that means."

"Bloody hell, Zak! Didn't you have a lawyer look at the contract before you signed it?"

"That was what my manager was supposed to do. Ricky said it was all cool, so I trusted him. And before you say it, Danny, yes, I know I'm an idiot," Zak said bitterly.

"I wasn't going to say that. I'm gutted for you."

Jules put her drink down. She was trying to get all this straight in her mind and the champagne bubbles going straight to her brain weren't helping.

"So does this mean you can't release any of your music if you don't sign this new contract and go along with what they want? And even if you do, they could change everything?"

"That's about the sum of it," Zak confessed. "I'm really pleased with the album, but Ricky, my manager, says Alchemist's big guns aren't happy. Apparently, the record company bosses have a different sound in mind for me now, more US country and less British. They say UK folk rock is over. The bottom line is that Alchemist want me to sign away all creative control and do what I'm told. I might end up very successful, but I won't be me any more. Sometimes I think I might as well have gone on The X Factor."

"So don't sign the new contract," said Danny, who tended to see things in black and white. It didn't always make him the easiest soul to live with, but Jules knew he was the most honourable man she'd ever met and it was one of the reasons she loved him. She could also imagine it was why his men would, and had, lay down their lives for him on the battlefield.

"If I don't sign, it's all over," Zak said quietly. He stared down at the table, his forefinger absently tracing the condensation rings from the champagne glasses. "I'll be a failure. What will the past two years have been about? It'll all have been for nothing."

"Of course it won't," Danny said sharply. "Nothing's ever wasted, mate, and take it from me – sometimes what feels like the worst thing in the world is actually the best thing that could ever happen to you. I should know."

He smiled at Jules as he said this and she felt her stomach fold over like cake mix in Alice's big ceramic bowl.

But Zak stared grimly into his champagne glass.

"Yeah, well, maybe. Anyway, do you know what's best of all? If I sign with them, they'll own me for the foreseeable. I'll have to do what they want and make the music they think I should make."

"You can't do that, mate," Danny said.

"What choice do I have? Say no and go home with my tail between my legs and get a job in the pub? Then what have I got?"

Danny gave him a long, hard look. "Your integrity. What else really matters?"

There was a pause. Jules found she was holding her breath. The sound of the bar seemed to fade, voices rising and falling and the beat of the music thudding in time with her heartbeat. She had the strangest feeling something very important was hanging on this moment.

Zak exhaled slowly. "Nothing."

"So believe in yourself," Danny ordered. "You're talented and your sound's unique. Follow your heart. 'Celtic Country and Western', you always said. That was what The Tinners were all about."

"The Tinners broke up," Zak said shortly.

"Maybe they shouldn't have?"

"Thanks for reminding me."

Danny looked exasperated. "I didn't mean to be tactless. I'm just gutted to hear what's happened to you. Don't let them exploit you."

"It's not exploitation. It's pretty standard in this industry. I've sold them my work, just like an author would to a publishing house, and what they choose to do with it is up to them. I guess it's the price I'll have to pay for wanting to be a musician."

"You've always been a musician, Zak. You packed out all the venues you played at back home," Danny reminded him. "Getting this far hasn't made you any better than you were before. The Tinners were great. You're great. People in the village still talk about how good you guys were. In fact, not just in the village, people in Cornwall still talk about the band. That's how good you guys were."

Zak sloshed more champagne into his glass.

"The record company didn't think we were marketable as a trio. They wanted me because I wrote the songs and sang the vocals. They thought the rest could be done by session musicians. Ned and Ollie said they understood."

Dan said nothing, but Zak couldn't look at him and his gaze slipped back to the glass as though transfixed.

"It's such a shame. I heard you guys play when I first arrived and you were brilliant," Jules said. "It was the village festival and you were headlining. I danced all night and I bought your CD."

"She's such a groupie," said Danny fondly.

"I'm only using you to get close to the band. Didn't you realise?" Jules dead-panned. "I'm going to run off with Zak now – if that's all right with you, Zak?"

"Anytime," said Zak gallantly. "Although, I must warn you, I'm not nearly as reliable as Danny. I'll probably forget your birthday and I'd make a terrible boyfriend."

"He really would," Danny agreed. "You wouldn't believe the amount of sobbing girls Granny Alice has had to comfort over the years."

Actually, Jules could. All the Tremaine boys were handsome, but Zak had that extra something that made you look twice and then a third time. He reminded her of Brad Pitt at his Legends of the Fall best: a little wild, a tad tortured and very definitely damaged; it was a potent combination that no woman could resist. Throw in faded jeans, battered cowboy boots and a guitar and there you had it – the perfect recipe for heartbreak.

"Wasn't that the festival weekend the talent scout saw you?" Dan recalled. His brother nodded.

"Yes. We went up to London to meet him the next week."

"It's a shame you can't play this year," Jules said. Somehow she'd ended up on the Festival Committee. Getting roped into these community events seemed to be a hazard of being Polwenna Bay's vicar, and already the village festival was starting to give her a headache. Big Rog Pollard was determined to run a talent show (Jules had told him several times that she was not having P Factor emblazoned on posters across the village) and yesterday their headline band had dropped out because they'd got a chance of playing Glastonbury. Jules didn't blame them, but now there was a massive gap in the programme which, unless she thought of something fast, Silver Starr was threatening to fill with ocarina playing.

Suddenly her move to London looked like a great idea.

Zak looked wistful.

"The Festival's always great. It would be so good to come home and see everyone too."

"Can't you come back for a long weekend?" Danny suggested.

"Your gran would love that," Jules added. She knew how much Alice missed Zak.

"I wish I could, but I've got this do and then I'm meant to be back in the studio. I'm not complaining, though. I know I'm lucky." Zak gave them a smile, but Jules noticed that it didn't quite reach his eyes. "I'm sorry if I've been teasy, guys. It's probably jet lag and I'm exhausted. I can't wait for this thing tonight to be over so I can have a sleep."

Zak had purple smudges beneath the bright blue Tremaine eyes, but these only added to his sexy, dissolute air. Ditto the golden stubble dusting his jaw and the dishevelled curls. Added to the DJ and loosened bow tie, the overall effect was like Christian Grey met James Bond, with a dash of Jagger thrown in for good measure.

"So much for sex, drugs and rock and roll," said Danny, doing his best to make a joke.

"Believe me, you can keep all that. I just want an early night," Zak was saying as he smothered a yawn. "Still, no chance of that when the awards ceremony starts in about twenty minutes and then there'll be interviews and an after-party. I've got to be there doing my bit for Alchemist Records like a well-trained artist." He hauled himself to his feet and poured the last of the champagne into their glasses. "Don't rush away on my account, guys. Finish this up and have a meal in the restaurant. Put it on my tab – the record company will pick it up."

Then Zak shook Danny's hand, kissed Jules on the cheek and was gone, swallowed up in the glamorous throng and leaving them staring at one another, totally thrown.

This was not quite the evening they'd anticipated and all of a sudden Jules didn't think the glittery celebrity world was quite so shiny after all.

"Can we go home to Cornwall please?" she said.

CHAPTER SIX

Zak wasn't sure how he got through the awards ceremony; it seemed to happen without him really noticing. Like raindrops on chalk pavement art, everything was blurring and dissolving around him as he replayed his conversation with Danny over and over again.

Out of all his brothers, it was Danny who Zak admired the most. Jake and Symon were driven and determined individuals and he had a lot of respect for them, but Dan had always had the dream of being in the army and, like Zak, had let nothing stand in his way when it came to reaching his goal. Dan's steely resolve and iron strength of will had seen him take the worst that life could dish out and still refuse to give in. Look at him now, house-hunting in the city with a fiancée who clearly adored him and about to start an exciting new job. He'd done all this on his own merits and with integrity too. Danny hadn't betrayed his friends or his principles along the way and could walk down the road with his head held high.

Zak knew that compared to what his brother had suffered, his own complaints were pretty pathetic. They won't let me play the music I like hardly compared to losing an arm and damaging your sight, did it? And having to attend industry parties and make small talk with record company bosses wasn't exactly on a par with clearing mines and facing roadside ambushes. He'd started to lose perspective and was in danger of becoming an utter tosser. He guessed it was a hazard of the job.

Or maybe there was no becoming about it? Perhaps he already was a tosser? The way he'd treated that pretty brunette backing singer the other week was thoughtless at best and cruel at worst and Zak wasn't proud of himself. She'd been a sweet girl really, and it wasn't her fault that she'd been thrust into a world where people were viewed as commodities and where the only currency that really counted was fame. He should have called her back at the very least and taken her for a drink to explain that he wasn't looking for anything more. Just ignoring her wasn't fair and Zak felt prickly with shame because he was better than that. Yes, he liked to have fun as much as the next guy, but Zak hoped he was usually a gentleman. This life was making him selfish.

There was a choice to be made here. Zak either signed the contract, did as he was told and saw the success that he'd been dreaming of for years, or he walked away, did his own thing and… and…

And what?

This was the sticking point. All Zak had ever wanted was to be a successful singer and songwriter. If he walked away now, what did the future hold for him? A bar job in the village? A bit of work at the marina with Jake? Gigging in pubs? Would it be enough when he had come this close? Or was he cursed either way, damned by whichever decision he did or didn't make?

Zak finished his drink and held up his glass to a passing waiter for a refill, knocking the drink back swiftly. It didn't seem to matter how much he drank tonight, because no amount of alcohol could stop Danny's words from playing on a loop. Was sacrificing his artistic integrity the only way to achieve success? If so, Zak knew that the only answer had to be to walk away because this was a price far higher than any he was prepared to pay.

"And the winner of Best Solo Female Artist is..." The emcee paused for dramatic effect. "Kellee!"

There was a shriek of delight from the adjacent table and the face of a delighted girl was beamed out of the huge screens that were arranged throughout the ballroom. She looked like she was wearing strips of tinfoil and dental floss and even Zak, who was generally a big fan of skimpy outfits, felt as though he ought to be offering her his jacket in case she caught cold.

"Oh my God! Oh my God!" she gasped, one hand pressed against her breastbone. "I can't believe it!"

Kellee wasn't alone; Zak couldn't believe it either. A pretty bottle blonde from Alchemist's stable with an average voice, and originally going by the far less exotic 'Kelly', she'd won a TV talent show and was being groomed for big things. Zak had met her at a couple of events and thought she was nice enough, but her musical ability was certainly questionable. She was up against some really class acts tonight – Alison Angel, for example, a former opera singer who really did have a voice from heaven and a genuine God-given talent. Ali was incredible, touted as the new Adele, and Zak had listened to her album with a mixture of awe and envy. Now he could add despair to the mix because how on earth had an artist of her calibre been overlooked for Kellee?

Then Zak glanced across the room to where Alison Angel was doing a sterling job of looking thrilled for her mediocre rival and was swiftly reminded that Ali, however fiercely talented, was in her late thirties and several stone overweight. Doh. This wasn't about talent, was it? This was about selling records and making cash.

It was all too depressing for words. Danny might as well have been sitting next to him saying, "I told you so."

While the audience clapped for Kellee and craned their necks to see just how good the losers were at pretending not to care, Zak started to feel horribly claustrophobic. As Kellee teetered onto the stage to collect her award, Zak could only just summon the energy to put his hands together. Christ. If his manager got him to sign the new contract, then Zak was only a few steps away from being her, wasn't he?

"Just pass me the bloody tinfoil now," he muttered, running a finger around his tight shirt collar. It felt like a noose and everything in him longed to rip the bow tie off. He felt hot and trapped and either the booze was taking effect, or he was having some kind of episode because it felt as though the walls were closing in. He used to feel like this a lot as a kid, especially when his father had gone travelling and he'd lain in bed at Seaspray wondering what he'd done to drive his parents away. It was only music that had made Zak feel better. Later on, girls had helped too, but Zak never let anyone get too close because he'd learned long ago that this was a sure way to get hurt. People always left you in the end. Singing about broken hearts and shattered summer promises was far easier than really feeling those things.

Sweat drenching his shirt and beading his brow, Zak rose to his feet and squeezed his way past the other tables, threading his way across the ballroom to the exit. He needed some air.

It was quiet outside the ballroom. Zak tugged off his bow tie and took a few deep breaths. How he wished Ned and Ollie were here with him. They'd have had a great time laughing at just how ridiculous the whole shebang was, and Ned, who was a brilliant mimic, would have had them in stitches with his impressions. It was impossible to take yourself too seriously when you were with those two and they always knew how to pull Zak out of these dark swamps of introspection – usually by embarking on a jamming session in The Ship. Just the memory was enough to make him smile. Big Rog Pollard who fancied himself as Cornwall's answer to Tom Jones would sing, Chris the Cod might fetch his guitar and contribute the two chords he'd mastered, and even Sheila Keverne had been known to join in with her tambourine. Throw in a couple of pints and a pasty and there you had it – happiness.

Homesickness hit Zak like a punch in the stomach, so he dived into the Gents to collect himself and splash some cold water on his face.

"Aye, aye! You look like you've lost a fiver and picked up a penny!"

Great. He wasn't alone. Instead, Ryan Kent, the lead singer of an indie band that had been huge in the nineties, was standing at the sinks busily chopping cocaine into neat white lines. Zak thought it a sad indication of just how jaded he'd become that occurrences like this no longer surprised him. The days of Coke being something that came from a bottle in The Ship were long past, as were the days of being impressed by stars like Ryan. Zak had been a huge fan once and he still thought the guy was super-talented even if he'd sold out long ago and was now more famous for naff duets with boy band members and novelty Christmas records than for his own brilliant music.

Ryan was also notorious for being off his face most of the time.

"Didn't get the award you wanted?" Ryan commiserated.

"Something like that," Zak said. He didn't want to engage with Ryan.

The older musician's eyes met Zak's in the mirror. They were bloodshot and world-weary.

"Want a pick-me-up, pal?"

Zak felt uncomfortable being here with Ryan. He might still be one of Alchemist's biggest stars, but as far as Zak could see, Ryan Kent was a real example of somebody who'd squandered his amazing talent. From penning biting political satire to making bland manufactured music – it was some fall from grace and Zak thought it was no wonder Ryan spent most of his time off his head.

"No, you're all right," he said.

Ryan shrugged one skinny shoulder.

"Up to you, pal. Personally, I can't get through these bloody things without a bit of help."

He leaned forward, covered one nostril and inhaled loudly. Then he straightened up and sniffed before wiping his nose with the back of his hand. Zak looked away, discomfited. Ryan Kent had written some of Britpop's classic anthems, hobnobbed at Number 10 and been the epitome of all things Cool Britannia. It felt wrong to see a musician hero he'd looked up to as a kid reduced to this, a bit like seeing your headmaster in his underpants.

"Don't look at me like that, man," grumbled Ryan, stuffing his plastic bag back into his waistcoat. "You wait till you've been in this game as long as me."

Zak shuddered. He was going to be having a very hard think indeed about whether he still wanted to play this game at all.

Leaving Ryan checking his nostrils for any giveaway telltale signs, Zak returned to the ballroom for the last few awards where he pasted on a smile and clapped and cheered with the best of them.

Once the final presentation had been made, he posed for photographs before hopping in a limo to head across town to the cool Docklands club where Alchemist were holding their after-party. To be honest, Zak would have rather gone back to the hotel and crashed out, but partying with the record company was expected. The music sometimes felt like the least important part of his job.

When Zak first arrived in London, he and the boys had been really excited by chauffeur-driven cars and beyond impressed by limousines with televisions and mini bars. Now, as he took his seat, Zak felt terribly jaded. Posing outside the club for yet more photos was exhausting too, and it was a relief to find himself behind the thick gold rope in the VIP area so that he could sink into a booth and catch his breath for a moment.

Around him the party was in full swing. Champagne flowed like the River Wenn after heavy rainfall and Kellee's album was thudding away over the speakers in perfect time with the thumping of his temples. Zak chatted to a couple of the record label bosses, sipped his drink and glanced surreptitiously at his watch. Almost half eleven. Maybe he could catch the sleeper train to Cornwall? How good would it be to wake up in his attic room at Seaspray with the early morning sun creeping across the floorboards and the gulls squabbling on the roof, their comedy yellow feet scrabbling on the slates above his head? Heaven.

"Zak! There you are!"

Kellee flung herself into the seat next to him. As she leaned forward and brushed his cheek with her lips, Zak noticed that her pupils were like dark pinpricks.

"Want to dance, Zakky?" she asked. "Come on! Let's dance! Yeah! Dance with me."

She was totally wired. As Zak watched her shimmy back and forth, he felt weary to his bones. Had Kellee taken something? She must have done.

"You need to sit down and have a rest," he said. Christ, he sounded like Granny Alice, but he couldn't help himself. At twenty-eight, Zak felt ancient and Kellee seemed impossibly young.

Young and vulnerable.

Kellee reached out and slid her hand up his thigh. A pink triangle tongue flickered across her glossy lips.

"No, I don't! I want to celebrate with the sexiest man in the room!"

Zak removed her hand gently. "Thanks for the compliment, sweetheart, but I'm going back to the hotel."

"Don't be boring, Zak! Let's party all night!" Now Kellee was grabbing his arm and trying to tug him to his feet.

"Come on! Dance! Don't be boring!" she cried, swaying to the sound of her own vocals. "Let's dance!"

Zak's patience was at breaking point.

"You need to go home and sleep off whatever you've taken," he said, but Kellee simply laughed and hopped from one high-heeled foot to another.

Feeling very weary, Zak hauled himself to his feet and was on the point of walking away when Kellee pressed her hands against her chest. She had turned very pale all of a sudden and her eyes were huge and dark against the ghostly pallor of her face.

"Are you okay?" Zak asked, alarmed.

Kellee fanned her face. "I'm just a bit hot. Oh! I do feel dizzy."

"Do you want to go outside and get some air?" Zak asked. "Or get a car to take you back to your hotel?"

She shook her head. "I just need another drink. Look, Harrison's over there! He knows how to have a good time."

A tall guy was waving at her across the club and holding up a bottle of champagne. Fine, thought Zak, as he snatched up his jacket from the back of his chair and slung it over his arm; he'd tried his best, but it was a free country. Kellee could party until dawn if she wanted to, but he was out of here. The earlier conversation with Danny was still at the forefront of his mind and the sordid meeting with Ryan Kent had unnerved him further; it was almost Dickensian. Talk about the Ghost of Musicians Yet to Come. There was definitely a lesson to be learned from all this.

"Have a good night," he said to Kellee and turned away. He could still make that train if he tried.

"Oh!"

Kellee had one hand pressed against her chest, while the other stretched out to clutch at the air. Her scarlet mouth was open as she tried to gulp in some air.

Zak stopped in his tracks. "Are you all right?"

But Kellee didn't answer. Her eyes rolling upwards, she lurched forwards, grabbing the table for support as her hands flailed wildly in the search for something to hold onto. As she caught the tablecloth, the whole lot tumbled earthwards and Kellee fell to the floor too, taking champagne bottles and glasses with her in a loud crash. All eyes were on her once again.

"Drunk," said somebody scathingly.

But Zak had seen enough drunks in his time to know this was something very different.

"Get help!" he shouted to the onlookers. "Someone call an ambulance! Now!"

"Don't be ridiculous," said someone with a nervous laugh. "The silly tart's only pissed."

"Don't let the press find out," said Zak's manager who had recently signed Kellee. "She's meant to be a sodding role model."

But Zak, crouched down by her side, knew straight away that Kellee wasn't drunk. He was no medic, but Zak feared any ambulance was going to be far too late.

The tinfoil pop princess crumpled on the floor was no longer breathing.

CHAPTER SEVEN

"Who's there?"

Jake Tremaine had almost jumped out of his skin. Late in to work after picking up an outboard motor from Plymouth, he was just about to make a coffee and eat lunch when a heap of blankets on the marina office sofa shifted and moaned. Seconds later, a curly head poked out, the chin thick with stubble and the eyes so bloodshot that the irises were shockingly blue as they gazed up at him blearily.

"It's all right, Jake. It's only me."

"Zak?"

Jake was taken aback. Although all the Tremaines knew where the office key was hidden (under a pile of crab pots by the harbour gate), this particular brother was the last one he'd expect to see bunking down on the sofa. Nick, maybe, if he'd got too drunk to attempt the steep walk up to Seaspray, or even Symon if he was waiting for an early tide to go out sailing, but Zak? Never. Apart from the fact that Zak was no longer living in Cornwall and was apparently about to become a huge star (according to Granny Alice, anyhow, who thought the sun rose and set from her middle grandchild's backside), Zak had never shown the slightest interest in boats. He could swim and sail and surf with the best of them, but any spare time he had was always spent making music.

"Yep," said Zak. "Afraid so."

He kicked the blankets off and stood up slowly as though every bone in his body ached. Jake was taken aback at the state of him. It was always the family joke that Zak would look good in a bin bag, but today, with his red eyes and hollow cheeks, he looked like death. He was wearing a crumpled tuxedo and reeked of stale booze too, but Jake knew better than to comment on any of these details or ask why he had appeared in the village unannounced and hidden away here rather than surprising them all at Seaspray.

All in good time, as Granny Alice would say.

"I'm about to make a coffee," was all Jake said. "Do you want one?"

Zak nodded. "Yes, please."

Jake filled the kettle at the metal sink and flicked it on before selecting two chipped mugs from the counter. They were sparkling clean, which meant Summer must have been in and given them a thorough clean. His girlfriend was convinced the welded-on tea stains harboured all kinds of dreadful germs and just the thought of her care made Jake's heart turn over with love. How the hell had he got so lucky? It wasn't so long ago that he'd been the one hitting the booze and passing out in the office. It was practically a Tremaine rite of passage.

The kettle boiled and Jake sloshed hot water onto the instant coffee, added a dash of long-life milk and then, darting a swift look at Zak, added two heaped teaspoons of sugar.

Zak wrapped his hands around the mug and inhaled deeply.

"You have no idea how much I need this."

"Heavy night?"

"Yeah, something like that."

Jake sipped his coffee and waited for an explanation, but Zak didn't elaborate; he simply sank back onto the sofa, staring miserably into the mug and with his shoulders slumped as though he had the weight of the world on them. Jake didn't think he'd ever seen his usually sunny-natured brother look so upset.

"Woman trouble?" he ventured finally. This would be a first. Usually girls flocked around Zak like seagulls around pasty crusts and his brother's biggest issue was which hopeful female to pick. "Don't tell me, I know! You're being chased by an angry husband and you've come here to hide out?"

A shadow flickered across Zak's face.

"That last bit isn't too far from the truth. Have you caught the news this morning?"

"I try to avoid it. It only gets me in a bad mood or into a row in the pub. The closest I get to news these days is what tribute act Big Rog is going as for the music festival. Apparently he's threatening to be Meatloaf."

"Right," said Zak listlessly.

Jake put his drink down and folded his arms. "All right, the engines are going to have to wait and I'm going to have to ask – what's going on? How come you're here and not in London? And why on earth are you wearing a tux?"

Zak glanced down in surprise as though he'd only just realised he was wearing evening dress.

"I left in a bit of a hurry," he said eventually. "I didn't know where else to go. I paid a taxi driver to bring me all the way here. Easiest grand that driver ever made."

"But why not come up to the house?"

"I didn't want to see Granny Alice. I've really let her down. I've let all of you down."

"Don't be daft. How have you let us down?"

"I've quit the music business for one thing. I've walked away from it all, Jake. I don't want anything to do with it ever again."

Jake wasn't quite sure what he was hearing. For as long as he could remember, all Zak had ever wanted was to be a professional musician.

"What do you mean, you've quit?"

"Exactly that. No more music and I'm not signing my new contract with

Alchemist. No bloody way."

None of this was making sense at all to Jake.

"But why on earth not?"

"Lots of reasons, but mostly because of what happened last night."

There was a catch in Zak's voice and his usually smiley mouth was downturned. Were his eyes red from crying?

"What happened last night?" Jake asked quietly.

Zak made a noise halfway between a sob and a cough.

"God, I don't know where to start. The papers are going to go mad, so it's probably best you hear it from me first. I want you to know the truth anyway, but it's not pretty and that's the reason I didn't go straight to Seaspray. I didn't want to attract any press attention to you guys or have you associated with it all. I'm not having any of you dragged into this mess."

Jake was worried now. This was exactly the way Summer had spoken when she'd returned to the village on the run from the press. She wasn't to blame for the scandal that had followed her, but she'd totally believed everything was her fault. It had taken Jake a long time to convince her otherwise.

"I think you'd better tell me what's happened," he said.

So Zak did exactly that and their coffee grew stone cold as he recounted the whole tale, from how disillusioned he'd been feeling with the industry through to the awards ceremony and the sordid encounter with Ryan Kent, followed by the shock of Kellee's collapse.

"She died?"

"Yes."

His brother's hands were shaking so much that coffee splattered onto his trousers, but Zak didn't seem to register this. Gently, Jake reached out and took the mug away from him.

"The paramedics did their best, but she didn't make it," Zak whispered. "She was only twenty, Jake. Jesus. She was just a kid."

Jake didn't watch much television, but even he had heard of Kellee. The talent show she'd featured on was one of Summer's guilty pleasures and it was shocking to think of all that youthful energy and promise being snuffed out. He had to look out of the office window and study the lemon wedge of beach, powder blue sky and the sparkling waves in order to ground himself. Life here was real and solid. The world his brother inhabited, the world that Summer had known so well, seemed a very brittle and ugly place.

Zak pressed the heels of his hands into his eyes as though trying to grind out the shock of what he'd witnessed.

"I tried mouth-to-mouth and the paramedics were amazing, but there was nothing anyone could do. She must have had a violent reaction to something."

"That's bloody awful," Jake said. "Poor, poor girl. But it's not your fault, Zakky. It's the fault of whoever supplied her with whatever she took and her fault too for taking it in the first place, if that's what did happen. They'll do an autopsy and find out what it was, but it isn't your fault, I promise."

Zak took a deep breath. He was shaking like a puppy out in a rainstorm.

"A girl died, Jake! She collapsed and died." He closed his eyes and his mouth twisted in agony. "She was crumpled on the floor like a rag doll and I couldn't help her. I was useless."

"It wasn't down to you, Zak. What about her manager? Her friends?"

"Her manager seemed more upset about the negative press and the messed-up tour. As for friends?" He gave a harsh laugh. "You really don't know what it's like in my world, do you? Friends don't tend to stick around when it all goes to hell."

Hearing all this, Jake wasn't surprised his brother was in such a shocking state. What had happened would be traumatic for anyone, but doubly so for a sensitive soul like Zak. Images of seagulls with broken wings camping in boxes by the Aga and mice rescued from the family cat to become pets flickered through his memory. Zak had always cared about the vulnerable, and beneath his fun-loving exterior, he felt things deeply.

"And that was when I knew it was all over," Zak said. He turned back to face Jake with a firm resolve, his blue eyes as bright as gas flames. "When I'd finished speaking to the police, I told Ricky where Alchemist could stick their new contract and then I walked out of the club, flagged down a cab and came here. I left my clothes, my career, everything, and I am never going back. Never. I don't want anything to do with that world. Not if this is how it works."

"I'm proud of you," Jake said.

"You might not be when this story hits the press."

"I will be," Jake promised. "We all will be."

But Zak was too busy blaming himself to listen.

"Maybe I should have got her away? Perhaps I could have done more sooner? I could tell she was as high as a kite."

"Kellee wasn't your responsibility, Zak," Jake said gently. "She was an adult and made her own choices."

"That's what my manager said when I told him about Ryan Kent. I said he could have easily given her something, but Ricky said that was just supposition. Then he pointed out I'd been seen with Ryan in the Gents. The implication was that I could be involved in all kinds of crap."

Jake's mind was already racing ahead. Did they need a solicitor? Wasn't Uncle Ed in London a barrister?

"Did you meet Ryan there?"

"Only because I went for a slash and he was already there. Christ, Jake! I've never touched anything. Ever. I've done a lot of stuff I'm not proud of, and I've behaved like an idiot far too often, but I swear to God I've never touched drugs."

"I believe you, Zak, but you're right – this story is going to break at some point," Jake said. "But when it does, you'll be able to hold your head up high because you haven't done anything wrong."

"It doesn't feel that way," said Zak sadly. "It feels like I've done everything wrong. I've made so many mistakes, Jake, and I hardly know where to start putting them right. I don't have a bloody clue what to do now."

The boat engine he was fixing for a wealthy second homer could wait, Jake decided. Some things were far more important than work.

He put his coffee cup down and laid a sympathetic hand on his brother's shoulder.

"Come on, let's get out of here."

"Out of here?" Zak echoed.

"Yep," said Jake. "You're not thinking of staying at the marina all day, are you? If so, I'm handing you a spanner."

Zak rubbed his forehead wearily. "I hadn't thought much beyond getting here."

"So come on then. Let's go."

"Go where?"

"Home, of course," said Jake simply. "I'm taking you to Seaspray. Where else would you go now, but back where you belong? We're here for you, Zak, and you're coming home."

And at these words Zak, exhausted and broken-hearted, sagged with relief. Home was the only place in the world he wanted to be. Home was safe. And home was the only place where maybe, just maybe, he might become himself once again.

Ruth Saberton

CHAPTER EIGHT

"So how's life at Seaspray?" Morwenna Carstairs asked Summer Penhalligan a few days later as they were sitting on the sunny terrace at Mariners and drinking coffee. "How's it going with Zak back at home? Groupies camped outside yet? Trails of knickers and broken hearts leading all the way to his bedroom? Can't be easy living there anyway, but having him rock up must be interesting?"

Summer wasn't quite sure how to reply. She loved living at Seaspray with Jake and the assorted members of the Tremaine clan who washed in and out of the place just like the tide ran up the beach. Some of her London friends had raised eyebrows and wondered how she could put up with the constant presence of other people. Didn't having his grandmother in close proximity make things awkward for her and Jake? Didn't this cramp their style? These were usually the first questions asked, as though if not for Alice's presence, Summer and Jake would be cavorting naked throughout the house and making love on the kitchen table/bathroom floor/staircase – delete as appropriate! Apart from the fact that Seaspray was an old house, filled with draughts and where Summer and Jake would die of cold if they even dared wander about naked in their bathroom, Jake worked long hours at the boatyard, a very physical job which meant he was asleep almost as soon as his blonde head touched the pillow. No, Alice Tremaine had never been anything other than a thoughtful and tactful housemate. Jake and Summer had a room at the far end of the house and Alice had never once intruded on their privacy, but generally they spent more time with the family than they did in their room.

As a teenager, Summer had loved spending time at Seaspray, chatting to Alice in the kitchen where she learned to bake bread and scones like plump pillows while pouring out all her worries. Alice Tremaine was a wonderful listener. Recently, Summer had been really worried about an upcoming and potentially very nasty court case with her ex, and Alice had been a wonderful sounding board.

"Bide your time," had been her advice. "Things have a way of working themselves out the way they're meant to, my love. You'll see."

Alice had been right too. Only a few days ago, Justin's solicitor had called with an offer to settle out of court. Summer hardly dared get her hopes up, but if this worked out, it would be a huge relief. She was so happy now with Jake, and just the thought of having to relive her past in court and having the sordid details dragged through the tabloids made her feel quite sick. Jake just got angry and wanted to throttle Justin, which didn't really help. Only Alice's calm words and sound advice had kept Summer from having a complete meltdown.

So, no, living with Alice was fine. Better than fine, it was wonderful because she and Jake were part of a big family unit here and Summer felt safe. Set high above the village at the foot of the coastal path and within steep terraced gardens, Seaspray was castle-like and had been Summer's protection ever since she had moved home. She loved waking up in the morning to see the waves tickling the sand and she loved wandering into the kitchen to place the kettle on the Aga. Sometimes she'd make pancakes for Morgan if it was Dan's weekend to have his son, although Morgan had to eat them fast; otherwise Nick would hoover up the lot. Even Jonny St Milton was easy to live with, tending to spend his time snoozing or with Alice. Generally, everyone rubbed along pretty well, Summer always thought, and Seaspray was a happy place to be. Any visitors who braved the steep climb up to the house loved to sit and chat at the kitchen table and the rest of the family were frequent visitors too. So, usually, if she was asked how it was living with her boyfriend's family, Summer would reply that it was great.

But now Zak was home, her answer might be a little different.

"Well?" Jigging her daughter on her lap, Mo gave Summer a searching look over the toddler's head. "I said, how's it going with Zak? I didn't ask you to explain the theory of relativity."

Summer thought it might be easier to have a stab at some complex physics. Since Zak arrived, it felt as though one of the storm clouds that often billowed across the horizon had changed direction and settled permanently above the house. Having grown up with the Tremaines, Summer had known Zak a long time, but it was hard to equate the sunny-natured and happy-go-lucky guy she knew with the brooding presence drifting around the place like something from Edgar Allen Poe. Zak wasn't eating, had shut himself in his room and was flatly refusing to take any calls from his manager. Summer only knew the bare bones of what had happened in London, but it was clear to her that Zak was blaming himself for the tragedy.

Alice was dreadfully worried about her grandson and after almost a week, his dark mood was weighing everyone down. Thankfully the papers hadn't mentioned Zak in conjunction with Kellee's death but, knowing the tabloids as she did, Summer doubted it would be long before journalists began to ask questions and knock on the door. The police had been in touch too and she knew how people always loved to speculate. Only this morning she'd overheard Keyhole Kathy Polmartin gossiping in the village shop, and Sheila Keverne had stopped her in the street to enquire, oh so caringly, about Zak. Was Zachary home for long? Was he unwell and was that why they hadn't seen him? Could she have a copy of his new record for her granddaughter? Was it true he was at the party where that poor young girl died?

Summer had felt like bashing Sheila and Kathy over the head with her wire shopping basket, but just about managed to refrain. Reminding herself that Justin's solicitor would clap his hands with glee if she lost the plot in public, Summer dredged up her old acting skills and sweetly said that Zak was simply home to rest after a busy time away. Then she'd forced herself to select some groceries and make small talk at the till before escaping up to Mariners to see Mo. After creeping around Seaspray, holding her breath and trying her best to be bright and breezy to perk Zak up, Summer needed a change of scene and topic.

She should have known better. One look at her face and Mo twigged instantly something was afoot. There was never any hiding from old friends – not even when you wanted to protect them from worrying or from hearing village gossip – and so Summer reluctantly recounted the conversation in the village shop.

"Those bloody old biddies!" Mo flared, her hands over Isla's ears. "One of these days, I swear I'll swing for them. How dare they!"

Mo's fiery temper matched her red hair and she was always quick to fly off the handle. Summer often thought it was amazing that Mo and her husband Ashley had ever managed to find a gap in their squabbling to fall in love and have a baby.

"It's not worth it. They'll be talking about something else tomorrow," she soothed. It was what she'd been telling herself during the long climb to Mo's house. "The Polwenna Festival is big news now and this talent show that Big Rog is organising. They're all trying to guess who will enter." Hoping for a way to divert Mo, she added, "Will you take part?"

"Nice try, but I'm not that easily sidetracked," said Mo. "Tell me more about Zak. Ash and I have only been back from London for a few days, so I haven't had a chance to catch up with the family yet. Sounds like we need to talk." She lowered Isla to the ground, wincing as she did so. "Go and find Daddy, sweetie, and ask him for a drink of milk and a biscuit. It's time he looked up from that computer screen anyway. No wonder he gets headaches." Meeting Summer's questioning gaze, she added grimly, "At least that's his story."

"Ashley's having headaches?"

"Either that or we have a Nurofen-guzzling poltergeist."

Summer lifted up her sunglasses and studied Mo carefully. Her friend's blue eyes were dark with worry, which was understandable given how unwell Ashley had been in the past.

"Has Ashley seen anyone about it?"

Mo rolled her eyes. "He just tells me he's fine and to stop nagging. Seems Ash is a neurosurgeon these days, as well as an expert on horses and childcare. I'd call his consultant and book him in myself, except it's not allowed apparently. Bloody medical ethics. Ashley's so stubborn I could scream. He won't listen to anyone."

"Oddly enough, that's exactly what he was saying to Jake that other day about you insisting on competing," said Summer, who didn't think she'd ever met a couple so well suited. Both were as pig-headed as the other – and they both loved each other desperately too. From bitter enemies to lovers, their relationship had seen more fireworks than the village's annual Guy Fawkes celebration. Now they were arguing about Mo's chosen career path.

"My eventing career isn't up for debate. Ashley knows that," said Mo.

Mo was a talented equestrienne who'd always wanted to reach the top of the game in three-day eventing. After having Isla, she'd taken a year off, but was now itching to get back out on the competitive circuit, an ambition that was causing all kinds of tensions with her husband who thought eventing was far too dangerous. Looking at Mo now, shifting her weight gingerly and grimacing as she topped up their coffee, Summer was inclined to agree with him.

"Horse-related injury?"

Mo shrugged and winced again.

"I fell off Dandy last night when he pecked on landing. Bloody stupid of me – a real rookie mistake. I can't believe I did it." Doubt flickered across her face. "I hope I haven't lost the ability to actually ride. Wouldn't that be ironic?"

"Of course you haven't," said Summer staunchly. "You've got natural talent and that won't go away. Look at me earlier, acting my heart out in the village shop! Practically Bafta-winning stuff."

"More like the start of an episode of Midsomer Murders. Who battered Sheila Keverne to death with the Duchy Originals biscuits? Or strangled Kathy Polmartin with the liquorice bootlaces?" Mo started to laugh and then clutched her chest. "Ouch! Christ! That hurts!"

"Are you okay?"

"It's nothing a few painkillers can't cure, or would cure if Ashley hadn't guzzled them all."

"Maybe you should see Dr Penwarren? Or go to A and E?" Summer suggested, but Mo just flapped her hand.

"Stop fussing, Summer. You're worse than Granny Alice. It's only a couple of cracked ribs or something."

Summer opened her mouth to say this sounded bad enough, but then thought better of it. Mo would take herself off to see Richard Penwarren soon enough. She just had to think it was her own idea.

"I don't have time to see a doctor anyway. There's too much to do at the yard. I really wish Emerald had stuck around a bit longer. I could have done with a hand right now." Mo was swirling her coffee impatiently. "Anyway, never mind me. It sounds as though Zak's the one we should be worrying about. You said he's hardly come out of his room in days? Not even to go on the pull with Nick?"

"Nick tried to persuade him to go for a drink, but Zak said he couldn't face going out."

"And he seriously hasn't played his guitar? Or even lifted the lid on the piano?"

"Not as far as I know. He told Alice that he's not in the mood to play music."

"That's very worrying," said Mo. "Music's always been everything to Zak." She looked out across the bay to the farthest side of the village where Seaspray clung to the hillside. "It's what I remember most about him from when we were kids. He was always singing or driving us crazy playing scales on the piano or strumming his guitar. He always wrote songs for birthdays too. Lord, I can't remember a time when Zak didn't sing or play. Music's everything to him – like horses are to me. I guess a psychologist would say we both looked for something to distract ourselves after Mum died. Granny was really busy with the little ones, so we older ones had to find our own way of not being alone. It might have helped if Dad hadn't pushed off, but there you go – that's Jimmy for you."

Mo focused on the sea, slipping back in time to that dark place of loss and confusion.

"But you did find your way," Summer reminded her. "And you have Ashley and Isla now. You're not alone."

"Zak doesn't have that though, does he? A person who loves him as much as he loves them. Someone who's his world, like Jake is for you and Ash is to me. And if he's going through something now, blaming himself for it all if I know my little brother, then without music, what has he got? He's all alone."

"From what I know of Zak, that won't last very long," said Summer. Keyhole Kathy's daughter had already quietly asked her if Zak was single, and Penny Kussell had walked up to Seaspray twice that week on the pretext of discussing festival business with Jules.

"I know Zak's got a bit of a reputation as a player—" Mo began, holding up her hand when Summer started to say that this was a bit like saying Hugh Hefner quite liked women. "No, hear me out! Part of that is playing up to the whole musician image. Plus, he's gorgeous, which I can say objectively even though I'm his sister and I know all his worst secrets, and he's a man too, so he's hardly likely to say 'no' when girls throw themselves at him, is he? And they've always chucked themselves at Zak and they always will. It's practically a law of physics."

All the Tremaines were beautiful, Jake most of all in Summer's eyes, but she had to concede, Zak was the most perfect of the bunch. The golden mane, ski-slope cheekbones and dimples you could lose your fingertips in, combined with dancing blue eyes, toned body and a cheeky devil-may-care attitude – the combination was lethal. Even with a forlorn expression, his eyes dark with unhappiness and the wild mane tamed into a ponytail, Zak had a broken man appeal women just couldn't resist. From Rochester to Christian Grey, it was a compelling challenge and they would soon be flocking to the front door. Summer knew that the hearts of Polwenna's young women were in big trouble.

"Can't you see what's really going on with him?" Mo demanded when Summer didn't reply. "Zak's a classic middle child; he's always looking for love and attention. I bet you that's what the fame thing's all about too."

"Believe me, that isn't what it's cracked up to be," said Summer with a shudder.

"You know that and I think Zak does too deep down." Mo looked thoughtful. "The last time Ash and I met up with him, we both thought he looked dreadful and his sparkle had totally gone. I know he misses home too and I reckon even before all this stuff happened, he'd figured out being famous isn't the way to find what he's really looking for."

"And what's that exactly?" Summer wondered.

"Love, of course!"

"Love?" Summer wasn't sure about this. Zak had never struck her as a man looking to settle down.

"Yes! L-O-V-E. Love!" said Mo. "My little brother's a true romantic. Out of all of us, I reckon he's the biggest romantic of the lot, and he feels things the most too. Where else do you think all those lyrics and heartbreaking melodies come from? He's only been through so many women because he's looking for 'the One'."

It was one explanation, Summer supposed. Whether or not it would be much comfort to all the weeping girls left in Zak's wake was another issue altogether.

"My God, I'm a genius," said Mo. "If the horses don't work out, maybe I should be a therapist? Or a psychologist?"

Summer laughed. "I think horses are less dangerous than your meddling! Symon wasn't too thrilled when you set him up with Tess Hamilton, was he?"

Mo grimaced. "Sy should have stuck with Tess and been a bit more grateful to me. Now look at him; saddled with Evil Ella. Doh!"

Symon Tremaine was actually blissfully happy with Ella St Milton, but Summer knew when to keep quiet. Mo showed no signs of wanting to bury that particular hatchet.

"So, it's down to us," Mo concluded with a determined look on her face that Summer recognised of old. It was the same expression she'd worn when she'd cut off Ella St Milton's plaits, told Ashley Carstairs he wouldn't be bulldozing a road through the woods (something Mo said she regretted now she had to push Isla's buggy half a mile along a muddy track in order to reach Mariners) or when she set her horse at a big cross-country fence.

"What's down to us?" Summer asked nervously.

"Sorting out my sad brother's love life, of course!" Mo's blue eyes shone with zeal. There was nothing she liked more than a mission. "We're going to help Zak find love, and since he loves Cornwall so much, where better to start looking than right here, at home in Polwenna Bay? And you've given me the best idea yet!"

Summer stared at her, alarmed. "I have?"

"Absolutely," beamed Mo. "Tess Hamilton, of course! She's perfect for him!"

CHAPTER NINE

While his sister was psychoanalysing him on the other side of the village, Zak Tremaine lay on his old bed and stared up at the ceiling. The same cracks that had been there for as long as he could remember still threaded their way over the plaster in a network of rivers and tributaries and there was a certain comfort in losing himself in the familiar patterns. The same comfort came from being back home again and high up in his old attic room where at night the house creaked and groaned around him like a storm-tossed galleon, while the sea far below teased the shore just as it always had and always would. This made his own transience – and Kellee's too – no less dreadful, but it did put things into context.

Nothing was forever, was it?

It was a Saturday morning in June. Sunshine strobed through the cracks in the faded curtains like the big searchlights which used to cut across the stage at the larger gigs he'd played, and he could hear the chug of engines from the harbour as the tripping boats carried visitors in and out of the bay. He didn't need to swing his legs over the side of the bed frame and pull the curtains apart to see what was going on; the rhythm of the tide and the comings and goings of the village were as familiar to him as his own breathing. He knew that the cliffs would bloom yellow with gorse, the sea breeze carry the taint of wild garlic, and that far below the twisting ribbon of the South West Way, seabirds would be nesting on ledges and squabbling noisily amongst themselves. It had always been the same and it would be the same long after he was gone. Time was a faithful, if cruel, lover.

That was a line for a song and for the briefest moment a melody shadowed the words. Once, Zak would have reached for a pen to jot it down. Some of his best work could trace its genesis to such moments when home at Seaspray, but today he turned his face to the wall in despair. What was the point of reaching down into the depths of his soul and dredging up music from the deepest and darkest places when the end result was that a record company would trade truth for sales? Why write at all?

Why do anything?

Zak closed his eyes. They felt gritty and heavy and to open them again was an effort. He'd been up for most of the night reliving the events of the past week, and it felt as though as soon as he managed to drop off into an uneasy slumber, the noise of the house waking had dragged him back to consciousness. The first sound was always the rumble of the boiler and the rattle of pipes as the antiquated heating system attempted to warm the house. This was followed by the padding of feet over bare boards and the clicking shut of bathroom doors. As taps were run, the water pipes groaned and the cisterns clanked when toilets were flushed. Voices drifted up from the stairwell, shortly followed by the whoosh of water as somebody filled the kettle. Over the years, these sounds had been woven together into the tapestry of life at Seaspray. Pans clattering, a door slamming, seagulls shrieking – everything sounded as it always had. How was it possible for nothing to have changed when everything felt so utterly different?

When Jake had taken him home, Zak had hoped that being at Seaspray would make everything all right again, but even the familiarity and safety of being with his family couldn't magically erase the past two years and the utter horror of Kellee's collapse. In a weird way, being home actually made him feel worse, if anything, because how could it all feel the same when he was completely changed?

Zak knew his grandmother was worried and he hated to think he was responsible for giving Alice any extra stress. He'd told her a little about what had happened – the bare bones really – but the story was already leaking out. Like prodding a wobbly tooth when you were eleven, Zak kept checking the newsfeed on his phone to see how much more dirt the press had managed to dig up. He wasn't naïve enough to think that they would leave Kellee alone for long. The gutter press didn't give a toss about respecting anyone, dead or alive.

It was only a matter of time before everyone knew he was the one who'd been with Kellee when she collapsed. Then the speculation and the gossip would really begin, and how could he protect Alice then? It didn't matter that he had never touched drugs and had no part in what had happened to Kellee; people would start to speculate and soon they'd point the finger. Zak didn't care about what they thought of him; he knew the truth and that was enough for his conscience, but he did care about how certain people might treat his grandmother. Alice had given up so much to care for him and the others and she should be taking it easy now, enjoying retirement and looking forward to her wedding. What if he'd only succeeded in bringing trouble to her doorstep?

Maybe he should have stayed away?

But Zak couldn't stay away because Cornwall was where his heart belonged. The scoured light, the rugged granite cliffs and the wind so sharp it could etch glass were a part of him and there was nowhere else he could imagine being. He heard music in everything, from the whispering of the waves to the chortle of the River Wenn as it gushed through the village and spluttered into the harbour.

Jake, as always, had not passed judgement. He'd let Zak talk himself hoarse before saying there was nothing Zak could have done. Summer too had been sympathetic, and the fact that she knew something of the shark-infested waters into which Zak had dipped his toes helped him feel less alone. Nick, being Nick, had simply offered to take him down the pub and get hammered.

"It's summer and the emmets are here! First sign of sun and there are girls in bikinis everywhere! You're bound to score and that will cheer you up," Nick had said happily.

Once, in what felt like another life altogether, this was exactly what Zak would have done to make himself feel better. He loved women and adored their company; there was no high to compare with that moment when you locked eyes with a stranger and knew instantly the fizz of attraction. Zak loved the whole process of smiling across a room, catching a gaze several times, buying a drink, introducing himself, the soft touch of lips and the sweet intake of breath at that first kiss, and then the wonder-filled holding and whispering until the moon and stars faded away and dawn rippled the sky blue and peach. Nothing else, not even music, made time recede so beautifully or the heart soar with the hope that this time, maybe, just maybe, it was something special...

Except that it never was, and then the disappointment was crushing or, even worse, not even a surprise. Lately, going out on dates with the models and actresses and wannabes that flitted through his world like a flutter of gorgeous butterflies had left Zak feeling lacklustre, so Nick's suggestion held no appeal. Just the thought of partying, flirting, drinking and, if he was successful, having a meaningless one-night encounter made Zak feel exhausted. He'd even found himself increasingly envious of Alex for escaping the music business and settling down with Kat. There were three missed calls from Alex on Zak's phone, and many more than that from Ricky, Zak's manager. All went unanswered. The last thing Alex needed was to be inflicted with his miserable mood, and as for his manager – Zak clenched his jaw. Their last conversation had been enough.

"I get that you're upset, man," Ricky Howard had said when Zak told him he was through with Alchemist, "but the police have cleared you of any involvement. It's all cool."

"Of course the police cleared me! It wasn't my doing," Zak said. The truth was that he blamed himself every minute of every day, but he knew in his heart this made no sense. What Kellee had chosen to do was her own affair and even if he had persuaded her to leave the party, it was unlikely the outcome would have been any different.

"I know, man! Of course I do. What I'm saying is that officially nobody can blame you."

"Do you seriously think that's what I'm upset about? A girl died," Zak said, hardly able to believe what he was hearing.

"Yeah, I know, and it's a shame, but she was off her head, Zak, and it wasn't the first time either. Everyone knew Kellee was into all kinds of stuff. You need to move on."

"Jesus, Ricky! If everybody knew, then why didn't they do something about it? Get her some help? Therapy?"

There had been an impatient intake of breath on the end of the line. His manager was trying to hide his frustration and Zak could picture Ricky perfectly, fingers drumming on the desktop and eyes rolling skywards.

"It's the music business," he'd said wearily. "Sex and drugs and rock 'n' roll, yeah? It happens. She's not the first and she sure as hell won't be the last."

Zak struggled to keep his temper.

"Well, it shouldn't happen and I'm telling you, I am through with all this shit."

"You're upset," Ricky said. "I get that, Zak, but you've worked too hard and come too far to quit now. You're on the edge of something huge."

"Yeah, a bloody cliff," Zak muttered.

Ricky chose to ignore this. Zak knew he had too much invested in his client to be inclined to push. He was probably thinking Zak would come around eventually. Well, Ricky was wrong. Once a Tremaine made their mind up, then that was it.

"Take a bit of time, get your shit together, and then we'll talk about that contract, yeah?" Ricky said finally. "I'll stall the big guys. Okay?"

Zak didn't bother to reply. He ended the call and switched his phone off, tossing it across the room as though just holding it contaminated him. Ricky's casual indifference had been the last straw. If he chose that life, Zak knew it was only a matter of time before he was as jaded as the rest of them. Then how did you cope? Drink? Sex? Drugs? The distance between him and Ryan Kent wasn't as great as he'd once thought. Thank God he was back in Cornwall.

The rap of knuckles on his bedroom door plucked Zak out of his thoughts.

"Zak, love? Are you awake?"

It was his grandmother, breathless from the steep climb, her voice threaded with concern. Zak heaved himself up into a sitting position and pushed his hair away from his face. He needed to sort himself out. He couldn't have his grandmother running around after him like this.

"I'm awake, Granny," Zak called back.

"I've brought you some tea," Alice said, edging a mug around the door. It was the same chipped one he'd used as a kid and Zak was touched that his grandmother had gone to the effort of hunting it out.

"I'm dressed," he said, sitting up.

"I should hope so too! It's almost lunchtime." Alice Tremaine bustled in and set the drink down on the bedside table. She was followed by Morgan who was carrying a plate piled high with toast.

"Are you depressed, Uncle Zak?" he asked, regarding Zak curiously.

Zak wasn't quite sure what to say to this.

"I don't think so," he said carefully. Zak was sure he'd heard that when people were depressed, they struggled to identify the reason why, whereas he knew perfectly well why he felt so utterly bloody.

"If you are depressed, then fresh air and exercise help. Fact," Morgan said solemnly. "Mo says that you need to get off your backside and stop moping."

"Morgan! That's enough!" Alice said sharply.

"But Mo did say that," Morgan protested. "Then Dad said it's hard to stop moping when you've watched someone die."

At least Danny understood. Zak wouldn't expect Mo to be sympathetic, as his formative years had been spent with his no-nonsense sister chivvying him along and scoffing at his nightmares of monsters under the bed and his need to sleep with the light on. Where Zak was a dreamer and a worrier, Mo was all about action and facing your fears and doing it anyway, which was probably just as well in her profession. If Mo imagined what could go wrong every time she set a horse at a fence, she'd never leave the starting box.

"I can see that they need to watch what they say in front of you, young man," said Alice.

Morgan was baffled. "But they did say that! And then you said you thought he was having a breakdown. You wanted Mum to speak to Richard."

Zak was rather alarmed. While he'd been quietly minding his own business in his room, it seemed his family had been holding some sort of pre-intervention meeting regarding his state of mind. Just great. The last thing Zak wanted, or needed, was Dr Richard Penwarren coming up to give him the once-over. As nice as Richard was, this was totally out of his realm of experience. Ironically, Morgan had just thrown Zak a small lifeline; maybe he should talk to Danny? Dan more than anyone would understand this overwhelming sense of guilt at being alive and the feeling of helplessness at losing the only goal you'd ever worked for.

"Downstairs, young man!" ordered Alice, relieving Morgan of the toast and setting it by the tea. She placed her hand on her great-grandson's head and spun him around. "Now!"

Morgan knew better than to argue and beat a hasty retreat.

Alice pulled open the curtains, flooding the room with sunshine, and pushed up the sash windows to fill the fetid room with salt breezes and the cries of gulls.

"You should go out and get some fresh air, love. Staying up here stewing won't do you any favours."

"Because I'm having a breakdown?" Zak asked.

"Oh, love, I didn't put it quite like that, but we're all so worried. You've hardly said a word to any of us since you came home. You hide away up here and you haven't touched a musical instrument since you arrived."

Perplexed, Alice sat beside him, and when he saw how tired she was, Zak felt bad. He took his grandmother's hands in his, taken aback that they were light as birds' bones and the skin so fragile like tissue paper. Oh! When had she got so old? His heart squeezed with love and he gave her a hug.

"Granny, I'm not cracking up. I'm just really sad and lost and angry and a million other things too, but I promise you I'm not losing the plot. I just need time to figure a few things out. I've decided I'm not going back to Alchemist."

"But your career!" said Alice.

A knot tightened in Zak's throat. He knew he couldn't sing a note as long as it was lodged there.

"I need a break from it all, Granny," Zak said, although this didn't come close to the feeling of wanting to run as fast and as far as he could. "It's all got... stuck and I don't even know if I want be in the music business any more."

"You've had an awful shock—" Alice began, but Zak shook his head.

"It's more than that, Granny. What happened to Kellee was awful, but things have been building up for ages. I know I should have helped her, made her leave the party—"

"Oh, love, it wasn't your responsibility. Please don't blame yourself."

Zak thought he could no more stop feeling responsible than he could stop the waves rolling up the beach, but there was no way he could explain this to his grandmother.

"I just need a bit of time to figure things out," was all he said. "I need to work out what I'm going to do and I don't know right now if music's going to be my future."

Or even a part of my life, he added silently.

"And what will you do until you decide?" Alice asked.

"Don't look so worried, I won't be staying in bed forever. Maybe I'll turn spanners for Jake at the marina? Be a part of the family business?"

Now his grandmother really did look concerned. Zak was a dreadful mechanic. It was a family joke that boat engines seized up as soon as he was within ten paces and, unlike the rest of the clan, he suffered dreadfully from seasickness. The future of Tremaine Marine was in grave danger if he was let anywhere near it.

"Perhaps I'll go travelling?" he added. "Like Dad?"

"I don't know if Jimmy's the best example to follow, love. Running away only causes a whole lot of other problems from what I've seen." Alice rose creakily to her feet. "But there is one thing I do know for sure and that is that life passes by a lot faster than we ever think it will. Don't waste precious time blaming yourself and feeling guilty. You can't change the past, but you can change the future."

Zak nodded. Changing the future was exactly what he was planning to do. Changing it as far as possible from the path he had been on.

Alice paused at the door. "By the way, love, Mo's invited you up to Mariners for supper tonight."

Zak groaned. "Would this be part of your master plan to get me off my backside and stop me moping?"

"You know I didn't mean it like that," huffed Alice. "And no, Mo's just being thoughtful. Anyway, it will do you good to have a change of scene. Jonny and I are going out for dinner tonight and Danny will be with Jules, so there won't be anything cooked here."

"I'll be fine," Zak said. Maybe he'd make some toast or send Nick out to fetch a takeaway or not eat at all? Anything was preferable to being bullied/interrogated/nagged by his big sister.

"I know you'll be fine, but it will do you good to get out," Alice said, and in the tone of voice that Zak knew from years of trying to skive from school or stay up past bedtime meant she wasn't to be argued with. "She's invited Alex and Kat up too. It'll do you good to see your friends."

Zak was even more horrified. "For God's sake, Granny Alice! I'm not feeling sociable. Christ!"

"We've left you in peace for days," Alice shot back. "I don't think it's doing you any favours. Don't shut your friends and family out, Zak, and don't take them for granted either. And while you're at it, don't blaspheme. I'm not so old I can't still wash your mouth out with soap and water!"

Once his grandmother had gone, shutting the door behind her with an offended thud, Zak walked to the window and stared out over the village. His tea and toast grew cold as the sun climbed higher in the sky and the tripping boats left and returned in a gentle rhythm. The tide retreated until the beach was a watermelon slice of shining sand, nibbled by waves and frilled with seaweed. Suddenly he wanted nothing more than to be outside in the fresh air with the sky arching above and the breeze whipping away his heavy mood. Grabbing his leather jacket, he dashed down the stairs and out of the front door before he could bump into any more well-meaning family members. Spotting Jules climbing up the garden path, her plump face pink and her hair sticking to her cheeks, he took the left-hand path that threaded through the rose garden and led to the cliffs. No offence to Jules, but Zak had had quite enough sermons for one day.

Once on the coast path, Zak took the steep route that led down to the rocks. This was a spot where he had always liked to sit and simply be. The march of the waves and the pungent incense of sea and kelp always soothed him, and there was something about observing the village from across the bay which always put life into perspective. He could certainly do with some perspective today.

Zak lay his jacket across a rock and settled down to watch the living painting that was the village. He spotted Jake down on the quayside and listened to the clank of the harbourside derrick as Eddie Penhalligan deposited iced-up fish boxes onto the deck of his trawler. The beach was dotted with tourists determined to pretend that the sun was warm enough to laze about on striped towels, and a solitary figure walked along the water's edge, long blonde hair blowing in the breeze and footprints speckling behind her. Zak recognised her vaguely as the local teacher Nick had briefly dated. She was intense, Zak recalled, and clever too. No wonder it hadn't lasted five minutes with his brother. This was the kind of girl who always appeared composed and a little aloof too, and even from this distance, she looked as though she had the weight of the world on her shoulders. It was a look Zak recognised instantly.

Nobody knew better than him just how heavy that weight could feel.

CHAPTER TEN

Most teachers lived for the school holidays, but for Tess, time off work posed a whole host of problems that she didn't have to think about during term time. One was that her parents invariably called and invited her home, requiring Tess to develop the creative skills of Caspar James in order to invent plausible excuses, while another was that rather than having her days packed fuller than the Circle Line in rush hour, she suddenly had hours and hours of free time stretching ahead. Without thirty small people to take care of, ringing bells to divide her day up into neat segments and hours of preparation to attend to in the evenings, Tess soon found herself at a loose end.

Having spare time was not something Tess enjoyed. In her experience, busy was best because that way she didn't find herself looking up at the shelf where her violin slumbered and wondering about what could have been.

Wondering was bad news. Wondering was when thoughts and regrets started to seep in through spare time's hairline cracks. Tess had worked hard keeping these at bay to be defeated this far down the line. So far this half term she'd tidied and reorganised her classroom, made a wall display, rewritten Polwenna Primary's e-safety policy, made a stack of new learning resources and marked all her books. The school caretaker had chased her out in the end, saying he needed time off even if she didn't. Tess supposed she could read a classic novel, maybe the copy of Middlemarch that had been languishing on the bookshelf since uni, or go shopping in Truro, but unlike a day in the classroom, she knew these activities wouldn't make her pass out with exhaustion almost as soon as her head touched the pillow.

Today Tess had been busy rearranging her kitchen cupboards and making sure her grade spreadsheets were up to date and colour-coded. There was nothing left to do, so when Mo Tremaine had called with an invitation to supper, Tess's inclination was to accept and pencil into her mental diary that the hours between seven and ten that night were now accounted for. Only the fact that she'd once been talked into going for dinner with Mo's brother Symon for a very similar reason – to kill time – made her demur.

"It's only a casual supper," Mo promised. "There's no need to dress up or anything – Ash is cooking spag bol for us and a couple of friends. He always makes way too much and I'll never get down to my riding weight if I scoff the lot. You'd be doing me a favour."

"What friends?" Tess asked, instantly suspicious. "You're not about to set me up with some single mate of Ashley's are you?"

"Of course not! I wouldn't dream of doing that," protested Mo.

"Anyway, Ashley doesn't have any friends. These are lovely people who'll be moving to the village. She's a teacher and he works in the record industry. You'll like them."

"Do you mean Alex and Kat?"

"So you've already met them!"

"I had dinner with them in The Ship," Tess told Mo. She'd thoroughly enjoyed her night with the couple and had a feeling they might be good friends once they lived in the village. It would be fun to see them again.

"Brilliant! See you at seven then," Mo had said and, taking this as an acceptance, rung off.

Now Tess had the evening sorted, all she had to do was fill the afternoon. Deciding it was time to go and enjoy the sunny day, she pulled her hair into a high ponytail, shoved her feet into her ancient Hunter wellies and set off to the beach. There was nothing like a walk along the seashore to blow the cobwebs away, and being able to do this regularly was one of the things Tess loved the most about living in Cornwall. It was a healing place where the seasons might come and go, but where there was a sense of timelessness in the granite of the cliffs, the shifting of the sands and the metronomic rhythm of the tide. She was on the brink of starting to think about things and a walk was exactly what she needed.

Tess crossed the bridge, followed the narrow street past the Cod Father, the Mermaid gift shop and lastly The Ship, before taking the steep steps at the foot of the quay two at a time. Once the sand was beneath her feet, she stomped across the beach towards the snaggle-toothed rocks that guarded the far end of the bay. Since it was sunny, families had set up for the day, pitching windbreaks and laying out picnics, and as she walked, Tess waved at children from school and exchanged pleasantries with their parents. Here she was Miss Hamilton the schoolteacher; she was respected, admired, a pillar of the community. In Polwenna, Tess was free to be herself rather than the daughter of gifted parents and something of a disappointment.

Here, nobody knew what had happened with Vassilly or could tell that he'd smashed her heart with more force than the waves pounded against the rocks of the headland.

Tess pushed that memory back down into the deep place where she locked away the past. She slammed the door on it, shot the bolts home and turned the key just for good measure. That was where the past was staying. She should throw away the key too, as there was no going back. Not ever.

She reached the far end of the beach and, having no desire to gamble with the tide and clamber over the rocks to the next cove, Tess retraced her footsteps. Her prints were already filling with water as the tide continued to creep away. Time didn't wait for anyone, Tess thought. People moved on. Things changed. Hearts mended.

But if that was true, why did she still find it all so hard? Why was it that whenever she stood still for just a moment, everything came racing back to her, the pain as raw as the day it happened?

Don't. Think. About. It. That was the best way.

Tess upped her pace and focused her attention on the horizon, but no matter how hard she tried to keep them at bay, the memories rolled in with the waves. The suck and hiss of the sea became percussion building up to the first sweet notes of the violin, the music as mournful and heart-rending as though pulled from the soul.

The beach faded away and the sand beneath Tess's feet became the cool boards of the concert hall stage. She was playing in front of the great and the good of the conservatoire, her father was conducting, the hall was packed and this was it, the pinnacle of everything she had trained for over the past twenty years. Tess's entire life to date had been simply a prelude to this very moment. As she played, Tess lost herself in the music, rising and falling with each plaintive note, and as though watching from outside of herself, she had known that this was the most perfect performance of her life. She was as talented and as full of possibilities as her parents could have hoped.

If your life can change in the beat of a minim, the querulous tremble of a quaver, then this was the moment distilled. If she had only focused on the music, kept her eyes away from the audience, then Tess would have never known the truth. Maybe even now she would be playing to packed auditoriums and wowing the classical world with her talent. But Tess had been scanning the front row of the audience because Vassilly had promised to be there. Her beautiful Vassilly with his sloe black eyes, raven dark hair and panther's deadly grace and of whom just the slightest glimpse had been enough to make her heart turn cartwheels.

Was there anything in the world more powerful and more intoxicating than first love? If there was, then Tess was yet to discover it. That feeling of every nerve being on red alert and every sense quivering when he was near. The exhilaration when he walked into a room and the crushing disappointment if he failed to appear. The way that a fleeting smile from him was the sunshine she wanted to bathe in and, like a flower, turn her face towards. The melting in her loins if he so much as casually brushed his fingers against hers or pushed a curl back from her face while they were studying a score.

It was such a cliché. The handsome music teacher who was her father's latest protégé, and something of a genius too, and the shy girl with a tendency to blush and a big talent that threatened to overwhelm her. When Vass had been employed to tutor her, Tess had soon come to live for her lessons with him.

And music wasn't all the handsome young man taught her.

For almost a year, the eighteen-year-old Tess had thought of nothing but Vass and her playing. Music was her world and she had a bright future ahead; everyone said so. As the daughter of the famous Hamiltons, it was practically a foregone conclusion, but with Vassilly as her tutor, and her secret lover, Tess knew her talent had reached a whole new level. Vass and music seemed to be one and the same and now she could no more listen to Mozart or Beethoven without thinking of him than she could live without breathing. Those hands sliding over hers to position her fingers were the same hands that slid the bra straps from her shoulders and caressed her naked skin. With the same skill that made the violin tremble, he'd drawn out sighs and gasps from Tess.

Vassilly was always careful not to declare their relationship, saying he respected her too much to do so, but that one day they would be together. Tess was flattered and frustrated in equal measure because her feelings for him were echoed in every note she played and the result was musical performances of such depth and dexterity that she had quickly come to the attention of the Royal Academy. Everyone said that he was an incredible teacher and Tess, the teacher in her appalled now by his lack of professionalism, had made astonishing progress.

Her parents had welcomed Vass into their home, and before long he was living in the staff annexe at the Richmond house, which meant he and Tess could see each other far more easily and much more often. Every day was charged with excitement, and the snatched moments in his flat or in the music room while her father was busy had been the most exciting of Tess's life so far. She'd been head over heels in love and it was the most wonderful and all-consuming emotion. Keeping her feelings a secret, which Vassilly insisted they must do, was hard because Tess – open and honest by nature – had wanted to tell the world.

"Why can't we tell anyone?" she would ask him. "I'm eighteen and you're only twenty-nine, so it's not such a big gap. We love each other, so why shouldn't we be together? I'm not ashamed."

But Vassilly would always stop her words with a kiss or a caress that turned her bones to jelly and then promise Tess that when the time was right, they would declare their feelings. Yet there was always a reason why they had to keep it a secret: his job with her father, his role as her tutor, he loved her too much for a scandal, she had to focus on her audition…

At the time, these had all sounded plausible reasons and quite romantic too – Tess was studying Romeo and Juliet and had been only too willing to cast herself and Vassilly as star-crossed lovers – but looking back, both as an adult and as a teacher, Tess could see how terribly Vassilly had overstepped their relationship and in the most unforgivable way. Like most unequal and illicit relationships, theirs had destroyed the future she should have enjoyed and had poisoned her early adulthood with lies. Even now, when her head told her that he had taken the worst kind of advantage of a young girl in his tutelage, Tess's heart said that she'd loved him.

Maybe she still did.

Well, falling in love was a mistake she'd never make again, and especially not with a musician. They were selfish to the bone.

Infuriated with herself for still being upset almost a decade on, Tess picked up a stone and hurled it into the water. If that was a voodoo pebble, then she really hoped Vass was clutching his head, or maybe an even more tender part. Yes, with any luck that.

The recital had been going beautifully. When Tess had glanced up from her playing, there Vassilly was, sitting at the end of the row where he had slipped in unnoticed, and her heart rose in time with a flurry of notes. He had coached her for months to play a Bartok violin concerto, the piece which they had agreed showcased her talent to perfection and would impress all the right people. It was notoriously difficult, but when Vass was beside her, Tess felt as though she could play anything. Spotting him sitting in the audience, so magnetically handsome with that intense dark gaze, haughty profile and panther's lithe frame, Tess knew she was set to give the performance of her life.

But then – and for a moment she'd thought she'd imagined it – she saw his hand slide into the lap of the woman beside him. It was just a momentary caress and as fleetingly substantial as a snowflake in the sunshine. It could have been a trick of the light, but Tess knew she hadn't imagined it when the woman turned her head to whisper something into his ear as her free hand traced the sharp hollow of his cheek. Her body language said they were familiar with one another, each minute gesture and caress speaking a dialect that existed only for them.

They were lovers.

Although she was young and inexperienced, every instinct in Tess was on alert and her skin prickled with horror. This woman was older than Vass, much older, but even so, Tess knew what she had seen. Her intuition was screaming at her that everything was wrong. There was danger. She knew her whole world was about to collapse.

Tess's bow had scraped across the strings, an ugly and discordant sound that shocked and killed the music. Her hands shook and her heart was thudding so hard that she thought she was having a heart attack. The concert hall had swum, noise burgeoned in a meaningless wave and her legs buckled. A panic attack was how the doctors described it afterwards, but Tess knew the truth; her heart had splintered. She'd not been able to play another note and it was at that moment, her mapped-out future had fled just as she had fled from the stage.

As her tutor, Vass had been sent to calm Tess down and encourage her back onto the stage. When she confronted him with the reason for her behaviour, he hadn't denied it.

"Marina is going to be my new patron when you leave," he had said, as though this wasn't a body blow. "It was wonderful with us, but it could never be more, Tess. You will move on and I need to think of my future. Don't spoil things. Let us be friends."

"Friends? We love each other!" Tess had gasped, unable to believe her ears.

Vass had smothered a sigh. "I adore you, of course, but I never promised you anything. It could never be more. You must have known that."

"But we love each other," Tess whispered again. Her heart was in pieces. Every touch, every kiss and every stolen moment had meant everything to her, and to have these most precious things so easily dismissed was beyond painful.

"Of course, of course," Vass said quickly, but the way his eyes kept slipping to the door told another story. "But our time was always going to be short. Beautiful but brief. Let us leave it as a wonderful memory, yes? Something that will never fade or grow tired? You will always be my masterpiece and when you are famous, I will be so proud that I, Vassilly Yolov, was your tutor. You must do that for me, Tess. You must make me proud and show how I have helped your talent to flourish."

"Your masterpiece?" Tess had whispered. Was that all she meant to him?

"Darling, what's going on?" The woman, Marina, Tess presumed, had joined them, threading her arm through Vassilly's in a gesture of ownership and ease. Although in her late forties, she was beautiful, slender with porcelain white skin, thick dark hair and dressed in expensive clothes. Tess, at eighteen, had instantly felt gauche and foolish, a spotty schoolgirl in comparison and lacking in every way. How could she have ever believed Vass could want her when there were women like this in the world?

"Nothing," Vass said quickly. "I was just telling Tess as her tutor that she needs to calm down and play."

"How can I play a note when you're being like this?" Tess half-sobbed, half-choked.

"Like what?" asked the woman, her fine brows meeting in a frown.

"Tess is upset because I have told her I am leaving to tutor your son. She is distressed," Vassilly said quickly and Tess gasped at the matter of fact manner in which he broke this news. "Attachments happen when you teach. It is an intense experience for all concerned. She is now refusing to play to spite me."

The woman looked at Tess with contempt.

"My dear girl, don't be so selfish. Vassilly has given so much of himself to nurture your talent. Put your silly crush aside and show everyone just how wonderfully he's taught you."

"Vass?" Tess whispered, but he couldn't meet her eyes. Tess felt as though she had been kicked in the stomach.

"Go back and play that piece as beautifully as I know only you can," Vass said softly. His voice was low, but Tess could hear the desperation lurking beneath. "You surely don't want people to think Vassilly Yolov has failed his student? You would not want that for me, would you, my Tess? You wouldn't want your father to be disappointed? David is expecting great things and we can't let him down. You are my masterpiece, remember?"

Tess stared at him as the ugly truth dawned. It had never been about love; Vass had simply been amusing himself while he tutored her, nothing more. No wonder he had wanted Tess to keep quiet – his job and his relationship with this Marina had depended on it. If Tess's father had suspected for so much as a minute what was happening, then – talented or not – Vass would have been sacked in a heartbeat. Tess was totally to be his creation, the masterpiece that would show the world how talented a teacher he was and showcase his own ability too. To have taught David Hamilton's daughter was a claim Vassilly would boast about for years, his association with the famous musical dynasty another rung scaled on his climb upwards in the cut-throat world of classical music. This was the only value Tess had ever held for him. She'd simply been too naïve and stupid to see it.

There was only one way Tess could think of to hurt Vassilly as much as he had hurt her: she wouldn't play another note. Ever. Tess would use her own failure to tarnish his name. It would be his fault, or so the Chinese whispers in the small world of classical music would say. His reputation as an inspired teacher and rising talent would be eroded over time, and since Tess's joy in music had been smashed along with her heart, what did it matter now if she destroyed her own future too? How could she play again when music and betrayal were forever linked?

It had never occurred to Tess that she could have told the truth and achieved exactly the same result. She had felt so humiliated and ashamed that in her mind, doing so would have broken her totally. At least she could keep her dignity.

So from that moment on, Tess Hamilton had turned her back on her musical career and she'd not played a note since. Stage fright, the psychologist had suggested. A deep-rooted inner fear of failure. Terror of success. She needed therapy and time. It was all nonsense, but how could any of the therapists her parents took her to help when they didn't know the truth? Tess had never spoken a word about any of it and she never would. She blamed herself for being taken in and not being good enough to keep Vassilly's heart. If she missed music, then this was no more than she deserved and it was worth her own loss to taint Vassilly's reputation with the stain of failure.

It was ironic that the only person she hadn't blamed back then was

Vass. Typical behaviour from a young person who had been groomed, Tess often reflected now. As an adult, she could see how she had been manipulated and taken advantage of, and from a moral and safeguarding perspective, this made her furious. Furious and suspicious because the world seemed to be full of opportunistic young men. Tess saw them in the pub, on the quay, at teacher conferences, and by all accounts on the dating sites her friends joined, and she recognised these men for what they were. Having had her heart broken once, she would make certain it never happened again. She had learned a very hard lesson and since then her heart had been well and truly kept under lock and key.

Tess had stepped away from music and put distance between herself and her family, changing her degree from music to English literature and becoming a teacher. London was still too full of memories and eventually she had relocated to Cornwall where nobody knew anything about her family or her musical past.

Vassilly had become fairly well known as a conductor in his own right and he had married Marina, or so Tess had heard. It didn't matter any more. Tess imagined she had only been one of many women he amused himself with and he probably hadn't changed his ways, married or not. Marina's wealth would bankroll him and the rest was immaterial. He'd left the Richmond house soon after Tess's 'breakdown', as her parents referred to this time in hushed tones, and David Hamilton had blamed Vass for driving Tess too hard. Vass had failed and David was furious. Tess had had some kind of revenge, but oddly it hadn't tasted as sweet as she'd expected. In fact, it had left her feeling rather queasy. If her father was angry with the tutor, his disappointment in Tess knew no bounds. Tess might have an impressive degree and a great career in education, even be tipped for a head teacher's post in the near future, but she wasn't a concert violinist. In his eyes, she had thrown her future away, and although he never said as much, Tess knew David Hamilton felt let down. That was why it was easier to live hundreds of miles away and keep her distance. Her sister had never played as well as Tess and so she imagined he was bitterly disappointed that their musical dynasty would end with him.

Well, tough, that was the way it was, Tess thought now as she stomped along the beach. Music was her past and if she did sometimes find herself longing to pick up her violin, set it upon her shoulder and reach for her bow, as long as Tess kept busy she could usually resist. Music was associated with heartache. It was over for her.

Teaching was her life now, and playing the violin, as much as she had once loved it, was in the past. And that, Tess told herself as she climbed the steps from the beach back to the quayside, was exactly where it was going to stay. Her talent, like her heart, was well and truly locked away.

CHAPTER ELEVEN

"This is a really bad idea, Mo. Call Tess right now and tell her something else has come up."

Ashley Carstairs stood in the kitchen at Mariners, a glass of wine held loosely in his hand, while various pots and pans bubbled away on the stove. The smell of herbs, garlic and rich tomato sauce filled the air and Mo's mouth was watering. If she didn't already love her husband to distraction, annoying as he could be at times, Mo would adore him for his culinary skills alone. Strictly a beans on toast kind of cook, Mo loved watching Ashley chop and simmer and create. It was actually very sexy.

What she wasn't quite so keen on was when he decided to give her a lecture about something, and from the expression on his face, Mo knew that he was about to launch into one now. She'd distract him. It usually worked.

"Mmm, this smells wonderful. You are clever, Ash," Mo said. She stepped forward and wound her arms around his neck, pressing herself against him – easier said than done when trying to dodge a wine glass and tomato sauce-laden spoon – and kissing him. In the past, the kitchen had been a scene for great fun and, glancing at the clock and seeing they had half an hour until their guests arrived, Mo wondered if they had time for a little more...

"Yes, I am," Ashley agreed, gently moving her aside so that he could stir the sauce. "Certainly clever enough to know when I'm being distracted. Much as I would love nothing more than to turn this off and give you a good seeing to over the kitchen table, Mrs Carstairs, we have guests due, one of whom I suggest you put off."

"I can't do that," Mo protested. "I invited Tess. Anyway, what's the problem? I thought you liked her."

Ashley gave her a sharp look. "I do like her. I just don't think matchmaking is your forte."

"Who says I'm matchmaking?" Mo did her best to look offended.

But her husband laughed. "Darling, subtle you are not. Last time you set her up with Symon. This time Zak is conveniently coming up for supper, which I expect you forgot to mention. How's it going to look when Tess sees the table laid for six?"

"Zak's my brother. He needs cheering up!"

"So you've provided a potential girlfriend to do the job? Did you run any of this by Tess or Zak?"

"I'm just trying to help! Don't you want Zak to be happy?"

Ashley put the lid on the saucepan, turned down the gas and placed the spoon carefully on the counter. No orange splatters all over the place when he was cooking, Mo noticed, whereas the last time that she – in an Annabel Karmel-inspired organic frenzy – made a batch of food for Isla, the entire kitchen had looked like a Jackson Pollock.

"I'm not sure that you can make other people happy, Mo. It's something they need to do for themselves."

"But they'd be perfect together! Just like us!"

"I applaud your good intentions, Red, but tell me this: how would you have felt if somebody had tried to push us together? Would you have liked being forced to have dinner with me?"

It was a good question. Since Mo had spent most of the time before they had got together devising ways of killing the evil property-developing and woodland-chopping-down Ashley Carstairs as slowly and painfully as possible, the answer was that she'd have been furious.

"You'd have been wearing the spaghetti on your head," she admitted.

"I rest my case," said Ashley, squinting at a packet of spaghetti, then waving it under her nose. "What does that say? Twelve minutes? The print is bloody tiny. Ridiculous."

"Yes, twelve minutes," Mo confirmed, having no trouble reading it. She wandered to the window and gazed out into the early evening. The shadows were lengthening in deep purples and greens across the garden and the tripping boats were tied up against the harbour wall. Mo twirled a red curl around her forefinger, something she always did when deep in thought. Oh dear, maybe Ashley had a point? Still, it was too late now because walking up the path to the house, bottle of wine in her hand and deep in conversation with Kat and Alex, was Tess.

"Oh Lord, they're early," she groaned. "I can't change things now, can I?"

"Not really," said Ashley. "Good luck, my darling. If I retire early with a headache, you'll understand, won't you?"

Mo would have liked to interrogate him further about this headache business, but the doorbell was ringing and unless she wanted Isla woken up, she'd better answer it.

"Oh ye of little faith," she said to Ashley. "It's all going to work out beautifully, you'll see."

At least she hoped it was. Crossing her fingers, Mo headed for the door and took a deep breath. Chill, she told herself firmly. It was only a casual kitchen supper. Ashley was overreacting. Tess and Zak would get on just fine.

Tess hadn't been up to Mariners for quite a while, but it was a house she saw every day since it stood sentinel on the right-hand side of the bay and watched all goings-on with the Cyclops gaze of its imposing glass wall. Since the Polwenna Action Group, headed by Mo at the time, had successfully campaigned to prevent Ashley from building a road through the woods, the only access to the property was a very steep walk up through the village, followed by another hike along the cliff path. Not wanting to be late or arrive hot and red-faced, Tess set off early, bumping into Kat and Alex who'd had the same idea.

"It's taking me ages to walk anywhere these days," Kat puffed, pausing to get her breath. She arched her spine and pressed her hand into the small of her back. "Crikey, this is a trek. How on earth do they manage to get anything up here?"

"Quad bike," said Tess. "If you like, I can give Little Rog Pollard a call? He's running a quad taxi service."

Actually, this was a slight exaggeration. What the Pollards were actually doing was moonlighting with their all-terrain vehicle and charging villagers handsomely to deliver them and their shopping to the front door. They were doing a roaring trade and, living in a house which was a steep climb from her own parking space, Tess totally understood why. However, the Pollards' latest enterprise wasn't going down well with everyone. For one thing, their vehicle was noisy and spat noxious fumes into the clean Cornish air, and for another, Little Rog was a dreadful driver, treating the narrow streets like his own private Monaco Grand Prix circuit and regularly taking out flowerpots and window boxes. Already the likes of Sheila Keverne and Ivy Lawrence were gunning for him, and poor Silver Starr was distraught because the din and pollution unbalanced her chakras. Having almost been mown down several times, Tess's concern was that one of her pupils might get flattened. It was only a matter of time.

Kat flapped her hand in front of her face. "I'm fine. We're almost there now and exercise is good for me."

"It won't be good for me if you give birth on the cliff path," said Alex.

They continued on their walk but by the time they reached Mariners, even Tess was feeling tired. Still, it was worth the steep climb for the jaw-dropping view. Ashley Carstairs really had bought the best property in the village; perched on the headland and guarding the village, Mariners was like a mini castle.

Alex whistled. "This is incredible. What does Ashley do again?"

"He's not a teacher, that's for sure," Kat said wryly.

Tess laughed. "So true! Something in the city, I think? Then property developing. I'm sure he'll fill you in."

The front door swung open and Mo Carstairs beamed at them.

"Come on in!" she cried. "Oh Kat, you poor thing having to walk all this way when you're so pregnant. I remember it well. I said to Ashley what a daft place this is to have a house."

"You could have had a road all the way to your front door," her husband pointed out mildly. "But no. That was a major problem, apparently."

"I have ethics and morals!" Mo flared and then laughed. "Although I must admit when I was at your stage, Kat, I would have happily traded those for a road to my front door!"

Coats and bags taken and everyone sorted out with drinks, Mo shepherded her guests through the open-plan ground floor to the seating area which boasted a stunning view of the bay. As they passed the big refectory table, Tess's sharp eyes noticed that six places were set and, unless her numeracy skills were failing her, there were only five of them present.

Oh no. She knew from bitter experience what this signified.

Tess's heart sank into her Skechers. She really hoped Mo wasn't playing Cupid again. She was just about to enquire as to the identity of the mystery sixth diner when a tall figure materialised at the window and slid the doors open. Warm air and the scent of hot male rushed in as the long denim-clad legs stepped into the room.

"Hope I'm not late, but you guys kind of sprung this on me," he said.

It was Zak Tremaine. Of course. Could Mo be any less subtle?

Tess recognised him from the brief times she had seen Zak in the village. Even glimpsed once, he was pretty hard to forget. A six-foot vision of muscular masculinity, thick blonde curls pulled back from his unshaven face and clad in black skinny jeans, baby blue shirt the exact colour of his eyes and a battered leather jacket, he was without doubt one of the most attractive men Tess had ever seen and as different from Vassilly's lean and hungry beauty as the sunrise was from the darkness of the night. Zak looked exactly as though he'd stepped into Mariners from the stage of a rock concert, which wasn't too much of a leap of imagination given his chosen profession. He probably spent hours in front of a mirror perfecting that exact look. Tess knew his type. Vass had agonised over getting his sweep of dark hair to fall over his eyes with just the right degree of nonchalance.

Zak smiled at the gathered guests. As well as having Mo's open and direct gaze, he had the Tremaine beauty in seaside bucket loads and amplified to the power of ten. In spite of her annoyance at Mo's latest interference, Tess couldn't help staring. This was sex appeal and star power to the max, if a little pale and with violet smudges under the blue eyes.

"Zak! Great to see you!" cried Alex, stepping forward and hugging him. Tess noticed that Zak froze for the briefest moment before hugging him back and then turning to kiss Kat. He seemed to be making a huge effort to hold himself together.

"Bloody hell, Zak. Why can't you use the front door like everyone else? You've trampled the flowerbeds," grumbled Mo.

"I'm here, Mo, okay? Don't start moaning about which door I use," said Zak, his brows coming together in a scowl which, if anything, only made him look more attractive in a mean and moody kind of way. He glanced across the room, spotted Tess and his mouth twisted into a cynical smile. As their eyes met, Tess knew he'd guessed instantly why his sister had invited him for supper and she felt humiliation wash over her because how desperate did this make her look? Spinster schoolteacher of the parish alert! The poor guy was probably already planning how to make a polite excuse to leave.

"You do it every time," muttered Mo.

"I'm more than happy to go home again if you want?" Zak suggested. Everything about his body language said he didn't want to be here anyway and Tess had every sympathy. She was feeling exactly the same.

"Don't you dare! I've cooked enough to feed half the village," said Ashley, draping an arm around his wife's shoulders. "Just ignore old crosspatch here. She's still sore from falling off that damn horse and it makes her tetchy. Personally, I couldn't give a hoot if you do the Dance of the Seven Veils across the flowerbeds. Just relax and have a drink." He held up the bottle in his left hand. "Red okay? Or is it all baths full of champagne these days?"

Shadows flickered across Zak's face.

"Just water for me, thanks."

"On a health kick?" Mo asked.

"Something like that," he agreed.

"You can join me with the fizzy water," said Kat, raising her glass and smiling. "I'm counting the days until I can have a Prosecco though!"

Zak smiled back, but Tess noticed that it didn't meet his eyes. Tension radiated from him and her sharp teacher's gaze noticed that the skin around his nails was bitten raw. Tess wasn't one for gossip, but it was impossible to live in a small place like Polwenna and not hear a little of the latest shenanigans via the local grapevine. Village shop gossip aside, Tess taught Morgan Tremaine who, wide-eyed, had told her that his uncle had come home because somebody had died. In front of him! Fact! Tess read the papers and it hadn't taken her long to work out that Zak Tremaine must have been at the party where that poor young singer died. Really, it wasn't such a surprise he looked haunted. He was probably on a major booze and drugs detox. Tess knew that the pressure in the music industry was immense and Zak was well known in the village for being a hard-living party animal.

What was Mo thinking, trying to set her up with somebody like him? Brother or not, she must know he was the last man on earth Tess would contemplate, even though he was without doubt the most beautiful man she'd ever seen. There was no way on earth Tess would ever have anything to do with Zak Tremaine.

This was going to be a long night.

"Have you met Tess? She teaches at the school," Mo was saying innocently to Zak. She might as well have said, "This is Tess and I'm setting you up with her! Tra da!"

Tess cringed. Mo was one step away from buying a hat.

Zak's blue gaze swept over Tess.

"I think we met in the pub once," he said. His voice was low and warm, like honey pooling on hot toast, and the musician in Tess could imagine just how it would sound set to a melody, the cadences rising and falling in harmony, making the hairs on the forearms stir. To her irritation, she felt her cheeks grow warm under his scrutiny.

"I'm afraid I don't really remember," she said. There was no way Tess was admitting she had ever noticed him. She was sure Zak Tremaine's ego was quite big enough without her help.

"Nice to know I made such an impression," Zak said slowly, still looking at her. He knew she was fibbing, just as he must know that any woman who saw him remembered the experience. "We've definitely met. I remember now. I think you were with Nick then? My younger brother?" There was an amused note in his voice now and his mouth curled into a smile as he added, "Was that another Mo set-up?"

Wow. What a smile. It changed his whole face and lit the eyes to the blue of the warmest Caribbean seas. Tess wasn't smiling though. Far from it.

When she'd first moved to Polwenna, Tess had indulged in the classic new arrival's initiation ritual of heading to the pub, partying hard with the locals and drinking far too much cider. Somewhere along the way she'd bumped into Nick Tremaine, a sweet guy who'd been a bit of fun for a few weeks and the perfect antidote to the intensity and secrecy of Vassilly. Of course, it hadn't worked out with Nick. It was only ever supposed to be a fun fling, but when you lived in a small village and invariably fished from the same pond, it was hard to forget the past. Nick Tremaine was a mistake Tess was determined not to make again. A convent was starting to look like an attractive option…

"I'm not setting anyone up!" protested Mo, but Zak just laughed.

"You're such a rubbish liar, sis. Your ears go bright pink!"

Sure enough, Mo's ears were looking rather rosy.

"Great tip, Zak," grinned Ashley. "Mo, you are so busted now. Never again will you be able to tell me that a saddle was cheap, you really need another horse or that your broken ribs don't hurt!"

Everyone except Tess was laughing. She couldn't even raise a faint smile.

"I don't want to be set up with anyone, thanks, Mo," she said sharply.

"Of course you don't," Zak agreed. "And neither do I, Mo. You hear me?"

"I don't know what you're going on about," huffed Mo, ears growing pinker by the second. "I was just being kind and feeding you while Granny was out. I should have let you go hungry. Anyway, isn't it time we ate? I think I can smell burning."

She gave Ashley a shove in the small of his back and they bustled back to the kitchen area while the others, feeling rather awkward, headed to the table.

"I hope I wasn't speaking out of turn," Zak said to Tess as they took their places. "I just thought I ought to nip any of Mo's mad schemes in the bud. Not that having a dinner date with you would be mad or anything. Hardly. The thing is, I know my sister and once she has an idea in her head, she's unstoppable."

He was as easy to talk to as he was easy on the eye, but Tess wasn't going to be fooled. The charm offensive was how men like Zak Tremaine operated. They reeled you in like the fishermen on the quay reeled in fish. Once hooked, they left you gasping and frightened. She'd learned her lesson.

"I'm far too busy working to think about anything else," she replied coolly. "I can't imagine having time for anything else but teaching."

"Very impressive and very noble," said Zak, holding her chair out so she could sit down. Nice manners were clearly another of his charms. "Make sure you write Mo a memo on that though or she'll be trying again and last I heard, Caspar James is in dire need of a muse. Trust me, Mo won't rest until we're all loved up and married off."

"I don't need a man or marriage to complete me," snapped Tess, who always baulked at this idea. After all, marriage hadn't made her mother happy. David Hamilton was always on tour and her mother generally complaining about being left alone and sacrificing her career. No, thank you.

"I'm quite sure you don't," said Zak evenly. "But the search to not find a relationship is sometimes fun."

Was he flirting with her now? Of course he was; flirting came as easily as breathing to guys like Zak.

"I'm far too busy to waste time having fun."

"That's a shame," Zak said quietly. "Life is very short."

There was a catch in his voice, but he probably rehearsed this for maximum benefit.

"Far too short to waste on people you don't want to spend time with," she retorted, more sharply than she'd intended. Oh Lord, that sounded really rude.

Zak stared at her for a moment and then nodded.

"Indeed it is. Well, at least Mo knows where we both stand on the matter now, so we can eat our spaghetti in peace. The night should just about be tolerable."

He took his seat at the table, pointedly angling himself away from her, and proceeded to spend the rest of the evening deep in conversation with Alex and Ashley.

Fine, thought Tess. It was easier this way. She hadn't meant to be quite so cutting, but finding herself next to Zak had put her on edge and made her sharper than she had meant to be. She decided to ignore him too, although this was easier said than done when his long denim-clad thigh was only centimetres from hers and the scent of his skin made her senses reel. Every now and then, her mind flashed back to that first moment his clear gaze had caught hers for just a few seconds longer than it should have done and she had to focus really hard on what Kat was saying about the new GCSE grading system. Ignoring Zak Tremaine took a great deal of effort and by the time the plates were cleared and the coffee finished, Tess was exhausted. If Kat and Alex had thought it strange she was so quiet and had made an excuse to leave early, then they were too polite to say so. And if Zak Tremaine thought she was a rude cow, then so much the better. The less Tess saw of him the better.

Fact. As his nephew might say.

It was only when she was back at home and in bed with the darkness of the Cornish night soothing her that something very strange struck Tess. So strange, in fact, that she sat bolt upright with shock.

She hadn't thought about Vassilly for hours. Not even once. What on earth was that about?

CHAPTER TWELVE

Jules often looked back on the younger version of herself who'd felt the calling to become a vicar with mingled affection and frustration. The days at theological college spent debating doctrine and writing essays on Bible history had been absolutely fascinating. Jules loved delving into scripture and studying the writings of the early church fathers and she was definitely committed to serving her Boss in any way she could. Nothing if not ambitious, the young Jules Mathieson had even harboured a secret dream about being the first female Archbishop of Canterbury (although she did worry that to have such a goal might be dangerously close to the sin of pride? Or was this down to gender? Did men worry about such things? Discuss), but God, it seemed, had other plans for her and a good sense of humour to boot.

Her Boss, it appeared, wanted Jules to serve Him in Polwenna Bay and this summer was testing her patience by making her the Chair of the Polwenna Festival Committee. As Jules attempted to open the latest meeting, and do her best to bring some order to proceedings, she was convinced that even Job would have struggled with this particular challenge. Thank goodness Mo Tremaine had agreed to be her deputy chairman. Jules didn't think she would make it through the summer without throttling someone otherwise.

Patience, she told herself desperately. Patience. So far, she'd had to wait while Sheila Keverne handed out agendas to everyone and insisted on calling a register. Then Big Rog needed the loo, an event which then prompted a lengthy discussion between Mrs Rog and Kursa Penwarren regarding the state of his prostate, and Silver Starr had insisted on moving her chair to the opposite side of the table because the energy had a better flow there. Silver was very fortunate that Jules was praying hard to Patience at this point; otherwise she and her chi might have found themselves out of the door, flowing down the River Wenn and out to sea.

If the committee wasn't enough of a challenge, then the festival was proving to be even more of a headache. Jules wasn't quite sure how it was that she'd ended up being in charge of it – something to do with being a vicar and therefore seen as a soft touch, she strongly suspected, but not having a musical bone in her body, she wasn't convinced she was the right person at all. As if she didn't have enough on with trying to house-hunt in London, look for a new parish, and keep up the I can't wait to move! act for Danny's benefit. Yes, Jules was certainly working hard on that score, and if this had been a drama festival, she probably would be more than well qualified to run it. Danny could be in no doubt that his fiancée could hardly wait to leave Cornwall for the big city and, even though nothing could be further from the truth, Jules was determined to keep it this way.

"Right! Let's begin, shall we?" she said, once Silver's magic crystal had found the right spot and Sheila had completed the register. "Item number one today: the venue. Now, as you know, the village green isn't going to be available this year since the water board are investigating the drains after the flood."

"Waste of bloody money. We all know how it happened and whose fault that was," interrupted Chris the Cod, giving Big Rog a very black look. Historically, the Pollards were meant to clear the village drains and, even almost two years on, there were still some very cheesed-off villagers.

"You blaming me?" said Big Rog.

Chris the Cod shrugged. "If the cap fits, mate."

"Come outside and say that!" bellowed Big Rog, hauling himself to his feet.

"Yeah!" added Little Rog, also leaping up and knocking his can of Coke everywhere. "Don't blame my dad. He does a good job."

"That's right, my boy!" agreed his father.

Jules sighed. The truth was that Big Rog did not really do a good job, spending more time in the pub than about his civic duty, but the drains were old and that particular winter had been very hard and so the flooding was probably caused by a combination of factors. An act of God even! Anyway, the last thing she needed was a village brawl.

"Look, we're not here to argue about why we've lost the venue," she said, pushing her chair back to escape the latest Pollard flood as it flowed towards her. "The point is we have lost it and we need somewhere else. Any ideas?"

"We could use the school playing field," Tess Hamilton suggested. She tucked a blonde curl behind her ear and smiled encouragingly at Jules. "I know it's not huge, but it could be a useful spot. It's flat for putting up stalls and the children could help decorate. It would be fun to include them."

"Can we pitch the beer tent there?" Big Rog asked and all the others nodded seriously.

"Is that a priority?" Jules asked, and as soon as the words had left her mouth, she could have kicked herself. Duh. Of course it was.

"Pol Breweries always donate ten barrels of Pol Brew. The yard of ale contest is a highlight of the day!" said Big Rog. "It's tradition!"

"I'll win this year," boasted his son.

"You can't even drink a can of Coke, you harris," said Chris the Cod.

"I'll walk it this year," boasted Caspar James. "I've been in training!"

"You're always in training," said Eddie Penhalligan. "You're a bleddy piss head, is why!"

There were guffaws at this, while Caspar pretended to be offended. Then the discussion veered right off track as they all debated who was the best drinker in the village, a dubious honour, but one they all took very seriously.

Jules closed her eyes and prayed harder. Somehow the gentle summer music festival, a time for morris dancing and folk singers, was morphing into a village booze fest. At the last meeting, she'd had her work cut out persuading the Pollards and Eddie that raising funds for the marquee hire with a charity three-legged pub crawl was a bad idea. Maybe she was missing something? Only the last time Jules looked, Polwenna Bay only had one pub!

"So the school field then?" Jules asked Tess, while the debate as to who could drink the most continued around them.

The teacher's pretty face was troubled. "I don't think a beer tent and a drinking contest at the school would really be very appropriate. Sorry, Jules. We'll have to think again."

"Could we use your place, Mo?" Jules asked. Mariners had a big garden, was set in the village and only a few minutes' walk from the pub where they could stage the all-important yard of ale.

"I don't think Ash will fancy that," Mo said. "You know how much he likes his privacy."

Jules didn't blame Ashley one bit. Mariners was perfect for looking at Polwenna without being embroiled in the everyday dramas and village politics. In the village, but not of it, so to speak.

"What about the bands?" asked Silver, totally skipping over the next three items on the agenda. "Did Skylark confirm?"

The headline band was another headache. With Glastonbury and other festivals all taking place around the same time as Pol Fest, bands were either committed to play elsewhere or enjoying the celebrations.

"They can't make it," Jules said, and there was a collective wail of disappointment. At this rate, Jules feared she'd be up on stage herself with one of St Wenn's tambourines and playing the comb and paper.

"What about your Zak?" said Eddie Penhalligan to Mo. "He's back, isn't he? Why doesn't he play? Ned Pavey's home from New Zealand now and Ollie Morris is always at a loose end. They could re-form The Tinners. It would be bleddy brilliant!"

There was a collective cheer at this suggestion. The Tinners had been hugely popular in Cornwall and the residents of Polwenna Bay had loved dining out on the fact that these regional celebrities came from their very own village. Jules hadn't seen much of Zak. In fact, she was pretty sure he'd actively avoided her a few days earlier when she'd been walking up to Seaspray, but she had the impression the last thing he would want to do was headline the village festival. Alice said he wanted nothing to do with music, which would be quite a stumbling block.

"He's here for a rest," Mo said.

"Tired after living it up in the city more like," Sheila Keverne scoffed.

"I heard he nearly died at that party where the girl overdosed," said Keyhole Kathy Polmartin, boot button eyes bright at the possibility of scandal. "Apparently his record company sacked him!"

"That's bollocks!" Mo flared. "Utter bollocks!"

"Language, Morwenna," admonished Sheila. "What would Alice say?"

"Oh, bugger off," Mo retorted. "And yes, by all means tell Granny Alice I said that too because I'll certainly be telling her what nasty gossip you're spreading about Zak!"

"I have never been so offended in all my life!" gasped Sheila, hand on her heart and eyes wide with feigned hurt.

"Actually, maid, that isn't true," said Eddie Penhalligan with a grin. "Remember when we were at school? And all the kids called you—"

"Eddie Penhalligan! Don't you dare start that again!" screeched Sheila, turning puce. "I'm warning you! If you say another word, then I am walking away from this committee!"

"Calm down! Don't get your knickers in a twist," said Eddie. "It was fifty years ago!"

"What did they call her?" asked Chris the Cod. "Just out of interest, like. We're all friends here, Sheila. Committee members shouldn't have secrets."

"Well..." began Eddie.

It was time to call for order before old feuds were resurrected and war broke out, decided Jules. Today was a serious patience overload.

"So far, we have no band and no venue," she interrupted in the ringing tones she'd developed in order to be heard in echoey medieval churches. It worked wonders and everyone fell silent. "At this rate, and unless we work together, we'll have no festival. Can we please all stop squabbling and think of some solutions? It's almost June!"

"What about the talent contest?" This suggestion was voiced by Mrs Pollard. A thin and rather unassuming woman, she was generally thought to be the brains of the Pollard building empire, which was either very worrying or a good thing depending upon who you were talking to.

"That's the third item on my agenda," Jules said gently. She was steering this meeting back on course if it was the last thing she did.

"I know that," said Karenza Pollard quietly, "but it seems to me that we've got lots of acts already. They may not be proper professional ones—"

"Hey! You be careful there, bird! My Meatloaf has often been mistaken for the real thing," Big Rog reminded her.

His wife ignored him. Jules guessed that she had seen the famous Meatloaf impression so many times now that it no longer amazed her as much as her husband felt it should. That was marriage for you!

"So why don't we have the talent show acts as our main event?" Mrs Pollard suggested. "A bit less Polwenna's Got Talent and a little more like

The X Factor?"

"P Factor!" bellowed Eddie. "I like it!"

Jules shuddered. No Way Factor, more like.

"It's an interesting idea," Tess said. "Can we pull it off? Do we have enough acts?"

"We did have fifteen at last count," Mo told her. "Sixteen if I can persuade Ashley to do a duet with me. So far, he's digging his heels in and saying there's no way he's going to be Danny to my Sandy! Not even if I promise to wear those tight trousers! But he'll do it in the end, you'll see."

"How will you persuade him?" Jules asked, intrigued. Ashley was a pretty determined man.

Mo winked. "I can't tell the vicar things like that, but you'll figure it out once you and Danny are married. Here's a clue – it's not by my cooking!"

Jules filed this information away for future reference. There were some things she couldn't ask the Bishop.

"I'll take part too," said Caspar. "I shall set my poetry to music for you all to enjoy."

"We want people to come to this, you harris," said Eddie. "Not scare them off!"

"I can play the guitar!"

"I'll sing!"

"My mum rings bells!"

Suddenly everyone had ideas and Jules felt a faint tremor of hope.

"Okay, this sounds like a plan to me. We can still have the morris dancing and the stalls and the other bits going on too – yes, Roger Pollard, I do mean the beer tent. Tess, you said the children were going to do some country dancing, so we could open with that."

Tess nodded and scribbled something in her notebook. "Absolutely."

"So now we just need to think of a venue," Jules concluded. "Any thoughts?"

At this, a hush fell. Jules could practically hear the grinding of cogs as everyone sought to come up with a solution. The problem was that the village clung to a steep valley and, apart from the green, there was very little flat land. The beach wasn't ideal for obvious reasons and the quay was far too narrow. The venue had to be somewhere that people could get to and spread out – safely! Clinging to the harbour wall or dodging the incoming tide would not make Jules's risk assessment easy.

"I've got it!" Mo cried. She leaned forward and her eyes shone with enthusiasm. "How about we change things a little bit and rather than calling it the Polwenna Festival, we call it the Summer Festival?"

"That's just semantics," drawled Caspar, yelping when Big Rog walloped him, yelling, "Don't be racist!"

"He means words, Rog," said Jules. She gave Caspar her sternest vicar look. "And it wasn't helpful, Caspar."

"No it bleddy well wasn't," grumbled Big Rog. "Him and his big words, showing off. This isn't bleddy Countdown."

"Caspar does have a point," Mo said. "It is just a change of name in one way, but it could also mean a new start for the festival."

"Go on, maid," said Eddie.

"Well," said Mo slowly, "I was thinking, and I'll have to run this past them, but Granny and Jonny are having their wedding reception up at Polwenna Manor in Symon's new restaurant. As they would love everyone to be there to celebrate with them, why don't we take the festival to them for their evening reception? We could have the music and the talent show at the Manor! Maybe a hog roast too and a marquee? That way everyone can celebrate, the festival goes ahead and Perry can see how the Manor works as a venue. He's bound to agree."

There was a lot of nodding and agreeing at this. The Manor was a beautiful setting, if still a little wild, and it could be the perfect solution.

"No passing trade would come to the chippy," said Chris the Cod.

"Or the pasty shop," said Patsy.

At this point, all the shopkeepers nodded sadly. The extra revenue that the festival brought to their respective establishments was always welcome.

"You could all have stalls up there," Mo pointed out. "Silver, you could read cards and sell things. Chris, you could do some mobile food, surely? And Patsy could sell pasties. Adam, you can have a bar. You'd have no competition and you'd probably make a killing."

"I don't know," said Big Rog. "It's not really in the village."

"It's a bit of a hike up," added Sheila doubtfully.

The Manor was only a short walk up the hill. Ten minutes at the most.

"Nobody will want to drive because then they can't have a beer," pointed out Eddie, and there was a ripple of agreement.

If she served pints of Pol Brew rather than communion wine at the Sunday services, would the attendance go up? wondered Jules.

"They could catch the Pollard Shuttle up, couldn't they Dad?" pointed out Little Rog. "We could do lifts up and down for a quid a time. Special rates."

Pound signs were practically flashing in Big Rog's eyes.

"That's right, my boy! But one pound fifty, I say. Fuel ain't cheap, is it? Yes, the more I think about it, the more the Manor seems by far the best venue for the Summer Festival! A very good idea, Mo. I second it!"

"Let's have a vote," said Sheila. "All in favour of moving the festival to Polwenna Manor, raise your hand."

Arms shot skywards as everyone thought of ways they could now make money. Oh dear, thought Jules. She'd better pen her next sermon on the evils of Mammon!

"It looks as though we have a venue and the festival sorted," she said to Mo and Tess once the unanimous vote was agreed and the meeting closed.

"The Manor is a great idea," said Tess. "I might get my class to do a project on the history of it. We could have a display up there. They'd love that. Perry could give us a tour."

"Just do a good risk assessment and check your insurance first though," said Mo. "You're quite likely to fall through the floor or have a ceiling come down on your heads!"

"Sounds as though we're all better off outside," Tess laughed. She had a lovely laugh, Jules thought, low and musical. It was a shame they didn't hear it more often. Tess often looked sad and as though she was keeping a huge part of herself back.

"I'll run the idea by Granny and Jonny right now and I bet they'll be thrilled," said Mo once the village hall was locked and they were walking along the main street back into the village. "Granny's been agonising about how to make sure nobody's left out of her big day. This way, the entire village is invited, the festival can go ahead and the newlyweds get to watch the village talent show!"

"I'm not sure that's a selling point," Jules warned. The thought of Big Rog in leather trousers made her feel quite queasy. "Maybe downplay that bit?"

"Chicken," laughed Mo. "Hey, Tess! What are you going to do for the show? Kat says you play the violin?"

Tess jumped as though she'd been shocked.

"What? No. I mean, I did but not any more. Not for years."

"You don't forget though, surely? Isn't it like riding a horse?"

"I don't know. I've never ridden a horse," Tess snapped.

Jules was taken aback. A model of patience, Tess never lost her temper.

"Same thing. It's all muscle memory. You'd remember it," said Mo, who wasn't much good at reading human body language. "Maybe Eddie's idea about reforming The Tinners isn't so daft after all? You could play the fiddle with the band, Tess. Wouldn't that be brilliant?"

"I don't think Zak wants to play at the moment," Jules said quickly, sensing Tess's unease. "Maybe just leave it?"

But Mo could never leave anything once she had an idea in her head.

"Of course he wants to play! Zak loves music. It's his life. He's just being a diva."

"Or perhaps playing brings back too many painful memories for him and he needs some space? Did you ever think of that?" Tess said.

"Not really," Mo admitted.

Tess didn't say any more, but she was clearly upset. Jules couldn't recall ever seeing her look so rattled.

"Fancy a quick drink in The Ship?" she suggested. This was usually the way Jules and Tess decompressed after the excitement of a committee meeting, but the teacher shook her head.

"Another time. I've got lessons to plan."

Then she swung her bag onto her shoulder and turned away, heading up the steep lane to her cottage and leaving Mo and Jules staring after her. Had Tess Hamilton just walked away without so much as a goodbye?

"What on earth was that about?" asked Mo. "Why is she being so weird about Zak's music?"

"I have no idea," Jules said slowly, "but I'm pretty certain it had absolutely nothing to do with how Zak feels about music. In fact, I don't think Tess was really talking about Zak at all."

CHAPTER THIRTEEN

"It's going to be a very different wedding reception, that's for sure," Alice Tremaine said to Jonny St Milton a few days later as they cleared away the dinner things. She straightened up from stacking the dishwasher and rubbed her aching back. "You are happy about it all, aren't you, love?"

"I'm marrying you! Of course I'm happy," Jonny reassured her.

"And you don't mind having our day hijacked by the festival? It won't be too much?"

Alice was fretting terribly about this. Although it was, as Mo had pointed out, a great way to make sure everyone in Polwenna Bay felt included in their celebrations, it was going to make the reception a lot bigger than she'd originally planned. When Alice thought back to her first marriage to dear Henry, a small post-war affair with only their parents and a few friends in attendance, this wedding seemed over the top and, she feared, even a little ridiculous given their ages. Oh dear. Maybe they should have plumped for the registry office after all?

In answer, Jonny put down his tea towel and took Alice in his arms. He was a little less steady on his feet these days, and a lot thinner too than when they'd first met, but the peace she felt when being held by him was just the same. Alice rested her head against his shoulder. He smelt of shaving soap, old-fashioned cologne and himself, and it could have been fifty years ago. Only the mirror on the dresser gave the truth away.

"Ally, please stop worrying," Jonny murmured into her hair. "All that matters is that we're getting married. I'd marry you on a beach, in a registry office or anywhere. The rest of it is totally irrelevant to me, but I do think that having most of the village there to help us celebrate will be a nice thing and make our day even more special."

"You don't think it's too much? That we're going over the top at our age? Being too extravagant?"

Jonny laughed and kissed the top of her head.

"Why shouldn't we pull out all the stops if we want? We can't take it with us when we go! Besides, I'm not planning on doing this again, Ally. Are you?"

"Only when we renew our vows on a Caribbean beach when we're one hundred," Alice said.

"Damn. I had an Elvis chapel in Vegas planned for that," Jonny countered. Releasing her, he sat down wearily at the table. From the way that just standing for a short while exhausted him, he'd be doing well to walk to the end of the village these days, never mind a flight to Las Vegas, thought Alice sadly. Suddenly the passing of the years, and the growing realisation that much of their life's currency was already spent, felt too painful for words. When she thought of all the years they'd missed out on and the opportunities that had slipped through their fingers, Alice could have wept. Time was mercurial; it passed slowly and almost without notice. Christmases, birthdays, endless golden summers all seemed to melt into one blur of images, flickering through time like the cine-films of her youth. There was nothing more painful than knowing that beautiful butterfly chances had fluttered before you, even settling in your hands when you'd scarcely noticed, and it was only when they were long faded to dust that you truly understood what had been at your fingertips.

Life was precious and not to be wasted – which was why Alice was determined Zak wasn't going to spend the whole summer brooding and why she would do everything in her power to make sure he didn't turn his back on his talent. Now was his time and it would never come again. Whatever Zak chose to do next would echo throughout the rest of his life.

Once Jonny had departed for an after-dinner rest, Alice finished tidying away before sitting down at the kitchen table with a cup of tea, always her preferred method of working through problems – and Zak was a problem, that was for sure.

On the surface, Alice's middle grandchild appeared the most straightforward of the lot. Sunny-natured, handsome, talented and popular, Zak Tremaine was truly blessed. He had none of the elder sibling's angst regarding responsibility that so tortured Jake, Mo's fiery temper had bypassed him and, unlike Danny, he was fit and healthy. He shared Symon's drive, Issie's social confidence and Nick's ability to charm anyone, but Zak's propensity for introspection and periods of deep and dark gloom were all his own. If Alice believed in astrology (which intellectually she didn't, but emotionally felt rather tempted by whenever she walked past Magic Moon), she would say that Zak was a typical Gemini with two very distinct sides to his personality; one as bright as the evening sunshine now streaming into Seaspray, and the other as dark as the deepest depths of the beach cave. Maybe it was his artistic temperament and these extremes of emotion that drove him to play and create? If he didn't feel things so acutely, then how could he write such beautiful music and play with such heart? Alice sighed. Was it wrong of her to feel that the price he paid for brilliance was too high? What did talent and genius really count for in comparison to being happy?

Alice knew that Mo had really upset Zak the other day. Attempting to set him up with Tess was a daft idea and it was typical of Mo to do something without thinking it through. Since that evening, Zak had retreated even further into himself, walking miles over the cliffs and spending hours in his room. His manager had left endless messages, Alex Evans had tried to coax him out and failed, and Morgan, never the most empathetic individual when it came to emotions, had lent Zak his old camera.

"Taking pictures will help him, Grand Granny," Morgan had explained earnestly. "I get a funny feeling in my tummy when I think about Dad and Jules moving away, so I take pictures and it gets better."

Oh dear. Poor Morgan. The Move was a whole different issue and one Alice couldn't deal with right now. Besides, it was Danny's choice, and Jules's too of course, and maybe it was the right thing for them? Just because Alice thought leaving Cornwall was a mistake didn't mean she was right. She was probably just being really selfish because she didn't want Danny and Jules to go. She sighed again as she hauled herself up from her seat to place her mug in the sink. It was just as well nobody told you that having children, and grandchildren too, only got harder the older they became. Sleepless nights and wobbly teeth were an absolute walk in the park compared to all this angst.

Alice knew she had to try and talk to Zak. She simply couldn't watch him spiral downwards. He was so lost and Alice was determined to help her grandson find his way. She'd thought long and hard and there was only one course of action which might possibly work, but it was a gamble. Alice was going to ask Zak to do something especially for her. Something that her grandson, with his kind and loving heart, would find almost impossible to refuse. In other words, Alice Tremaine was going to resort to emotional blackmail…

Zak realised he couldn't hide at Seaspray forever. At some point he'd have to decide on his next course of action, if for no better reason than because there was only so much studying the plaster cracks in the ceiling that a man could take before he started to go round the twist. Since coming home, he'd managed to keep a low profile and hadn't been very sociable. He'd yet to visit the pub, much to the disappointment of Nick who'd been hoping to have his drinking buddy back, and hadn't braved the village shop or even Patsy's Pasties. With the exception of Mo's kitchen supper, which was hardly a roaring success with the snooty Tess looking down her perfect nose at him all evening, Zak hadn't been sociable at all. He'd ignored several calls from Alex and even one from his old bandmate, Ned.

Especially the one from Ned…

Zak rose early every day, heading out of the house when the sky was stippled pink like a mackerel's belly and the gulls were still slumbering. Lots of long walks over the cliffs were helping clear his mind and to some extent the guilt about Kellee too as he rationalised the events of that evening, but Zak's feelings about the music business were still as tangled as the fishing nets piled on the quay. He missed being in the studio creating and he knew that very soon he would crave the buzz which came with performing, but whether or not he wanted to do these things on the same scale as before and in a commercial capacity were questions Zak couldn't answer. There was something missing from it all, but he'd never quite been able to identify what it was, and having seen firsthand with Ryan Kent what happened when you filled that gap with drink or substances, endless thoughts were running through Zak's mind about the direction his life could take.

There were so many questions, but he still had no answers. Zak suspected that these would come in time, but he also knew that his manager and Alchemist weren't going to wait indefinitely.

"It's time to piss or get off the potty," had been the last delightful message from Ricky. Even though he'd erased it, his manager's crude phrase kept ricocheting through Zak's mind like a malevolent squash ball. The record company had given him a month's break, had even offered a stay in The Priory, and Zak knew they had been patient, but time was money and Alchemist was a business with lots of hungry mouths to feed. If Zak Tremaine wouldn't play ball, then there was a queue of wannabes who would be only too happy to take his place.

Zak had walked miles today, almost as far as Fowey, but even so, the fresh air and exercise weren't enough to dredge up a solution or, maybe he should more accurately say, a cure? When Zak told Alice that he was through with music, he hadn't quite been truthful. It was more that the music was through with him.

Ever since that fateful evening at the awards ceremony, it was as though something deep within him had changed. The joyous ease with which melodies flowed through his mind, sweeping in like the tide and filling the rock pools of his imagination with notes and lyrics and themes, had totally deserted him. Now when he sat at his old desk and tried to write some lyrics down, nothing came, no matter how hard he tried. Zak had gone to pick up his guitar countless times, but his hands had shaken and, afraid he might not be able to play a note, he'd placed it back into its case, flipped the lid shut and shoved it under the bed where it lay out of sight but not out of mind, a slumbering rebuke constantly reminding him of what he'd lost.

Why couldn't he write any more? He was home, where the music had been as much a part of life as the sweeping beam of the lighthouse through the night or the clattering of his grandmother in the kitchen. There was more than enough inspiration. The waves. The sky. Weathered granite and ancient myths. The clawing of grief in his heart. Misery as unyielding as the rocks and dangerously compelling, drawing you closer to your watery end – he could draw countless parallels and forge links in his mind, but even so, the magic had evaporated and he couldn't write. The well of ideas had totally dried up and after several more failed attempts, Zak admitted defeat, balling the paper up in his fist and lobbing it into the bin with a howl of despair.

Maybe this answered his question? If he couldn't compose any more and was too scared to play, then he may as well turn his back on music and turn spanners for Jake or wash dishes for Symon. He could even muck out for Mo. What did it matter?

The cautious rap of knuckles on the door broke into his thoughts. Alice, of course, checking he hadn't topped himself. Zak felt bad that he was making her tiptoe about in her own home and cast a shadow over what should have been the happy run-up to her wedding. His granny didn't deserve this extra stress. Maybe it would be better for everyone if he did just push off travelling? The thought of leaving it all behind and just walking away certainly appealed. Maybe he was more like Jimmy than he thought?

Usually, Alice waited to be asked to come in, but this time she pushed open the door and walked straight into the room. Zak sat up hastily and ran a hand through his tangled hair.

"I've been walking—" he began, but Alice held up her hand.

"I haven't come to lecture you, my love. What you choose to do with your time is up to you."

It was? Zak was surprised to hear this, since for the past couple of weeks Alice had been constantly on at him to eat/go and see Alex and Kat/help in the garden, and whatever other activities she could think of to gee him up.

"I've come to ask a favour," Alice continued. She sat down beside him and Zak's stomach lurched when he saw how cautiously she did this, her hand pressed into the small of her back and her mouth making a small grimace of discomfort.

"Are you all right, Granny?"

"Oh, I'm just a bit creaky, love. The joys of getting old. Everything hurts."

"Don't say that. You're not old," said Zak staunchly.

"Darling, I am. I'm eighty, hardly a spring chicken. These stairs take it out of me. I can't run up and down them like I used to when you were small and had a nightmare. Goodness, I must have been fit then. I practically need a Sherpa and supplies these days. It's getting harder every day."

After his mother died, Zak had been plagued by night terrors. It was all a faint memory now, maybe not even a memory of the events themselves but just of being told about them, but he did know how hard Alice had worked to bring up five motherless and confused grandchildren. He hugged her hard and tried not to notice how frail she was. If Zak didn't admit that Alice was getting old, maybe she wouldn't; a bit like hiding beneath the duvet from the monster under the bed – if you couldn't see it, then it wasn't real.

"What can I do to help? I'll do anything you want."

"Are you sure about that, love? Maybe you should ask what it is I want before you make rash promises!"

"No, I mean it. Just say the word and it's done."

Zak imagined Alice needed help gardening. Seaspray had two acres of steep clifftop grounds, all terraces and steps more easily accessed by mountain goats, and it was truly horrible to maintain. Alice did all the weeding and planting, while Jake and Nick did the rest, but Zak was sure he could help too. Or was it shopping? He'd even go into the village and fetch the groceries if this was what she wanted, brave the gossip and the stares if it made her life easier. There was nothing, nothing, he wouldn't do for his grandmother.

"I've been planning the wedding," Alice said. "Oh, love. There's so much to do and it's exhausting. We're just trying to finalise the reception now and I'm really hoping you can help me out."

"Of course I can," Zak told her. "Do you want me handing out canapés? Putting up the marquee?"

Alice laughed and kissed him. She smelt the same as she always had, of Chanel Number Five and baking, and Zak's heart twisted with love. She smelt of home and Granny Alice was his home. He would do anything for her. Anything.

"No, love, it's nothing that difficult, not for you anyway, but it is something only you can do for me and it's the one thing that would make my day extra special. I've wanted to ask you for so long and it would really mean the world to me. It would be the best wedding present and something I could treasure for the rest of my life, however long that may be. So will you? For me?"

Zak stared at Alice, alarmed. This sounded almost like a final request.

"Of course I will, Granny. I'll do anything you need. Just tell me what it is."

And then Alice looked him right in the eye and delivered the request that was a sucker punch to Zak's heart.

"I want you to write a song especially for Jonny and I and perform it at our reception. Do you think you could do that for me, love? I'm old now and I know this will be the last song I'll ever ask you to write. Will you do this for me? Will you make my wedding day extra special?"

CHAPTER FOURTEEN

Zak was floored by his grandmother's request. Hadn't she understood when he'd said I don't want anything to do with music any more? Didn't she get that he had no choice in the matter? That not being able to write and play wasn't an option?

This was what he got for not telling Granny Alice the entire story. As far as she knew, Zak had chosen not to play. He'd turned his back on music. He was refusing to write. His grandmother had no idea that it was the other way around and that since that evening when Kellee collapsed right in front of him, music had turned its back on Zak Tremaine.

For a moment, Zak was poised to tell her the truth. It would be a relief to confess that his gift was gone, along with the joy he'd once felt in music, and explain that everything felt tainted by commercialism and the cynical machinations of powerful bosses. Alice would listen and would know the right thing to say. She would be able to… to…

To what? Make everything better again? Mend his heartache with a kiss and a biscuit? Zak knew his grandmother was a formidable woman and never baulked at facing problems head on, but he knew this was something even Alice couldn't fix. Maybe nobody could.

"Well, love?" Alice asked when Zak failed to reply. "Do you think I could have a special song as my wedding present?"

Her faded blue eyes were filled with such hope that Zak knew he couldn't let her down. She asked so little of them all, but did so much. What did Alice ever receive in return? And when had she ever asked anything of him? Zak couldn't think of one single occasion.

"Wouldn't you rather have a Louis Vuitton bag or some bling? That's what women usually ask me for," he half-joked.

Alice tutted. "If you're spending time with such materialistic young women, I'm not surprised you haven't found a nice girl yet, Zachary. Anyway, what on earth would I be wanting a Louis Vuitton for? This isn't The Only Way is Cornwall! And I can't imagine I could fit all my shopping in it."

Zak would have commissioned LV to make Alice a bespoke wheelie trolley if he thought it got him out of having to write a song, but he knew that she wouldn't be interested. What she wanted was going to cost him far more than a designer bag. Somehow he'd have to think of something.

"I don't want things or designer items," Alice said firmly. "Homemade presents mean the most and I treasure everything you children have ever given me. Why else do you think the Christmas tree still has that dreadful papier maché star all these years on?"

Zak had to smile. Mo's brush with art was about as successful as her matchmaking, but each year, and with great ceremony, out came the lumpy star to shed yellow paint dust all over them.

"Or why I wear that clay necklace with the sunflower seeds in it, even though most of them have fallen out? Nick made it, that's why," Alice continued. "Shall I go on?"

There was a lot more treasure tat to list. She might be in the attic room for a while.

"No, I get what you're saying. You want something personal from me on your wedding day. Something written just for you and your special occasion."

Zak had often done similar things in the past for friends and family. The song he'd written for Nick's twenty-first birthday was still sung in the pub (and away from his grandmother's ears) and Morgan's Theme was the only tune his nephew ever played on the recorder. The only difference was that back then, writing and playing came as easily as breathing, whereas he now had the musician's equivalent of writer's block, or in this case, more like total constipation. Maybe he should sound out Caspar and see if Polwenna's resident bestselling author had some tips?

"Oh, yes! Exactly that," said Alice, beaming at him. "It would make me so happy. And Jonny too, of course."

Zak would have needed a heart of stone to refuse. Once his delighted grandmother had left, full of excitement, he buried his face in his hands and groaned. How the hell was he supposed to write a song that would mean this much to Alice, a song which needed to sum up the joy of a teenage romance recaptured, yet the sadness of a reunion distilled by the bittersweet passing of the years? How could he write a song which should be the most important composition of his life when he couldn't even put a line down on paper or string two notes together? His gift had deserted him and without it Zak had no idea what to do.

It was the worst scenario imaginable.

Suddenly the walls of his bedroom seemed far too close together and the air was too warm. He was in a box with the lid slowly shutting and he needed space to breathe.

Actually, stuff that. He needed a drink.

Zak picked up his jacket, grabbed his wallet from the desk and before he could think better of it, headed out into the warm evening. It was still light, the sea a peculiar turquoise blue stitched to a raspberry ripple sky, swifts darting through the air like arrows fired from a crossbow, gorging on insects as they rode the breeze. It was beautiful and the kind of scene that once would have had him reaching for his guitar, but now all Zak could think about was getting to The Ship and downing his first drink. A pint of Pol Brew was well overdue.

Zak took the steps up to the pub two at a time, gave the door a shove with his shoulder and ducked his head under the low lintel as he had a thousand times before. After the brightness of the evening, the pub was dark, lit by an assortment of white fairy lights, lamps and candles shoved into bottles. As his eyes adjusted to the dimness, Zak saw the place was packed with an eclectic mix of out-of-season holidaymakers, easily identified by their Joules clothing and delight at the low beams and real ale, and the usual crowd of locals colonising the far end of the bar. It didn't matter that he hadn't stepped into the pub for almost a year, everyone still occupied their usual positions and nothing had changed. Little Rog was elbowed almost under the stairs with the coats, while his larger father took up most of the space, Caspar James held court by the pork scratchings and a crowd of fishermen perched on the bar stools or stood with hands braced against the beams as though expecting the scuffed floorboards to shift and lurch beneath their feet. One of them was Nick, who waved delightedly at him.

"About time, fam! Look, you lot! Zak's here!"

There was a chorus of "Geddon!" and "All right?" as Zak found himself being clapped on the back by salt-hardened hands and welcomed back with genuine pleasure. Within moments, a pint of Pol Brew was pressed onto him and the drinking crowd had shuffled up to make space at the bar. As the first gulp of beer trickled over his taste buds, Zak felt the tension he'd carried about for what felt like forever start to slip away. Nothing had changed here, nobody in The Ship was impressed by his adventures up country and they were far more excited about Polwenna's Got Talent than they were about any scandal he might have been embroiled in. He should have remembered just how down to earth it was here, more proof if he needed it that the world he'd been living in was made of smoke and mirrors.

"About time you got your arse down here, you harris!" said Bobby Penhalligan, raising his glass.

"The party never starts until you arrive," added Joel Trewithen, a wiry lad who always wore a woolly hat, even in the height of summer. There was much debate in the village as to why this might be. Was he bald? Did he keep his cash under it? Drugs? Nick had once tried to pull it off and had been punched on the nose so hard that Dr Kussell had been called to treat him for concussion. No one had ever tried that again.

Zak laughed. "I think I'm getting too old to party."

"That's rubbish," said Little Rog's voice from the alcove under the stairs. "Dad's old and he still parties, don't you Pa?"

"That's right, my boy!" nodded his father. "And no time to party like on blessed Friday night! End of the working week."

Caspar James snorted. "Working week?"

"And what's that supposed to mean?" demanded Big Rog.

Caspar shrugged velvet-clad shoulders. "You used the word 'work'. It amused me somewhat."

"That's rich from the likes of you, writing that porn all day. Hardly a job for a real man. Real men build things and catch fish. They don't ponce about with laptops," taunted Eddie Penhalligan.

"I don't ponce about and neither do I write porn. I write historical romance!" huffed Caspar. "I'm a Romantic Novelists' Society winner 2013, I'll have you know! I've met Richard and Judy too, so there. I leave writing filth to self-published amateurs like Alice Tremaine."

Zak spluttered into his pint. "I don't think Granny sees her novel as filth."

"Yeah! Come outside and say my gran writes porn," said Nick, squaring up to Caspar.

"Am I to suffer the same fate as Kit Marlow?" Caspar said to the room, a theatrical hand to his brow. "Alas, another literary talent cut down too soon."

"Kit Marlow? Who's that? Does he live in Fowey?" asked Eddie.

"You don't half talk some bollocks, Cas," said Big Rog.

Judging by the amounts of empty glasses, the locals must have been stuck into the beer for a while and feelings always ran high after a few drinks. Zak, the only sober one of the bunch, deflected the situation the only way he could.

"The next round's on me! What are you all having?"

Personal differences were swiftly forgotten in the rush for a free pint and by the time the drinks were poured, the conversation had turned back to the music festival and everyone was friends again. Maybe if Zak couldn't compose and play any more, he would have a whole new career negotiating world peace?

"Nice to see you back," said the barmaid, passing Zak his change and smiling up at him Princess Diana style from under mascara-laden lashes.

Zak smiled back. He was feeling so much better after a pint. Maybe things had been so rough lately because he'd knocked the booze on the head? Going from drinking heavily to drinking nothing had probably put his body into a state of shock or something. The muse was probably gagging for a beer, that was all. Feeling cheered by this thought, he knocked back a second and then a third. By the time Nick had bought him a fourth, the place was a little fuzzy around the edges and all his jagged thoughts had been well and truly smoothed away. Zak flirted with the barmaid (Mandy? Sandy? He couldn't quite recall, but she was quite pretty) and felt on top of the world. He'd stop soon, before melancholy started to seep into the mix, but partying in the local with his old friends and neighbours was working wonders.

As the evening wore on, customers ebbed and flowed through the pub.

The holidaymakers tended to stay for a few drinks before walking back to their rented cottages, the local crowd staggered home for dinner, while the die-hard drinkers, namely Nick and his fishermen pals, pushed on through to closing time and, they always hoped, beyond.

"If we're lucky we'll get a lock-in," Nick said to Zak.

"Not with Mandy in charge. She always says we're drunk and to bugger off home," said Bobby Penhalligan sadly. His green eyes were crossing with drink and as he went to lean on the bar he missed it, crashing into Nick and sloshing Pol Brew everywhere. Even in his not entirely sober state, Zak thought Mandy probably had a point.

"She'll let us stay if Zak asks," remarked Joel Trewithen from beneath his woolly hat. A man of few words, people tended to listen when he did speak.

"That's true," agreed Joey. "Mate, chat her up for us. Get her to give us a lock-in!"

Zak glanced across the bar where, sure enough, Mandy was checking him out. He vaguely recalled that they'd had a thing a couple of summers ago; at least he thought it was with her. When you were in a band, lived in a county full of holidaymakers and partied hard, lots of evenings started out like this and ended up a little hazy.

Zak held his glass up. "Tide's out."

"Christ. You're drinking faster than me," said Nick in awe.

Zak had actually lost count of quite how many pints he'd had. Was he nudging double figures? He was at that stage in the proceedings where he was feeling almost too full to drink any more. Maybe it was time to move onto shorts?

"Buy you another if you get Mandy to have a lock-in," said Bobby.

"I'm not sure we need a lock-in," Zak replied. The pub was starting to dip and roll. Maybe he should hang onto a beam?

"You don't think you can pull her, you mean," scoffed Joey. "Lost your touch, Zak?"

Zak had forgotten what an idiot Summer's brother could be when he was drunk. Time to go home – if he could make it up to Seaspray. Lord. Just how much had he drunk? Unlike the others, who were well practised and had been pacing themselves, Zak had been knocking the beer back like orange squash.

"Zak could pull her if he wanted to," flared Nick. "He could pull any girl in this pub. Couldn't you, fam?"

Zak shrugged. "Whatever."

But Nick was happy to continue boasting. In the past, he and Zak had hunted as a pair and both being tall, handsome and sociable, it hadn't been hard for them to collect holiday romances and broken hearts. Zak had loved the chase and the stomach-looping anticipation of a first kiss, with all the promise and novelty. But he was twenty-eight now, not eighteen, and all of a sudden, the time warp of the pub felt claustrophobic rather than charming. He wasn't that person any more. He didn't want to be that person any more.

"So prove it, Nicky," taunted Joey. "One hundred quid says he can't!"

"Done!" said Nick. "Easy bloody money."

Zak rolled his eyes. "How old are we?"

Nick grinned. "Old enough to still need some cash! Don't let me down, fam. I'm skint and the Tremaine honour is at stake here. I'm counting on you."

This was the point in the proceedings where, if he was sober, Zak would have told Joey and Nick to grow up and gone home (with or without Mandy, depending on his mood), but because he was drunk, he simply bought another drink and let Nick carry on bragging. While his friends were squabbling, he couldn't lose himself in his thoughts, which was very good news indeed.

Joey cracked his knuckles. "Right. The bet is on and I choose…" He glanced around the pub, eyes narrowed as he sized up the potential target. "Her!"

Zak peered through the crowd to see who Joey had spotted. They were all so drunk, it was probably Sheila Keverne or Ivy Lawrence. There were certainly several older women drinking, but Joey was looking beyond them and at the slim blonde standing by the window who was deep in conversation with Zak's ex sister-in-law, Tara.

Bobby whistled. "Tess Hamilton? Good choice. She's well off blokes since Nick, and who can blame her the way he farts."

"Sod off," said Nick mildly.

"She's a right ice maiden. You've no hope of scoring there," crowed Joey.

"May as well collect your winnings now, mate," Joel said.

Zak gripped the bar. It felt as though it was dissolving beneath his fingers and the voices of his drinking companions seemed to come from very far away. Tess must have sensed him looking because she turned slowly, her brown eyes meeting his for a brief moment, before they flickered back to Tara. Even in his drunken state, Zak had to concede Tess was beautiful even if she was icy, aloof and, judging from the way she'd totally snubbed him at Mariners, loathed him for some mysterious reason. In the past, he'd have been straight in there with a glass of wine and upping the charm offensive because there was nothing like a challenge.

In the past, he was an utter arse.

"Bet you double the cash you can't pull her by the festival, Zakky," said Bobby.

Zak sighed. "I don't want to pull her, as you so nicely put it."

"Are you mental? Who wouldn't want to pull that? She's hot," said Joel, looking rather warm himself beneath his woolly hat.

"Me for one," Zak said. "I don't fancy her."

"Never stopped you before," said Bobby.

"Well, it's stopping me now," he replied. "She's snobby and stuck up. No thanks."

Nick spun around, his face taut with emotion and his blue eyes narrowed.

"Watch your mouth! She's none of those things. Tess is great, actually, and way too good for you. Jesus! This is a stupid conversation."

"You started it, you twatting harris," said Joel amiably.

Nick couldn't argue with this. He had.

"Should have stuck to pull a pig, mate. Play to your strengths," added Bobby. "I bet you'd win easily."

Zak's head was starting to spin. The conversation was taking on a woolly slant. Pigs? Winning? What were they discussing again?

Nick slammed his glass down on the bar.

"You're a bunch of tossers and the stupid bet's off, okay? It's bloody well off!"

He stormed out of The Ship, slamming the door so hard behind him that the stacked glasses rattled and dried hops pinned above the bar rained down on the drinkers.

Zak knew he ought to go after his brother, but his legs were so heavy he didn't know whether he could even get off the bar stool, let alone stand up. Besides, Nick was known for his volatile temper; he took after Mo in that respect, and he'd probably calm down as soon as the cool air hit him and be back within quarter of an hour. When Joel passed Zak another drink, the decision was made. He was at the tipping point between being pleasantly drunk and being totally and utterly slaughtered and it was too late to care. Anyway, a heavy night in the pub was working wonders on the oblivion front. Everything was forgotten – including, once he'd finished the pint and then his first, second and third whisky chaser, the stupid and immature bet to pull Tess Hamilton.

It hadn't meant anything anyway. At least, not to Zak Tremaine.

Ruth Saberton

CHAPTER FIFTEEN

Mo knew that going riding with broken ribs wasn't generally advocated by the British Horse Society, but at the time it seemed a good idea. She'd ridden since she was tiny and had taken to the saddle with cracked ribs on several occasions, once even to compete, so it was no big deal. Everything would have been fine too if she'd only stuck with her training programme and ridden Dandy in the safety of her sand school, but since it was such a glorious morning, she'd played hooky from dressage and gone for a hack around the fields.

With the early morning dew still sparkling on the ground, the wind-whispered grass rippling like the sea and the only sounds birdsong from the hedgerows and the distant rumble of a tractor, Mo had given Dandy a loose rein and enjoyed their quiet meander through pastoral bliss. Deep in thought about Ashley and his ongoing headaches, the cause of yet another row the previous evening, her mind was miles away from the horse beneath her when a pheasant exploded from the hedge and Dandy executed a top-speed turn of the haunches with extra game bird-powered bucking effects thrown in for good measure. Her reins held at the buckle and her concentration several miles away at Mariners, Mo was totally taken by surprise and consequently ended up hitting the deck. Hard.

So hard, in fact, that she'd broken her stupid ankle.

"I'm not going to say I told you so," said Ashley as he drove Mo home from the hospital.

Mo, her ankle in a big plastic boot, glowered at him from the passenger seat.

"Go on, say it. You know you want to."

"No, it wouldn't be kind, darling."

Mo gritted her teeth. "Just say it, darling."

Ashley flashed her a smile, his teeth white against his dark stubbled skin.

"Oh, very well. If you insist. I told you so, Morwenna! Eventing is dangerous."

"I wasn't eventing. I was pootling along a bridleway," muttered Mo. "I can't believe I fell off. I'm worse than a novice. Maybe we could just tell everyone I was jumping a four-star course somewhere?"

Her husband ignored this.

"No body protector. No mobile phone. No note to tell anyone where you were. Poor Penny was in a dreadful state when Dandy came back without you – and so was I, incidentally."

Penny Kussell worked part time at the yard as a groom and Mo felt bad about giving her a fright. Independent by nature, Mo was so used to doing things alone that she sometimes forgot that other people worried about her.

Ashley, for example, fretted dreadfully. It was sweet, but also very annoying – especially now she'd proved him right. All his concerns about her safety and Isla needing her mother in one piece, which Mo had dismissed as fussing, suddenly felt very real. What if she had been really hurt? What would happen to Isla? Especially if Ashley—

No!

Mo applied her mental brakes with a screech. She wasn't even going to think about that. It felt horribly like tempting fate.

"I'm so sorry."

Mo felt dangerously close to tears all of a sudden and because Mo Carstairs never cried, she looked out of the window and forced herself to concentrate on the green blur of the passing Cornish countryside. She curled her hands into fists and dug her nails into her palms. Pain was a great distraction.

Ashley released one hand from the Range Rover's steering wheel and placed it on her knee, squeezing gently. His tender touch undid her and Mo closed her eyes in defeat.

"I love you, Red. I can't bear to think about you getting hurt."

"It was just a silly spook, Ash. I wasn't concentrating. It wasn't as though I was doing anything risky. I was only hacking like I've done a million times before."

"I know, my darling, but when Penny called, it felt like all my worst fears were coming true. I'm not asking you to give up riding, I'd never do that, but just to step it back for a few years. It's not as though we need the money."

Mo bit her lip. If she stopped now, she might never reach the top of her game, might never again know the thrill of riding the big tracks. On the other hand, just lately she'd started to wonder whether this was meant to be her journey after all. Mo would rather leap out of the car right now and roll down the hill into the harbour than admit this to a soul. Surely she couldn't have lost her competitive drive? She'd been working for this since she was a teenager.

"If I don't compete, then who am I?" she wondered aloud.

Ashley's storm-grey eyes flickered to hers.

"You're the woman I love," he said quietly. "You're my wife and Isla's mummy. You're the most important person in the world, Mo, and we can't lose you. Isla and I need you. We love you."

Now the tears did spill over.

"I love you too," Mo sobbed. "Both of you, so much."

"So stop taking risks! It breaks me to think of what might happen."

"But don't you see, Ash? That's exactly how I feel about you! Isla and I can't lose you."

Ashley slipped his hand away and turned his attention back to guiding the big car down the narrow lane leading to the entrance of Fernside Woods. His hawk-like profile was stony and his mouth set in a grim line.

"You're not going to lose me."

"So you say, but how am I meant to know that?"

"You trust me, that's how."

"Trust! When you've been having headaches for months now and trying to hide it? No, don't deny what's happening," she added, sensing that her husband was about to protest. "You've been gobbling painkillers like they're Smarties. So, unless you have an addiction I don't know about, something's wrong."

Ashley didn't say anything, but he put his foot down and the car surged forwards.

"Ashley! Tell me the truth!" Mo cried. "Are you getting ill again? If you are, then bloody tell me!"

Her husband took a deep breath. His hands gripped the steering wheel so hard that the knuckles glowed chalky white through his flesh. The car slowed.

"I've been having headaches again. Nowhere near as bad as before, but they are getting worse."

The world seemed to slow on its axis. The car veered around a sharp bend in direct time with the lurching of her heart. Mo felt the blood drain away from her limbs and for an awful moment she thought she was going to be sick. The silent stalking fear that shadowed her when she woke in the small hours had finally caught up with her.

"I've been hoping they would go away, but they haven't. It even hurts to look at the computer or watch telly."

Mo couldn't speak. Terror had zipped her throat up. Silent tears dripped off her chin and splashed onto her breeches.

"I've already made an appointment to see my consultant," Ashley continued, staring straight ahead. "I'm going up to London on Wednesday. He's going to run some tests. Scans. That kind of thing."

"Were you going to tell me?" Mo whispered. Her voice sounded brittle, as though it was about to shatter.

"I was waiting to hear back from Stephen's secretary and I really didn't want to worry you until I had a date and knew what was going on. I guess I was also hoping he'd tell me not to panic and that it was nothing."

"But Mr Oliver didn't say that, did he?"

Ashley shook his dark head. "I'm afraid not. He called in person this morning and asked me to come straight in. I was going to tell you when you got home from the yard."

Mo crooked her little finger at him. It was their private code and, silently, Ashley linked his with hers. The gesture said that they were joined, even in the most fragile of touches, and that they were a unit. Stronger together than apart. Never to be parted.

Her stomach was in free fall. She couldn't be without Ashley. She wouldn't be without him.

"It's going to be okay," she said.

"I hope so, Red, but I need you to be safe. I need you with me. Is that selfish?"

"No," said Mo softly. "I'm the selfish one for not thinking about you. Sometimes I get so carried away with things that I can't see the wood for the trees."

Ashley laughed. "Wasn't that how we met?"

The happy memories of those early days, days spent sparring and squabbling and frantically trying to deny their attraction to one another, was enough to lighten their hearts just a little. Neither ever wanted to bring the other down.

"Hmm," said Mo, gulping back the sobs and focusing on her injured foot. "Now I'm wishing more than ever I'd said 'yes' to that road through the woods."

"You wouldn't be the woman I love if you'd done that," Ashley replied. "Besides, you would have missed out on the amazing experience you're about to enjoy."

"Which is? Hopping along the track on crutches? You giving me a fireman's lift all the way home?"

"Nope, much better than that. I've called the Pollard Express to take you through the woods to Mariners. You can thank me later, darling."

"Oh I will," Mo said grimly. "Have you seen either Rog drive? I thought you wanted to keep me safe?"

"Always," said Ashley fiercely. "Forever."

At this point, their car broke out of the sunken lane. Sunlight flashed through the windscreen, gilding Ashley's profile and making Mo's heart squeeze with love. She would do anything to help him through this. Anything. The light turned into dancing dapples as they turned left into the small clearing on the edge of the woods, which was as near to Mariners as a car could get. Here, Little Rog waited, perched on top of his quad bike and waving excitedly. This was a big gig for him since Fernside was a private woodland and no vehicles were permitted through the gates. He was probably having all kinds of rally-driving fantasies.

"Your chariot awaits," said Ashley, leaning across and kissing her before helping Mo out of the car and carrying her over to the quad. He was as strong as ever, Mo thought as she desperately attempted to clutch straws. He couldn't possibly be sick if he could lift ten stone of her plus her boot. No way.

While Little Rog made a big deal about fitting a helmet onto Mo's red head, clamping her crutches down with bungees and revving the engine,

Ashley cupped her face in his hands and brushed her mouth with his.

"I'll fetch Isla from Alice and then I'll be straight back."

"You promise?" Mo heard her voice wobble, and Ashley folded her into his arms, holding her close.

"I promise. It's going to be fine."

"I don't know if it is," said Mo. She gave him a watery smile and attempted a joke. "I mean you were worried about me riding my horses! Have you ever seen Little Rog drive this thing?"

"I can get from one end of the village to the other in three minutes," boasted Little Rog.

"So could Teddy St Milton and it didn't do him any favours," pointed out Ashley, tugging Mo's chinstrap tight. "You look after my wife, Roger Pollard. One trip to A & E in a day is quite enough."

"You don't get rid of me that easily," said Mo, and Ashley kissed her.

"Or you me," he said. "And that, Mrs Carstairs, is a promise."

Ruth Saberton

CHAPTER SIXTEEN

Zak Tremaine was having the hangover he well and truly deserved. Everything hurt, from the ends of his hair to the backs of his eyeballs, and when Alice's giant fry-up failed to tempt him, he knew things were bad. Just the smell made his stomach slosh and his mouth taste dangerously metallic. With a groan, Zak pushed the plate away. It was kind of his grandmother to have left his breakfast in the warming oven until he'd finally staggered into the kitchen, but he couldn't eat a thing.

"Good night?" grinned Danny from across the kitchen table where he and Jules were huddled over the laptop in the latest round of the search for London rentals.

Zak massaged his pounding forehead with the heels of his hands.

"I can't remember," he confessed.

"Then that sounds like a very good night," Danny said. "Or it could have been a very bad one and you've just blanked it all out?"

Zak honestly had no idea either way. His memories of the previous evening's proceedings made Swiss cheese look solid. He vaguely remembered having tequila slammers with Caspar James at some point and he thought he might have kissed Mandy the barmaid outside by the beer barrels, but after that it was all very hazy. He didn't remember walking home or going to bed, but he must have managed both because he'd woken up in his attic room fully clothed. The light sneaking in through the thin curtains had sliced into his brain like a chisel and he'd hauled himself into a sitting position more creakily than Jonny St Milton ever did. Once the room stopped rolling sufficiently for him to stand, Zak had shuffled to the sink which he'd filled with cold water, into which he then plunged his face, gulping thirstily before straightening up with a gasp.

"Good, I think," he ventured. "My wallet's empty, anyway."

"That's to be expected if you must go out drinking with fishermen," Alice said disapprovingly. She had Isla on her lap and was spooning in scrambled eggs which the little girl opened her mouth for like a baby bird.

"Nick's a fisherman. Fact," pointed out Morgan.

"I know that, love, and I number him as one of those who drinks more that he needs to," said Alice. She scooped up another spoonful of egg, zooming the load towards Isla's mouth in the style of an aeroplane, something Zak vaguely recalled he'd once loved. Maybe Alice could try this for him now? It could be a way of managing to force down some sustenance.

Morgan gestured to Zak's laden plate. "Can I have that if you don't want it?"

Zak pushed it across to him. "Be my guest."

"It's nearly lunchtime, Morgan," said Danny automatically.

"I know that. It's now eleven forty-two and we have lunch at one pm sharp. That means I have seventy-eight minutes exactly to wait and I will never last that long," replied Morgan.

"Fact?" teased Jules.

"Opinion," said Danny firmly. "Morgan will make it through to lunch without scoffing Zak's leftovers. Fact."

Morgan thought about this for a moment. "It's good not to waste the world's resources and that is a fact. Miss Hamilton said so."

A quicksilver memory flickered like a fish through the silty depths of Zak's memory. Tess Hamilton the snooty schoolteacher had been in The Ship last night, hadn't she? He recalled seeing her blonde head across the pub and feeling her cool gaze sweep over him, finding him lacking in every way. Did he speak to her? Zak didn't recall a conversation, not that this meant anything given the amount he'd had to drink, but seeing as she'd utterly blanked him at Mo's, it seemed unlikely. There was something, though. He was sure of it. And hadn't Nick stropped off for some reason?

Zak frowned, but the memory of what may or may not have taken place simply circled his mind like water around a plughole before draining away to emptiness.

Nope. It was gone.

"Who am I to argue with Miss Hamilton?" Danny was asking now, with an eye roll aimed at the ceiling. "You'd better eat up and save the planet, son."

While Morgan began to fork up his second breakfast of the morning, Alice was frowning.

"You really ought to eat something, Zak, love."

"I will once I feel a little bit more human," Zak promised, although the way he felt right now this might not be until at least Christmas. Instead, he reached for the mug of black coffee Jules had made, her secret 'wake up' weapon, she'd said, and took a big gulp. Instantly caffeine punched his nervous system and Zak spluttered his drink all over the table. This coffee was so strong it was a miracle the mug hadn't dissolved! What on earth was it doing to his insides?

"Bloody hell, Jules! That's lethal! Are you some kind of sadist?"

"You try getting up for matins after a big night out in this village," Jules said. "We vicars are harder than you think."

Danny passed Zak a wad of kitchen roll. "Drink up, fam. You need all the help you can get this morning. You look awful."

Zak mopped up the coffee, thinking to himself that if Dan thought he looked bad now, then it was just as well his brother hadn't bumped into him first thing. Zak's travelling artist's emergency kit of Resolve, eye drops and Clarins Beauty Flash usually did the trick, but even they were having their work cut out this morning.

"Have you checked your social media feeds, Uncle Zak?" Morgan asked through a mouthful of fried bread.

Zak shook his head – not wise when his brain seemed to swivel inside his skull. He hadn't been anywhere near his Instagram or Facebook or Twitter since... well, since that terrible evening. Prior to this, and in what felt like another life, he'd logged on almost as soon as his eyes opened in the morning, periodically checking throughout the day and only leaving it alone when his head touched the pillow. His enforced digital detox had actually proven to be a big relief and the only good thing that had come out of this sorry mess.

Morgan's eyes were wide. "But what if someone's posted a picture of you drunk? Or looking silly?"

Zak shrugged. "It wouldn't be the first time. Anyway, my manager sorts all that out for me. Or at least he did. He's probably sacked me by now."

"If he has, can I be your new manager?" asked Morgan. "I'm media proficient because I am young and growing up in the digital age. Fact. And I've set up all Uncle Symon's social media and I'm helping Jules make a website for the church."

"That's a great offer and I'll definitely consider it," Zak promised. He took another sip of coffee and winced as it karate-kicked his taste buds. "Although I'm thinking I might give up the music business for a bit."

"And live here in Polwenna?" Morgan's face lit up like the Wembley arch at this idea, which made Zak feel ridiculously pleased. However, he was soon put in his place when his nephew added, "All my friends at school think you're really cool. I could probably sell them tickets to meet you and make enough money to buy a better camera."

"My son, the budding capitalist," said Danny, ruffling Morgan's hair.

"Opportunist, you mean," corrected Alice, shaking her head in amused despair.

"Entrepreneur, actually," said Morgan, not in the slightest perturbed. "I can split the money with you if you like, Uncle Zak? If you are going to be poor now you aren't a rock star."

"I'm all right for now, mate, but thanks for the offer," said Zak.

Alice sighed. "What with Mo falling off her horse, you looking like death and Morgan hatching schemes, you children will be the death of me."

Morgan looked up in alarm. His cutlery clattered against the plate.

"We're going to kill you?"

"It's just a saying, mate," Danny reassured him hastily. "Grand Granny means that we are all very hard work some days."

"Most days," Alice corrected. She dabbed Isla's mouth with a baby wipe and lifted her back into the high chair so that she could fill the kettle and place it on the Aga hotplate. "At least Mo isn't badly hurt. Ashley says it's just her ankle and her pride that are injured. He's going to make sure she rests by taking her away to London with him for a bit."

Zak's killer hangover meant that he'd missed out on the morning's excitement, but he had managed to glean that his sister had taken a tumble from that big scary horse she liked riding. Now, as he fought a rising spring tide of nausea, Zak listened to Jules fretting about who could take Mo's place to help her run the music festival. In the past, he would have leapt at the chance to be involved, loving the challenge of booking great bands and whipping up publicity or even headlining himself, but not any more. Zak's music mojo had been well and truly lost.

Jules sighed. "I don't want to sound selfish, but I really needed her to help me with the festival. I've got so much on with the wedding season and organising our move to London. Oh Lord. Maybe we should just cancel the whole thing?"

Zak wasn't sure if it was his hangover playing tricks with his hearing, but it sounded to him as though Jules was trying very hard to be enthusiastic about the move. She didn't look like a woman who was brimming with excitement about starting a new life in the city.

"But what about my wedding reception?" Alice asked. Her face crumpled and she sat down at the table again. "Oh dear. Maybe putting the two together wasn't such a clever idea after all? What ever shall I tell Jonny?"

Sensing the atmosphere, Isla began to cry. The thin wail almost split Zak's brain in half.

"Jonny only cares about marrying you, Alice," Jules said, scooping Isla up and rocking the little girl backwards and forwards until she started to giggle.

"But the reception was supposed to be very special! I was so looking forward to it. Zak's writing me a song especially," Alice said shakily. Her hands were clasped tightly in her lap and she looked as close to despair as Zak had ever seen her. "I so wanted to share my day with everyone too. We can't cancel it, Jules. That would let everyone down. Oh dear. What am I going to do?"

Zak wasn't sure what came over him at this point. Maybe he was still drunk? Or perhaps he simply couldn't bear to see Alice so upset? Or had an alien taken him over for a few poorly timed seconds? In any case, it was a little like an out-of-body experience to hear himself say, "Don't panic, Granny. I'll give Jules a hand to sort the festival and the reception."

"You will?" Jules looked stunned.

"That's good of you mate," Danny said. "We're so pushed for time now with the house-hunting that I don't think Jules could take on any more."

"No, I couldn't," Jules agreed. "Thank you, Zak! Brilliant!"

Zak wasn't convinced his rash offer was brilliant at all, but it was nice to see how happy his grandmother and Jules seemed to be. It was only a tiny village affair, he told himself. Nothing to stress about. Pol Fest was hardly Glasto. All he'd need to do was organise a few pissed-up locals, find a marquee and hire some bands. Compared to the challenge of writing his grandmother a special song, just the mere thought of which made him want to reach for another beer, this was a walk in the park. How hard could it be?

"Thank you, love!" said Alice.

"This is going to work out really well," Jules beamed. "Now all I need to do is convince a couple of other people to help and I think we'll be able to pull it off." She passed Isla to Alice. "I'm going to go and ask Tess right now."

Zak stared at her. "What?"

"I'm going to ask Tess Hamilton to help," said Jules patiently. "The teacher."

"I know who she is," said Zak. "In fact, I'm finding it hard to avoid her. Are you lot trying to push us together?"

"No! Of course not!" cried Jules, looking so horrified that Zak believed her. Besides, Jules was a vicar and they weren't allowed to lie, were they?

"So why her?" he asked suspiciously.

"She's super-organised, knows everyone, has great ideas and she's also very clever," Jules said, ticking off Tess Hamilton's virtues on her fingers. It was a vomit-inducing squeaky clean list. The woman was so dull that in comparison watching paint dry would be a thrill a minute. Kill him now, why not?

"She'll be an asset and save us hours of work too. Getting her on side was going to be a job for Mo, but I may as well walk over to hers now and see what I can do to persuade her. Then we can really get going. Oh!" Jules gave Zak a strange look. "You are all right with this, aren't you? There's not a problem with you and Tess. You haven't... you didn't..."

Poor Jules turned as red as Alice's Aga. Zak knew she was wondering if he'd slept with Tess, but was too coy to ask.

"Haven't what?" he asked, his blue eyes wide and innocent.

"Dated her?" Jules offered feebly.

"That was Uncle Nick. Fact," piped up Morgan. "He was punching well above his weight. That was what Uncle Jake said. What does it mean, Dad? Who was Uncle Nick punching?"

Again, Zak had the odd sensation something was floating through his memory, just out of reach. He was sure it had something to do with the aloof blonde in question, she of the serious brown eyes and distinct lack of humour, but what this might be he simply didn't know.

"It's a metaphor, love. Nobody is really punching anyone," Alice told Morgan with a wry smile. "Although I may come close to it when I next see

Jake!"

"Don't blame Jake," grinned Danny. "It's totally true. Nick can moon about all he likes, but Tess is never going to be seriously interested in him. If a guy doesn't listen to Radio Four, have a Mensa admittance intellect and read Chaucer in the original, then there's no hope. Nick spells like Chaucer, but that's as far as the list goes with him."

"Stop it!" Alice scolded. "Don't be so mean!"

"It's true, Gran! She's out of the league for the remaining single Tremaine men," said Danny.

Once upon a time, a comment like that would have been the ultimate challenge for Zak and it was a sad sign of the times that he couldn't be less interested. He had nothing to prove to anyone now except himself.

"Zak, is it all right with you if I ask Tess to help?" Jules was looking worried and Zak knew she was waiting for a definitive answer. What else could he say but that it was fine? If he said it wasn't, then they would all jump to all sorts of crazy conclusions.

"It's not a problem for me," he said nonchalantly. "Miss Hamilton isn't my greatest fan, but I don't have an issue with the woman. She's a bit miserable, I suppose, and she's way too superior for my liking, but we're only working on an event together so I can put up with her for a few weeks. It's not as though you're asking me to marry the girl, is it?"

What? Where on earth had that come from?

Jules looked as taken aback by this remark as Zak felt by uttering it.

"Err, no. Of course not."

"She is very pretty, though, Uncle Zak. Fact," said Morgan. "She looks just like Princess Elsa in Frozen. Especially when she has her hair in a plait."

Oh, great. Now every time he saw Tess, Let It Go would be playing on a loop in his head, thought Zak. Still, his nephew did have a point. Tall, slim Tess with her soft and musical voice, cloud of golden hair and ballerina's willowy grace was a dead ringer for the popular Disney Princess even if she found it hard to let her dislike of him go!

Well, that was all fine, but one thing was for certain; Zak Tremaine was not inclined to waste any time trying to melt the chilly heart of this particular ice maiden. He had far more important problems to deal with than Tess haughty Hamilton.

Polwenna's answer to Frozen was welcome to stay that way.

CHAPTER SEVENTEEN

Tess wasn't sure how Jules Mathieson managed to convince her to take on some responsibility for the Polwenna Festival. Working with Zak Tremaine of all people and on something to do with music was the worst idea Tess had ever heard, yet here she was about to join him for a festival meeting. The vicar's powers of persuasion were wasted in the church, that was for sure; Jules should have been a lawyer.

It was Sunday afternoon and rather than lesson planning or doing housework or even going for a run, Tess was getting ready to meet Zak at the Harbour Tea Room, a spot that was too public and busy to stay at for long and where hopefully Zak wouldn't be tempted to get stuck into the beer the way he had when she'd last seen him in The Ship. He might be all about the rock and roll lifestyle, but Tess had children to teach the next day. She had responsibilities.

Tess teased her hair into a loose plait and checked her makeup in the hall mirror. She'd normally wear mascara and lipstick to go out and it was a warm June day, so a strappy sundress and wedge sandals were totally appropriate. It wasn't as though she was making a special effort just because she was meeting Zak Tremaine. She would have dressed just like this if she was meeting Jules for coffee or the Chair of Governors. Even so, Tess felt a flutter of nerves deep in her belly. Ridiculous, she told herself sharply, peering critically at her reflection and curling a stray strand of hair around her finger. There was no need to feel this anxious about a silly festival meeting! Still, her mind flashed back to seeing Zak in the pub the previous evening, his intense blue eyes meeting hers across the crowded bar and sending a jolt right into the very core of her being. A man like this was dangerous and Tess would have to constantly remind herself of that. It was lucky that she was immune to his charms.

Too much lipstick. Her mouth was far too bright. Annoyed, Tess scrubbed away the pink hue until her lips were bare. That was better. A sweep of mascara over her lashes, peach blush and spritz of Mademoiselle wasn't overdoing it, surely? Tess frowned at her reflection. Maybe she should have worn glasses rather than contacts? There was a certain safety in hiding behind spectacles. However absurd it sounded, the associated connotations of intellectualism and seriousness were a sound second line of defence and one Tess often used. Being young and female and blonde didn't always count in her favour, and when she'd started her teaching career she'd often suspected these personal qualities went against her being taken seriously and being respected.

And Zak Tremaine was going to take her seriously and respect her if it was the last thing he did.

Oh, why had she agreed to help Jules with this?

Her aversion to all things music-related aside, Tess already had quite enough on her plate without signing up for any extra jobs. The summer term was always hectic with sports day to organise, reports to write and the transition to secondary school for Year Six to co-ordinate, and the threat of an Ofsted inspection was always a dark cloud on the sunny horizon, requiring all her policies and records to be absolutely perfect. Added to this, her parents were threatening to come and visit and her sister was also dropping hints about spending the holidays in Cornwall, boys and surf being high on Chloe's list of summer must-haves. The last thing Tess needed was the extra stress of having to co-ordinate bands and quarrelling villagers.

Actually, make that the second last thing she needed. Having to work alongside Zak Tremaine was number one in the chart of the last things Tess Hamilton needed or wanted. She'd seen him the previous night drinking heavily in the pub with his drinking buddies and several times had felt his blue-eyed gaze appraising her. Tess had strongly suspected she was the topic of discussion too, some stupid laddish remarks about teachers and canes probably, a thought that didn't exactly make Zak any more endearing. Add to this the rumours about his wild London life, and even wilder Cornish ones, and there you had it: somebody she would far rather stay away from.

Why on earth had she agreed?

The simple answer was that Tess liked Polwenna's vicar and had a lot of time for her. Jules was also a school governor and always willing to go the extra mile to help out. She took fantastic assemblies, helped to raise money for additional resources and could always be counted on to be the voice of reason at meetings. Several times when the head teacher, the ancient and set-in-her-ways Miss Powell, had wanted to push through an idea that Tess disagreed with, it had been Jules who had managed to talk her round. Jules also did a huge amount in the village and always with a smile and good humour – easier said than done when you were having to gently shepherd the Pollards or stop Eddie Penhalligan from falling out with his own shadow.

So when the vicar knocked on Tess's door, out of breath from the steep climb and upset about Mo's accident, Tess had very soon found herself agreeing to help out.

"This isn't another matchmaking attempt, is it?" she'd asked suspiciously, Mo's dinner party still fresh in her mind.

Jules had shaken her head emphatically. "Goodness, no. I'd never presume to do that, Tess. That kind of stunt is definitely Mo's department. This is purely me being totally desperate – not that I'm only asking you because I'm desperate!"

"Fibber," Tess had said.

Jules laughed. "Well, maybe I am a bit desperate in the sense that I'm rushed off my feet with parish business and the move to London. I was counting on Mo to knock everyone into shape for me. She's good at that and so are you."

"Bossy you mean?" Tess suggested. "Once a teacher, always a teacher?"

"The job does come with some authority. A bit like mine," Jules agreed. "Although I can't give my parishioners detentions, sadly, although I often feel like it! You have such great organisational skills, Tess, and it's those I want to borrow. And if you can deal with thirty squabbling children, I'm sure you can handle Big Rog and Caspar James."

Tess thought about this for a minute. "I think I'd rather deal with the children."

"I don't blame you," sighed Jules. "But seriously, I'd really appreciate your help and I promise there won't be too much to do. Zak's going to take care of the practical side – after all, he's got all the right contacts – and all I need you to do is work out the running order and organise the events. The Pollards are doing the morning duck race and Silver says she'll do the treasure hunt on the beach, so that's sorted. The yard of ale is at lunchtime in the pub. All you need to do is help with the talent show and the set-up."

"And that's it?"

"That's really it,' Jules said. "Honestly, you'd be doing me the biggest favour. I wouldn't have asked if I wasn't at the end of my tether. I do know how busy you are."

The truth of the matter was that, apart from school, Tess wasn't actually very busy. It was closer to the heart of the matter to say that her personal life was so empty that tumbleweed blew through it on a regular basis. She went running, attended a book group, sometimes met friends for a drink, but apart from this her diary was looking blank, something she worked very hard to avoid. It was the thought of filling in more time, time when she might start to think about the past or when her parents might suggest a visit, that finally swayed her.

She could handle Zak Tremaine, Tess told herself sharply as she gave her appearance one last check before heading out into the afternoon sunshine. It was only three weeks of planning a festival. Hadn't she already proved that there was nothing she couldn't do when she put her mind to it? She swung her bag onto her shoulder, squared her shoulders and raised her chin. There. She was ready for anything.

Tess's walk down to the harbour only took minutes. The village was buzzing with seasonal visitors so she wove her way through them until she reached the waterside where the café was busy with groups of people basking in the sunshine and nursing lattes. The steps down the slipway were colonised with day trippers enjoying impromptu picnics, some even dangling their feet into the murky water of the inner harbour, while others perched above on the harbour wall to enjoy the best views of the village. No matter what mood she was in, the picturesque village never failed to put a smile on Tess's face, even if she had been roped into helping with the festival. She felt so lucky to live here and be a part of the place.

The sunshine on her face and the holiday atmosphere also made Tess feel a little more relaxed. Even when the café queue shifted a little and she caught sight of Zak, Tess still felt upbeat. She was armed with a notebook, the list of jobs Jules had emailed over and a schedule that had to be followed – organising and delegating was what Tess was good at, so if Zak could manage to do his part without getting drunk/pulling holidaymakers/attending wild parties, then all would be well. It was only a few weeks. She could get through this.

As Tess threaded a path through the tables, she noticed how all female eyes were drawn to Zak. Dressed in blue jeans, a white tee shirt and with his perfect jawline thick with golden stubble, he was leaning back in his chair with the obligatory wrap-around shades in place as he raised his face to the sunshine. A cinnamon dusting of freckles danced over the bridge of his nose and his skin was the same warm gold as honey, while his wild blond ringlets were tucked behind his ears and brushing those broad shoulders. He could have been a living advert for Calvin Klein. No wonder people kept glancing at him.

All of a sudden, Tess wished she'd left the lipstick on.

"Zak," she said.

He started at the sound of her voice before pushing the shades into his thick golden hair and blinking up at her with bloodshot eyes. Yes, he'd clearly enjoyed a heavy night.

"Tess, hi!" Zak rose to his feet, a little unsteadily, Tess thought, although this might be because the café was on a slight slope. He leaned forward to kiss her cheek before thinking better of it and extending a hand instead. "Great to see you again. How are you?"

His arm muscles contracted beneath the tanned skin, a tribal-style tattoo moving in perfect contour with the bicep it traced. As his fingers closed over hers in a brief but firm handshake, Tess caught the scent of a delicious aftershave. Okay, she admitted grudgingly, he was attractive in a clichéd dishevelled bad boy way, but when he smiled at her, it was abundantly clear he possessed the Tremaine charm in bucket loads because she couldn't help smiling back.

"You caught me napping," he said.

"Your heavy night in the pub was obviously tiring," Tess replied.

She hadn't meant to sound quite so scathing, but the words leapt from her mouth before she could stop them and Zak looked taken aback. Then he shook his head in despair.

"Oh dear. That's what I get for drinking with Nick and his crowd. I take it you were there too?"

"Afraid so. I left shortly after you and Sheila Keverne started doing karaoke," Tess dead-panned.

He laughed. "Karaoke? I could never be that drunk! Ah, I think I remember now. You were at the far end of the bar, weren't you?"

Tess pulled out a chair and sat opposite him. "Good to know I'm so hard to forget."

"Oh, you're certainly that," Zak said slowly. His eyes, startling blue against the bloodshot whites, met hers for a second before he slipped his sunglasses back on. "That evening at Mo's is one I won't forget in a hurry. I may even need counselling. How is it, by the way?"

Tess was puzzled. "How is what?"

"That cold shoulder of yours? Come on, you could hardly bear to speak to me at Mariners. I had to go home to check my aftershave and totally rethink my grooming routine. You had me seriously worried I might have a personal hygiene issue."

"I don't know what you're talking about," fibbed Tess.

"Yes you do," said Zak, sounding amused rather than offended. "But I totally understand. That whole 'accidental set-up' thing was really awkward and I'm sorry you were upset by it. I promise it wasn't any of my doing. Blame Mo. She never learns or listens."

Tess was thrown that instead of ignoring the elephant in the room, Zak was inviting it to sit down and have a cream tea with them.

"Mo can be a little insensitive," he continued, "and I get it that I'm not your type. It's fine. You're not mine either – I prefer my women to actually like me! At first, anyway. The wanting to stab me to death part usually comes much later on!"

Tess laughed. Zak was funny and self-deprecating, not qualities she would have attributed to him. Had she been too quick to judge? Too hasty to listen to rumours and jump to conclusions?

"I'm sorry if I was rude. It's just that I get a lot of that kind of thing and it's beyond annoying. It isn't the first time that Mo's pulled a stunt like that either. Symon was the last victim and he wasn't thrilled either."

"God, no. Sy would hate that. He's so shy. What was Mo thinking?"

"The usual? That nobody can possibly be happy unless they're coupled up? I'm more than happy being single and concentrating on my career, but some people seem to find that really hard to accept."

"I feel your pain," Zak agreed. "If it isn't Mo playing Cupid, then it's Alex and Kat or, heaven help me, my dear old gran."

He pushed his shades up into his hair once more and their eyes met, for longer this time and with a flash of mutual sympathy. He was nicer than she'd thought, Tess admitted to herself. Maybe working with him wouldn't be so awful.

"I didn't actually think you'd show up today," Zak said quietly. "I wouldn't have blamed you either, I honestly wouldn't. I couldn't imagine you'd be too keen to spend any time with me after Mo's antics the other evening and now I know you saw how plastered I was last night, I'm even more surprised."

"We all get drunk from time to time. Besides, Jules needed a hand and I couldn't let her down."

He nodded. "To be honest, I'm only here myself because I want to help Jules out and because this is in effect Granny Alice's wedding reception. How can I not lend a hand after all she's done for me?"

Tess understood. The Tremaines were famously close to their grandmother and Alice was one of the most generous people she had ever met. You would need a heart of stone not to want to make her wedding day special.

"I know I've caused her stress by coming home too," he continued. "Maybe having to take part in the festival is my penance?"

"Nobody could have done anything bad enough to deserve that," said Tess.

"That's where you're wrong." Zak stared down at the table, crumbling lichen between finger and thumb as though this might squash what had gone before. "I've got a lot going on right now and I came here for a break. Something happened that changed everything for me. I won't spell it out because I can imagine the rumour mill's been in overdrive."

Tess wasn't sure what to say. He was right; the rumours had been flying around the village and, depending on who you listened to, Zak was either a raging alcoholic, a drug addict or suffering from a mental breakdown. Sitting with him now, she suspected the truth was adrift in the middle of the ocean of rumours. She'd read the papers too and had a fair idea, but even so, Zak Tremaine wasn't coming across as the arrogant rocker she'd pegged him as. She'd met far more conceited classical musicians in her time.

"So in terms of penance, the last thing I really needed was to be involved in a music festival," he continued, "or to have to work with you, no offence meant. I just don't work well with others. I'm better alone, especially right now."

"I'm not offended. I work best on my own too," Tess said. "And I nearly didn't come today. I'm still embarrassed after Mo's little stunt. I'm tired of that kind of well-meaning interference."

Tess didn't look at him as she said this, focusing instead on the snowy white seagull intent on rummaging through the litter bin. She didn't need Zak to know just how humiliated she felt to have been so obviously set up with a guy who was as out of her league as the moon. When she did manage to glance back, she saw that he was regarding her thoughtfully.

"I'll understand if you'd rather not work with me. I'd hate you to feel awkward."

Oddly enough, Tess was feeling less awkward by the minute.

"No, I'm good with it if you are? Unless you'd rather I stepped away and let you work with someone else?"

"Christ, no. You come highly recommended. Morgan sings your praises, Mo – as we know – wants you as a sister-in-law and never mind which brother you pick, and Jules says you're super-organised."

"That's true," sighed Tess. "I even colour co-ordinate my pencil tin."

"While I'd struggle to locate a single pencil. Organising isn't one of my greatest strengths, but I promise I'm really good at calling in favours and old contacts. No, the way I see it is that this job has to be done and we're doing Gran and Jules a favour. In return, while we're working on the festival together, mad matchmaking Mo will leave us in peace," said Zak. "We won't be complicating matters by fancying each other, since we're both happily single, and we're helping out the local community. It's a win-win for us both."

"How very Machiavellian," said Tess.

"I'm sure it is, if I knew what that meant! Tell you what, I'll get you a coffee and some cake, shall I, while you think it over?"

He smiled at her again, then headed into the café. Tess watched him make his way through the visitors and although she could admire him aesthetically, there was comfort in knowing she wasn't attracted to him and he, by his own admission, wasn't interested in her. That took a whole lot of pressure off. Zak Tremaine was turning out to be surprisingly good company and she had a good feeling their skills would complement one another. By the time he returned with a latte and two huge slices of chocolate cake, Tess's mind was made up. She could do this. As long as Zak handled the music side and she took care of logistics, this would work. There were only three weeks to endure before the whole thing was over. Simple.

And Zak liked chocolate cake, so just how hard could working with him possibly be?

Ruth Saberton

CHAPTER EIGHTEEN

"I really appreciate you helping, love. It's a big weight off my mind, especially now Mo can't lend a hand. I hope it isn't too much trouble for you," Alice Tremaine said to Zak a couple of evenings later.

Zak glanced up from the kitchen table where, surrounded by piles of homemade shabby chic bunting and handwritten wedding invitations, he'd been sitting for the past two hours making phone calls and doing his best to put together a makeshift stage and sound system. This was easier said than done in the summer when most equipment was already in use or booked up, but after following a chance lead he'd finally got somewhere. Trying to pull something like this together in such a short time was a huge task, and although when he'd met Tess at the café he'd been nothing but positive, deep down Zak had been concerned. The last thing he wanted was to let Alice down.

"It's fine, Gran," he assured her, crossing his fingers under the table. So far so good, anyway, and if his sound engineer contact came up with the goods they'd be sorted.

"And how's my song coming on?" his grandmother pressed. "I'm so excited about it, Zak love. It'll be the highlight of my day."

Jonny cleared his throat loudly. "Ahem! I think you may have overlooked something."

"My second highlight after getting married to you, of course," placated Alice. "Have you written it yet, Zak?"

"It's getting there," Zak hedged. "I've lots of thoughts."

This at least was true. Zak did have a lot of thoughts about the song, mostly panicked ones because he still couldn't write a note. It was a nightmare and he didn't dare glance at his grandmother because she would take one look at him and the game would be up. There was no way Zak was letting her down. No way at all.

"And you're happy working closely with Tess?" Alice asked.

Working closely with Tess was an innocent enough phrase, so why on earth did it fill his mind with such exciting thoughts, wondered Zak? They'd both admitted they weren't attracted to one another and, as gorgeous as she undoubtedly was, aloof and brainy women weren't really his type.

"Tess and I will get along just fine," he said.

Alice looked delighted. "I'm so glad to hear it. She's such a lovely girl, isn't she? Really lovely."

"Alice," said Jonny warningly, looking up over the paper from his spot on the kitchen sofa.

"What?" Alice said, wide-eyed and innocent.

"You know exactly what, love," chided Jonny. His eyes meeting Zak's, he added, "Although I must admit she is a cracking-looking girl and if I was fifty years younger I'd not say no! Aargh! Ouch! What was that for?"

His yelp of pain was caused by Alice flicking her fiancé with the end of a tea towel, an old trick always guaranteed to get her grandchildren moving when they dawdled on school days or stop them in their tracks when they were squabbling and World War Three was on the brink of breaking out at Seaspray.

"You know what, Jonny St Milton! I'll give you fifty years younger!"

"I was speaking hypothetically," muttered Jonny, rubbing his arm. "You know I only have eyes for you, Ally. Always did and always will."

"And you can hardly see with those!" Alice pointed out, hands on her hips. "I don't know, Jonny St Milton. Can I trust you? Should I be having second thoughts? Or are you going to run off with another woman?"

"I think you're safe, Granny. Tess is very happy being single," said Zak, powering down the computer and glancing at the kitchen clock. Crikey. It was almost six thirty and he was supposed to be meeting her at the beach café for a catch up. Persuading Tess to venture out on a school night had taken some doing. The girl had a work ethic like no other and she was also well and truly immune to the Zak Tremaine magic, something of an intriguing first. In honour of what felt like a major victory, he'd even put on a fresh white shirt teamed with smart indigo jeans, something his granny hadn't missed.

"Nonsense. She just hasn't met the right person yet," said Alice, happy to shoot Zak a very unsubtle hint. "That makes all the difference."

"Wise words indeed," said Jonny, heaving himself out of the chair and reaching for his walking stick. "Care for a turn around the garden, Alice? The jasmine's glorious at this time of day."

Alice took Jonny's arm and together they made their way out of the back door and into the garden. Warm air, birdsong and the heavy scent of the evening garden drifted in with the breeze. Zak sighed and gathered up his papers, stuffing them into a bag. His grandmother's blatant matchmaking aside, the truth was that Tess Hamilton was on his mind a little bit more than she maybe ought to be. When she'd rocked up at the harbour café in that white sundress which clung to her curves in all the right places and showed off her light tan to perfection, it had been all he could do to stop his jaw dropping. What had happened to the trouser suits, glasses and the hair bullied into a bun? Her blonde hair had been loosely gathered into a plait which fell over one shoulder, and Zak had been disconcerted to find himself thinking Morgan was right and she did look just like a princess. Or maybe even an angel, although the way the sun shone through the cotton dress to outline slender limbs and the sweet swell of her hips was pure temptation.

An angel girl with the promise of sin...

Fragments of a line and the fleeting notes of a half melody had drifted through Zak's mind, as insubstantial and as impossible to grasp as the mist which cloaked the river in the early morning. He'd had to gather his wits swiftly and for a while Zak hadn't been certain whether he'd made any sense at all. It had been all he could do not to stare like a teenager. He'd certainly revealed far more about himself than he'd intended. He'd had to make a dash into the café on the pretext of cake in order to collect himself.

In any case, Zak was looking forward to seeing her again. He might even make an effort and have a shave. Although Zak had no intention of trying to defrost Polwenna Bay's snow queen, it never did a man any harm to look his best.

The beach café was bustling when Tess arrived at seven o'clock. Now it was summer time, evening meals were being served on the salt-silvered decking and, as the sky turned to indigo and the sun slipped over the headland, white fairy lights trembled in the sea breeze. It was refreshing after the walk through the village and Tess let her powder blue wrap drop from her shoulders, enjoying the silky kiss of the cool air.

She was wearing jeans and a strappy top and had piled her hair, still damp from her post-run shower, onto the top of her head with a glittery clip. Tess had thought she'd make an effort because it never hurt to do so, but when she spotted Zak her mind went blank and her pulse went crazy. The clean-shaven man sitting alone at the far end of the decking, the man with razor-sharp cheekbones and thick golden curls falling to his shoulders and who was dressed simply in a white shirt undone at the neck to reveal his tanned throat and glimpse of muscular chest was a far cry from the dressed-down guy she'd had coffee with on Sunday. That guy had been attractive, but this incarnation was devastating and suddenly Tess understood the legendary Zak Tremaine magic. It was that special something that some people had – the power to draw all eyes to them and to command attention wherever they went, even without seeming to do a thing. He must be incredible when he played, she found herself thinking. Magnetic and compulsive. No one would be able to look anywhere else.

Catching sight of her, Zak waved and in reply Tess mimed a drinking gesture. He gave her a thumbs up and mouthed coffee, before returning his attention to the pile of papers in front of him. Coffee for him and a bucket of ice cold water for her, Tess thought as she queued for their drinks. She'd pour it over her head and bring herself to her senses. Musician. Unreliable. Hard living. Selfish. Career minded. Just like Vass.

Zak is a player, she told herself sharply. Everyone knows it. She knew it. This was just some primeval response to an alpha male, a throwback to the caveman days. There was no logic to it and Tess loved logic and felt unnerved when her pulse and libido didn't play ball. Right. If in doubt, assume schoolteacher mode, always better than full body armour when it came to dealing with men like Zak Tremaine. This approach had certainly worked with Nick.

"Don't let those papers blow away," Tess tutted when she joined him. "You need to weigh them down with something."

Zak laughed and placed the big beach pebble emblazoned with their table number on top of the paperwork.

"How's that, miss? Do I get a merit?"

Tess narrowed her eyes critically. "Hmm. It will do. Full marks for improvising, but marks off for sitting outside where it could all blow away."

"Ah, no. That's where you're wrong," he replied. "I get full marks for sitting us outside where we can watch the evening fall and the fishing boats come in. Look, there's one on the horizon. Don't you love the way the green and red lights spill like ink over the waves? Like a map for the trawlers to follow? They're the fishing twine of home and heart, luring them back to safety."

Now he'd described such a familiar sight this way, Tess knew she could never look at the returning boats in the same way again; Zak's description would stay with her forever. He had the eye of a poet and a skilled way with language that distilled a scene and emotions into one perfect image. Zak also had foresight and vision; where she would have tucked them into an inside booth where the wind couldn't snatch at their notes and where the light was brighter to write by, practicalities rather than poetic sensibilities taking priority, he was driven by atmosphere and setting.

He'd been right. How crazy to miss being outside on such a perfect summer's evening. She must try and loosen up a little.

"That's a gorgeous image," she said warmly. "It's just so vivid. You should jot it down and use it in a song."

Zak flinched and his smile slipped away like the condensation was slipping down her cold glass of wine.

"Yeah. Maybe."

Tess said nothing more. She slipped into her seat and decided to change the subject. If music was also a touchy subject for Zak Tremaine, then they were in big trouble.

"Well, I really need this," she said, raising her glass at him. "What a day. I'm exhausted."

"I bet it's full on being a teacher, isn't it?" Zak asked and Tess laughed.

"That's one way of putting it. Some days I literally don't even stop for a cup of tea or the loo! And then there's the workload I take home. It's not great for a social life."

"I did worry I was losing my touch when you resisted coming out tonight."

"Don't take it personally. Teachers rarely venture out on school nights.

We're pretty much useless for the next day if we do and I'll probably pay for this tomorrow when your nephew is asking me a challenging question!"

He chuckled. "I can imagine Morgan keeps you on your toes."

"They all do, but the kids are fantastic and they make every busy moment worthwhile."

She took a sip of her drink and caught Zak's intense gaze regarding her over his coffee cup. Something about the way he was looking at her made her flush. Was he checking out her top? Surely not. It was just her imagination.

"It must be amazing to make a difference," he said thoughtfully. "To know you're doing something that's really worthwhile, something that actually counts, must be incredible."

"It doesn't always feel that way when you're up all night trying to plan and prepare or when the Government decides to lob a daft new initiative at you," Tess reflected, "but yes, you're right. It's the little everyday achievements that mean so much. Like when a student finally understands something after trying really hard or a parent tells you how much their child loves coming to school. That makes teaching the best job in the world."

And then words spilled from Tess as she told Zak about her work. Teaching was her absolute passion and she couldn't imagine doing anything else now. Although she'd come to her profession by accident, she knew how lucky she was to have found her vocation.

"I'm talking far too much," she said finally. Even the light had faded away now and his coffee was long gone. "Sorry."

"Don't apologise. I'm impressed by your passion for your work – impressed and a bit jealous too. I wish I was as enthusiastic about my job."

Tess was surprised. "I thought you loved music? Everyone here is always saying how incredibly talented you are."

"I bet that's not all they said about me either." Zak pushed his coffee cup away with a rattle and a bleak expression settled on his face. "It's fine. I've lived here long enough to know how people love to gossip. Anyway, you've read the papers and you've probably worked it out for yourself. It's not a pretty story."

There was no point pretending to be clueless.

"The girl who died at the party? So you really were there?"

"Yeah." Zak ripped a packet of sugar open and tipped it onto the table, swirling his index finger through the bone-white grains. "She collapsed right in front of me and there wasn't a bloody thing I could do to save her. She was only nineteen."

Tess started at him, aghast. "That's awful!"

"Yeah, it was, and I think that was the end of it all for me. Maybe I've had a mini breakdown or something? That's what my manager thinks, but the truth is there's so much bullshit in that world and I was growing tired of it all anyway and I was pretty disillusioned too. My record company want me to write the music they think sells and I don't think that's the music I was writing. I've reached a point where I just can't do it any more, no matter what they promise me. I can see exactly where I'm headed if I go along with it. I've seen what I might become."

"It feels like selling your soul," Tess said softly and Zak's head snapped up as though on elastic.

"Yes! That's exactly it, Tess! I'd already sold my friends down the river and for what? For absolutely nothing. It was an absolute farce. The dream wasn't what I thought it would be. Maybe nothing ever is…"

His voice was bleak and Tess remained quiet. He wasn't really talking to her, was he? Zak was confessing something to himself and she was there to listen to him, as much a part of the background as the sigh of the waves breaking on the beach and the chink of cutlery on china from the diners seated around them.

"So here I am back home and without a clue what's next. All I know is that I can't write any more. Not a note and not a word. It's all caught up in my head and no matter what I do, I can't set it free." He placed his head in his hands and exhaled wearily. "So there you have it, Tess. The sad truth about Zak Tremaine. Whatever gift I had has gone and the music's left me. Maybe it's just as well? I'd rather not be a part of it at all than be a poor shadow of what I could have been and a man who sells out for cash."

In an instant, Tess's heart went out to him. To turn your back on the talent that had defined you was something she understood only too well. Stepping away from her musical career hurt so much sometimes that it was like a physical pain, leaving her breathless and doubled over even after all this time and no matter how much she adored teaching. Some day, something would come along that might staunch the wound for him, but there would always be those remaining gaps where regrets would seep through, as vivid and shocking as blood.

Zak raised his head and gave her a dismissive shrug, but Tess noticed that his finger still traced tight circles in the spilled sugar.

"I've no idea why I just dumped all that on you. I bet you wish you'd stayed in and marked books. Well, now you know what a screw-up I am, please feel free to leave."

Over and over went the sugar circles, the glistening granules tracing the endless torment in his mind. Tess worked with children, but their psychology wasn't a world away from that of adults and she could see how Zak was driving himself crazy with blame and self-loathing. He'd been lured into a glamorous world, tempted into abandoning his friends and shown a snapshot of what really went on beneath the glittering surface. It wasn't an unusual story; after all, how many celebrities and musicians and models ended up on drugs or with addictions or came to tragic ends? Jim Morrison,

Michael Jackson, Whitney, Prince – the list went on and on. Zak Tremaine, for all his startling beauty and talent and reputation as something of a player, was a sensitive soul and tortured by his experiences and Tess could see how close to the brink he was.

No wonder he couldn't write. Tess was no psychologist, but she reckoned Zak was probably so traumatised by what had happened to Kellee that he couldn't see beyond it. Lord. Who wouldn't be? The poor girl had collapsed and died right in front of him.

Without thinking, she lay her hand over his to still the compulsive circling.

"I know what it's like when something you love becomes too painful to bear," she said softly. "It's easier to cut it away totally than to only have a slither of what you once took for granted. Better to be nothing than a sad echo."

Zak's raised his eyebrows questioningly. "Sounds as though you know what you're talking about."

Tess slipped her hand away, sipping cool wine to buy herself thinking time. Zak had laid himself wide open and maybe it was only fair that she did the same? Yet Tess made a point of never talking about the past and had closed the door on music a long time ago. Having made such a mess of her musical career, and made such a fool of herself too in the process because Vass had never been worth vandalising her own talent, the subject had become so entwined with feelings of humiliation that, like a ruin infiltrated by ivy, she didn't think the two could ever be separated.

"I guess I do," she said eventually. Her heart was hammering against her ribs because this was something she did her best not to think about – her entire adult way of life had been deliberately designed in order to avoid ever having a spare moment to think about it – and as soon as the door on those memories was even a crack ajar, the old feelings of panic returned. Telling him even a little of this made Tess feel as though she was back on that stage, dry-mouthed and hands shaking as she realised she couldn't play a single note as her entire world shattered, and she hesitated.

Zak didn't push or prompt her, but simply sat quietly, his eyes holding hers, as he waited for Tess to continue. She took a deep breath.

"I used to play the violin," she said finally. "I was good, very good I think, and my parents were really pushing for me to make it my career. They're musical, you see, and music's everything to them. My father's a wonderful violinist and conductor and my mother's a mezzo soprano, or rather she was until she gave it all up to have a family – as she never stops telling us. They must have spent a fortune on lessons and coaching and ferrying me about to junior academy and I was all set to follow in their footsteps. I'd never even imagined myself doing anything else."

"Wow. Proper musicians," said Zak. "I'm impressed. As a self-taught pub singer, I feel a bit inadequate."

"Don't be," said Tess. "You're the professional, not me. I totally blew it."

She knocked back her last mouthful of wine and set the glass down with far more of a thud than she'd intended since her hands were trembling. She'd never breathed so much as a word of this to anyone and Tess couldn't quite believe she was telling Zak Tremaine. What was in the wine here? Truth serum? He wasn't pressing her to say any more, but there was something about Zak which set Tess at ease and invited confidence. Perhaps it was because he didn't ask or expect anything? Or because she sensed he felt the same aching loss? Or maybe a mixture of both? It made no sense at all, yet Tess found she wanted to tell him more.

"I had the biggest performance of my life and I literally couldn't play a note," she continued, seeing again the vast auditorium, the audience an anonymous ocean blanked out by spotlights, and then Vassilly's indifferent face and how she pleaded with him. "I was on the stage for my big audition and playing a piece I knew inside out, that I could have played in my sleep, and I froze. I just couldn't go on."

"You poor thing." Zak's blue eyes were sympathetic. "Stage fright is bloody awful and you're not alone. Nerves happen to us all. Christ, I once forgot the whole first verse of a song. I looked a right idiot, just had to 'la la la' and 'ooo' until the bridge!"

It was kind of him to try and make her feel better, but forgetting your words at a pub gig, however awkward, hardly compared to the utter humiliation of your lover and the classical music world's greatest watching you fail. Still, as easy as Zak Tremaine might be to talk to, dare Tess mention the real reason why she'd not been able to play? Stage fright was a far easier label than I was a naïve idiot in love with a narcissist.

Then she looked at Zak and knew she couldn't keep any secrets from him. Didn't want to keep anything back. Slowly and hesitantly, she told him all about Vass, not stopping until she talked herself to a standstill.

"So that was it," she finished. "I couldn't play a note. I ran off the stage and that was it. Budding career over."

"Oh, Tess. On behalf of the male gender, please accept my apologies," said Zak. "The guy sounds like a total arse. Men are idiots – take it from me because I've been one far more times that I care to count, but what he did was unforgiveable. If he was here right now, I'd push him in the harbour!"

Tess laughed at the idea of Vass, always neat and groomed, sloshing about in the murky green harbour with the ducks and the weedy mooring ropes. It was so strange, but telling Zak hadn't been nearly as hard as she had thought and the story, even to her own ears, was simply sad. She felt sympathy for the girl she'd once been. Telling it aloud and to a friend had taken away the shame and the power. It was simply the tale of an opportunistic young man and a naïve girl.

"Join the queue," she said.

"No, seriously, me first. Not only was he unforgivable to treat you like that, but he's also the biggest moron on the planet. Any man who walks away from you must need his brain checking," said Zak gallantly.

"Hmm." Tess wasn't convinced. "Anyway, that's my story. Music became all muddled up with betrayal and a teenager's daft idea of revenge. By the time I came to my senses, I'd missed my chance and too much time had moved on. So I moved on too."

"And you haven't played since?"

"No. My parents sent me to lots of counsellors and therapists, but I just couldn't do it. Each time I tried, it was as though I was back on the stage with everyone watching me and unable to play a note. In the end, everyone gave up, including me."

And Vassilly, of course, who had simply moved on. Without her musical success to reflect his own, Tess had been absolutely no use to him. Her self-sabotage hadn't hurt his career in the slightest because nobody had blamed Tess's tutor for long. The failure had been seen as hers and hers alone. By the time Tess had worked this out for herself, it had been too late to make a U turn. Her chance had passed and playing the violin was forever linked in her mind with heartbreak and humiliation.

"Poor you. It must have been like a waking version of one of those dreams where you're naked in a public place," Zak said slowly before clapping his hand over his mouth theatrically. Taking it away again, he raised his eyes to the twilight sky where Venus was scurrying after a slither of moon. Starlight silvered his hair and shimmered on his perfect face and Tess was struck anew by just how beautiful he was.

"That was just a very unfortunate figure of speech," he said. "I wasn't thinking of you naked. I promise!"

His horrified expression made Tess giggle. Zak was funny and cheeky and easy to chat to. She certainly hadn't expected him to be like this.

"And I promise I'm not picturing you having a Red Hot Chilli Peppers moment," she shot back.

"They don't make socks big enough – otherwise I might have tried it in The Ship and given Sheila Keverne a fright!"

Tess wagged her finger at him. "That's quite enough of that kind of talk, young man. Settle down!"

"Yes, miss," Zak said with a cheeky wink. "Will you cane me? Or is that extra?"

This was better. Back to banter. Tess could cope with this far more easily than soul baring.

"It'll be lines and a note to Alice."

"Christ! I don't need Granny on my case. I'll behave myself. Besides, I'll have to respect you even more now I know you're a serious musician."

"I was a serious musician. Now I'm just a failure."

"You're never that," Zak said hotly. "You're one of the most successful people I know, Tess! Talented. Hard working. Successful. Beautiful. Good at her job. Morgan thinks the world of you. He's always repeating what you say at school. Word for word. Fact! No wonder I'm totally intimidated."

Beautiful? Did he really say that? And intimidated? By her?

"I think if Dan hears, 'Miss Hamilton says' one more time, he may combust," Zak continued. "Seriously, Tess, all the other stuff aside, you're Morgan's heroine and you make school a happy place for him which makes you a big success, much more so than jumping around in tight leather trousers – that's me, by the way, not you! Although I bet you'd look great in leathers! Oh dear, I'm doing it again, aren't I? Maybe I should fetch us some more drinks? With lots of ice for me!"

He was teasing her, Tess knew, and he didn't mean it, but even so, she felt her face grow warm at his playful words. Time to return to teacher mode where the ground was firm beneath her feet.

"I'll get the drinks while you look at my notes," she said, swiftly steering the conversation back to safer ground. "I've got a running order for the talent show now and it's top secret, so don't tell a soul. I could have retired on the bribes Big Rog and Patsy Penhalligan have been offering me to find out who's going as what amongst the competition."

Zak nodded and tapped his nose. "It's safe with me. Anyway, I thought everyone knew Big Rog is Meatloaf?"

"That's a double bluff. He's really Tom Jones," Tess shuddered. The thought of the builder singing Sex Bomb while wearing an unbuttoned short and being pelted with knickers (his description, not hers) made her feel a bit queasy. Patsy as Cher wasn't much better. And then there was Keyhole Kathy as Madonna. Talk about people unleashing their alter egos. Some fantasies really should remain as just that.

"Next time I see Tom Jones, I'll tell him he's got competition," Zak said. He reached for her paperwork and started to flip through it. "I'll have a Diet Coke, and lots of ice, please. I'm overheating from all the talk about leather trousers!"

As Tess returned to the café, she was smiling. Telling Zak a little about her past hadn't been nearly as painful as she'd feared. He hadn't told her that she should try again or could work through it either because he understood implicitly that these were only decisions she could make. Instead, he had listened and reminded her of where her strengths did lie. It was kind of Zak to say these things and Tess knew she was a very good teacher, 'outstanding' according to Ofsted, but there was still that small childlike part of her that wanted to impress her parents and she knew her chosen career was never going to do that. After her 'episode', as they'd chosen to refer to it, the Hamiltons had spent a fortune taking Tess to see therapists and counsellors in the hope that she would play the violin again. Of course, she had never breathed a word of what had really happened, and the more time that passed, the deeper she hid her secret.

She was happy to have left that world behind. Music was the past and a reminder of how close she had come to letting someone else control her heart and her future. No longer playing was also symbolic and a constant reminder to never again allow herself to be such a fool. Once the festival was over, Tess would step away from Zak Tremaine, no matter how much fun or how easy on the eye he was. He'd got far too close already.

Drinks purchased, she headed back to the table determined that for the rest of the evening they would talk of nothing else but the arrangements and logistics. Even when Kat and Alex joined them later, she would keep the conversation strictly to the festival. Zak Tremaine was the last person she would allow to slip under her guard. But when she stepped outside, he smiled at her across the terrace, a delighted smile warmer than all the patio heaters combined and a smile that was for her alone, and Tess felt her stomach do a slow forward roll.

Oh no. It was far too late to worry about Zak Tremaine slipping under her guard. Somehow, and without Tess even noticing, he'd already done that. If she wasn't careful, Tess realised with a jolt of alarm, she could end up in big trouble here.

CHAPTER NINETEEN

"What about this one? 'A top floor self-contained studio apartment presented in excellent condition. The property benefits from an abundance of natural light. Spacious room and with a fully fitted kitchen and bathroom. Excellent transport links with an underground station across the road.' Here, have a look."

As Tara Tremaine pushed the laptop across the table to reveal a rabbit hutch-sized attic boarded out in lurid orange pine, Jules realised she was starting to go Rightmove blind. After a whole afternoon trawling property sites with Morgan and his mother helping, and even Alice chipping in too when she wasn't writing out wedding invitations, Jules could no longer process anything she was looking at. Had she seen this one already? Oh dear. All these tiny flats with massive rents were starting to blur into one. She really must try and be more enthusiastic, but this was very hard to do when your heart wasn't truly in it.

Please help me to be more excited about this move, Lord, Jules prayed. It means so much to Danny and I really want to support him.

Jules wasn't the only one in the family who felt it was important to show Danny how behind him she was. Tara had given up her evening off to help search, while Morgan had spent hours devising a spreadsheet and formula to find the perfect property. He'd explained the science of this to Jules at great length and, although she hadn't understood a word, she'd been impressed by both his ingenuity and the way that he was doing his very best to be excited for Danny. Tara had privately mentioned to Jules that although he didn't show it or talk about it, Morgan was very upset by the thought of his father moving away. Tess Hamilton had already noticed a few issues at school and some of his routines had become more extreme. He was more focused than ever on his photography too and refused to be parted from his camera even at bedtime.

"You know how much change upsets him," Tara had confided to Jules, biting her lip and looking very worried. "When we moved away, it was dreadful for him and I really do regret that because it's taken ages to get him settled again. It's one of the reasons I keep telling Richard I can't marry him yet. Morgan doesn't need any more changes and upsets in his life."

"I hope you didn't put it to Richard like that?" Jules asked, alarmed. Sweet-natured Richard would be truly hurt by such a remark.

Tara simply laughed. "Of course not! Don't worry, Jules. In spite of everything Mo might tell you, I'm really not that much of a cow! Richard understands the situation and he loves me, and Morgan too, so he's happy to take things slowly. We're in no hurry."

"But us moving away is upsetting Morgan?" Jules had to know the truth and Tara's weary sigh was all the answer she needed.

"I think so, yes. You guys are a huge part of his world but, Jules, please don't feel guilty. You have your own lives to live and I know how much the army means to Dan. It's wonderful he'll be able to be a part of it again and I'd never want to stop that. Morgan will get used to it. We all will."

Jules had almost said that she wasn't so sure. Most nights she lay awake until the small hours fretting about the move to London. Why couldn't she be more enthusiastic? She'd had an informal chat with the bishop of her potential new area who was more than happy to find her a position when the time came, and their conversation had revealed that there was certainly a need for her there. When she finished at St Wenn's, and once she and Dan were married, there was a whole new life waiting in London. There would be new challenges and new adventures. She should be counting the days.

Only she wasn't. Instead, she lay awake in bed and prayed hard for ages before trawling Rightmove and (her guilty pleasure) rereading some of Caspar James's bodice-rippers to distract her shuttling brain. Even so, it was usually almost light before Jules nodded off. No wonder she couldn't focus on the property hunt and had almost overslept for early morning communion.

Now, on this warm June evening in the kitchen at Seaspray and where the back door was open to let in the salty air and laughter of gulls as they danced on the evening breeze, Jules was doing her very best to wear her excited face. If Tara and Morgan and Alice – who Jules knew was very sad to see her grandson move away – could do it, then so could she. Danny was the love of her life and Jules would do anything, anything, to make sure he was happy.

Morgan was waving a sheet of coloured paper at his father and bouncing up and down with excitement.

"This one is number three on my list of houses that matched your criteria, Dad. My spreadsheet says it fills six out of the eight cells in the table. Fact!"

Danny, standing at the window and looking out over the village, didn't reply. He'd been in a strange mood all evening, saying little and seeming to be half a world away, but he did this sometimes – went deep into himself – and Jules had learned to wait until he was ready to make his way back to her rather than diving in and asking what was up. It was another of her lessons in patience.

Morgan, however, didn't do patience.

"Dad! Did you hear me? Come and look at this one!"

Danny turned around and he looked so bleak that Jules's stomach lurched. Was there something wrong? Was he in pain? When they'd first met, Danny had been in a very dark place and Jules knew he was always only a few steps away from returning. Trauma and injury and painful memories walked side by side with Danny Tremaine. They were his constant companions.

Dan smiled at Morgan, a slow smile that tugged at his scars just as it tugged at Jules's heart strings.

"Coming, son. Let's see what you've got."

Danny limped across the kitchen and pulled out a chair, sitting down heavily at the table and reaching out for Morgan's spreadsheet.

"Wow. This is detailed."

"I spent two hours working on the formula," said Morgan proudly.

"Your dream house has to be in here somewhere," Tara told him.

"If it exists,' Danny shrugged. "I'm starting to wonder."

"Let's start here. The price is right and it's really well placed for you to get into town easily, Dan." Tara slid the laptop across the table.

Danny's good eye narrowed critically. "I'm not sure, T. It's a bit small."

"One bedroom, you said. Near a station." Morgan stood behind his father and pointed at the screen.

"It's on the top floor. I'd have to walk up three flights of stairs," said Danny.

Jules and Tara exchanged surprised glances. Danny never alluded to his injuries.

"You climb all the way up to this house from the coast path and that's much more strenuous than a couple of flights of stairs," pointed out his grandmother.

"Hmm," said Danny. He couldn't argue with this. The climb to Seaspray was steep and even the village postman needed a rest when he arrived with the mail. Danny, who walked miles over the cliffs on a daily basis and lifted weights too, never thought twice about it.

"It's near to a good parish for me," said Jules, standing beside him and studying the details. Golly. Almost a thousand a month for such a small place? It seemed a fortune. She really hoped the Church would find them a vicarage once she was in her post.

"It's far too pricey," said Danny.

"But it's in your budget, Dad!" cried Morgan, looking agitated. "I put the data in. I didn't get it wrong, did I? I did have the right numbers?"

"Of course you did, love," Tara said quickly, shooting her ex a sharp look. "He's done a great job, hasn't he, Dan?"

"Yeah, yeah, great," said Danny automatically, but he didn't sound convinced and Jules noticed Morgan start to tap his fingers on the table top, never a good sign.

"You've done brilliantly," Jules told Morgan warmly. "I think this could be one to look at next week. What do you think, Alice? Isn't it nice and light?"

"It's lovely and sunny," said Alice Tremaine, obediently. "They must have had beautiful weather when they took the pictures. There's not a cloud in the sky."

"They've Photoshopped it, Grand Granny. Fact!" said Morgan, looking happier.

Alice was shocked. "But isn't that cheating?"

"They can't always take the pictures when the sun's out so they use filters," Morgan explained. "I can show you if you like? You can have a try. Shall I show you now?"

"Thank you, love," said Alice. "Maybe after supper? Dad needs the computer now to look at the houses."

"There's no second bedroom for Morgan to stay in," Danny pointed out.

"He'll happily sleep on a sofa bed," countered Tara. "He can't wait to come and see the sights in London, can you Morgan?"

"I want to go to the Science Museum and the Natural History Museum," Morgan said. "Will you take me, Dad?"

"Sure," said Danny, but he didn't sound very excited at the idea and continued to scroll listlessly through the pictures of the flat, while the rest of them discussed all the London attractions they were planning to visit once he had relocated.

Danny wasn't saying much. Did he think she wasn't interested, wondered Jules? Was she ruining things for him? She couldn't bear this idea. It was time to up her game.

"It's in the right area and I think we should view it," she declared. "I spoke to the Bishop about working near there and he's very positive about the possibility of a place for me."

"It's near a tube station too, Dad, and that was on your list," added Morgan, jabbing his finger onto the spreadsheet. "Look!"

"It sounds just right," said Alice.

"Shall I email and request a viewing for you?" asked Tara, pulling the laptop back across to her side of the table, fingers hovering above the keyboard.

"Good Lord. You're all very keen to get rid of me," said Danny. "Shall I go now? When's the next train?"

On the surface he was joking, but there was a barb lurking beneath the words as sharp as any fish hook and Jules was jolted. Here they all were going the extra mile to prove to Danny how happy they were for him, twirling the conversational equivalent of huge stripey gold umbrellas so as not to let it rain on his parade, and in return Danny was being acerbic and, if she was truly honest, downright disagreeable. Now he hadn't even waited to see what was next on Morgan's list, but had stomped out the door and into the garden.

What was the matter with him?

"Was that a 'yes' or a 'no'?" Tara asked. "I never could tell when he's in one of these moods."

Jules wasn't sure either, but she wasn't going to admit this in front of Danny's ex-wife, no matter how much she liked Tara. Pride might well be a sin, but even so...

"Yes, book us in for Saturday," she said firmly. "And that garden flat in Hayes too."

Leaving Tara and Morgan in charge of the logistics, Jules stepped into the evening sunshine to find Danny. There was no sign of him in the garden where the shadows were stretching over the lawn and the scent of Alice's jasmine hung heavy in the air, so Jules wandered around to the terrace. Here, the sun, tightrope-walking on the horizon to gild the sea and blush the sky, drenched Seaspray and created the perfect spot for gazing out over the evening village and Danny, sitting on a weathered bench, was doing exactly this. Without saying a word, Jules sat beside him and slipped her hand into his. Danny tightened his fingers on hers and for a few moments they sat in companionable silence, watching the waves ripple towards the land. Then Danny exhaled.

"Jules, do you really want to move to London?"

Ah. So this was what was troubling her fiancé: Dan was worried that she didn't want to relocate. Every night, Jules had prayed for guidance because in her heart the answer was a resounding 'no'. She loved it here, was happy in Polwenna Bay and felt that there was still work to be done at St Wenn's. Yet her great love for Danny surely had to be a part of that guidance because she wanted to be with him. Every atom of her being knew they were meant to be together and right now this was the clearest answer she could find.

"Of course I do," she said.

"Really?"

Danny turned to look at her and the anguish on his face brought a lump to Jules's throat. He was so worried that she was unhappy that it was ruining everything for him. How could she let that happen? Danny had suffered so much and given so much that he deserved every happiness. The army meant the world to him and to be given a chance to become a part of it again was something Jules could never deny him. Sometimes love meant making sacrifices.

"Really," she said, squeezing his hand. "There's so much to look forward to. I'll have new challenges and a chance to do God's work in a new area where there's so much need."

"There's need here," Dan reminded her. "You're always telling me that Cornwall has some of the worst levels of poverty in the country."

Ah. Yes. This was true. Jules often thought of Cornwall as a contradiction; Doc Martin, Poldark and idyllic holidays masked unemployment, lack of housing and poor resources. She was certainly very busy in her pastoral capacity.

"True," she said, her brain working fast to think of an answer, "and it's been a really great foundation for inner city outreach. But my work aside, it will be fun to be in London. Think of all the museums and art galleries we can visit! And the shopping!"

"Since when were you interested in museums and art galleries and shopping? Whenever we go to Plymouth, it's all about pizza and the cinema!"

Ah. She'd been rumbled. In reality, the nearest Jules came to art and shopping was chatting to Perry when he delivered her organic veg box.

"I'm looking forward to getting cultured and I'm going to spend a lot of time in museums," she said. Visiting museums might well help to take the edge off missing the cliff paths and the wide skies, so it wasn't a fib, was it? "I'm really looking forward to it."

"Right," said Danny slowly. "Well, that's great."

She rested her head on his shoulder. Being close to Danny always felt like coming home and with this thought Jules knew her Boss had given her the answer she was looking for. Supporting Danny and being with him, for better or for worse, was what she was meant to do. Everything else would fall into place and all she had to do was trust.

"I'm totally behind this move," she said firmly. "London here we come."

CHAPTER TWENTY

There was a lot to be said for working in a garden, Zak had discovered since he'd started giving Perry a hand with his organic produce business. Although digging beds, thinning out seedlings and removing weeds might not be the most glamorous of tasks, there was an honesty to it and satisfaction too in seeing tangible results. Plants didn't bicker, or manipulate people or have hidden agendas, and at the end of the day, Zak walked away with the job done and without any worries about the following day hanging over him. A couple of evenings a week he pulled pints in the pub and, when Jake was brave enough to allow him, Zak helped out at the marina too.

All activities kept Zak busy and helped to distract him from the disaster area of his professional life. It was true to say that since he'd walked away from his music career, Zak had felt a huge weight lifted, a weight he hadn't even realised he was carrying, and the heavy wings of doubt beating against his peace of mind had flown away into the cloudless June sky. The relief of not having to fret about his musical direction or the integrity of his art was hard to describe, but it made Zak feel light enough to blow away on the sea breeze like seeds from the dandelion clocks nodding in the hedgerows. Those things could all wait. For now it was enough just to be. Record deals, artistic vision and impending contracts receded just as the tide slipped down the beach, and slowly Zak's day-to-day life was taking on a new pattern.

It no longer felt quite as hard for Zak to venture into the village, especially since growing anticipation for Polwenna's Got Talent rendered his reappearance old news, and when Symon had mentioned that Perry was looking for someone to lend a hand at Polwenna Manor Organics, Zak had been happy to volunteer his services. His sabbatical from Alchemist wouldn't continue indefinitely and, much to his manager's frustration and his own, he'd yet to come up with any plans for his future. Even worse, he'd failed to write a single note of the song he'd promised his grandmother. Every time he reached for his guitar, it felt as though a blanket of fear wrapped itself around him, fear that he couldn't write or, worse still, that he didn't deserve to be able to write. Working for Perry bought him space from thinking about all this and there was something meditative about tilling the soil and watching plants grow. It was also lucky for Perry that Zak seemed to be a better gardener than he was a mechanic and so far hadn't killed a single seedling. If he couldn't write and play any more, then perhaps he would become a gardener? In Perry's world, there was no need to rush and Zak was finding this very refreshing.

"Everything has its season; all we need to do is be patient and see what happens," Perry said as they worked their way along lines of peppery rocket and curly kale. "These were seedlings only a few weeks ago and now look. Time will bring answers."

This was a great philosophy and Zak admired Perry's ability to let anything – even living on a permanent knife-edge of bankruptcy – faze him, but this approach wasn't particularly helpful when time was the one thing he didn't have the luxury of having. Every dawn which saw Zak trudging out of the village and up the hill to the Manor was another dawn bringing Alice and Jonny's wedding closer with not as much as a note of the song written. At this rate, he'd have to ask Alex to write it for him, which was cheating and not at all what Alice was hoping for, but what choice did he have?

He'd lost his gift and probably forever.

At least he was out and about again. After his period of self-imposed isolation at Seaspray, something inside Zak had shifted. At first he'd thought this might simply be that he couldn't bear to stare at the ceiling cracks for another minute or star as the subject of yet another concerned discussion between Alice and Jonny, but as he worked in Perry's market garden, every thrust of his fork or tugging of weeds untangling the events of the past few weeks, Zak was starting to wonder if there was more to life than this? Being alone with just his thoughts and the plants, and with the repetitive action of his allotted tasks, had helped him reach several conclusions.

The first was simple: he was beyond relieved to be home and away from the pressure of the music industry. Zak wasn't sure when his dream had spiralled into a nightmare, but like ink dropped onto wet paper, his cherished design had shifted and blurred until it became distorted and bore no resemblance to the original. Writing and playing was Zak's passion and, looking back, he realised that nothing that had followed the initial euphoria of being signed by a record company compared with the joy of playing with The Tinners. Of course, he'd enjoyed the buzz of success and the gloss that came with it, but after eighteen months, one hotel room looked pretty much like another, as did a recording studio, and he missed the camaraderie of his friends.

Did this mean fame and fortune weren't for him? Zak wondered as he re-potted seedlings in the listing glasshouse, the late afternoon sunshine bathing him in golden warmth. Was everything he'd worked for and dreamed of since he was a child nothing but smoke and mirrors, an illusion of what would make him happy when, irony of irony, happiness had been under his nose all along? Did he want to be here in Polwenna Bay rather than travelling the world? And if so, and if he wasn't going to be a professional musician, then what was he going to do with the rest of his life? There was only so much gardening Perry needed and, after a disastrous attempt to fix an outboard motor, there was no way Jake would let Zak anywhere near the workshop in a hurry. It was official: he was utterly useless.

Maybe Symon needed a pot washer? And Mo was always happy to rope people in to muck out. Patsy Penhalligan might want a hand in the pasty shop too now it was high season. There were opportunities here in the village if you looked for them; they might not be glamorous, but there was another kind of wealth that wasn't material, riches that weren't measured by the size of your bank balance or the kind of car you drove. Here, it was possible to have the wealth of waking up every morning without a leaden weight pressing down against your chest, with birdsong as the backing track to the morning and clear light streaming through the window. It was walking for miles over the cliffs with terns and gulls and shaggy ponies the only company, and it was watching the waves march forward to break against the cliffs as they always had and always would. It was looking in the mirror and not despising the reflection that gazed back at him. It was waking up without a hangover or a dishevelled girl beside him. It was this feeling of peace.

It was starting to like himself again.

Zak had also thought long and hard about Kellee and everything that had taken place that night. Logically, he knew that what had happened to her was a tragic accident and not his fault, but in his mind it had become entangled with the world he'd been a part of, and no matter how hard he tried to unpick the threads, the pattern was forever changed and the dream forever tainted. Enough people had come forward to say that Kellee had often taken substances, several artists had mysteriously gone away for a 'rest', and Ryan Kent had been packed off to rehab where rumour had it he was writing his autobiography. The police were satisfied and once the inquest was heard, the matter would be closed, everything would be signed off neatly and life would move on.

Yet try as he might, Zak couldn't do the same. Something had changed that night and he knew that deep down inside, within that same small and often very inconvenient part of him that told him when he was behaving badly, there was no going back. He'd had a glimpse of something that night, almost like Scrooge seeing the Ghost of a Life Yet to Come, and it had altered him forever. No matter how much time his manager gave him, Zak knew he wouldn't be signing a new contract. He felt bad for letting down his family, the musicians who'd worked with him, Alex who'd co-written many of the tracks on his album and everyone else who'd ever supported his dream, but there was a roadblock in his mind now that could never be passed.

Zak wasn't going back. This particular stretch of his journey was over.

There was a sense of relief at reaching this conclusion and, although he hadn't shared it with a soul, Zak knew he'd have to tell his manager very soon and Alice too. He'd been very surprised to discover that his instinct had been to tell Tess first. He hadn't known her for long, but her musical career had stalled too and she was the one person who he knew would understand how it felt to turn your back on something that was a part of your soul. Part of you. Tess's decision had been enforced by stage fright and his would be a choice of sorts, but for both of them the sense of loss stung like sea salt on barnacle-scraped knees. Tess Hamilton had made a huge success of her life since. Everyone in the village, from the Pollards to the vicar, sang her praises, but without music, who was Zak Tremaine? In the family, he'd always been the musical one, Jake was the responsible one, Mo the equestrienne, Symon the chef, Dan the soldier, Issie the reckless one, while Nick was the party animal. These childhood identities had served them well into adulthood and fitted as easily as worn slippers. Reinvention was exciting but terrifying too. Tess had already said as much.

Tess.

Zak straightened up, earth crumbling from his fingers and a seedling suspended between soil and sky as he caught himself thinking about Tess. It was strange how often Miss Hamilton was on his mind lately and how much he looked forward to meeting up and filling her in on the latest developments. At odd times during the day, Zak found himself musing on things that he needed to tell her and details she'd find interesting. He kept a notebook now and jotted down any ideas which occurred to him or that he wanted to run by her – as well as keeping track of the tasks he needed to complete and had committed to. Tess's mind was as quick as the turning tide and sharper than a gutting knife, and she could spot an excuse at one hundred paces and wasn't afraid to call him out on something either – which Zak found oddly attractive. When her hands were on her hips, her full chest rising and falling with agitation, and the eyes behind those school mam specs flashing with anger, he wasn't hearing a single word, but was instead imagining wanting to kiss that crosspatch mouth until it stopped telling him off.

What was he thinking? The only reason they were friends was because he'd made it clear to Tess that he wasn't interested in relationships or in her. He couldn't blow their friendship because it was coming to mean more to him with every day that passed. Zak only hoped that mind-reading wasn't on Tess's alarmingly long list of talents.

A few nights ago, Zak and Symon had been Perry's guinea pigs for testing the latest batch of rhubarb gin, an activity which they had all bitterly regretted the next day. As well as suffering the mother of all hangovers, Zak had totally forgotten he was supposed to be overseeing the evening rehearsal for the talent show. A more appropriate description would be refereeing since each performer furiously guarded their stage time and chaos erupted when Chris the Cod overran by ten minutes. Jules had been fetched to calm the situation and Silver Starr had felt driven to do some emergency smudging of the village hall, which had set off Sheila Keverne's asthma. All in all, it wasn't the most successful night and, according to Tess, totally Zak's fault for failing to show up. She'd torn a strip off him and, used to women adoring him, Zak had been taken aback to find himself apologising and organising two extra rehearsals to make amends.

Dealing with fame-obsessed villagers was worth every minute though to get him back into Tess's good books. She had the sweetest smile and when she turned it on him and her eyes lit up, Zak felt the strangest tugging sensation in his chest. It had happened several times now and Zak was growing concerned. Did he have a heart murmur? Was it stress or a strange side effect from all the plants here?

It couldn't be anything else, he told himself firmly. Prim and proper Tess Hamilton with her smart suits, classical music background and practically OCD attention to organisational matters was definitely not his type. Zak liked boho babes with long beach-waved hair, flowing skirts and chilled-out attitudes, or leather trouser-clad rock chicks with kholed eyes or older women who knew what they wanted or fans high on atmosphere and excitement... oh, anyone really, except bossy teachers with clipboards and an attitude! Tess Hamilton might be seriously sexy, but she was not a woman he would usually be interested in. No way at all.

So, why then, did his thoughts keep pinging back to Tess as though magnetised? It didn't make any sense. Zak wasn't sure if it was his imagination, but the days when they were due to meet up seemed to drag on forever, knowing that she would be joining him in a coffee shop or the pub with her face set in a serious expression, her teeth worrying that full bottom lip, and that curvy, sexy body hidden beneath a prim trouser suit but with the curve of her hips or the swell of her breast hinted at as the soft fabric clung to her. His mind was constantly drifting in very inappropriate directions and several times he'd totally lost the thread of what she was saying. Luckily, he had managed to nod in all the right places and if he had accidentally agreed to drive Keyhole Kathy to Par Market to stock up on bits for costumes, then it was a small price to pay for seeing Tess look pleased with him.

Lord. He was almost thirty and desperate to please the teacher. Only it wasn't house points or an A grade he'd like Tess to give him...

Zak sighed. Okay, so he did fancy her. He was only human, but he had to accept that there was no way it could ever be anything more than a fantasy. Tess wasn't a fan of musicians, and at Mo's dinner party she had made her feelings about him abundantly clear. She'd also said many times that she was all but married to her classroom whiteboard and Zak was no fool. He knew this was her way of telling him she wasn't interested.

So why, then, did he sometimes get the exact opposite impression?

Occasionally Zak caught her looking at him from beneath those long lashes and she would flush and get all flustered, pretending that she had something to ask him. If he didn't know better, he'd think she was checking him out.

Dream on, Zak told himself. A brainbox and a beauty, Tess Hamilton was way, way out of his league. Anyway, he had enough on his plate without getting involved with anyone, especially a girl that he suspected his brother Nick still held a torch for. Now that would be complicated. Nick might give the impression of being as shallow as a flea's paddling pool, but Zak knew this was an act. Like all the Tremaines, when Nick fell, he fell hard and fast.

Zak never did like heights or drops much and he was making sure he had a harness and ropes. This growing attraction he had for Tess was probably just the music festival organiser's equivalent of Stockholm Syndrome. Forced together, they had no choice but to make the best of a bad situation and once it was over, everything would go back to normal.

Whatever normal was these days…

Disconcerted, Zak returned his attention to transplanting lettuces, a job which was every bit as repetitive and as soothing as he could have wished. Another strange development was that although arranging the festival had started off as a chore and something Zak would have avoided like the plague if he was a) brave enough to say no to Alice and b) had thought of a good excuse not to be involved, in reality it was proving to be great fun. His contacts had been really helpful and Zak was touched by how willingly they'd pulled together to help him provide staging, light and sound. Nobody seemed to bear a grudge that he'd been off the scene for so long and neither did they question the fact that he was back in Cornwall.

"No better place to be, man," was how one put it, and even inside a tumbledown greenhouse, potting salad for the perpetually skint Perry who would probably pay him in rhubarb gin and radishes, Zak had to agree. He was also pleasantly surprised to discover that he was enjoying the process of organising the practicalities and logistics and solving the problems which cropped up. Squabbling villagers aside, with Tess's attention to detail, it seemed as though everything was coming together beautifully. Alice and Jonny's wedding was going to be perfect.

Or it would be, if only he could write the bloody song. Would he ever feel like writing and singing again?

"What are you doing hiding away in here? Sy's been looking for you everywhere."

Ella St Milton, his brother's girlfriend and business partner, had strolled into the glasshouse. Dressed in a white sundress and big Chanel shades perched on her immaculate blonde head, she was the epitome of summer chic. Zak, dressed in mud-splattered Levis and faded Levellers tee shirt, was instantly alarmed.

"Don't come any further. You'll get filthy!"

Ella raised her neat eyebrows. "I wasn't planning to start gardening, Zak. God forbid! You're supposed to be helping Alice and Jonny with the menu, remember? The taster session? Everyone's due to arrive in the next half an hour."

Zak groaned. More reception planning, which meant more discussion about the song that he was nowhere near writing. Talk about under pressure; he practically had the Queen track playing on a loop in his head.

He jerked his head at the trestle. "I'm only halfway through this lot."

"They'll keep," said Ella. "Come on, Zak, Alice is wondering where you are. We've set up some tables out in the courtyard, Sy's slaved over the samples and Perry's cracked open some pear wine. Even Jake has managed to bear the sight of me and come up. It's practically a family party. Besides, we need you to tell us where the stage and the pavilion are going to be. Tess hasn't a clue."

Zak's head snapped up. "Tess is here?"

"Yes, of course she is. She came straight from school and brought Morgan. She's got the evening menu for the hog roast and is working out the best place to set it up. She did tell you, didn't she?"

Tess had certainly told him, but Zak suspected he'd been too busy imagining how her soft skin would feel against his and picturing tracing the sweet curve of her throat with his lips to take in a single word. He couldn't remember the last time he'd been so distracted by a woman. It was very odd and totally out of character. Zak liked women, enjoyed their company, mercurial moods and exciting bodies, and he seldom left a gig or a party alone, but he'd never obsessed over anyone like this.

What Zak needed was a good night out. Maybe Nick would be up for some partying? But first he'd better haul ass to this menu tasting and another round in the game of 'dodge Granny Alice's questions about her song'. Tomorrow he'd phone Alex and just lay his cards on the table. This was way too stressful.

He brushed earth from his hands and nodded at Ella.

"Fine. I'll be with you in just a minute when I've cleaned up here and fetched my notes."

If Tess was here, he'd better make sure he got his act together. It was crazy, but he'd never wanted to impress a woman more in his life.

Weird.

Ruth Saberton

CHAPTER TWENTY-ONE

Tess rarely left school before five o'clock in the afternoon, but she was making an exception today. Alice and Jonny were having a run-through of the arrangements for their wedding reception and she wanted to be present to make sure everything was just as it should be. As she drove to Polwenna Manor, with Morgan chatting away beside her, Tess ran through her mental checklist even though her head was still spinning from the mad dash to clear the school gates in time to meet the Tremaines.

There was so much to think about. Would the timings work? Would the hog roast fit in the area she'd chosen? Would the stage arrive? What if Alice hated the evening menu? Would the Pollards ever talk to each other again?

Relax! Tess told herself sharply. She was good at organising things, at making order appear from chaos. It was what she did best. Tess was fairly certain there wouldn't be many nasty surprises because everything had seemed to fall into place just beautifully. Her only worry was Zak, who had seemed really distracted recently. He kept drifting off into day dreams and a couple of times he'd been staring right at her, but not seemed to have heard a single word she'd said. Then there was the evening when he'd been so busy drinking with Symon and Perry that he'd totally forgotten to attend the rehearsal. Tess shuddered every time she thought about how chaotic that had been. Big Rog and Chris the Cod still weren't talking and Sheila Keverne was adamant that she had permanent lung damage thanks to Silver Starr.

Oh, for peaceful days when league tables and Ofsted were all she had to stress about! These were nothing in comparison to the worry of the Polwenna Festival. After this year, never again, and she certainly wouldn't offer to work alongside Zak Tremaine. For Tess, this was proving to be the biggest challenge of the lot.

Could she rely on Zak? Tess still wasn't certain. He was a contradiction. On the one hand, there was something about him that inspired utter confidence – she couldn't quite believe how much she had told him about herself – and when he turned those bright blue eyes on her, she was almost unable to dredge up a sensible sentence or pull her thoughts together. He was beautiful. That was a given. Yet there was more to him than that. Beneath the golden looks was a heart that felt things keenly and a sharp mind that wrestled with the rights and wrongs of a society that was off-kilter. Tess recognised this because in Zak Tremaine she glimpsed her own angst and saw snatches of the soul-searching she recalled only too well. There was more to him than a good-time partying playboy, but he teetered on the edge and Tess feared he might topple. Had he organised everything? He promised her that he had and that everything was under control, but what if he was distracted again? He was a musician, and who knew better than her how self-absorbed and unreliable they could be?

One evening out with his brother and Perry is not the end of the world, Tess reminded herself sharply. Zak deserved to kick back a little after what he'd been through and everyone knew Perry's home-brewed gin was lethal. The last time Tess had allowed herself a glass, she'd been hung over for days.

"You keep sighing, Miss," observed Morgan who was riding shotgun beside her and fiddling with the car clock which was yet to catch up with British Summer Time.

"Do I?" sighed Tess. "Oh dear. Maybe I do. I've got a lot to think about, I suppose."

"My dad keeps sighing too. And Jules," Morgan told her. "Have they got a lot to think about too?"

"I'm sure they have. They must have an awful lot to do for their move," Tess said gently. She knew Morgan wasn't keen on the idea.

Morgan didn't reply, or even acknowledge her remark, but instead turned his total attention to the clock, jabbing at the buttons over and over again, while counting beneath his breath. Eight seemed to be his magic number and Tess knew this was some kind of control for the little boy. Her heart went out to him. Who could blame Morgan for feeling unsettled? Nobody liked change, not truly, and it was always hard when adults made decisions beyond a child's understanding.

Actually, it was just as hard when they made decisions that were beyond an adult's understanding too. Even after all this time, Tess still couldn't fathom why Vassilly had behaved as he did. Did he feel nothing? Was it all just a game to him? She hadn't taken up tapping but, like Morgan, she'd found her own way of wrestling back control and if that made her obsessive or anally retentive or a control freak, then so be it. Guilty as charged. She wasn't about to change now.

Tess turned the car out of the village and past the vicarage, where Jules was apparently doing a lot of sighing, before heading up the hill to the Manor. The afternoon sun was shining through the trees and throwing dancing dapples onto the lane. She wound the window down to fill the car with the scent of mown grass and the trembling calls of wood pigeons from the shadows of Fernside Woods. It was a perfect early summer's evening, the sort that kept you going through long rainy winters and cold nights, and as she headed along the drive to Polwenna Manor, Tess felt as though she could have been taking part in the opening sequence of a Merchant Ivory production. The house looked perfect from this distance, nestled in a fold in the hillside and surrounded by lawns. With the distant sea view and an air of grandeur, it didn't matter how dilapidated the Manor itself might be because it was a glorious spot and simply perfect for a summer wedding reception and festival. Tess's heart rose a little. How could she have doubted?

She pulled up outside the house, the wheels of her little car scrunching on the gravel, and parked alongside Jonny's stately old Bentley. Several other cars were already parked and the sounds of laughter and chink of cutlery, as well as mouth-watering aromas, suggested the food tasting was already well underway. Morgan was off almost before she'd killed the engine and Tess smiled to see him so excited. As she grabbed her bag and folder, she reminded herself that this was meant to be fun. She must stop taking everything so seriously.

The courtyard behind the Manor backed onto Symon's new restaurant and it was here that an assortment of tables and chairs had been set up. Alice and Jonny were already seated with plates piled high, Jake and Summer were chatting to Symon, and even Teddy St Milton, currently charged with dangerous driving and due to appear in court, had made a rare appearance. His face wore its usual sulky expression, but his arrogance was muted and Tess, having been the focus of his unwanted attention on more than one occasion, was glad when he could barely bring himself to mutter a greeting. Tara and Nick were scurrying backwards and forwards with plates and Danny was talking into his mobile. Tess glanced around for Zak and when she saw him, her pulse missed a beat.

He was simply dressed in scuffed Timberlands, torn jeans and a faded grey tee shirt that clung to his torso. His long curls were loose, falling into his blue eyes and brushing his broad shoulders, and when he saw her and smiled, she felt her mouth dry. He was scruffy, dishevelled and dreadfully sexy, and all of a sudden Tess's mind could only hold one terrible thought.

She was totally and utterly attracted to Zak Tremaine.

How had that happened? A womaniser. A musician. Too good-looking by far. He was exactly the type of man she should avoid and had been actively working to avoid. What kind of cruel midsummer's joke was Fate playing on her?

"Hello, you," Zak said, smiling at her and brushing soil from his jeans. "Excuse the filth, but I've been working in the garden for Perry."

Instantly, Tess had a Lady Chatterley-style scenario playing out in her imagination. No! This had to stop!

"I haven't got time to wash, although I guess I could dip in the lake like we used to as kids," he added. "Want to come for a swim? You must be roasting in that suit. You poor thing. What a day to be stuck indoors."

Swimming? Seriously? Now she was having a Mr Darcy moment and Tess's face grew warm at the mere thought of wet shirts and breeches. Zak Tremaine would make a devastatingly sexy Regency rake. The cover artists for historical romance novels would be queuing up to use him and his muscular chest for inspiration.

For goodness sake! The heat must be getting to her.

"We've got far too much to do to waste time swimming," Tess said quickly, covering her awkwardness by rummaging in her bag for her trusty notebook. "Anyway, I haven't got my costume."

"Who said anything about costumes?"

She tutted. "You are such a kid."

Zak grinned. "I can be a grown-up if you like?"

He didn't say any more, but Tess saw something flicker in those blue eyes and it was answered by a swooping sensation deep in her belly. Although she knew he was just messing about, she couldn't help feeling wrong-footed because the mere thought of being naked with Zak Tremaine in the silky waters of the lake made all common sense combust, and beneath her smart suit she felt lava hot. She really must start dating again and get out more if the only single guy she'd come across in months was making her feel like this.

"I've got too much to do. Some of us have to make sure this all goes to plan," she said.

"Well, I'm going to have a dip," Zak replied, thankfully oblivious to her thoughts. "If I can't tempt you to come too, why don't you go and chat to the others and run some of your thoughts past them while I clean up? That should also give you lots of time to make sure I haven't messed anything up. Again."

Tess felt bad now. "Ignore me. I'm just being grouchy in the heat. A swim in the lake would have been lovely. Maybe next time."

"Sure," he said easily. "I'll catch you in a bit. Save one of the mini lamb kebabs for me. And don't drink Perry's homemade wine. It's lethal."

He turned and walked away from her, his long legs striding across the shadow-darkened lawn for a moment before he was sprinting down the hill towards the lake. Tess turned away. She thought it was just as well Zak had no idea just how tempted she was to throw her inhibitions (and clothes) to the wind and join him.

"Everything okay, Tess?"

Tara Tremaine was headed Tess's way. The laden tray in her arms suggested that she was en route to lay out the taster menu and had made a fair detour across the lawn to check on Tess. Oh dear. Did she look as wobbly as she felt?

"I'm fine," Tess said quickly. "Just catching up with Zak about a few bits."

Tara raised a delicate eyebrow. "And what bits would those be exactly? Or shouldn't I ask?"

"Festival stuff, of course!"

"Why 'of course'? I thought you and Zak were getting on really well. He's a nice guy and, you must admit, he's pretty easy on the eye."

"Hmm," said Tess, who was still drowning in her lake fantasy. "I guess so, if you like that kind of thing."

"See, you do like him! I knew it! I'm never wrong about these things."

"You are this time." Tess was nipping this snippet of gossip in the bud right now. "I am not interested in Zak in the slightest. He is not my type."

"Fibber," grinned Tara. "He's every woman's type. Relax, Tess! There's no shame in having some fun. The last time I looked, you were a schoolteacher, not a nun."

Tess certainly felt like a nun at times. Apart from her ill-judged fling with Nick when she'd first arrived in the village, she'd done her very best not to get involved with anyone, something that she thought was very sensible in a small community where people had very long memories.

"We're just sorting out the final arrangements for the festival. There's nothing more in it than that and there never will be," she insisted.

"Well, you must be mad then," said Tara. "If I was young and single, and not his ex sister-in-law, then I definitely would and so would most girls around here. Besides, Zak likes you."

Tess rolled her eyes. "He puts up with me because of the festival. I drive him mad with all my lists and my nagging. He'll be glad to see the back of me when it's over."

"Rubbish. Alice is adamant it's you we've got to thank for him not festering away in his room in some kind of artistic decline," said Tara. "She says that it's only since he's been seeing you—"

"He is not 'seeing' me!" Tess corrected, shaking her head. Honestly. This was so typical of Polwenna Bay. People were forever putting two and two together and making five. Old Miss Powell, who'd been head of the primary school since Adam and Eve went to school, should be ashamed of the villagers' mathematical acumen!

"You fibber! You've been spotted all over the village together. You had coffee in the beach café, ate cake at the Harbour Tea Room and Patsy says he bought you a pasty the other day!"

"Well, that's it then. We must be having a torrid affair if he bought me a pasty. Who caught that on their CCTV?"

"Nobody. It was on Facebook. Keyhole Kathy has her own group: The Only Way is Polwenna. You must have seen it."

"I don't use social media. Surely it can't be that exciting that Zak bought me a pasty? We all eat pasties. This is Cornwall."

"It's not the pasty but what it signifies, oh naïve and innocent one! The village school mistress has been seen out and about without a chaperone and with Polwenna's most eligible bachelor to boot. Tongues are wagging. There's probably a sweepstake running on when you'll get married."

Tess was frustrated. "For heaven's sake! We're working together and it's only because Jules made me feel so guilty."

Tara knew when to stop teasing.

"I know, I'm just being silly. But it is true that since you've been working together, Zak's been much more like his old self. Alice really does say she has you to thank for that."

Since Zak Tremaine's 'old self' was usually busy drinking, partying and pulling pretty girls, Tess wasn't sure Alice should be thanking her. Besides, Tara and Alice and the rest of the Tremaines had no idea that Zak was tortured by not being able to write a note or not wanting to play; only she was party to that morsel of information. The truth was that he had probably never been further away from being his old self.

"If there is a difference, it's because he's had something more to think about other than what happened in London," she said firmly.

"Whatever you say," Tara shrugged. She paused for a minute as though debating something before adding, "but I've seen the way he looks at you and I've known Zak a long time. He's definitely interested in you, Tess. I can tell. Anyway, that's enough chat from me. These Cornish cheese swirls have a date with the happy couple."

Even though she knew Tara was talking nonsense, Tess's stomach was twisting itself into knots.

Was Tara right? Did Zak like her? Did she like him? Were they becoming more than friends?

And if so, how did that make her feel?

Her insides did a flutter and beneath her sensible school suit her heart rattled against her ribs. The answer was: nervous, scared and dangerously excited. Even Tess's hands tingled with it.

This was a worrying new development. Maybe she should be the one to jump into cold water?

CHAPTER TWENTY-TWO

The afternoon sped by in a glow of golden sunset, delicious food, chatter, and too many glasses of Perry's homemade wine. By the time only crumbs remained of the taster dishes, Tess was feeling far less fraught. Tara had just been teasing and, as usual, she was too uptight to take a joke. Zak wasn't interested in her and she was daft to have even thought for a moment that he might be. He'd returned from his swim, barefoot and with his golden hair slicked back as he ran his hands over his wet face, but hadn't joined Tess or looked her way once. Instead, he'd walked past her, choosing to sit with Danny and Morgan. If the idea wasn't so ridiculous, Tess would have said she'd upset him by not joining him for a swim.

That was utter nonsense. He simply wasn't that interested and this evening was proof that Tara was totally wrong. Tess was actually very relieved and not disappointed in the slightest that Zak hadn't sought her out or even asked if she was having a nice time.

Talking of time – Tess checked her watch. Almost half past five. She'd make her excuses in a minute and walk home. There was a lot to do this evening. Like… like…

Well, she was sure she could think of something. It might be a Friday night, but there were always preparations for school and lesson planning and marking to be done. She'd left her classroom in such a hurry too. Perhaps she could pop back there for an hour and do some tidying up?

"Was the food all right, Granny?" Symon was asking as he and Tara collected the plates.

Alice, seated next to Jonny at a trestle table, nodded and placed her hands on her stomach.

"Delicious, my love! You are so clever."

Tess would second that. Somehow Symon had managed to create a mini feast using all the fresh local ingredients that were his hallmark: miniature lobster crostini, salsa mussels on seaweed crackers, aubergine and Yarg pastries, churros dusted with icing sugar and petals, and sugar-coated apple twists served with caramelised pears and crushed walnuts, topped with rich clotted cream. Everything was mouth-watering and Tess thought she wouldn't need to eat for a week.

Symon blushed to the roots of his red hair at this praise.

"Thanks, Granny! I'm so pleased you liked it."

Jonny St Milton dabbed his mouth with a napkin. "We more than liked it! This is fantastic. Do I also sense Ella's hand in this somewhere? She knows how much I love seafood."

"Absolutely," nodded Sy. "We wrote the menu together. Hopefully we ticked all the boxes."

"These dishes are just for the afternoon's reception, aren't they? The festival food will be different?" Alice asked, looking concerned. The thought of feeding lobster to the whole village was clearly alarming her. Eddie Penhalligan could easily eat most of the mini crostini by himself.

"There'll be a hog roast at the far side of the lawn," Tess said quickly. "It's far enough away so nobody gets covered in smoke. There's a candy floss machine and popcorn too, as well as all the stands. Then the stage will be directly opposite. Everyone should have more than enough food and places to go."

In between sampling dishes, Tess and Ella had circled the venue to make sure that every location was clear in their minds. From the flower bower where Alice and Jonny would meet their guests, to the converted horsebox gin bar (Perry's latest venture) to the flat paved area where the stage would be set up – every detail had been logged and Tess was happy she knew exactly how the event would work. Ella certainly knew her wedding planning, even arranging a photo booth where people could dress up in silly hats and take pictures for their Instagram and Facebook accounts, very important if Tara's comment about Keyhole Kathy was to be believed, and had organised take-home goody bags. Ella's hard work made Tess's contribution of the hog roast and morris dancers seem like nothing.

"The stage is arriving on the morning of the wedding and I'll come up here with Jake and Nick to get it sorted," Zak added, joining them. "It's all arranged and it will be fine, so you don't need to worry about a thing. I promise I won't let you down."

"So everything's sorted?" Danny asked. "We don't need to do anything else?"

"Totally sorted," Zak promised. "All we need to do is look forward to the wedding. And the festival, of course. I can hardly wait for Polwenna's Got Talent."

Tess thought she could happily handle the anticipation. If she heard Eddie Penhalligan make one more crack about doing his elephant impression she would swing for him.

"Hey! Are we too late? Tell me you haven't guzzled all the grub, you greedy bunch!"

Mo Carstairs, clutching Ashley's arm and hobbling on a plastic-booted foot, was making a beeline for the table and waving her free hand at them all.

"Isn't Mo supposed to be in London?" Alice asked Symon. "I thought Ashley had a check up?"

Symon raised his eyes to the heavens. "I can't keep up with her and Ashley, Granny. You know me. I like the quiet life."

There was certainly nothing quiet about the Carstairs family. Mo was shouting and waving, Ashley was telling her to calm down and not to strain her bad foot, while Isla, shrieking with excitement, charged towards Alice. Within seconds, the little girl was scooped up onto her great-grandmother's lap and eating churros, her face and hands covered in icing sugar, and chattering away at the top of her voice.

"So much for the healthy snacks you insisted on feeding her all the way back," Ashley said to Mo. "We could have stopped at KFC after all."

"KFC?" shrieked Mo. "When Symon's food is on offer? Are you mad?"

"Yes, I sometimes think I must be," Ashley replied wryly. "But it helps, as they say."

"This is a lovely surprise, darling. I didn't think you were due back for another few days?" Alice said to Mo.

"We weren't, but it turns out we didn't need to stay in London for nearly as long as we thought we might have to. We've had some news," Mo told her.

Alice's hand fluttered to her throat. "News? What kind of news?"

"Good news!" Mo said quickly. "The best!"

"I need to sit down if Ashley's finally settled his marina bill," deadpanned Jake.

"With the prices you charge? Just how rich do you think I am?" Ashley shot back.

"You are very rich, Ashley. Fact. Have you bought a helicopter? Is that the good news?" asked Morgan.

"No, sorry, mate. It's not quite that good," said Ashley. Turning to Mo, he added softly, "Maybe we should stop with the guesses, Red? They'll all be bitterly disappointed at this rate."

"Yes, and before anyone gets the wrong end of the stick, I'm not up the duff again either," added Mo. "Oh, come on you lot! Look at Ash. I mean really look at him! What's different?"

Everyone looked. And looked some more. Then Tess got it.

"He's wearing glasses!"

"You've got such an eye for detail," said Zak admiringly.

Tess certainly knew every detail of him. She knew Zak often smelt of Bleu de Chanel, that his jaw was sprinkled with golden stubble and that the backs of his tanned forearms were corded with sinews and dusted with golden hair. She knew he had freckles on the bridge of his nose and that when he smiled the dimple in his left cheek was higher than the right. She knew every swirl of the tribal tattoo that decorated his right forearm.

Yes. When it came to Zak Tremaine, it was true to say that Tess Hamilton really did have an eye for detail, although this wasn't necessarily a good thing.

"That's the good news?" Morgan wasn't impressed.

"It is when you've been getting headaches and you think something bad might be happening," said Ashley. "Luckily for me, it turns out I've just been straining my eyes with all my computer work. You've never seen a man so happy to be told he's got dreadful eyesight. I could have kissed the optician except that he was about seventy and had a moustache."

"Sounds just your type, Ash. We all know Mo has a great 'tache!" grinned Nick.

His sister flipped him a V sign before going on to explain how Ashley had been suffering from headaches for several months and, given the state of his health in the past, had been terrified this could mean the return of his brain tumour. After going to London to see his consultant and undergoing some routine tests, Ashley was over the moon to learn his headaches weren't caused by anything more sinister than poor eyesight.

"That's wonderful news," said Alice. "Darlings, you must have been so worried. Why didn't you tell us?"

"We didn't want to worry you unnecessarily," Mo said. "And wasn't it a good job we didn't?"

Alice didn't look convinced and Mo added quickly, "Isn't Ash handsome in his glasses, Granny? I think they make him look quite brainy."

"Thank you, darling," said Ashley, shaking his head and laughing. "I'm glad I look quite brainy."

At this point, Perry decided what they really needed to celebrate was more of his homemade wine. Tess found herself having a glass thrust upon her, which quickly turned into several glasses, and by the time the sun was setting, all thoughts of going home to do her marking had vanished. The evening soon slipped seamlessly from menu sampling and wedding planning to a full-blown family celebration. Purple dusk smoked in across the lawns, light spilled from the manor house windows and Tess tipped her head back to look up at the stars, gasping when one flew across the heavens.

A shooting star!

"Have you made a wish?"

Zak was at her shoulder, so close that she could feel the warmth of his skin.

"No," she said.

"Shall I make one for us?"

At the word 'us', Tess felt a sensation in her chest like champagne bubbles popping. She curled her hands into fists and fought to anchor herself rather than spinning away into the stars. It was Perry's wine making her feel all loose-limbed and swimmy-headed, nothing else. She'd been this close to Zak many times since they'd become friends. Nothing had changed.

Nothing except for admitting to herself that she did find him attractive, but that was allowed! Zak was beautiful and admiring him was no different to admiring a work of art or well-crafted poem. It was just aesthetics. Her reaction was totally understandable.

Zak tilted his face up to the sky and closed his eyes. "Done."

"Did you wish for the festival to go well?"

"Come on, Tess. You know I can't tell you my wish. It won't come true if I do that."

"You don't really believe that, do you?"

He lay a hand over his heart. "Totally."

"In that case, I really hope you wished the festival runs smoothly," Tess said. "I'm actually wondering if it really was such a good idea combining it with Alice's wedding?"

"Have faith. It will turn out just fine. And can you imagine the hell up in the village if people hadn't been involved? Alice and Jonny have lived here forever. They're as much a part of it as the quay or the cliffs."

"You are too. You're a Tremaine and everyone here knows you."

He grimaced. "Trust me. That isn't always a good thing. They think they know me, but I'm not the same person I used to be. The only one who knows the real me is you. I've told you the truth, Tess. You know what a failure I am."

"You're nothing of the kind!"

"I am. A musician who can't play or write. A man of nearly thirty who has no idea what to do with his life. Someone whose plans have fallen apart."

"That's life, Zak. It's what happens to us and it doesn't always work out the way we want it to." She touched his arm gently in a gesture of sympathy. "Sometimes things aren't meant to be the way we want them to be. No matter how many stars we wish upon."

For a moment, Zak looked as though he was about to argue. Then he just smiled sadly.

"Yeah, maybe. Look, shall we have a last check of our venue? Make sure that at least is the way we want it?"

Topic closed, thought Tess. Years in the classroom had taught her when to push for more and when to back off.

"Sure," she said.

As she turned to follow him, the world seemed to dip and spin. The stars whirled by. Oh! Who moved the ground?

Zak grabbed her elbow. "Whoa! Steady!"

"Perry's wine," Tess gasped as she clutched his arm.

"Don't say you weren't warned. Everyone knows that stuff should be illegal. The trouble we got into once as kids!"

"Thank goodness it's not school tomorrow," said Tess.

With Zak still holding her elbow, they wandered away from the noise and light of the gathering and into the darkening grounds. Tess said nothing, partly glad of the support and partly liking the feel of being close to him, their arms and thighs brushing as they strolled across the rough grass. They were close in height and their strides evenly matched; there was no scurrying to keep up or sense of having to slow her pace. It felt a little like walking in beat with a metronome perfectly set to her own rhythm.

Together they paced out the sites earmarked for the festival. The sun had slipped far beneath the world's edge now and the night bloomed in from the wooded hills, the air heavy with the scent of the honeysuckle woven through the hedges and the leaves stirred by only the flutter of moths and the scurrying of hidden creatures. It was so still that when a disturbed pheasant shouted his displeasure at their approach, Tess's feet almost left the earth and she stumbled against Zak.

"Oh! Sorry," she said.

Instantly his arms closed around her.

"Don't be," Zak said.

And then he kissed her.

His mouth was the perfect alchemy of firm and soft, and as her lips parted beneath his, Tess sensed his touch was bringing her alive in ways she'd never even imagined. His hands were slipping into her hair and pulling her closer as the kiss deepened, slow and teasing at first before building to a crescendo of longing.

How could a simple kiss have the power to make her feel like this? The warmth of his body, the taste of icing sugar that lingered on his tongue and the racing of the blood around her trembling body all made Tess's head spin. She slid her hands over his chest and then beneath the tee shirt, loving the sensation of muscle and warm skin beneath her fingertips and wanting nothing more than to tumble deeper and deeper into the kiss. After years of clinging on to control and fighting to hold on to every aspect of her life, just one kiss from Zak Tremaine was enough to send her plummeting over the edge. Butterflies fluttered inside her and when Zak gently pulled away, Tess felt dazed and lost, as though she had found her way home after a long journey only to be turned away.

He stared down at her. In the darkness, his eyes were inky and his hair silvered by the starlight as he cupped her face in his hands and brushed his mouth against hers once more, so slowly and so deliciously that shivers rippled her skin.

"Well, who'd ever have thought it?" he said softy. "Wishing on a star really does work."

CHAPTER TWENTY-THREE

Zak hadn't set out to kiss Tess. Although when the shooting star had zipped by and he had sent up a fleeting wish that something might happen between them, he genuinely had been intending to do one last check of the festival site in order to put her mind at rest. He'd never had some dastardly plan of leading her into the dark garden to seduce her, but when she stumbled and he felt her soft body against his, he'd been unable to stop himself. Kissing Tess had come as naturally to him as breathing.

And now they were staring at one another, partly in wonder and partly in shock, and Zak was very glad he hadn't touched a drop of Perry's wine. Although his head was spinning and the earth was shifting beneath his feet, this was nothing to do with alcohol and everything to do with the woman in his arms.

Zak had never felt like this before. He was stone-cold sober yet intoxicated, the head rush and the racing of his heart like nothing he'd ever known. Tess's head rested against his shoulder and Zak closed his arms around her, holding her close and wanting nothing more than this moment to last forever. He could hardly believe this was really happening and Zak wanted nothing to break the spell. Such magical interludes came along maybe once or twice in a lifetime and that was only if you were very lucky. As he held Tess close, Zak knew even when he was old, so old that girls and passion and kissing were long past, he would pull this memory out and relive it. He would carry it close to his heart for the rest of his life, and the darkness of the night, the heavy scent of honeysuckle and the smile of the moon would be just as vivid then as they were right now. This was a perfect moment and one that was meant to be, the stuff that dreams were made of.

The snatch of a lyric darted through his mind like the silver flicker of darting fish in rock pools and was traced by the faintest ripples of a melody, and Zak's heart, already full, felt as though it would burst. The world had turned on its axis. Everything had changed. It sounded nonsensical and dramatic, the stuff of bad teenage poetry, but Zak didn't care because suddenly he understood. This was what Shakespeare and Keats and countless other writers had been on about.

Suddenly he got it.

Zak had wanted to kiss Tess for a while and spent more time than he cared to admit imagining how she might taste and feel. She was a beautiful woman, but more than that, she was intelligent and interesting too and he'd come to enjoy the time they spent together. In the short time he'd known her, Tess had become the closest thing to a true friend Zak had ever had. She saw him – the real him – and she didn't judge. When he spent time with Tess, Zak knew he didn't need to be the returning hero or the big success, but could simply be himself.

Had he ever been truly himself with a woman before? Many different versions of himself, perhaps; the party animal, the drinker, the fun guy, the lead singer. Zak had certainly played all of these parts, but the role of a lost, fearful and, let's be honest, messed-up loser, was a new one. Yet Tess never judged. Instead, she listened and opened up too, sharing her own experiences and insights. She'd shown him her vulnerabilities and her fears in order to help him face his own and he loved her even more for it.

Wait a moment. What was that? Love? Surely not.

Zak was poleaxed by this possibility. He liked women and spending time with them. He'd dated sporadically, although this was hard to do when you were on the road and even harder when pretty girls constantly threw themselves at you and he was, after all, only human. Although he'd enjoyed more than his fair share of them, Zak wasn't a huge fan of one-night stands either. A romantic at heart, he liked the idea that there was a special someone out there waiting for him, destined to be his perfect match. Seeing his siblings settle down (and even Granny Alice!) had given him hope that his soulmate was waiting for him too. He just had to find her and, if he was honest, so far the hunt had been a lot of fun.

Zak had a vague idea of his ideal woman. She would be gorgeous, of course, but also funny and clever and have her own career too rather than seeing his growing fame as her next foothold on the showbiz ladder. She wouldn't resent his music or the time he spent writing and playing because she would have her own thing going on too, but neither would she put up with any nonsense from him. Zak was honest enough to know that he could be temperamental and difficult to live with at times, so his soulmate would have to be a strong woman. A woman he could respect.

Tess Hamilton was all these things. She was single-minded and driven, honest and conscientious and utterly gorgeous, yet their conversations occupied his thoughts just as much as her pretty face. From the outside, she was every inch the career-obsessed ice maiden, but Zak knew the real Tess. She was as soft beneath her shell as any crab hauled up from the ocean floor and showed her vulnerable side to very few people. Zak counted himself beyond privileged to be one of them. He was honoured to be trusted.

"Are you okay with this?" he asked softly.

Tess's answer was to step back and look up at him. Her hair was drifting loose from the plait, her lips were swollen with kisses and her mascara smudged beneath her eyes. She'd never looked more beautiful.

"What happened there?"

"It's pretty simple really," said Zak. "You kissed me."

"I most certainly did not! You kissed me!"

"I think you'll find that you started it? When you hurled yourself at me?"

"I didn't hurl myself at you! I jumped when I heard that noise! I was scared."

"Scared by a pheasant? A likely story, Miss Hamilton. We both know that was just an excuse to throw yourself at me. I must say, I feel utterly taken advantage of! Fancy dragging me into the woods just to have your wicked way."

"I didn't! I never—" Tess stopped and shook her head. "Oh. You're teasing me."

"Maybe a little," Zak said gently. He took her hand and raised it to his lips, kissing it tenderly before adding. "I'd like to tease you a lot more."

"And why's that?" Tess asked.

Zak took a deep breath. This was far more terrifying than stepping onto the stage.

"Because you're amazing, Tess. The most incredible woman I've ever met."

Tess raised her eyes up to the stars. "How much have you had to drink?"

"For your information, I'm stone-cold sober. I know better than to touch Perry's homemade wine. I'm fairly certain I once caught him using it as paint stripper when he had a decorating business."

"Please tell me that's a joke." shuddered Tess.

"You know Perry. What do you think? Remember the organic mushrooms grown in matter from his composting loo?"

She wrinkled her nose in a cute way that made Zak's heart melt even more. He loved the way they could laugh and joke together. Tess Hamilton was the whole package, that was for sure.

"Let's not go there! So if you're not drunk, isn't this where you say we should forget this ever happened because you don't want to spoil our friendship?"

"No," said Zak. "We're still friends. Even better ones now."

Her brown eyes flashed with suspicion.

"Friends with benefits, you mean?"

"No! Do you really think I'd say that?"

She shrugged.

"Well, I wouldn't," he said fiercely. "You are worth far more than that, Tess. Don't you realise?"

She stared at him and he knew she was trying to make up her mind, asking herself whether or not she could trust him. That she even needed to stop and consider this cut him deeply.

"I'm confused, Zak. You know all the lines, surely? I was giving you a get-out before you had to come up with one."

Zak did know all the lines. He may have even used them once or twice, but they couldn't have been further from his mind right now. And as for needing a get-out – no way.

"I don't want to forget this just happened and I certainly don't want a 'get-out'. I don't have a problem with what has happened tonight," he told her. "Quite the opposite, actually. Although you have had a couple of glasses, so maybe…"

"Maybe what?"

"Maybe we should talk about it tomorrow? Once you're sober?"

Tess looked staggered. "Are you saying I kissed you because I'm drunk? I'm not drunk!"

"You've had a few drinks though, so maybe your inhibitions aren't quite what they were? I don't want you to think I've taken advantage of you," Zak said.

"You just said I took advantage of you, remember?" Tess shot back. "Make your mind up! Which one is it?"

"How about you kiss me again and we make an informed judgement? Would that do?"

It was a cheeky punt, but Zak had to try. He couldn't have Tess walk away now thinking this was just a game. Zak couldn't bear her to walk away at all.

For a moment Tess looked as though she was in the middle of a huge mental battle before she started to smile.

"Fine. That might settle the issue," she agreed. "Purely for argument's sake, of course."

"Of course," said Zak solemnly.

He reached out and pulled her against him again, loving the way she swayed against him, all warmth and curves. Their bodies fitted together perfectly.

"So how does this work?" Zak asked. "Do I kiss you again and then we make an informed decision? We could make a chart with some of those colour-coded pens of yours."

Tess rose onto her tip toes.

"You said I was kissing you, remember? And please leave the marking and the logistics to me!"

Zak was about to come right back at her with a witty retort when Tess wound her arms around his neck and pulled his mouth back down to hers. Then Tess was kissing him and Zak was kissing her, all thoughts of replies and banter vanishing as he was lost in a million sensations. Lips met, hearts collided and nerve endings sparkled like Catherine Wheels while the Milky Way turned above them. Zak had no idea how much time had passed, and didn't care either because he never wanted this moment to stop, but gradually he became aware of voices calling his name.

"Sounds like they're sending a search party out for us," he said as they broke apart, both wide-eyed and giddy with longing. "They probably think we've fallen in Perry's lake. Or been eaten by those scary pheasants."

"I guess we have been a while," Tess replied. She glanced at her watch and gasped. "It's almost half past ten!"

"Time flies when you're having fun. I guess we should head back," Zak said. He wished they could stay forever in this magical night garden of velvet darkness and stars. More lyrics danced through his mind, as bright and as full of promise as shooting stars.

What was happening to him?

Tess smoothed her hair and smiled shyly up at him. "Do I look okay? Am I respectable?"

"You," said Zak, "look absolutely wonderful. You are wonderful. I just hope you still respect me in the morning!"

Tess widened her eyes. "Whoever said I respected you in the first place?"

Laughing, they retraced their steps back to the manor house. Every now and again their fingertips brushed and Zak was consumed by a ravenous need to feel her skin against his once more. Keeping a distance was torture and it took more willpower than Zak ever knew he possessed to carry on when all he wanted to do was kiss Tess again and again, trailing his mouth down to the hollow of her collarbone and below. It had felt so good to hold her close. So totally and utterly right.

How had he not noticed what was right under his nose? What had taken him so long?

He was an idiot, but one thing was for sure. Now he'd found Tess, Zak wasn't letting her go in a hurry.

"Where did you guys go? We've been having a party!" cried Mo when they broke out of the gardens and into the warm light that spilled from the house.

"We were just checking out some of the locations for the festival," Zak said. It was true – they had been doing that before the evening had taken a far more interesting turn.

"Is that what they call it these days?" chuckled Jonny St Milton.

Alice shot her fiancé a sharp look. "I'm sure it's all going to be just fine. Why don't you just relax now and enjoy yourselves?"

Zak and Tess had been enjoying themselves and all of a sudden laughter was rising up inside him like champagne bubbles. He didn't dare catch her eye.

"Yes, come on!" said his sister, shoving a glass into Zak's hand and sloshing in some Moët. "We're celebrating Ashley's good news!"

Zak thought that Ashley Carstairs must have bought up the local supermarket's entire stock of champagne and judging by the amount of empty bottles, everyone had been stuck in for some time. The party was only just starting and if Zak knew the Tremaines, it would be going on for some time yet. His heart sank. Usually he loved a party, but tonight all Zak wanted was to be alone with Tess. He needed to know how she felt, make certain she was all right with what had happened and he wanted to ask her what she was thinking.

And yes, if he was honest, he wanted to kiss her again... more than he had ever wanted to kiss anyone. In fact, he had never wanted anything as much. What on earth did fame and fortune matter? What he had found with Tess made him rich beyond his wildest dreams and happier than he had ever known it was possible to be.

Zak Tremaine had fallen head over heels in love and it was the most wonderful and terrifying thing that had ever happened to him.

CHAPTER TWENTY-FOUR

The party continued well into the small hours. At some point, Alice and Jonny must have slipped away, taking Isla and Morgan with them, and Jules arrived after youth club. The Penhalligan brothers, who had a talent for sniffing out parties, rocked up with Little Rog in tow and were soon throwing shapes on the makeshift dance floor, aka the weed-strewn courtyard. Just the sight of their energy was enough to make Tess feel exhausted and she smothered a yawn.

"Tired?" Zak asked softly. He was sitting down opposite her on the tartan car rug which someone had thoughtfully tossed onto the damp grass.

"I'm shattered. It's been a long week."

He nodded. "It feels to me like it's been a very long evening. Do you think we've stayed long enough to be sociable and not attract too much attention?"

The 'we' and the implication that they were partners in crime, linked together by a magical secret, made Tess's skin ripple with shivers. The longing to repeat the experience of kissing Zak Tremaine was overwhelming and utterly terrifying. Did he feel the same? Or was he hoping that they hadn't attracted attention and that nobody would ever find out what had taken place? Did it mean anything to him?

Did it mean anything to her? And did she want it to?

Yes, whispered her heart, and Tess was alarmed. Having learned a very hard lesson when she was eighteen, Tess had done her utmost not to let anyone since get close, but somehow Zak had ducked beneath her guard. Until she'd felt his arms close around her, Tess had no idea just how much she wanted him. Now she couldn't think about anything else. Her brain was stuck on repeat.

Although he wasn't touching her, or even sitting that close, every atom of her being was aware of his proximity and Tess's heart was racing. Their starlight kisses kept replaying themselves through her racing mind. How had this thing, this impossible, wonderful, terrible thing, happened? One moment they'd been walking through the gardens and chatting away as always, and the next she was lost in the most incredible bone-melting kiss of her life. Tess needed time to process it.

"I think it's time I went home. I've had too much to drink to drive back and it's a bit of a walk," she said.

Zak stood up and stretched, his tee shirt riding up to reveal a slither of taut stomach. "Cool. Let's get going."

Tess dragged her eyes away from him because the lurch of desire she felt was dizzying. There was no way she could blame this on Mo's champagne or Perry's wine.

"You don't have to leave."

"I'm not letting you walk back on your own."

"That's very kind, but we're in Cornwall. I think I'm as safe as anyone could be."

"I don't care where we are, you're not walking home alone at one in the morning," Zak said firmly. "Besides, my sister was knocked down out on this back road. I wouldn't forgive myself if something happened to you."

This was a fair point. It wasn't so long ago that Emerald Tremaine had been hit by Teddy St Milton, Jonny's grandson. Although it was fair to say that the night-time lanes were inky black, it hadn't helped matters that Teddy had been speeding home following a boozy night out. The back lanes were always popular with certain locals coming home after a few too many.

"Thanks, that's really kind," Tess said, touched.

"It's not kind at all. I wouldn't be much of a gentleman if I didn't offer and besides, I don't want the evening to end just yet," Zak said softly. "Do you?"

Her mouth was dry. If Tess was honest, she wanted this strange and beautiful night to carry on forever.

"No," she whispered.

Their eyes met and she knew he felt exactly the same way. How was it even possible? On paper, Zak Tremaine was everything she should be running away from.

Should.

"I've only had a couple of sips of champagne, so I can drive you back if you like?" He continued. "That will save you walking back up tomorrow to fetch your car."

Tess had to admit that the thought of being driven back to the village was very welcome indeed. Her eyes were heavy and it had been a long day.

She rummaged in her bag and pulled out her car keys.

"It's only a Ford Focus," she warned him as he pushed the keys into his jeans pocket. "It's nothing like the Astons and Porsches you pop stars drive."

"Firstly," said Zak, "I'm not a pop star. 'Country folk' I think was how they put it the last time I asked. Secondly, you should be ashamed of yourself for stereotyping me as a shallow petrol head. I could be a vegan planet-saving Morrissey type who rides a push bike."

"Are you?"

He grinned. "No. Afraid not. But it's motorbikes for me, not cars. I've got a Ducati and it's my pride and joy."

"Really? I've never seen you on it."

"Granny hates motorbikes so I don't tend to ride it here. I keep it in London. To be honest, I don't use the bike much and it'll probably be the first thing to go. Granny certainly won't want me parking it at Seaspray, although it could be handy for getting old Jonny up the hill. Perhaps he could sit in a sidecar? We could be like Wallace and Grommit!"

Tess laughed at the thought of Jonny St Milton in goggles and with long ears.

"Now I'll never be able to look at him the same way!"

Zak gave her a sidelong glance. "I was kind of hoping you would say that about me. But Jonny? Not so much!"

He pulled the keys out of his pocket, clicked the central locking and opened the door for her. Once Tess was settled into the passenger seat, he adjusted the driving position for his longer legs and started the car. Moments later they were sweeping through the Manor's gates and heading towards the village.

"So you're going to stay in Polwenna Bay?" Tess asked. She couldn't help herself.

"Everything I want is right here," Zak said softly.

The intensity in his voice stopped her words, but when his left hand stole across to cover hers for a moment, his index finger skimming the soft skin, there was no need for Tess to speak. His touch said it all.

The car journey back to the village passed in a daze. Tess was stunned. How could just the brush of a fingertip be this overwhelming? If she'd once thought that Vass could turn her to jelly, Tess realised that she'd known nothing about desire. The strength of longing that Zak had awakened within her showed her feelings for Vass to be little more than a teenage crush that, nurtured by the intensity of secrecy, had grown monstrous and out of all proportion. It was both a liberating and depressing realisation.

How many years had she wasted on a man who wasn't worth one second of her time and who had taken advantage of his position in the worst possible way?

When Zak eventually eased the car into her parking space, Tess felt a stab of regret that the evening was almost over. Would the magic of the night-time garden fade away when the day crept in? Would the dawn's pure light cause the events of the past few hours to be little more than a strange dream?

"Not bad for a car that isn't a Porsche," remarked Zak as he locked the car.

"Never doubt a Focus," Tess said, patting the bonnet.

They walked up the hill to Tess's cottage. When Zak reached for her hand, Tess didn't resist. It felt so natural and so right to have her fingers enclosed by his. Being with him was breathtakingly easy.

"This is me," she said once they reached her cottage. The door key felt unwieldy in her hand and she fumbled to fit it into the lock, so Zak gently took it from her and the door swung open.

"Do you want to come in for a coffee?"

Oh God. How lame did that sound? What a cringeworthy cliché. Tess may as well have just asked him if he wanted to rip her clothes off, pin her to the bed and make love to her until dawn painted the sky pink. Of course, now she couldn't think of anything else but this and her face grew hot. What if he said 'yes', thinking this was what she really meant? And did she really mean sex? If so, was she ready for this?

Yes! screamed her libido.

No! scolded her common sense. You've been drinking. He's not your type. He's a player. You don't want to get involved with anyone, remember?

But Tess's libido wasn't listening to the voice of reason. It was far too busy worrying whether her bra and pants matched and trying to remember when she'd last shaved her legs.

Luckily Zak couldn't hear her internal monologue.

"I think I'd better make tracks. It's really late and you've had a long day."

Tess wasn't quite sure what to make of his response. Should she be offended? Relieved? Her sinking heart told her that she'd been hoping he would agree to come in and this alarmed her dreadfully. That he'd declined worried her. Was Zak giving her the brush off? Was this his way of letting her down gently, and if so what did it say about her that Polwenna's playboy wasn't interested?

This was suddenly so complicated. Tess simply hadn't dated enough to know the etiquette for these things.

"Fine. Thanks for seeing me home," she said. Even to her own ears, her voice sounded tight and odd.

Zak ran a hand through his thick blonde curls and gave her a shy smile.

"You don't have to thank me, Tess. I wanted to, and to be honest I really don't want to leave now. Trust me, I'd like nothing more than to pretend I'm desperately in need of caffeine and then spend the rest of the night with you."

"So why not come in?" Tess whispered.

Zak exhaled slowly.

"Because you are worth far more than just one night, Tess. Far, far more."

He placed his hands on her shoulders before lowering his mouth to hers in a kiss as soft as the brush of a butterfly's wings.

"There's no pressure and no rush. We've got all the time in the world," he whispered.

Then, and after one last cashmere-soft kiss, he melted into the darkness and it was as though she'd dreamed the whole strange evening. Tess stared after him, straining her eyes to try and decipher his form, but it was impossible to see beyond the shadows. Puffs of deep indigo cloud had blown up from the west, shrouding the stars and casting the village into darkness. He really had gone.

Tess shook her head. Zak Tremaine was a gentleman. Whoever would have thought it? She wasn't sure whether to be pleased or disappointed.

She wandered through the cottage, so agitated and brimming with questions and need that she was quite unable to settle. She'd never sleep now. Instead, she rattled around the kitchen making tea she wouldn't drink and replaying his words over and over again.

Zak had said they had all the time in the world. Did that mean that he wanted to see more of her? That Zak saw a future for them? Could this be the start of something wonderful? And did she feel the same? Did she want this to be the beginning of a relationship?

Tess's heart was racing. She didn't do relationships. She couldn't be hurt again and yet there was something about Zak that, in spite of his bad boy reputation, made her feel safe with him. Oh! It was so confusing. This was all so out of the blue, unexpected, probably ill-advised and without a doubt not something she was looking for, yet being with Zak had felt so right, which was why she hadn't paused to question it. On paper, you would never have put them together – the sexy musician with the wild reputation and the dull schoolteacher – but in reality they matched like two sides of the same coin. It didn't make sense. At all. Tess guessed that for once she would have to ignore logic and simply trust what her heart was telling her.

She tipped her cold tea away, put a load of washing on and even started to tidy her desk – all routine tasks that usually distracted her from thinking too hard. But tonight, when her lips were still tingling from kisses, nothing could stop the thoughts from pinballing around her mind and sleep felt very far away.

Tess was energised. Crackling with energy. Wired.

How was it possible that everything could look the same when she felt so different? Nothing could soothe the chatter in her head and calm the racing of her thoughts or make sense of the swooping and diving of her heart.

Nothing except for…

Except for…

Tess froze mid-pace, unable to believe the notion that had darted through her mind, if even for a millisecond. She hadn't come anywhere near thinking like this for years. From the very moment that the bow had become a dead weight in her hand and the music had ceased to flow through her heart and mind, she had shut the lid, literally and metaphorically, on what had once been the biggest part of her life. Her heart had been locked just as tightly as her violin case.

As though in a trance, she crossed the room and there it was on the shelf – the dark brown case with the worn handle that fitted her hand like a lover's. The faded stickers on the scuffed leather were curling with age and dryness, but Tess knew the Giovanni Schwarz was slumbering within like Sleeping Beauty and just waiting for the right touch to awaken her. It had been a decade or so rather than a century, but tonight something forgotten, something almost despaired of, had awoken in Tess.

It felt a lot like hope.

She reached up to the shelf, her hands tingling with anticipation and her heart thudding as though she'd just stomped up the hill. The cottage was quiet, as though holding its breath, and even the hallway clock seemed to tick extra quietly as though not wanting to startle her away from this moment.

Tess closed her fingers around the handle. The leather was cool to the touch and as she slid the case forward, the sudden jolt of weight into her hand was as familiar as her own breath. Before she had time to think about it or halt herself with arguments about not being able to do the beautiful instrument justice and worries that it might be too out of tune to salvage, she was slipping the cloth away from the wood and holding the instrument in her hands. Just as Zak's body had felt so right held against hers, so too did her precious violin, and Tess knew with absolute certainty that in some inexplicable way the two were linked.

She sank to the floor and placed the violin across her lap. An old friend, familiar in every way, it seemed to look up at her as though saying, here you are at last!

"Hello, you," Tess whispered, caressing the glowing wood with shaking fingers.

Of course there was no answer, but when she plucked the A string, the trembling note felt like a greeting of sorts. She turned the pegs and worked her way through the strings and with only her ear to guide her, it was harder than she recalled. She could attempt a fine tune, but in the past she'd always done this by using the grand piano in the music room at her parents' house. Vass would be seated at the piano with his beautiful musician's fingers resting on the ivories, while she tuned her violin at his direction – just as he had tuned her to his direction too, if only she hadn't been too blind to see it. Tess had always feared that repeating the process alone would be too painful, but the truth was that her focus was trained solely on her violin, her ear trained to hear the pitch, and any thoughts of Vass were incidental as she tuned the precious instrument. Suddenly Tess understood that he always had been second to the music. She had simply been too young and too hot-headed to see that. He no longer had any hold over her or her gift. There was no need to punish him or herself for a mistake made so long ago.

She was free.

When she was happy that the violin sounded as true as she could make it, Tess reached for the bow and rose to her feet. Her entire body was shaking.

How could ten years feel like ten seconds? As she tucked the violin between her chin and shoulder, it felt as though it had never been away, as much a part of her as her breath or her racing heart. Fear coursed through Tess when she lifted the bow. Could she do the beautiful instrument justice or would it sound like a scalded cat, nothing more than a poorly played fiddle? Would the gods punish her for turning her back on her gift by snatching it away from her?

There was only one way to find out. Now she had come this far, there was no turning back.

Tess closed her eyes, took a deep breath, drew the bow across the strings and began to play.

CHAPTER TWENTY-FIVE

Zak walked the half mile home to Seaspray in a daze. He still wasn't quite sure how events had taken such a surreal turn. Tess was gorgeous and definitely as beautiful as any of the models he'd partied with, but he'd never for one moment assumed that anything would happen between them. It was certainly true that over the past few weeks he'd stopped regarding Tess as the standoffish and mildly disapproving woman he'd been saddled with for the purposes of sorting out the music festival and now considered her a friend who surfed his wavelength. At some point, she'd started to fill a great deal of his waking thoughts – and quite a fair few of his dreams too – and he looked forward to the time they spent together.

But had he been looking for anything more? Absolutely not. Zak's life was upside down and the last thing he needed was any more complications.

Zak had tried hard to convince himself that the clever and in-control Tess with her career plan and penchant for lists was the last woman who would ever be interested in a chaotic and unemployed musician who had thrown his career away. He'd also given himself several stern lectures about why getting involved with anyone was a bad move right now, and he'd almost believed it too until she'd jumped when the pheasant cried and stumbled against his chest. But when she looked up at him with those big brown eyes, he'd been totally and utterly lost.

He should never have walked into the gardens with her, alone and in the starlight. That had been asking for trouble. The problem was it had been such a perfect night and he'd just wanted some time alone with Tess, away from the constant chatter and interruption of his friends and family. She was definitely popular. Tess and Mo were great friends, Morgan hung on her every word, while Nick clearly still held a torch for her. All Zak had wanted was to have her to himself for a few minutes. He must have become far too used to that since they'd been planning the music festival.

Then he'd kissed her – something he genuinely hadn't planned on doing, but something which came as naturally as breathing – and all his logical and rational arguments had flown right out of the window. Tess was different to all the girls he'd dated before: holidaymakers in the village for two weeks and in search of a summer romance, or casual flings when on the road with no expectations or promises made. Tess was different. She was serious and thoughtful and Zak knew she was as deep as the ocean beyond the harbour wall. She'd been hurt badly in the past and she kept her heart well guarded; that she'd offered it to him this evening meant far more than any Grammy or Brit award.

So he could tell himself all he liked that he was the last thing that Tess needed or that they were friends or that it was the wrong time to get involved, but it was far too late for logic now; Zak was involved. More than involved. He was falling for her and they were no longer just friends. They were more than that. Leaving her only moments ago to walk home had been the hardest thing in the world when all he had wanted to do was step inside, scoop Tess into his arms and spend the night with her. Only the fact that he knew she had been drinking and he liked her far too much to want her to ever feel that her judgement had been less than sound had made him step away.

But it was bloody hard, thought Zak as he let himself into Seaspray. Being the good guy was not nearly as much fun as being the bad boy, and as great as the moral high ground was, it was a little lonely there all on your own. He sighed. Was Tess laying awake thinking about him and wishing he'd stayed? Or was she now sobering up and thanking her lucky stars he'd gone home?

God. It was terrifying just how much he hoped it was the latter…

Wandering into the kitchen and lost in a fog of thought, Zak's feet nearly left the floor when a figure lurched out of the gloom.

"There you are, Zak!"

"Jesus, Danny! What are you doing creeping up on people?" Zak's heart was hammering against his ribs like a pneumatic drill.

Danny switched the table lamp on. He looked exhausted.

"I couldn't sleep so I was making a drink."

"In the dark?"

"I didn't want to wake Granny. The last thing I need is her worrying about me. Anyway, never mind me. What about you creeping in during the small hours? I didn't think we'd see you back tonight."

"Where else would I go?"

"Come on, Zak! I've only lost my sight in one eye. I saw you sneaking away with Tess."

Zak couldn't stop a daft grin from spreading across his face at just the mention of her name.

"I didn't sneak away with her. I drove Tess home and then I walked back here. It's all above board."

Danny whistled.

"Who are you and what have you done with Zak Tremaine?"

"And what's that supposed to mean?"

"It means that this sudden bout of chivalry is totally out character," Danny observed as he lifted the kettle from the Aga hotplate and sloshed hot water into two mugs. "Don't you usually sneak girls in here once Granny's out of the way and then boot them out nice and early the next morning?"

Put like this, Zak thought his past conduct sounded terrible. He was sure that most times he'd at least made any overnight guest a cup of tea and some toast before asking her to leave.

"I don't do that," he protested.

"Yes, you do," said Dan firmly. "I'm not having a go, mate. Bloody hell, I used to feel dead jealous. I had all the responsibility of a wife and kid, while you had all the no-strings fun. You might even go as far as to say it's your trademark. Love 'em and leave 'em, right? Don't get tied down? Have fun and move on? I'm sure I've heard you say all those things."

Zak sat down at the table and placed his head in his hands. If he was honest, there was a grain of truth in this. Maybe several.

"You make me sound awful," he said.

"You're just being a bloke. What man honestly wouldn't do the same in your position?" Dan said as he pummelled the tea bags. "You're young, free and single and a musician. Girls love that stuff. Pulling a different one every night is practically obligatory behaviour in your line of work, I would have thought?"

Zak had thought along similar lines not so long ago, but now that kind of behaviour seemed shallow and, truth be told, a little sordid. Walking up the hill with Tess earlier on, kissing her on the cottage doorstep, then walking away longing for more was a million times more exciting. He couldn't stop thinking about her even though nothing more than kisses had passed between them.

It was the oddest thing.

"So your point is?" Zak asked.

"My point is that it's very unusual to hear that you've just walked a girl home and left her there! You must really like Tess," said Danny. He pulled out a chair and sat down opposite Zak. "Seriously, mate, I don't blame you in the slightest. Tess is great, and she's a good-looking girl too, although I wouldn't have had her down as your type."

"Why not?" Zak asked, before adding quickly, "Not that I'm saying she is my type, or anything."

Danny leaned back in his chair and raised his mug in response.

"Okay. Here's my opinion. Tess is beautiful and a challenge, which certainly makes her your type, but I don't think she's the type of girl you can pick up and drop on a whim. She's not a girl to dick about, Zak."

"She's porcelain," Zak said softly. "Outwardly resilient and yet as fragile as bone china."

"Poetically put and spot on, so don't mess her around, Zak. Apart from the fact it's not cool, Jules would kill me if you do that. She's told me to make sure you treat Tess right."

"Jules asked you to have a word with me? Seriously? The vicar is sending me a warning?" Zak couldn't believe it. "What's next? Flaming crucifixes?"

"Don't be so bloody overdramatic. You do know that you practically come with a government health warning in these parts? Falling for Zak Tremaine can seriously damage your heart. Jules is concerned for her friend, that's all."

Stung, Zak glowered at him. "Tess is my friend too. She's just a friend."

A friend he kissed. A friend he couldn't wait to see. A friend whose clothes he longed to peel off and whose every inch of soft white skin he wanted to explore and touch. A friend who made his heart sing and whose face caused melodies and lyrics to whisper though his mind.

"Great," said Danny. "Glad we cleared that up. So you don't want to be with her then? You wouldn't mind if she was seeing another guy? Nick again maybe?"

"Tess would never see Nick again." The thought alone was a dart of jealousy straight into Zak's heart.

Dan shrugged. "What about a colleague? A serious teacher type who reads The Guardian and wears sports jackets with leather elbow patches?"

Zak knew his brother was trying to goad him into admitting he had feelings for Tess. After years of sibling mind games, Danny knew exactly how to press Zak's buttons. It was working too because the thought of Tess with anyone else but him made Zak's insides writhe.

"Does that thought make you burn with jealousy?" asked Danny. "Actually, you don't need to answer – I can see by your expression it does and I've never seen you react like this before. I think it's safe to conclude you really do like Tess and that my work here on Jules's behalf is done."

"Tess is my friend," Zak repeated.

"Good," said Danny. "That's the whole point because when you meet the right woman, she is your friend. Your best friend and the one person you want to be with above all others. You'll find you don't care about all the crap that you once used to and you'll wonder what the hell you were once playing at. You'll realise that before her you really were an utter idiot. Being out there on the loose isn't nearly as much fun as being with the right girl."

Zak had never heard Danny speak like this, but his brother wasn't finished.

"Even in tatty jeans and a hoody, she'll take your breath away and her jokes will make you ache with laughter even if you've heard them a thousand times before. You'll find yourself working out how to make her smile and when she does, you'll feel like the King of the World."

"Is that how you feel about Jules?"

Dan nodded. "She makes my heart calm and she sees me with all my faults and still loves me anyway, even when I'm being an idiot. I know she's the one."

The brothers sat in companionable silence, Dan sipping tea and Zak lost in thought. Words and images were threading their way through his mind, linking to snatches of melodies and shimmering with promise. Something was starting to awaken deep down inside him, yawning and stirring, and it felt terrifyingly like music. Suddenly Zak wanted nothing more than to retreat upstairs to his attic room, pick up his guitar and see what happened next. The blankness and the dread which had been his constant companions had vanished. Falling in love with Tess had filled his heart with melodies.

Danny finished his tea and stood up, the chair scraping the floor.

"There's one more thing," he said quietly. "Something that is maybe the biggest clue of all that she's the one, and that is that you'll do anything you can, anything, to make her happy. Even if it breaks your own heart. Especially if it breaks your own heart."

Once his brother had gone upstairs, Zak sat at the table feeling perplexed. What was all that about? It wasn't really about him; he knew that much. Danny spoke in riddles sometimes, Zak decided, and it wasn't always helpful. What could possibly make Jules happy but would break his brother's heart? That made no sense.

Pondering this, Zak rinsed their mugs, checked the door was locked and turned off the light. Once upstairs in his attic room, and with the door shut firmly behind him, he took a deep breath and reached for his guitar with shaking hands. The relief of holding it again, the strings familiar beneath his fingertips and weight just right in his arms, was immense. It might be a battered old instrument, but it had played in hundreds of pubs and must know every folk song, country tune and Oasis cover. The sound it made, and the memories the old wood had absorbed over the years, made it better than brand new to Zak. His guitar knew him and it understood that sometimes the only way Zak Tremaine could figure out what was in his heart was by picking it up and playing.

Zak sat on the edge of his bed. Words flittered through his mind like the moths beating their wings at his lit window.

Moonlight smile

Porcelain

Night garden

The images merged with musical notes and Zak's breath caught. Oh God! It was back! The music was back!

His right hand strummed a chord, the air trembled with sound and slowly, Zak Tremaine began to play and sing once more.

Ruth Saberton

CHAPTER TWENTY-SIX

It was unusual for Jules to have a lie in. Although it was Saturday, she had a packed schedule and when her alarm clock dragged her awake at half six, it took almost all her willpower not to turn it off and go back to sleep. It had been a late night at the Manor, if a fun one, and she'd had far too much champagne. As she sat up and rubbed her eyes, Jules's brain rattled inside her skull and her mouth felt as though half the beach had been tipped into it.

Great. A hangover when she was due to meet the Bishop. Just what she didn't need. Celebrating Ashley's good news – an answer to her prayers if there had ever been one – had seemed a good idea at the time, but she really should have stopped at one glass.

Still, she hadn't been the only one who'd had a few too many, Jules reflected as she clambered out of bed and, temples pounding in perfect beat with her footsteps, headed for the bathroom. The Penhalligan brothers would have sore heads today for certain and even Tess had drunk several glasses. She'd vanished with Zak Tremaine at one point and returned all sparkly-eyed and flushed. Interesting. Jules liked Zak, but she knew he had something of a reputation when it came to breaking hearts, so she was alarmed for her friend. She hoped Danny had been able to have a quiet word with his brother; Tess was far too special to be messed about with.

Still, that would have to wait. Today Jules was meeting the Bishop and she couldn't be late. He was a busy man with the whole of Cornwall to think about and she was touched that he had agreed to see her at such short notice. After weeks of wrestling with the idea of moving, praying hard, and constantly telling herself that a new life in London was perfect for Danny, Jules knew she couldn't prevaricate any longer; she had to hand in her notice.

The problem was that although her head was very good at telling her all the reasons why moving to London was a fantastic opportunity, Jules's heart was telling her something very different and this was tearing her apart. What was the right decision? How could she know for sure? She loved Danny with every fibre of her being and she couldn't wait to marry him in December, but she also loved her work in the parish and felt the calling to stay for longer and see it through. She was growing her congregation – and having saved St Wenn's from closure was a huge achievement – and Jules also loved the work she did in the community. Being a vicar wasn't all floaty robes and Sundays; in fact, Jules often thought church business was the least of what she did. She was equally as busy within the community. Or was this her vanity speaking? Should she pray to be more humble? Less proud of what she had been building in her small seaside parish? Nobody was irreplaceable and there was huge need in the cities. Was this where God wanted her?

"Please give me a sign, Lord!" Jules said to the bathroom ceiling, but the crumbling polystyrene tiles didn't answer and neither did a heavenly voice boom down at her. It seemed that she was going to have to listen harder in order to figure this one out. If only Danny wasn't so excited about their next adventure. Jules knew she ought to sit down with him and tell him how torn she was feeling; after all, they had always promised that there would be no secrets between them, but she couldn't bear to be the one to tarnish his happiness.

Jules sighed and turned on the shower, bracing herself for the arctic experience that was only seconds away. It wasn't that she was a fan of hosing herself down with cold water, as Jules was more a wallow in the bath with a romance novel kind of girl, but more a case of the hot water system having been on the blink ever since the Pollards re-plumbed the vicarage. Jules suspected a new boiler was the answer, but Big Rog seemed to think it a matter of pride that he fixed the issue. Unfortunately, doing this did actually require him turning up and spending time working on the boiler, hard to do when the Pollards, obsessed with Polwenna's Got Talent, spent most of their time rehearsing and any spare moments left over upping the ante on their new luggage delivery business. Only the day before, Sheila Keverne had almost been mown down by a speeding quad bike driven by what sounded like Tom Jones being strangled. Never mind sex bombs; Big Rog's driving was going to cause mass destruction at this rate and the villagers were up in arms. Sheila had already tasked Jules with tackling Big Rog about his driving. Traffic control was another vicarly duty nobody would know about, Jules reflected. If she left the village, there would be carnage!

She also feared that the Church of England might not replace her and then St Wenn's would fall under the jurisdiction of the next parish. Most rural vicars had more than one church to look after, so Jules was well aware just how lucky she was to only have St Wenn's in her care. In these days of dwindling congregations and making economies, consolidating Polwenna Bay's church with another parish would certainly be a sensible move, in terms of accounting anyway.

Jules's head, already aching, was really pounding now. What was the right thing to do? Why wasn't she able to see it? When she'd prayed all those years ago about what to do with her life, the answer that she should be ordained had come so clearly that she'd looked up to see where it had come from! So why was there no answer now?

Jules really hoped the Bishop would be able to help. Danny was off to London today, on another flat-hunting expedition, and she hated to think that he might guess how she really felt.

As she endured the daily blasting of icy spray, Jules tried hard to be positive. She reminded herself that her Boss had a habit of working in mysterious ways. Take the Rectory water issue, for example. Her Christmas wedding did feel a lifetime away though, so a daily cold shower to ward off carnal thoughts was probably just the thing! It was also true to say that there were few things in life more mysterious than the workings of the Pollards. Sometimes they arrived to fix things and sometimes they didn't show at all. Sometimes what they did worked and sometimes it didn't. Lunch began at eleven, home time was at three and dreckly really did mean a parallel time zone, one in which things were done months, if not years, later.

At least once she and Danny moved to London and started their new city life she wouldn't freeze to death every morning, Jules decided. It might also be nice to step out of the bathroom without her skin having a blue tinge and texture of a plucked chicken! There. She'd found another positive point to moving. That made at least three.

Three? Was that all? Bathrobe on and her feet thrust into the fake Uggs she'd found in the market, Jules headed to the kitchen to thaw out over toast and tea. That there were only three good points to moving was alarming and being able to have hot water hardly counted really. Maybe during the drive to Truro she'd come up with a few more?

It was a beautiful June morning, one of those where the heat of the day was already promised by the shimmering haze hanging over the sea and the scent of warm earth. The stillness of the early morning village could have given Wordsworth's Westminster Bridge a run for its money, and as she walked to her parking space, Jules wondered if this was another plus point for staying? God's creation touched her soul every day here in Cornwall and she was never far from giving thanks for all that was around her – except maybe Big Rog thundering by on his quad and definitely shattering the peace.

"Morning, Vicar! Handsome day!" he hollered, as Jules flattened herself against a cottage wall and hoped that her toes wouldn't be squashed. Her backside was wedged in a window basket.

"It would be more handsome if I wasn't run over," she said darkly, but Big Rog was long gone, roaring up the street and singing loudly above the engine, blissfully unaware that the vicar's bum was now planted in Kursa Penwarren's prize-winning window box. Jules squeezed out and stepped back into the street, brushing nasturtium petals and earth from her trousers and hoping her outfit wasn't marked in an unfortunate way. Only the Pollards could ruin her day twice before half past eight in the morning!

The journey to Truro passed in a blur of A roads, Radio Four, stunning countryside and a sneaky stop off at the services for a latte and a muffin. Telling herself that she had months yet to worry about fitting into her wedding dress, Jules continued on the last leg of her journey. Driving always felt meditative to her, and as the miles passed and the road ribboned beneath the bonnet of her trusty little car, Jules thought about Jonny and Alice's upcoming wedding. They already had the service planned; it would be simple and fairly short, and the order of service was printed and waiting to be picked up. Jules and the WI would decorate the church in the early morning with the cream and pink roses that Alice had chosen, Danny as chief usher would make certain that everyone was where they were meant to be, and Sheila Keverne, who had been busy practising Ave Maria on the church organ, would be waiting for the bride. With Jake giving Alice away, Isla as the flower girl and Teddy – rather ironically – as best man, each one had their role to play. All Jules needed to do now was write her homily and as she drove west, ideas came to her with every mile that passed. Changing seasons, travelled roads, changing Cornwall, and God's grace were the themes that would stitch the sermon together, and by the time she parked beneath the cathedral's timeless shadow, Jules knew exactly what she would say.

If only the same were true of this visit to see the Bishop. Would he be expecting her to resign? Realistically, this was what she ought to be doing so that over the coming months she could help to make the transition smooth for the next incumbent, but each time she had sat down to draft her reply, something stopped her. Five minutes on Facebook. A quick tweet from St Wenn's. A phone call. Anything, it seemed, except writing the letter that would be the final piece in the puzzle of moving to London. Oh dear. What was wrong with her?

Jules loved Truro. Its centre was a treasure trove of winding back streets, radiating from the cathedral like bicycle spokes, and filled with magical shops. Stepping into these felt like travelling back in time as the noise of the twenty-first century receded, replaced by the gurgle of water channelled away by gullies and the clack of heels on cobblestones. There was the hiss of a coffee machine from an open doorway, the bitter scent of grounds and the murmur of voices as people sipped their drinks and chatted. Usually, Jules sought out her favourite venue, a quirky coffee shop housed in a mellowed red brick building, all twisty barley sugar banisters and sloping worn floors, but today there was no time. Instead, she headed for the diocese office where she took a seat and waited to be called through. Although the place was drenched with sunshine and the secretary welcoming, it felt dreadfully like being in the dentist's waiting room and Jules felt her headache start to beat in her temples once again.

What was she going to say? What could she do? Perhaps she should make an excuse and leave, come back when she knew what she wanted to do? Yes! That was a plan.

"Jules, my dear. How good to see you again. Come on through."

The door to the inner sanctum had swung open and Bishop Bill was beckoning her. There was to be no escape after all. Jules tried her best to squash a rising sense of panic. It was daft to be nervous since the plump and smiley Bishop was always kind and welcoming, and had also forgiven her for a multitude of rookie vicar mistakes such as the infamous Polwenna Bay calendar and accepting money from the royalties of Alice Tremaine's bodice-ripper. This was just a chat. There was nothing to fear and before she could do a runner, Jules found herself seated at the far side of the Bishop's big desk, exchanging pleasantries and sipping coffee fresh from his Nespresso machine.

"We like to move with the times in the Diocese of Cornwall," he said when she'd looked surprised (mashing a tea bag in a chipped mug was the modus operandi at St Wenn's, and if Sheila learned that the Bishop of Cornwall had a Nespresso machine, she wouldn't cease nagging until Jules had one for the vestry). "Now, tell me, how are things at St Wenn's? You have a lively flock as I recall!"

He said this with a ghost of a smile and Jules blushed. The Bishop had last visited the village to break the good news that St Wenn's wouldn't be closed and had nearly been lynched when the parishioners mistakenly thought he'd sacked Jules. Sheila had looked close to walloping him with a hymn book and Alice had almost exploded with fury. Luckily matters had calmed down eventually, but the Bishop had looked rather alarmed.

"They're all well, thank you," she said, crossing her fingers under the table. Squabbling, quad bike near misses and talent show competitiveness aside, they were all well. Put it this way; nobody was posing naked any more or writing racy novels to raise money for the church roof, which was surely an improvement.

"Good. Good. I've been very impressed by the work you do there. Not an easy parish at all and very much a closed shop, but they've certainly taken you to their hearts."

"Yes." Jules stared miserably down at the table top. "They have and I love working there. I do."

"Yet you feel called to take your gifts to another area and serve God in a new capacity."

It wasn't a question. Jules had spoken to Bishop Bill several times and it was he who had put her in touch with a possible parish in London.

"You have a heart for this work, Jules, and although we will be sorry to lose you in Cornwall, I know that you will continue to serve God," the Bishop said when she didn't reply. "There will be new challenges ahead, I am sure, and there are also changes for you on a personal level. It's an exciting time."

"Yes. Yes, it really is." Even to her own ears, Jules didn't sound convinced. She put her coffee down and tried her hardest to articulate what she was feeling. "I can't wait to marry Danny and I am so excited about our life together."

The Bishop leaned back in his chair and folded his hands together. "But?"

She shrugged. "I don't know. I mean, I know I want to marry Dan and that it's the right thing to do. I know that with all my heart."

"Yes. Your fiancé is a thoughtful man with a heart for supporting you in your work," he agreed. "You'll make a good team, I'm sure, and wherever you go, you'll demonstrate God's love for the community where you live and serve. I've no doubt of that."

"Thank you."

His words were a balm in one way, but in another Jules felt even worse. What did it mean that even with the Bishop's blessing and encouragement her heart wasn't filled with enthusiasm? "I guess I'm just a bit nervous," she suggested. It sounded lame even to her own ears.

Bishop Bill nodded. "It's only natural to feel nervous. When you join a new congregation it's always difficult at first, but you learn as well as lead. That makes you grow. Frontline ministry is filled with challenges, as I'm sure you know, and it will call upon many of your skills and test your faith. Yet you have nothing to worry about. You are more than qualified and you will be an asset to any parish."

"So why doesn't it feel right that I go?" Jules blurted out, unable to keep her fears to herself for a moment longer. "Why am I not more excited? Why do I feel so sad at the thought of leaving? Why aren't I racing up the motorway to house-hunt and have interviews? Why doesn't God tell me what I should do even though I ask and ask Him? Where's my answer? Why isn't He guiding me?"

Oh great. Now she was crying.

"Sorry," she sobbed.

The Bishop pushed a box of tissues across the desk.

"Don't be. You'd be surprised how many people cry in here. It must be something to do with me."

"Maybe it's because once we're in here we tell the truth? I haven't breathed a word of this to anyone. Not Danny. My friends. Or even myself." She took a tissue and mopped her eyes. "I didn't even tell God!"

"He already knows what's in your heart," said the Bishop.

"So where's my answer? My signs?" Jules demanded. She was actually quite cross about this. "Didn't I show enough faith to have any?"

"I can't answer that because I don't know God's mind. In fact, I think I know less about my faith now than I did when I was first ordained, but that doesn't mean my faith is less solid. I believe the closer we are to God, the more He reveals of Himself and the less we understand. The more we have to trust."

Just great, thought Jules. She'd been hoping this would all get easier as time went by, and that one day she would have all the answers. If even bishops were stumped at times, then what hope was there?

"Yet it seems to me that you do have the answer to your prayer," he continued, leaning forward now and smiling at her. "You came here today because you were intending to resign. You felt that was the next logical step. Hand in your notice, look for a new job, move house, start afresh. Am I right?"

"I guess so."

"Yet in your heart you felt burdened. You couldn't quite manage to feel the excitement you wanted to feel. The jobs you looked at didn't feel quite right. The houses you've viewed haven't quite worked out. Your work in Polwenna Bay isn't quite done. The words you should have said didn't quite come out the right way," he concluded with a smile.

Jules laughed at this because her deluge of words certainly didn't bear any resemblance to what she'd intended to say.

"Hardly!"

"So you have your answer, I think? The Lord is telling you that it isn't quite time to leave yet. Sometimes our lack of answer is the very answer we were seeking all along."

Jules stared at him. Of course! This made perfect sense. If every door closed and every instinct you had was a 'no', then this was the answer. In her heart she had known all along that leaving Polwenna Bay wasn't the right thing to do. She'd just needed to listen. Suddenly Jules felt a peace descend, a sensation she hadn't enjoyed for a very long time.

She was meant to stay. Of course she was.

But there was one big problem with this answer to her prayer.

"What about Danny?" Jules whispered. "What shall I tell him?"

The Bishop smiled at her. There was compassion and understanding in his eyes and Jules knew there wasn't much he hadn't come across in his time as a pastor.

"The only thing you can tell him, and you already know what that is, I think?"

Jules did, but saying it aloud was going to be one of the hardest things she'd ever had to do because she was going to shatter Danny's dreams and make their future very complicated. Yet what choice was there? If their marriage was to work, if they were to grow as a team and as husband and wife, then they had to be honest with each other. Without honesty, what was there?

There was nothing else for it. She was going to have to tell Danny the truth.

Jules was going to have to break the news that she didn't want to move to London.

CHAPTER TWENTY-SEVEN

Like Polwenna Bay's vicar, Tess never slept in either. On weekday mornings, her alarm pinged her out of bed at six o'clock so she could have her run, shower and get ready in time to arrive at school by eight o'clock, and at the weekends she automatically woke at exactly the same time. If asked, Tess would have said that she was naturally an early riser and a morning person, although the truth was probably more along the lines that lolling around in bed was no fun unless there was someone special to snuggle up with. As much as she loved her big sleigh bed with its plump white duvet and marshmallow pillows, being alone in it wasn't much fun. Better to be up and about keeping busy.

So when the warm sunshine stole through the crack in her curtains and kissed her awake on Saturday morning, Tess was amazed to discover it was almost eleven o'clock.

Eleven! How was that possible?

She sat bolt upright, shocked at herself. Then, as the memories of the night before came racing back, she was even more stunned. The walk through the starlight garden with Zak Tremaine and limb-melting kisses, his tender words on her doorstep and the promises wrapped within them, and finally the thrill of reaching for her violin and playing again.

What an incredible and magical evening. Was it really true or had she dreamed it? The fact that she was still in bed while the sun climbed high above the village, wasting time sleeping when there was still so much to be done, seemed to suggest the events of last night really did happen, as did the violin case resting on her chest of drawers. Unless it had magically grown legs and walked itself up the narrow stairs, then it really was true; she had played again and until the early hours of the morning too. It was lucky that the adjoining cottages were second homes and currently empty; otherwise the neighbours would have been complaining this morning! After all this time, she'd probably sounded like a scalded cat.

Still, the quality of her playing aside, it had felt wonderful to hold her violin once again and experience the alchemy of instrument and soul-forged music. Now she had found it once again, Tess wondered how she had managed to live without it for so very long. Music had been her joy and her passion and even without the glittering career or having Vassilly by her side, Tess knew she still loved music as much as she always had. What a shame she'd allowed incidental things and bitterness to obscure this passion. What a waste. Tess understood now that the pure pleasure of playing was what music was truly about. The rest of it had been about pleasing her parents and later punishing Vass who, of course, had never really cared about her sacrifice. The only person she'd hurt was herself. Tess now understood that as long as she remained true to her heart, she would never lose music again.

Did she regret giving up music for teaching? In some ways perhaps, but arguably her ultimate choice had made far more of a difference. The children that she taught meant everything to Tess and she loved her job. You simply couldn't put a value on the satisfaction that came when you saw a child finally grasp a concept or make progress that was above and beyond what was expected. Teaching was the best job in the world and Tess could never regret her chosen career even if it did come at the expense of another one. Some things were meant to be and this was her journey. Perhaps she was meant to have followed this path all along? Was Vass just a twist in the road which had brought her to this point? A part of a greater design? A footnote in her history rather than the key driving force behind her decisions?

This was an unexpected shift in her perception.

Usually when she thought about Vass – something Tess tried very hard not to do – she was filled with anger, and the pain of his betrayal stung as sharply as always. Yet today there was nothing. She tested her feelings in surprise. Her memories of him were still clear, his dark eyes and raven wing hair as beautiful as always, but the accompanying pang was noticeably absent and her feelings for him seemed distant, as though they had belonged to another woman entirely. She could see now that they were the all-consuming emotions of a teenager; emotions forged in the crucible of secrecy and given more importance than they had really deserved. First love, always painful and invariably a beacon of what could have been, had grown into something quite different altogether, something monstrous and destructive which had held her captive for far longer than the reality had warranted. If she saw Vass now, Tess knew that she would feel little more than a flicker of nostalgia for the girl she'd once been.

And a great deal of anger towards him for his lack of judgement.

Tess sat up in bed, the sunshine dancing over the covers, and yawned. Something had changed, that much was for certain, and when she tried to recall those precious stolen kisses and the snatched hours in the music room at the Richmond house, the images were as faded as though viewed through an Instagram sepia filter, and instead her mind kept leapfrogging the distant memories to the vivid events of the previous night. Closing her eyes and sinking back into her pillows, she relived Zak's kisses. How a few curls of blonde mane fell across his brow. The dangerous glitter of his eyes in the starlight. The way that when his mouth brushed hers, little sparks of electricity had fizzed throughout her body. Tess wasn't a nun. She'd dated since Vass, even had a few short-lived relationships, but there was nothing that compared to the chemistry she'd shared with Zak. Each kiss had the intensity and the breathtaking wonder of the first time. As he'd buried his hands in her hair and pulled her closer, Tess's heartbeat accelerated, and when his thumbs caressed her neck, shivers had rippled down her spine. She had never wanted a man more in her life.

This was crazy! This was Zak Tremaine. Wild Zak with the bad boy reputation, a musician and a rolling stone. He was the kind of man she had sworn to avoid at all costs. So how was it that he alone had the power to make her heart sing and music play – in all senses of the expression?

Tess kicked off the duvet and swung her legs out of bed, her eyes widening when she realised she was still wearing yesterday's outfit. She must have played herself into exhaustion and simply passed out. Nonplussed, she tugged off her crumpled garments and pulled on her bathrobe, wandering downstairs to make coffee and attempt to make sense of her well-ordered life being walloped by this wrecking ball of unrequested emotion.

The sun was streaming in through the sitting room window. Over the higgledy-piggledy jumble of lichen-speckled and seagull poop-spotted rooftops, Tess made out glimpses of sparkling sea and a small sailing boat dancing towards the horizon. What was Zak up to this morning? Was he fast asleep or was he sitting on the terrace at Seaspray and gazing out at the seascape? It made Tess's heart lift to think that they might be watching the same sailing boat; it linked them in some small way even though they were the last two people on earth who should be together.

A buzzing from the window sill jolted Tess out of her musings. Her phone, propped against the glass to catch a faint pip of 4G, had an incoming text. Before she'd even picked it up, Tess knew it was Zak. The rush of happiness caused by seeing his name on the screen was terrifying.

Morning! Are you about for lunch?

What was the etiquette here? Everything in Tess was longing to text back at once with a resounding yes, but was that too keen? Was she supposed to play it cool?

The phone buzzed again.

Not sure I can wait until lunch to see you! So much for playing it cool!

Tess laughed. He was right. Who cared about playing it cool? Playing games of any kind was the opposite of cool, surely? She liked Zak, she enjoyed being with him and she couldn't wait to see him again. Who gave a hoot about playing it cool? He must know she liked him – the way she'd kissed him last night was probably quite a giveaway. With a smile, she typed back.

Are you encouraging me to skive off from my marking?

Within seconds, the phone buzzed again.

I'd like to encourage you to do far more than that ;)

in the meantime, Harbour Café?

half eleven?

Tess glanced at the sitting room clock. She had about twenty minutes to shower and try to look presentable. Could she do all that in just twenty minutes? On the other hand, this meant only twenty minutes until she would see Zak again…

Of course she could do it.

Sending back a text confirming she'd be there, Tess flew up the stairs and dived into the shower. Just over twenty-five minutes later, she was walking down the steps which led to the small sun-drenched seating area alongside the marina with hopefully only her flushed cheeks and damp hair any indication that her walk down had been anything other than leisurely. Her outfit of skinny jeans, glittery sandals and floaty white top was casual enough to not appear that she was trying too hard, yet Tess also hoped it would make him look twice. Tara had been with her when she bought the jeans and had said that they made her legs look model long, and since Zak had dated real live models, Tess felt a little under pressure. Her usual tracksuit bottoms, running vest and tatty trainers probably wouldn't cut it!

Catching sight of Zak now, Tess was very glad she'd made an effort.

"Hey you," he said. "Wow. You look amazing."

Zak, dressed in a pair of faded denim jeans, a blue and white striped shirt with the sleeves rolled up to show off his tanned arms and his bare feet thrust into a pair of deck shoes, looked good enough to eat. Dark wrap-around shades were rammed in his thick curls which were swept back from his face and secured at the nape of his neck. Tess saw both Penny Kussell and Mandy Polgooth staring and looking put out when Zak greeted her.

"You look great yourself," she said. "Late nights clearly agree with you."

Zak stood up and stepped towards her, slipping his arm around her waist and pulling her in for a peck on the cheek. It was so natural and effortless and she leaned into him, loving the smell of his skin and his scent.

"You agree with me," he said softly. His breath was warm against her ear, but it made Tess shiver.

"I've ordered some coffee," he continued, pulling out a chair for her and then sitting back down himself. "I didn't get to sleep until late."

"Me neither," Tess told him.

"For the same reasons as me?"

"I'd need to know your reasons to answer that question," Tess countered.

Zak looked shy all of a sudden. The bravado was a great front, she was learning, but the real man beneath it, the man who'd been broken by tragedy and scalded by the industry he'd been a part of, was honest and vulnerable. Seeing this made Tess love him even more.

Wait. What was that?

Her thoughts suddenly tangled like fishing wire and Tess was flustered. Luckily their coffee arrived at this point so she was able to busy herself with the cups and pouring.

"I didn't know you took sugar," said Zak.

Tess looked down in surprise. Somehow she'd managed to tip in several sachets.

"I don't."

But Zak knew this already. Over the past two weeks, they'd glugged gallons of coffee while drawing up lists, making calls and trying to come up with ways to persuade the Pollards to help out for free. Zak knew Tess liked her coffee black and bitter.

He placed his hand on hers and the simple gesture was enough to calm her.

"The reason I didn't sleep wasn't just because of what happened between us, although believe me that would be quite enough to keep me wide awake, but there's no pressure, I promise. This really is just coffee between two friends – although I did think maybe once we've caffeined ourselves into consciousness we could grab a couple of pasties and have a walk on the beach?" He pulled a face. "I'm gabbling, aren't I?"

Tess smiled. "A little."

"See? Guys get nervous too, you know. But seriously, Tess, I wanted to tell you something else. Something amazing which I know is down to you."

"Go on," she encouraged.

He wove his fingers with hers. Tess didn't slide her hand away or remind him she was the local teacher and couldn't be seen holding hands with a man. She was far too intent on what he was telling her and the touch of his hand on hers to care about anything else.

"Last night after I left you, Tess, I was on top of the world. You're amazing. Incredible. I have to be honest; you've been all I can think about for weeks."

Tess raised her eyebrows. "I'm shocked. What about the festival?"

"Don't tease me," Zak begged. "I'm trying hard to get the words out here and I'm just a man at the end of the day. We're not so good at this stuff. Tess, I love spending time with you and chatting to you. I look forward to seeing you no matter if I've only seen you a few hours earlier. Even if I've just popped up the road to check with Granny Alice about something! You've changed everything for me, even before last night, and I just wanted you to know that. I'm no longer in the dark place I fell into after what happened in London and that's in no small part down to your friendship. It means the world to me and I would never want to jeopardise it."

Tess felt exactly the same way about him. She hadn't sought to find whatever it was that they had, but now that she'd come to know him, Tess couldn't imagine not being Zak's friend. He knew more about her than anyone else she knew. He knew the real her, not just the cool and collected schoolteacher side the rest of the village thought they knew.

Zak squeezed her hand. "There's more, Tess. Last night when I went home, I had this melody playing in my mind, so I went upstairs, picked up my guitar and I started to play. Can you believe it? I was able to write that music down and play again!"

She stared at him in utter disbelief. How was it possible? She had told herself there was no such thing as a soulmate and had worked hard to convince herself that love was a myth, yet how could she deny these things now? Zak and she were two halves of the same soul. She'd already felt this way after that beautiful evening, but that music had come back to both of them was proof beyond all doubt. Tears filled her eyes.

"Hey, don't be sad," Zak said, slipping his hand from hers and brushing her tears away. "This is happy news. I can't even start to tell you how I feel."

Tess nodded. Her tears were tears of happiness for him and wonderment too. If she'd needed any signs or, as Silver Starr might say, nudges from the Universe, then they couldn't have been any clearer.

"I know exactly how you feel. It happened to me too," she said.

Now it was Zak's turn to stare. "You played your violin again? Last night? Seriously?"

Tess nodded. "It was like being in a dream, but yes, I went home and played. Very badly, I should think, but it didn't matter. All I wanted to do was play my violin. I couldn't not play it, if that makes any sense?"

But Tess knew it made perfect sense to Zak. Out of all the billions of people on the planet, he was the only one who knew exactly what she was saying and understood the significance of the event. Tess was crying with joy and amazement and hope and happiness, and when she looked into Zak's eyes she saw the same emotions shimmering there in a perfect reflection of her own.

Zak Tremaine was the other half of her. There was no other explanation.

So when Zak pulled her towards him and kissed her, in broad daylight and in front of everyone at the café, Tess didn't pull back or worry that she'd been spotted. Instead, she closed her eyes and kissed him back, her very soul spilling into the embrace and telling him exactly how she felt. There would be no more holding back, or self-protection or ancient worries about being hurt. All of these things were as nothing now because in spite of everything, against all logic and all her best resolutions, Tess knew that this man was her mirror image and her soulmate. She could trust him with her heart.

She could trust him with everything.

CHAPTER TWENTY-EIGHT

Her penultimate wedding dress fitting completed, Alice Tremaine set off to meet Jonny for lunch. There was only so much standing on the Penhalligans' coffee table while Susie pinned and tweaked her dress that an eighty-year-old woman could cope with, and as Alice strolled along the harbour, she couldn't quite shake the fear that making so much fuss about a wedding was rather foolish at her advanced age. The modest wedding she'd originally had in mind was morphing into something very different.

Was it all getting out of hand? Her stomach curdled with nerves each time she thought about the whole deal, something Alice couldn't recall happening when she'd married Henry Tremaine. Of course, that had been a lifetime ago and times and circumstances were very different now, but even so, there hadn't been anywhere near so much to do. She'd worn a simple dress, carried a small posy which dear Henry had picked himself from Seaspray's garden, and then they'd had a simple afternoon tea at the hotel with just a few friends and family. Their honeymoon had been a few days in a guest house before they'd returned to Polwenna Bay and their new life together. Henry had never been one for fuss or going far from home and unlike Jonny wouldn't have dreamed of springing an exotic venue on her. Jonny was certainly being very secretive about the location of their honeymoon and this also made Alice feel worried. As much as she would love the travel, she knew his health wasn't good and the last thing she wanted was for Jonny to put himself under pressure. Oh! She wished he was more of a homebody like Henry. That would be one less thing to worry about.

Alice knew it was daft to compare the two men and her two weddings. This was a different time of her life. She wasn't twenty now, was she? Far from it. But even so, was this wedding, with its musical entertainment, hog roast and village celebrations, a little over the top for a couple in their twilight years? And was a white wedding dress, however simple and elegant, plain ridiculous for a woman of her age?

"Sounds like a classic case of wedding jitters to me," Susie Penhalligan had said through a mouthful of pins when Alice mentioned her concerns. "It's only natural to be nervous about getting married."

But Alice wasn't nervous about marrying Jonny; she loved him dearly and besides, she'd known him all her life. She was looking forward to the adventures that lay ahead and was thankful every day that they'd been given a second chance. No, it wasn't that at all. It was just that the villagers were getting very excited about her wedding and wherever Alice went, somebody else had a new idea or suggestion. Alice was realistic enough to know that it was really the talent show, free food and partying that they were looking forward to, but even so, she had a sense of events starting to gather momentum. As much as she wanted her friends and neighbours to share her day, Alice was starting to wish she had gone along with Jonny's suggestion that they elope. Even an Elvis chapel in Vegas would probably be more peaceful than Polwenna Manor, with the Pollards zooming about on their noisy quad bikes and the talent show in full swing.

"Oh dear. Maybe I'm too old for all this?" Alice said to a beady-eyed seagull perched on the top of a net bin.

The seagull cocked its head thoughtfully, as though considering the question, before swooping away over the harbour. Maybe the seabird was telling her to just spread her wings and go with events? Head for the horizon and simply go for it? Although seeing omens was all a bit Silver Starr, it was too late now to do anything else because the wedding was fast approaching and soon Alice would be Mrs St Milton. How excited her teenage self would have been at this thought! Her octogenarian self was excited too, but knew that this wedding came complete with many decades of baggage, not the least of which were all her worries about the grandchildren. Grown up as they were, Alice often thought that they needed her more now than ever, especially now their problems couldn't be solved with a cuddle and a biscuit.

Take Danny, for instance. Engaged to a lovely girl, father of a wonderful son and now with an exciting new job on the horizon, her grandson should be jumping for joy at his good fortune instead of drifting around Seaspray with a face longer than a wet bank holiday weekend. He'd left the house this morning, London bound for more flat-hunting, looking as though he was off to his execution. Alice had almost said something but, knowing how touchy Danny could be if he thought anyone was interfering, had managed to bite her tongue just in time. Whatever the problem was, he would come to her if and when he wanted to and until then Alice would just have to fret quietly.

She sighed and turned towards the café, leaning heavily on the handrail as she descended the steep steps. Jonny, seated at a table overlooking the marina, waved cheerfully and Alice raised her eyes to heaven. How had Jonny navigated these steps? Sheer bloody-mindedness probably, as he would never ask for help. Honestly! The stubborn old fool! If he fell and broke a hip now, it would put their special day back months and that would never do – who knew at their age how much time they would be granted?

Of course, nobody ever knew the answer to that question. Just look at Jimmy's poor wife. One minute she was as fit as a fiddle and busy with the children, and the next she was gone. Life seemed so cruel sometimes, and even all these years on, Alice struggled to make sense of this loss. Losing his wife had broken her son's heart and changed his life forever, so Jimmy was yet another worry on Alice's long list. He was as restless as the waves rolling across the bay and as unsettled as the Cornish weather. Would he even make it back to Polwenna for her wedding, or would yet another Jimmy disaster take place and thwart his attempt to come home? Over the years, Alice had seen them all, from running away to California to springing a surprise adult grandchild on her, so nothing that her son did could surprise her now. Jimmy might be in his sixties, but he was as much of a worry now as he had been as a child.

Alice also hoped she hadn't put too much pressure on Zak. He'd been very quiet recently, and whenever she asked him about her wedding song, he evaded the question with all the skill of a cabinet minister on the Today programme. Not being John Humphrys, Alice didn't like to press too hard for an answer, but she was starting to suspect Zak was struggling. Asking him to write a song had seemed such a good idea at the time – a wonderful lever to force him to start composing and playing again – but as far as she could tell, he hadn't written a single note. He certainly hadn't touched the piano and the constant hummed snatches of melody which had always marked his presence about the place were silenced. Poor Zak must be very unhappy. Had she inadvertently made things worse?

Then there were the flowers. Had she made the right choice? Would Symon really cope with feeding everyone on the day? Could Susie finish the dress in time? Would Morgan take good enough pictures? Would Teddy St Milton behave himself at the reception? And would the villagers? Alice hoped she hadn't taken on too much by combining the festival and her evening reception. At least the yard of ale competition was taking place in the pub. That was one less worry.

Oh Lord. There was so much to think about. Alice's head felt fit to burst. Thank heavens that lovely Tess was in charge. Nothing ever seemed to flap the girl and she had such a quiet air of authority that even the Pollards scurried to do her bidding. Yes, if anyone could take control of the festival, then it was Polwenna Primary's outstanding Miss Hamilton.

As she made her way through the busy harbourside café to join her fiancé – stopping briefly to tell Big Rog for the third time that she didn't need quad bike transportation to her own wedding reception, no matter how beautifully he decorated the vehicle or how cheap the price – Alice's head started to pound and elopement looked ever more attractive. Everyone from the Pollards and their quad to Silver Starr, who was desperate to perform a pagan blessing, wanted a say in her big day and it was making everything feel like very hard work. Still, Alice knew she couldn't complain since she was the one who'd insisted on involving the local community.

This was all her doing.

"After all these years, you'd think I'd know better," she muttered.

"Sorry, my love? I didn't quite catch that." Jonny stood up as she joined him and, leaning on the table for support, shuffled around and pulled out a chair for her. Alice really wished he'd remain seated. He was looking very tottery just lately, but her fiancé had impeccable manners and he'd sooner hurl himself into the water than not act in a gentlemanly fashion. So she pushed away her concerns and simply offered up her cheek to be kissed.

"I was just thinking out loud, love. Talking to myself."

Jonny raised a bushy white eyebrow. "Talking to yourself? You do know what they say, don't you, Ally? It's the first sign of madness."

"What's the second one? Planning a big wedding when you're eighty and involving the entire village?"

"Ah. I take it you've just been accosted by the Pollards?" said Jonny. "White ribbons and bows on a quad bike and a few tin cans too for effect? I must say, I'm rather tempted. If he'll add a Just Married sign, then I'm in! Shall we call Big Rog over?"

"Don't you dare, Jonny St Milton!"

He winked. "Where's your sense of adventure, Ally? Besides, I'd like to see you on a quad. Maybe even in biker gear? Perhaps we could both ride it?"

Alice laughed at the very notion. "You, ride a quad? You can't even get up the stairs without keeling over!"

He placed a hand on his heart. "Ah, shoot my dreams down in flames, why not? I just wanted to see my fiancée in leathers!"

"You'll give yourself a funny turn having thoughts like that!"

"It'd be worth it," Jonny sighed. "Fine. We'll just have to use my Bentley as agreed and one of the hotel staff as a chauffeur rather than Little Rog. Maybe Tom Elliot can do it." He reached across the table and took her hand in his, caressing her palm with his thumb. "Seriously, Ally. If it's worrying you, then we can call the whole thing off and run away to Gretna Green."

"Don't tempt me," said Alice grimly. "No, love, it's fine. I'm just fussing. I was just worrying about it all."

Jonny leaned back in his chair and regarded her thoughtfully over the top of his glasses. "Anything in particular? Or should I say anyone? Is this a grandchild-sized worry?"

He knew her far too well, thought Alice.

"I was worrying about Zak," she admitted.

"Zak?"

"He's so lost without music."

"He's had a hard time, Ally, and he's got some huge decisions to make, but at least he's got space here to do that. Hopefully he won't get to his seventies and realise where it all went wrong and then panic because time's slipped away. I think that young man's got his head screwed on."

"But he's so unhappy."

"Take comfort in this, my love; Zak didn't look too unhappy to me earlier on when I saw him walking through the village with that pretty schoolteacher. I can't blame him either! If I was a few years younger…"

"Should I be jealous?" Alice teased. "You seem to have quite a crush!"

Jonny patted her hand. "If we were young again, I'd only have eyes for you, my love. I wouldn't mess up twice. I just think she's a lovely girl. They make a nice young couple."

"You've been in the sun too long," Alice said. "Or else your imagination's in overdrive. Tess and Zak are working on the music festival, that's all."

How Alice wished it was otherwise. Tess was perfect for Zak. He needed somebody proper, a real person with her own opinions and her own career rather than the vapid butterflies who followed him from gig to gig. Deep down, Zak craved acceptance and security and when he finally fell in love, Alice knew he would fall hard and this made her tremble for him. With her middle grandson, there were no half measures. He could be very badly hurt.

"Really?" Jonny raised a bushy white eyebrow. "So that was why they were eating pasties and heading down to the beach? Interesting way to organise an event. He looked absolutely ecstatic to me. Incidentally, so did she. They were so wrapped up in each other, they didn't even notice me walk by."

"Really?"

"Really," nodded Jonny. "Besides, didn't they slip away together last night?"

Alice frowned. "Weren't they simply checking locations?"

Jonny raised her hand to his lips and kissed it.

"In the dark? Alone? Come, my sweet, we're not so old that we don't recall what it was like to be young! I would have slipped away with you given half the chance."

"Slip over, more like," teased Alice. Her brain was whizzing about now. Come to think of it, Zak had seemed happier lately, and last night when she'd woken to get a glass of water, she'd thought she'd heard the soft strumming of a guitar, something which she'd put down to being half asleep. Now she was starting to wonder and even hope…

He smiled. "Oh, Ally. If I was twenty-five again, I'd have slipped away into the woods with you, don't you doubt that for a moment. We might be old now, but I promise I couldn't love you any more even if I was young again. You're as beautiful now as you were when we first met."

"Oh, Jonny, what nonsense. I'm an old woman."

"You're still the girl I fell in love with," he said staunchly. "I love you, Alice, and I've always loved you. Life took a few twists and turns and, like most young men, I messed it up, but I'm here now and I promise you that I won't mess it up again. I'm going to spend the rest of my life making you happy and I couldn't give a hoot how or where we get married. All I care about is marrying you." His grip tightened on her fingers and his voice grew hoarse. "You're everything to me."

Alice's vision swam. "And you to me," she whispered.

It was so easy to lose sight of what this wedding was really about. It wasn't the venue or the dress or the reception that counted; these things were immaterial. This wedding was about celebrating their love and sharing the rest of their lives together, however long or short that time would be. If the arrangements didn't go smoothly and if she looked daft in her dress, did it really matter? She would still be marrying the man who had been her first love and who would be her last.

"Here we are, Mrs Tremaine. One cream tea for you," announced Pippa Penhalligan who was waitressing, placing a tray laden with floury scones, pots of glistening jam and thick clotted cream in front of them. "My mum says to let you know she's making a hundred for your wedding, as her present to you, and Keyho— I mean, Kathy Polmartin says she's going to supply the cream and jam."

"That's very kind of them," said Alice, touched. As if Patsy didn't have enough baking to do in the summer season and Kathy Polmartin was busy with the shop too. People had really taken her wedding to their hearts and suddenly all her worries seemed daft. All that mattered was marrying Jonny and sharing their happy day with all their friends and family.

The knot of worry that had been tightening for weeks was suddenly undone and for the first time in longer than she cared to admit, Alice found that she wasn't dreading her big day. Quite the opposite, in fact.

As she sat opposite the man she loved, Alice Tremaine could hardly wait to get married.

CHAPTER TWENTY-NINE

Jules had spent her weekend feeling very worried. Her meeting with the Bishop, followed by lots more hard prayer, had certainly made up her mind that she was meant to stay in Cornwall, and while she was at peace with the knowledge that this was the right thing for her as a pastor, what about Danny? What would this mean for their relationship and their future together?

It was Sunday evening, the six o'clock communion service was long over, and now Jules was in the vestry attempting to write the latest edition of the parish newsletter and failing miserably. Each time she tried to jot down an entertaining line about the bell-ringing club or the upcoming produce market, she was overcome with dread about the inevitable conversation she would need to have with her fiancé and the words simply dried up. So far, the Jules's Jottings section was blank and the piece on the Memory Café looked as though it had been well and truly forgotten.

Jules picked up her pen and started again.

My jottings this month are all about how much the community is looking forward to the wonderful blend of wedding day and festival taking place on Saturday the...

Wonderful blend? That made the whole event sound like a jar of coffee. Besides, was it really such a wonderful blend? As the day grew ever closer, Jules was starting to wonder about the wisdom of combining the two events. Like so many things that went badly wrong, it had seemed such a good idea at the time, but somehow Alice's plans for a quiet wedding, followed by an evening celebration for the village, had morphed into something else entirely: a Frankenstein's monster of music, hog roast, talent show and now a massive cream tea extravaganza put on by Patsy Penhalligan who was not to be outdone by Chris the Cod and his chip van or the Pollards and their quad transport. Whatever one villager wanted to do for Alice, there was another determined to top it and there was no knowing where their competitiveness was going to end. Frankenwedding was a far better description than wonderful blend, thought Jules despairingly, as she deleted her only line before shutting the laptop lid with a frustrated thud.

It was starting to feel as though all areas of her life were slipping out of control. She was just about clinging on by her fingertips and even that was debatable.

"Is this about surrendering, Lord?" Jules said out loud. "Is that what I need to learn?"

But St Wenn's was quiet and her only reply was the stillness of centuries and the creaking of the ancient building. The setting sunshine streamed through the vestry window, bathing her desk in gold, and the scent of newly mown grass filled the place. Somewhere a woodpigeon called and in direct contrast to the churning sensation in Jules's stomach, all was peaceful at St Wenn's. It was as though she was being told to just trust and let things be.

But Jules, like most people, wasn't very good at doing this. Instead, she was fretting and worrying, chewing at her nails until they were worn down again, and comfort eating far too many custard creams. Nails and waistline wrecked, it was only a matter of time before her own wedding was ruined too, she thought sadly. How on earth was she going to break the news to Danny? He'd be heartbroken that she wasn't choosing to go to London with him. She gnawed at the nail of her index finger, lost in gloomy thoughts about what this might mean for their relationship and their future together. She knew only too well from her pastoral work just how much hard work marriage could be at the best of times and when a couple spent all their time together, so what chance did they stand of making it work if they were hundreds of miles apart? Did this mean that marriage wasn't the right step for them after all?

Jules couldn't believe this was the case. She loved Danny with all her heart and she knew he loved her too. They were made for one another and the blessings that had flowed into her life since they had met were simply too many to count. She knew he felt the same way because he told her so all the time. They were stronger together, happier together and a great team too. Why would God have brought them together only for them to have to part again? Jules believed He had a plan for her, indeed for everyone, but if this one went the way she feared it might, then it seriously sucked.

"Oh, Lord, why couldn't your plan be for me to be desperate to go to London and for everything to work out?" Jules asked her Boss for the one millionth time. "Wouldn't that have made more sense? There's lots of need in the city. It would have been a no-brainer! What do you want me to do? Why do you want me to stay?"

She waited a moment in case there was a booming voice from above or the spider plant burst into flames (unlike Moses, Jules didn't have any undergrowth conveniently to hand inside St Wenn's), but there was nothing. No obvious direction. No simple solutions. No clear sign. Only a very difficult conversation lying ahead and one she knew there was no avoiding. It was best she got it over and done with.

Jules checked her watch. Half past eight on Sunday evening. She'd been staring at her laptop for almost half an hour and to no avail. If she carried on like this, the newsletter would never get written, she'd gnaw her nails all the way to her elbows and eat her own body weight in biscuits. She needed to go and see Danny and tell him her decision. They told one another everything and were best friends with no secrets, so keeping this from him was eating her up inside.

She stood up and gathered up her jacket from the back of her chair. There was no time like the present. Danny had already texted to say he was back safely from London and wanted to catch up with her. As she locked the vestry and walked through the church, Jules felt even worse because he'd probably found their dream flat and couldn't wait to tell her. He'd be in the kitchen telling Alice and Morgan all about it and making excited plans for the next stage of their lives. It was truly awful knowing she was about to burst his bubble, shatter his dreams and a million other clichéd sayings which basically meant ruin everything.

The walk to Seaspray was always beautiful and never more so than in the midsummer when the warm days seemed to melt into one another in a hazy blur and the air was still. By the time Jules reached the house, twilight's watercolour wash was painting the world in evening hues as dusk came billowing in across the bay. The garden was filled with the scents of lavender, rosemary and jasmine, whose sweet top notes were carried upon the soft breeze. As Jules climbed the path to the house, the perfumes lightened her heavy heart, as did simply being at Seaspray, somewhere she had come to see as her second home. Jules really hoped this wasn't about to change.

It was strange how you could feel at peace in some places. Seaspray was a mother; it reached out to gather you close and there was a wonderful comforting energy to the house. The kitchen truly was the heart of the home, a hub of chatter and laughter and warmth, presided over by Alice who was forever making tea and producing wonderful cakes from the Aga. The room was filled with clutter too; paintings with curling edges were pinned to cupboards – treasured works of art sploshed decades ago, cookery books were piled on the window sills, postcards were Blu Tacked to the fridge or held on by colourful magnets, candles were wedged into empty wine bottles and herbs hung from the saucepan racks. Usually Alice was somewhere to be found, or Jonny would be sitting on the battered sofa with a cat on his lap and a book in his hand, but today only Morgan was present and, judging by the books spread out on the kitchen table, stuck into his homework.

"Dad's talking to Mum on the phone," he said, barely glancing up. "She says I can stay tonight if I like since he's been away all weekend."

"Cool," said Jules. She sat down next to him. "It'll be good to catch up with Dad and hear if he's found anywhere to live, won't it?"

Morgan ignored this. He was staring down at his exercise book. Maths, Jules observed, and even at his level probably way beyond her. Possibly a little beyond Morgan too if all the crossings out and the hard pressing down of his pen were anything to judge by. He was working hard on something. Tess must have the patience of a saint to decipher such scrawl!

"Mum says I need to make the most of Dad still being here," Morgan said eventually. "I won't see him so much when he's in London. It's two hundred and thirty-one point eight miles from Polwenna Bay to Ealing. Fact."

Jules wondered what the fact was. The exact distance or that Morgan wouldn't see so much of his father once Dan lived in London? That was certainly a fact, as much as Danny might try and protest otherwise; distance and time made it so and Jules's heart was granite heavy as the reality of what lay ahead sank in.

"Dad will be down to see you all the time and you'll spend a lot of time staying with him. It'll be great fun," she offered, but even to her own ears this sounded rather lame. How could seeing Danny at weekends or in school holidays compare to seeing him every day? Jules could only guess how Morgan would be feeling about this impending change to his routine, and Tess had mentioned several times that he was agitated and unsettled at school. She felt agitated and unsettled too and, unthinkingly, she started to chew her thumbnail.

Morgan looked up. "Aren't you going too?"

"What makes you say that?" Jules asked, jolted. Did she have a sign floating above her head or something?

"You said I would have fun staying with him. You didn't say with us. Don't you want to go too?"

Morgan was too sharp sometimes.

"It's complicated, Morgan," Jules said.

"Why is it? You go to London or you don't go. Fact."

"Well, yes," Jules conceded since it was a fair point. "But sometimes it isn't that easy."

Morgan put down his pen and frowned. "Why not?"

Where did she begin?

"Well, sometimes you want to do something, but you know that it won't be the right thing so you have to choose to do something different. Like you might want to eat chocolate for breakfast, lunch and supper, but you know it isn't really a good idea. It might make you happy at first, but in the end it will make you very sad."

As parables went, this was hardly up there with the Good Samaritan and the Lost Sheep. No wonder Morgan was confused.

"Eating chocolate all day would be silly. You'd be very sick."

You certainly would, and Jules should know since every Easter she gave this particular diet a very good try.

"I'm not really talking about chocolate, Morgan. What I'm trying to say is that sometimes you want to do things very much, but you can't do them because you know they're not the right thing to do. That's what I meant."

Morgan stared at her for a moment before returning his attention back to his exercise book.

"Grown-ups are so weird," he said. "Fact."

They certainly were, Jules thought. Even trying to explain her dilemma in simple terms was confusing, so no wonder poor Morgan was struggling with it all. If in doubt, make tea, Jules decided. Putting the kettle on and fetching mugs was a good distraction, and by the time she'd filled the teapot, Danny had finished his call and joined them. He looked tired and he'd lost weight too. All this commuting up and down to the city was exhausting him. As he folded her into a hug, Jules leaned against him and breathed in his delicious scent of spicy aftershave and pure Danny, and felt something deep inside unwind. When she was with Dan, everything always felt so right. Surely it couldn't be that they would split up?

"This is a nice surprise," Danny said.

"The tea?"

He kissed her nose. "Seeing you, of course, although tea's great. I was going to pop over to the Rectory."

"You've travelled enough for one day, so I've come to you," said Jules. "You must be exhausted."

Dan yawned. "You're not kidding there. I think I'll be seeing railway tracks in my sleep."

"Can I stay the night, Dad? Can I? Can I?" demanded Morgan.

"Yes, Mum says that's fine, but only if you go to bed by half nine," Danny told him. "Scoot up now, mate, and get your pyjamas on and brush your teeth. I'll come up and read to you in a bit, okay?"

Morgan punched the air and leapt down from the table.

"Yes!" Pausing in the doorway, he added, "Can I stay here every day until you go to London? Please?"

Jules felt Danny tense. "I think Mum would miss you far too much for that, mate."

Morgan shrugged. "I know, but she'll see me every day when you've gone and most of the weekends too. The days I am here now will add up to equal those she gets when you move. I've been doing sums in my book to work it out and percentages too. I can even make a graph if you like?"

Danny swallowed. "No, mate. You're all right. It's a clever idea, and I bet the maths is brilliant too, but I don't think Mum will like it much."

Morgan looked right at Jules. "Sometimes grown-ups have to do things they don't like. Fact."

Then with this parting comment he was gone, leaving Jules and Danny staring after him, floored.

"What," said Danny, "was all that about?"

Jules sighed. "Me messing up. I was trying to explain something to him, but I didn't do a very good job."

"Sounds to me as though you did a really good job. Grown-ups are always having to do things they don't like. Fact! And, Jules, I'm afraid that

I'm going to have to do just that right now. There's something I need to say to you."

Jules felt her legs turn to water. It was time that she took her own advice, sat down with the man she loved and told him the truth. She needed his support, his love and his strength to help her stand firm in her choice, even though asking him to do so was going to be so hard.

"And I need to talk to you too, Danny."

He gave her a searching look. "That sounds ominous. Let's go to the sitting room. We can talk there without any of the others barging in."

The sitting room connoted seriousness and something out of the ordinary. Tea in hand and her stomach in knots, Jules followed Dan down the passageway and into the large oak-panelled room with its comfy sofas, blue velvet curtains and views over the bay.

"Were any of the flats good?" she asked as they sat down. She was making small talk because what she wanted to say was all clogged up in her throat and as much as she wanted to shove the words out, they seemed to stick. Jules was afraid, afraid that once the words were spoken and out in the world, she would lose Danny forever. But if she didn't speak, she would lose her integrity. She had to tell him. Now.

She took a deep breath, but just as she was about to speak, Danny, who was pacing the room, stopped and turned to face her.

"I'm really sorry, but there's something I need to say right now and I'm sorry because I should have told you earlier except I've been too much of a coward."

"You could never be a coward, Danny!" Jules said fiercely. "You're the bravest person I know. You've been in combat."

He laughed harshly. "It's different in a war zone. Trust me, this is way harder so I'll just come out with it. Jules, I haven't found us a flat. I'm afraid I cancelled all this weekend's viewings."

She sat bolt upright. "What? Why?"

There was silence. Then Danny exhaled slowly and came to sit beside her. His entire body slumped into the sofa and he looked utterly defeated.

"Because my heart isn't in it, Jules. I just couldn't bring myself to go through the motions."

Jules stared at him. "I don't understand."

He swallowed. "I know that I'm going to really disappoint you now, and believe me, that's the last thing I would ever want to do, especially when I know how excited you are about moving to London, but I can't do it. I just can't. I thought it was what I wanted and it felt like the right thing to do, but as the time gets closer, I just know that I don't want to leave. No matter how much I love the army and how much I've missed being a part of it, I can't bring myself to leave Polwenna. I've spent all weekend trying to decide what to do, but in the end, I knew there was only one thing I could do – tell you the truth. The answer became quite clear on Saturday morning when I was sitting outside yet another flat and literally counting down the hours until I came home."

Saturday morning. Just when she had been about to see the Bishop...

All of a sudden, Jules understood exactly why she'd not had the answers to her prayers she'd been looking for. She'd been looking for all the wrong answers when her Boss had been giving her the right ones all the time!

Whoever said God didn't have a sense of humour?

"You don't want to move to London, Danny?"

"No. I don't." Dan was emphatic. He took her hand and squeezed it as he spoke, so tightly it hurt – not that Jules cared about that. She only cared about what he was now telling her and in a torrent of words that must have been dammed up inside him for longer than she could have ever guessed. "I really don't. I know it would have been exciting and a whole new adventure for us and a great career move for me and given you all kinds of new avenues as a pastor too... Oh, Jules, I know that on paper it all makes perfect sense, but in here..." Still holding her hand, he pressed it against his chest and Jules could feel the racing of his heart beneath his tee shirt. "I just can't feel it in here. I'd miss Morgan dreadfully, and home and my family. I came so close to losing them before and I can't let that happen again, even if it means turning down wonderful new opportunities. I don't want to live in a crowded city where nobody knows us. I want to live in a place where I'm part of a community and where people care about each other. Where the air is fresh and there are open spaces. Where nobody gives a damn what I look like or that I limp. I want to live somewhere where people know my family and who I am and where I know the names of my neighbours. Where I can name all the boats and the cottages and even the bloody seagulls if I have to! My roots are in Polwenna Bay, Jules, and I love it here. I'm sorry that it's not exciting or glamorous or exotic, but it's where I want to be. I love this place more than any glittering career."

"It's home," Jules said softly. Tears were prickling her eyes.

"It is," Danny agreed, his voice hoarse with emotion. "So I spoke to my superior on Saturday afternoon and I told him as grateful as I am for the chance of a second career in the army, my son and my family have to take priority. I can't leave them behind, no matter how much I love the army. I'm sorry, Jules, because I know I should have discussed this with you, but I simply couldn't wait. I just had the strongest feeling that this was the right thing to do. Can you ever forgive me? Can you still love me after letting you down like this?"

She threw her arms around him and hugged him tightly. "Oh, Danny! There's absolutely nothing to forgive. Do you hear me? Nothing! And you haven't let me down. You never could. Of course I still love you! I couldn't stop if I tried." Jules was half laughing and half sobbing with relief and happiness and the pure joy of knowing her prayers had been heard, and answered, all along.

"And I love you," said Danny, burying his face in her hair. "So so much, Jules Mathieson, even if you are totally crazy."

"I'm the crazy one?" Jules had tears running down her cheeks now. "Me?"

"Yes, you! Why on earth are you laughing when I've just ruined everything you've been looking forward to? You're totally within your rights to throttle me!"

At this, Jules sat up and did her best to collect herself, hard to do when she was so overwhelmed with happiness and relief and gratitude. It was time she levelled with Danny.

"Ah. I think we need to have a bit of a chat about all that actually," she said. "The thing is, Dan, I don't want to move to London either. Not really. Not at all, if I'm honest. I've been doing my very best to support you with it, but tonight I was plucking up the courage to tell you the truth about how I really feel."

"You don't want to move to London? Really?"

"Really," said Jules. "I want to stay here in Polwenna Bay. I thought you were desperate to go."

"I was at first," he admitted. "It seemed like a great idea and I thought it was what I wanted, but as time went on I realised just how much I already had here."

"Me too!" Jules cried.

Now it was Danny's turn to laugh. He rained kisses down onto Jules's wet eyelids, cheeks and even the tip of her snub nose.

"So you've been encouraging me because you thought a move was what I wanted, while I've been doing exactly the same because I thought you were desperate for an inner city parish? We've both been trying to protect each other when really we both want to be here in Cornwall?"

"Sounds like it to me," Jules nodded, smiling up at him. "Maybe in the future we have a rule that we just tell each other the truth? It could save a lot of time and motorway miles!"

"Sounds like a deal to me. Unless it's about my cooking, of course, which we must all agree is brilliant."

"Hmm," said Jules. Danny could burn water. "Perhaps I'll rethink that rule? Your cooking is—"

To silence her, Danny kissed Jules soundly and she kissed him back, lightheaded with happiness and still giggling at the craziness of the entire situation. There were so many lessons to be learned from all this that she didn't know where to start. Jules guessed it was one to talk to her Boss about later, that was for sure. She really should know from all her study of the scriptures that a life lived doing His will was one crazy ride. Being eaten by whales, thrown in a lions' den, building an ark – it was all in the job description. Perhaps her non-move to London should be added to the list?

"What are you thinking about now?" Danny asked.

"That Morgan was absolutely right," Jules said. "Grown-ups are weird. Fact!"

Ruth Saberton

CHAPTER THIRTY

Tess always loved the summer term. The warm weather meant the children could enjoy PE outside and play on the field at break times, which they thought a real treat, and she could take them to the beach for nature walks or creative writing activities. After-school clubs felt far less exhausting when the sun was shining outside, and getting up early for a run was a joy when the sky was already blue and the air sweet with warmth. The days always flew by in a flurry of trips out, assessments and end-of-year activities, yet even so, Tess couldn't remember a summer term racing past like this one.

Wherever had the time gone? It seemed to Tess that it had vanished as though conjured away by a magician; one moment she was in the garden at Polwenna Manor, kissing Zak beneath the star-freckled sky and with acres of time until Alice's wedding, and the next they were only days away from the big event itself. Time was in fast-forward mode, that was for sure. How was it possible that it was now mid-June?

Tess knew the answer; happiness was giving time wings and she was floating through the days in a haze of joy. When she wasn't at work or engrossed in her planning, Tess was spending every spare moment with Zak Tremaine. They walked across the cliffs, whiled away long, light evenings with beachcombing and, best of all, hid away at her cottage where they cooked dinner together and talked until the light faded, when the sleepy seagulls tucked their heads beneath their wings and the hot air balloon moon rose over the village.

Tess had never known anything like this absolute affinity with Zak. They never ran out of things to talk about and as each day passed, they discovered that they had more and more in common. How a man who, on paper, was so totally wrong for her could turn out to be so right was a mystery, but not one she felt inclined to question. Instead, Tess chose to view it as a wonderful surprise, and if she needed any confirmation other than her heart, then the return of her love for music told Tess all she needed to know. It made no sense and it wasn't something she'd sought out, but being with Zak was totally and utterly right. Tess woke up smiling every day just with the pure joy of being alive in a world that had Zak Tremaine in it. Even when they were apart, his bright image walked through the silent rooms of her mind, and when their eyes met at a festival meeting or across the pub, they spoke volumes in a silent and secret language only they understood.

Tess knew she could trust herself this time.

She also still couldn't believe how, after years without playing a note, she was hardly able to tear herself away from her violin. Tess's love of music had returned in a torrent and she played and played and played. She didn't think she could stop even if she tried. Zak would listen, leaning forward on the sofa and watching with an intensity that made her heart quiver. He was playing and writing too, but unlike Tess, and rather ironically given the career he'd chosen, Zak was intensely private when it came to his own music.

"I guess I'm just shy," he'd offered when Tess asked why he didn't bring his guitar up to her cottage. She'd thought it might be fun to play together, but Zak was horrified.

"Shy?" she'd echoed. "You play to huge audiences, Mr Rock Star!"

"Mr ex-Rock Star, actually. I'm a gardener now, remember? Just ask Perry."

"You'll have to come up with a better excuse than that," Tess said.

"Excuse? That's a very valid reason! Those salad greens rely on me," Zak had replied, pulling an outraged face.

Tess's answer was to make a clucking sound and mime wings and so he'd dived for her and tickled her until she'd begged for mercy. Then he'd kissed her and they'd forgotten all about music for quite some time...

"The thing is, it's totally different playing to an audience," Zak had tried to explain later on when they lay wrapped in one another's arms and watching the velvet night sink over the village. "There's a kind of anonymity to it, but when there's someone there you really care about, and whose opinion means the world, it's absolutely terrifying. You don't want to let them down or disappoint them."

Tess had nodded and held him tightly. After all, who understood this better than she did? Vassilly's expression of scorn couldn't have hurt more if he'd plunged a knife right into her heart. No wonder it became impossible to play after that. Every time she had reached for her violin, she saw again the look of utter contempt on his cold and beautiful face and felt once again the sting of failure. It had been less painful to put music aside than to relive those emotions each time she opened her violin case.

"I will play for you," Zak had whispered, tracing the curve of her shoulder with his lips and looking up at her with eyes turned indigo by the darkness, "and soon too. I've almost written Granny's special song and once it's finished, and I'm happy I'm not about to totally embarrass myself in front of a real musician, you'll be the first to hear it."

And with this, Tess knew she had to be content.

In any case, hearing him play or not, Tess had spent the past weeks with a permanent smile on her face. This unexpected thing that was happening between them – 'thing' being the only word she could come up with since 'relationship' sounded very serious and 'fling' too casual for something which felt so significant – had sprinkled her world with magic dust. Every day, she awoke with that delicious tingly sense of anticipation which felt as though Christmas had arrived early. Everything in her world felt special now, from making tea to cooking supper to simply chatting as they walked along the seashore. Tess found it hard to believe how everything could look the same and yet feel so different, and it was wonderful. She hadn't planned on finding romance. In fact, she hadn't planned on Zak Tremaine at all, but now that she had found him, Tess knew life was never going to look the same again. Everything had changed.

Was there a future with Zak? Did she even want a future with him? Tess wasn't sure what the answers were to these questions, but she wasn't fretting about what would happen next; instinct told her that it would evolve naturally. She would enjoy every moment and turn her boat downstream to see where life took them. Everything inside Tess told her that a wonderful adventure lay ahead. Her bitterness towards Vass had vanished and she felt compassion rather than anger towards her naïve eighteen-year-old self. Suddenly there was more in her life than relentlessly pursuing her career, but rather than finding that this was detrimental to her teaching, Tess was discovering happiness made her a better practitioner in the classroom. Bathed in a warm glow of contentment, she was more relaxed, and everything she did, from the mid-term assessments to practising for the summer concert, seemed to flow effortlessly. If the children commented that she was smiling a lot more too, then that could only be a good thing!

"So is it love?" Tara Tremaine teased when she collected Morgan from school.

Tess blushed. "Don't be silly."

"I'm not being silly! You look so happy and, according to my son, Zak has a grin like a Cheshire cat too. Fact!"

"I do not have a grin like a Cheshire cat!" Tess had protested, but later that day she'd caught a glimpse of her reflection in the classroom window and realised that her friend was right. There was nothing she could do though; Tess simply couldn't stop smiling. This felt like the start of something wonderful and she wasn't going to question it or try to suppress it. The truth was that she couldn't have done so even if she'd tried.

Zak was adamant that he wanted to stay in Polwenna Bay, that he was finished with trying to make it as a professional musician, but Tess knew he was far too talented to spend the rest of his days working in Perry's garden. At some point he would want to share his talent again and it was only right that he should do so. But when that time came, would he want Tess to go with him? And would she want to? Committed to her teaching job and her life in the village, Tess had loved putting down roots in Cornwall. She had no burning desire to travel the world as part of a star's entourage and neither did she wish to be the partner who was left behind to hold the fort. No, thank you. She'd seen from her parents' marriage just how high the cost of this lifestyle could be. There were many questions that would need to be answered, the first one being whether a quiet life here with her in Cornwall was what Zak really wanted? Or was it just what he wanted for now? How serious was he?

Tess knew she was racing ahead. Zak hadn't made her any promises, not verbally anyway, although his kisses had spoken volumes and his every touch was filled with tenderness. Although they'd not yet spent a whole night together, Tess knew there was no need to rush. This was something life-changing and they both knew it. Questioning it or worrying wasn't necessary and things would unfold the way they were meant to. Take the festival, for example, which had started off as such a drama, almost fated to be cancelled, and had seemed so much work when Jules had talked her into helping. Yet somehow it had morphed into a musical celebration with all the villagers coming together to help. If Tess had ever needed an example of trusting the Universe, as Silver Starr might put it, and allowing things to take their natural course, then here it was. If she just went with her heart and allowed things to fall into place, maybe all would be well.

She'd laughed out loud at this. Going with your heart and allowing things to fall into place were not usually expressions that the super-organised – and, if she was honest, slightly neurotic – Tess Hamilton would use! She was well known for planning everything, from her weekly shop to her schemes of work, with military precision. What had Zak done to her? At this rate, she would soon stop colour co-ordinating her sock drawer or arranging the tins in her food cupboard so that the labels all faced the front!

These were some of the thoughts running through Tess's mind on the Sunday before Alice and Jonny's wedding. Up at first light, the world beyond her bedroom window was breathless with the promise of another beautiful day, and with under a week to go until the big day, she ought to be driving herself insane checking details and racing about doing errands rather than wandering downstairs to drink coffee in her small garden and watch the sun rise over the rooftops. Even the seagulls were yawning at this time of day.

Not Tess. She was filled with energy and could hardly sit still. Nothing could quash this surge of happiness either. When Miss Powell, the ancient and very crotchety head teacher had reprimanded Tess for spending too much of the budget on reward stickers, Tess had simply apologised and offered to pay for them herself, a feat little short of miraculous seeing as usually she wanted to throttle the bloody woman. Even when her father had phoned, making the usual thinly veiled digs about how she was wasting her time and talent teaching in a rural backwater, Tess wasn't downhearted. David Hamilton had no idea just how happy she was or even what it was like to feel like this. Rather than being hurt by his comments, the barbed words slipped from her like seawater from a seagull's feathers and Tess had actually felt rather sorry for her father. In fact, she felt sorry for anyone who didn't feel as happy as she was.

Tess rinsed her coffee cup under the kitchen tap and left it to drain. She was due to meet Zak at the beach café for breakfast in an hour's time, but she was buzzing with energy and there were only so many times you could walk around a small cottage. The adjacent properties were currently occupied by holidaymakers who probably wouldn't appreciate a spot of early-morning Vivaldi, so playing her violin was out of the question. Tess decided she'd walk down into the village and make the most of the empty streets and the quiet shops before the tide of day trippers swept through. Maybe she would go for a short run along the cliff path while it was still free of hikers and people setting up picnics? Already there was heat in the morning sunshine and the cloudless sky promised yet another stunning day which would bring visitors flocking to the coast. The tripping boats would be busy, Patsy would be baking as many pasties as her ovens could hold and Chris the Cod would be laughing all the way to the bank. The Cornish winter could be long and lean, and the people of Polwenna Bay had learned to make the most of every day which the summer offered. So far, this year's season was looking promising and, like all the locals, Tess was hoping very hard that the weather held. Alice's wedding would be wonderful if it did.

The walk down the hill never took long, and even with a few pauses to admire the view, Tess was soon in the main street. Already a few early-bird tourists were wandering through the street all set for a spot of low-tide rock pooling as the children swung brightly coloured buckets and the fathers brandished pristine fishing nets. Tess smiled to see them. How she and Chloe would have loved such a holiday when they were children. Polwenna Bay with its sandy beach, diet of chips and ice cream and days spent building sandcastles and scrabbling over the rocks to go crabbing would have been utter bliss. Even the sting of sunburn or the inevitable pouring rain wouldn't have mattered because it would have been such an adventure, but Tess's parents had more sophisticated tastes. Prague and Rome and Budapest were their destinations of choice, holidays mostly tied in with rehearsals and the endless shopping trips that Tess's mother employed to plug the empty gaps in her marriage. Maybe this was another reason she had avoided relationships for so long, Tess wondered? Vass was just a symptom, another reason to steer clear of commitment and music. The two had been long entwined in her mind and the disappointment and resentment which characterised the Hamiltons' marriage was hardly a good advert for the institution.

But there were good marriages too, Tess reflected as she headed towards the village shop. Look at Kat and Alex, for instance; they seemed blissfully content, as did Ashley and Mo in their own unique spiky and squabbly manner, and the soon-to-be-married Jonny and Alice were wrapped up in each other and bright with happiness. Marriage wasn't all bad and maybe...

Whoa! Tess slammed on her mental brakes, shocked at herself. Was she seriously thinking about marriage? That was ridiculous! She'd only been seeing Zak a few weeks! It was far too soon to think about marriage.

But even so...

Half horrified and half intrigued by her musings, Tess stepped into the village shop to buy some water to take up onto the cliffs. As always, Keyhole Kathy was behind the counter and holding court to a bunch of customers. Tess grabbed an Evian and made her way to the till, but, deeply engrossed in one of the Sunday tabloids, none of the locals glanced her way.

"It says here that they were all taking drugs," Keyhole Kathy breathed, her beady eyes firmly glued to the text as her finger prodded the paper. "They were all as high as kites, according to witnesses."

Penny Kussell's head was obscuring her view, so Tess had no idea what they were looking at, but everyone was certainly riveted. She sighed and shifted from one trainer-shod foot to the other, knowing she'd be waiting a while to be served at this rate.

"So was she taking drugs too?" Penny breathed.

"According to the papers, she was out of her head. It's all here and several anonymous sources say her crowd are well known for being party animals. But what would you expect from those types?" said Keyhole Kathy.

There was much nodding and murmurs of agreement.

"Too much money, that's the trouble. As the Bible says, money is the root of all evil," tutted Sheila Keverne sanctimoniously.

Personally, Tess thought gossiping old biddies were the root of all evil. They certainly were in Polwenna Bay. Whatever red-top exposé they were reading today was certainly proving them all with a great morning's entertainment and she felt rather sorry for the unfortunate celebrity they were pulling apart.

"I wouldn't mind giving being a pop star a try," said Mandy, The Ship's barmaid. "I'd love to be rich and get to wear all those clothes and go to swanky parties. She even got to meet One Direction too, lucky cow."

"Kellee always seemed such a nice girl. I loved watching her on UK's Most Talented. What a shame that she was led astray," sighed Sheila. "Satan is so pervasive."

"I think we all know who else was there helping lead her astray, don't we?" said Kathy. "Who came back here as fast as his legs could carry him and has been hiding away ever since? I knew something was fishy about that! Alice won't say a word about it, but who would throw away being a big music star unless there was a reason? Maybe he didn't leave of his own accord? Perhaps he was fired?"

There was a collective intake of breath as Keyhole Kathy paused for emphasis. Tess found she was holding her breath too and her stomach tightened because she could guess who it was that the shopkeeper was alluding to now.

"Do you mean Zak Tremaine?" asked Kursa Penwarren.

"Mo never mentioned that," Penny said.

"And neither did Alice," added Sheila with a frown.

Kathy regarded them all as though they were stupid.

"Well, of course they didn't mention it. It's hardly something to brag about, is it? But now it all makes sense. That's definitely Zak in the picture. I'd recognise him anywhere with all that hair. He needs a trip to see you at Kosi Kuts, Kursa."

They all leaned forward to confer.

"It does look a bit like him, I must admit," Sheila admitted.

"So they went into the party together, but Kellee never left. Now tell me if that isn't fishy?" continued Kathy, the bit firmly between her teeth now. "I'm telling you, Zak Tremaine's come scuttling home because he's up to his neck in it. Alice has been very odd lately too; she's hardly had time for anyone."

"She's getting married and she's had a lot to do," pointed out Penny, but everyone else ignored her. The last thing they wanted to hear was reason.

"Do you think he's on drugs?" whispered Sheila, her hand pressed against her heart.

"I expect Zak was sent back to Seaspray by the record company to go cold turkey," said Kathy knowledgeably, although the closest she came to this was slicing chicken roll at the deli counter.

There was a collective gasp and Tess would have laughed at the idea of Zak doing a Trainspotting-style detox up in his attic if the gossip hadn't been so hurtful. She knew just how much he'd agonised over what had taken place in London and how terribly disillusioned he was, disillusioned to the point where he hadn't been able to think of much else or even lose himself in the solace of his music. To hear Zak's private pain dissected for the amusement of Sheila and her cronies was more than Tess could stand.

There was a sharp crack, as loud as a pistol shot. The gathered women spun around. In an unconscious attempt to keep control, Tess realised she had gripped the bottle of water so hard that it split. Icy mineral water gushed everywhere, but didn't cool Tess's red-hot fury.

"How dare you say such unkind things!" Tess said in a low but deadly tone which silenced assembly halls, difficult colleagues and naughty nine-year-olds alike. "You should be utterly ashamed of yourselves spreading such vicious gossip!"

"We were only reading the paper, and having a chat," Kathy began, but her words were like a match to touch paper and Tess exploded.

"A chat? Is that what you call it? I don't suppose any of you would have the courage to actually have this chat if Alice or Zak were present. I know;

why don't I accompany you up to Seaspray right now and you can ask them yourselves what really happened. Who's up for that? Anyone?"

There was deathly silence. Nobody could look Tess in the eye.

"I thought not. Bullies never like to face up to what they're doing. All of you ought to be thoroughly ashamed." Scorn dripped from her words like the water was dripping from the split bottle.

"We're not bullies! We were just talking," muttered Mandy, even her badly dyed hair looking sullen. "And anyway, it is weird that Zak's come back, because he couldn't wait to get out of here and be a big shot. And now he's working in Perry's garden? It doesn't make sense."

Kathy Polmartin nodded. "You're an incomer, so you don't know him like we do. He's always been... wild."

"I might not have lived here for six generations, but I know enough to tell you that what you were saying is a pack of lies! Zak had nothing to do with any of this! He's a good person!" Tess cried.

"You have to say that seeing as you're shagging him!" Mandy shot back. "Don't deny it. We all know. He sleeps with everyone, so it was only a matter of time. Well, I don't suppose you'd be quite so keen on good old Zak Tremaine if you knew he only shagged you for a bet."

"Shut up, Mandy!" hissed Penny.

Tess felt as though she had been punched in the stomach. Hard.

"What?"

"It's true," Mandy said with a careless shrug. "I was working that night and they were all at the bar getting pissed, so I heard every word. Bobby Penhalligan told me about it too. They made a bet with Zak that he could sleep with anyone and you were the challenge. 'Ice maiden', that's what he called you. Ask him yourself if you don't believe me."

The shop was swooping and dipping around Tess and there was a horrible whooshing sound in her ears. For an awful moment, she thought she might pass out right there in the middle of the shop.

She had to get outside.

With the split bottle still clutched in her hand, Tess stumbled into the street. She was icy cold all over and shaking, and the warmth of the bright sunshine felt like a shock. For a moment she sagged against the wall of the shop, the rough Cornish ripple stonework rough against her cheek, but this harsh sensation was almost welcome and far preferable to the acid sting to the soul caused by Mandy's words.

He only shagged you for a bet.

That wasn't true! It couldn't be true! Zak would never speak about her that way and he could never be so cruel. What they shared went deeper than the physical; it was a true meeting of hearts and minds and Tess had never, ever known anything like it. The very thought that it might not mean the same to Zak was unbearable and the notion that she could have been deluding herself beyond painful. Surely it couldn't be possible that all the time she had believed they were falling in love, he was laughing at her behind her back? Tess wouldn't – couldn't – believe it.

Yet in the back of her mind, a memory was swimming up to the surface – a distant and murky one, yet a memory all the same. It was a recollection of being in the pub and chatting to Tara, while conscious that Zak, with his face of a fallen angel, was watching her from across the bar. She'd hardly been able to focus on their conversation, so much so that Tara had noticed and teased her about it. Tess seemed to recall Zak had been with Nick and Bobby and the rest of their crowd that evening. Had they been making the bet? Was all this really just a game to him? If so, Tess wanted to curl up and shrink away. If she had ever believed that Vass had hurt her, it was nothing, nothing, compared to this. This was a pain like no other.

Tess had to see Zak. She had to find out the truth.

Somehow she stumbled her way through the narrow streets, across the bridge and into the beach café. When she spotted Zak already sitting at one of the tables, all Tess wanted to do was hurl herself into his arms, bury her face in his chest and let being close make everything all right – a bitter irony when it could be him who'd made everything so totally and utterly wrong.

"Tess! You're early. Brilliant!" Zak half rose in that old-fashioned and polite way of his that always made her melt. He pushed his shades up into this thick blonde hair and beamed at her. When she didn't smile back, confusion settled over his features like clouds suppressing sparkles on the dancing waves.

"Is everything all right?"

Tess had to know straight away. There was no way she could sit down and go through the farce of having coffee and croissants before she said anything. She would choke on it all anyway.

"Did you make a bet that you could sleep with me?" she demanded, her voice shaking.

There was no need for Zak to answer because the look of horror on his face told Tess everything she needed to know. If he'd been a child in her class, she would have said he was totally and utterly busted, but since he was the man she had been falling in love with, the man she had started to believe was the other half of her soul and the one person she trusted above all others, Tess took no pleasure in catching him out. With just that one guilty look, he'd destroyed everything – her faith in him, her trust in her own judgement and the joy in everything around her.

He'd been laughing at her all along.

Tess turned on her heel and, with her head held high and her heart breaking, walked away.

Ruth Saberton

CHAPTER THIRTY-ONE

"Tess! Please! Let me explain!"

Tess was almost past the marina by the time Zak had caught up. Anger and hurt, coupled with the urgency to put as much space between them as possible, had given her a turn of speed which even years of running couldn't take credit for.

She spun around to face him. Anger made her savage.

"What is there to explain? You bragged about being able to sleep with anyone you chose and picked me as the challenge, didn't you?"

Zak's blue eyes were wild with emotion. "No! Of course not! That wasn't it at all."

Tess made a noise halfway between a snort and a sob.

"Please don't take me for even more of a fool. It seems that the whole village knows about your bet to 'shag' me as Mandy so nicely put it."

"It wasn't like that, Tess. I swear I never said that. There was just some stupid throwaway comment made when the lads had a bit too much to drink. I can't even remember what they did say. I was totally hammered that night."

"You could always just ask Bobby or Mandy," Tess suggested icily. "They seem to know all the details." Her heart lurched and she blinked scalding tears away. "How could you do that? I thought we had something special."

"We did! We do! Please, Tess!" Zak stepped forward as though about to take her in his arms, but Tess recoiled, holding up her hands to ward him off.

"Don't touch me!" Tess yelled. "You must have really felt like the big man when I was stupid enough to fall for it. How much did you win? Or was it just an alpha male thing? Wow, they must all really look up to you now. You must be quite the man."

Zak looked stricken.

"Tess, whatever you think of me right now, I promise I would never, ever do that to you."

"Oh, really? Bobby Penhalligan's told everyone something very different."

"It wasn't like that! You have to believe me. Tess, it was just drunken lad talk, and I swear to God I wasn't even involved. I was so drunk that night, I could hardly see straight."

"Oh well, that's all right then. If you were drunk, it excuses everything," said Tess bitterly.

Zak ran a hand through his thick blonde hair, the same hair that in another lifetime she had loved to run her hands through.

"It was just stupid pub talk and I'm sorry I was ever a part of it, but you have to believe me when I tell you that I had absolutely no intention of ever getting involved with you. You'd already made it more than clear at Ashley and Mo's that you didn't have time for me."

Tess wished now that she'd stuck to her first instincts.

"But then we ended up working together on the festival and I saw a whole new side to you and I loved every moment we got to spend time together," Zak continued. "Bloody hell, Tess, I even found myself engineering meetings on the slightest of excuses just so I could see you. And the more time I spent with you, the more I ... I..."

"Thought you'd see if you could make an idiot of me? Win the bet?"

"No! Of course not!"

"See if you could prove yourself to your pathetic mates?"

"No," he said quietly. "Never. I just wanted to spend time with you and be your friend. I wanted to get to know you better."

"You certainly did that," Tess said. The misery in her voice was acid on her tongue and, unable to bear the sight of him any longer, she turned away.

Zak caught her arm.

"Tess! You mean everything to me!"

But Tess shook him off.

His touch appalled her because even in this hurt and angry state, being close to Zak Tremaine still filled her with longing. Her hormones needed to wise the hell up.

"Let go of me, Zak! Go and play your games with somebody else! I can't stand to be anywhere near you!"

Tess stormed away, blinded with tears. Somehow she managed to negotiate the warren of streets and weave her way through the tourists heading to the beach. Tears blurred the village into a Monet. Her chest was so tight with grief she thought she might explode.

This was all her own fault. Tess had nobody to blame but herself. She knew better than to trust a man. They always proved false in the end, so why on earth had she let herself believe that Zak Tremaine might be any different? Like a fool, she had let herself come close to falling in love again and with a man who was just as much a liar and a disappointment as Vassilly. Worse, really, since Vass had never pretended to be anything other than self-absorbed and single-minded – she'd just been too young to see him for what he was. She'd been Vassilly's passport to the next level of his career, and in a weird way Tess understood this, but with Zak she'd truly believed there was no hidden agenda. He'd got so close so fast and Tess had told him things about her past that she'd never shared with anyone else. She'd trusted him.

What was she meant to do now? Where did she go from here? They lived in a small village and were still involved with the festival. Avoiding one another would be difficult at best and impossible at worst. There would be no escaping bumping into him or hearing what he was up to or, a thought which made her feel physically ill, seeing him with the inevitable next girl.

Her phone buzzed in her pocket, but she didn't need to see the screen to know that it was Zak. Tess switched it off with trembling hands. She'd delete his number later. Block it if she had to. She'd put her violin away again too, because it was another link to him and what she'd thought her life could be. Tess thought she would leave the case on the shelf and just in the line of sight as a constant reminder to her that men and music were a very bad combination. Once the festival was over, she would have nothing more to do with music or Zak Tremaine.

That part of her life was well and truly over.

Zak was beside himself. He simply didn't know what to do. Tess wouldn't speak to him or let him explain. She'd simply walked away with her head held high and with a fury that had taken his breath away.

The speed of how fast everything had unravelled made Zak's head spin. One minute he was basking in the sunshine and looking forward to spending another day with Tess, the next she was shouting at him and accusing him of using her for a bet. Zak was totally floored because he would never have done something so crass, at least not now, although when he was a teenager it was the sort of stupid boast he and his mates always made. Who'd be first to pull the pretty holidaymaker staying at the campsite with her parents? Who could get to first base with her plainer friend? Who could kiss the most girls that summer? It was all immature teenage stuff and Zak wasn't proud of being part of it, but he would never treat Tess like that. No way! Zak knew he was beyond lucky that a woman like Tess would even give him the time of day. He might have been the village golden boy, in his youth anyway, but Tess was beautiful and talented and clever and kind, and just about any other positive adjective you might care to add to the list. She was everything – and more – that he had ever hoped to find in a girl.

And he'd utterly blown it.

Zak knew he would never forget the expression of pure scorn that twisted Tess's beautiful face when she'd confronted him. Each one of her scathing words were seared into his memory. Yet as painful as these things were, more unbearable still was when Zak imagined how Tess must be feeling, it was as though someone had kicked him in the stomach. He couldn't stand to think of her being unhappy, and knowing he was the cause was unbearable.

The irony was that, probably for the first time in his life when it came to a girl, Zak genuinely was telling the truth. He really couldn't remember exactly what had been said that night in the pub. He vaguely recalled a conversation about his legendary ability to pull any girl (grossly exaggerated and also not particularly difficult when you were the lead singer in a band performing in a small holiday town) and at the back of his memory, Zak seemed to remember something had been said about Tess, but these were the usual stupid bottom-of-a-pint-glass comments that he tended to ignore. Everyone knew that once Bobby and Joey and the rest of their crowd had a few, they turned into even more idiotic versions of themselves, and Zak was mortified to have been caught up in their stupid bar room bragging. He'd been a total idiot going drinking with them in the first place. Hadn't he learned anything from what had happened to Kellee?

He'd let Tess down. He was no better than that tosser of a music teacher who'd dicked her about all those years ago. Actually, he was worse, because Zak knew better than to treat a girl this way. He'd been raised by Alice and grown up with sisters, so knew that women were his equals, or – if Mo was to be listened to – his superiors, and he was better than this. He had to show Tess that she'd got it all wrong!

He pulled his phone out of his jeans pocket and dialled Tess, but inevitably the call went straight to voicemail. She'd probably switched her phone off or maybe she'd already blocked his number? Zak considered leaving a message explaining himself, but knew that Tess would only delete it and who could blame her? Instead, he sent a brief text asking her if they could talk. She'd probably ignore that too, but he had to try something. He wouldn't give up. He couldn't give up. Zak had to put this right. He couldn't lose Tess. She meant everything.

There had to be a way he could put this right.

Deep in thought, Zak walked along the quay. Think! He told himself. Think!

Since it was Sunday morning, the fishing boats were in, tied alongside the harbour wall and tugging at their moorings like restless horses. There was no sign of the Penhalligan brothers, which was lucky for them since Zak would have strangled them with his bare hands, but he spotted Nick striding towards him from the direction of the village. For once, his younger brother's usually sunny face was set in a scowl, and before Zak could register what was happening, Nick landed a bruising right hook to his chin.

"That's for Tess!" he hissed. "How could you, Zak? How could you?"

CHAPTER THIRTY-TWO

Zak staggered sideways into a net bin, literally knocked for six and clutching his throbbing jaw. It was lucky Nick was a good head smaller; otherwise Zak's nose would have been splattered across his face. Even so, his younger brother was strong from hours of hauling nets and lifting fish boxes and the power of the blow made Zak feel close to vomiting. A galaxy of stars spun before his eyes.

"What was that about?" he gasped as he clutched his face.

"You know exactly what!" Nick spat. "I've just come from the village shop and everyone's full of it."

"Full of what?" Zak asked, nursing his jaw. There was going to be a beauty of a bruise now and if it showed for the wedding Alice would go spare. She'd go spare anyway if she caught wind of this because she hated it when her grandsons scrapped.

"Of you saying that you shagged Tess for a bet," Nick hissed.

"What? Don't be stupid! Of course I didn't!"

His brother glared at him. "Of course you did, you mean. You never could resist a challenge. How could you, Zak? How could you do that to her? I made a stupid comment and I wish to God I hadn't."

Zak stared at his brother.

"Do you really think I'm that much of a bastard?"

Nick's face was twisted with misery.

"I was there that night. I bloody started it."

Like patchwork squares randomly stitched together by a crazy tailor, snatches of the evening had started to come back to Zak. Nick and the boys laughing, stupid comments whizzing them back to their teenage years more effectively than a time machine, the pathetic challenge and Nick's encouragement, followed by the lads' choice of Tess. Zak didn't recall much more than this, but he did remember Nick storming out and after that he'd got as drunk as he'd ever been in his life.

Which was saying something.

Nick was still glowering at him. "Couldn't you just have amused yourself with Mandy or some emmet looking for a holiday romance? Did you really have to make a fool of Tess?"

"Nick, I hardly remember anything about that night or the conversation. It's a total blur. What happened between Tess and me happened naturally. It had nothing to do with a bet. For God's sake! Of course it wasn't."

Nick regarded him through narrowed eyes. "Swear to God?"

"Yes, I swear to God!" said Zak. He felt the warm trickle of blood on his skin. "I like Tess very much and I was hoping it was going somewhere, and I still do if she'll only hear me out, which seems unlikely right now. She probably hates me and who can blame her? I've ruined the best thing that ever happened to me."

Nick stepped. "You really do like her, don't you?"

"Yes," said Zak bleakly. "I do." Oh, sod it. There was no point pretending. What did he have to lose by being proud since he'd already lost it all? "I'm in love with her, Nicky. Totally and utterly in love with her."

"Bloody hell," said Nick. "What a lash up."

Zak laughed bleakly. "Yeah. What a lash up."

The brothers stood in thoughtful silence. Eventually, Nick pointed to Zak's face.

"Maybe we should get some ice on that? It's going to swell."

Zak rubbed his jaw and winced. Yep. It was going to swell up an absolute treat.

"Sure you're not about to deck me again?"

"No," said Nick. He held up his hand which was also looking a little swollen. "Once is enough because it bloody hurt. I need ice too. Let's get some from the machine on the fish market."

"Granny's going to flip when she sees this," Nick remarked once they were inside the fish market and Zak was holding a bag of ice to his jaw.

"And if she finds out how I got it, then she'll really freak," said Zak.

Nick paled. "You're right. Don't grass me up, fam."

Zak shifted the bag and winced.

"What do I get in return for my silence? Your football stickers? Your skateboard? Anyway, someone's bound to have seen us. Granny probably already knows. It'll be on Facebook by now."

Nick sighed. "I'll tell her the truth."

"And what is the truth exactly?" Zak asked. "Why are you so angry about it? Do you still have feelings for Tess, Nick? If so, you should have said something. I would have backed off."

"Would you?"

Zak considered this for a moment and then shook his head.

"To be honest, I don't think I could have done that even if I'd wanted to. She's the one, Nick. I love her."

Zak's heart clenched with terror. What if Tess wouldn't forgive him and never wanted to see him again? How could he live with that? Spending the rest of his life knowing that he had lost something that was so precious he hadn't known its worth until it had gone?

"Just as well I'm not in love with her too then," said Nick. He rubbed some ice against his knuckles.

"Sure about that?" Zak asked.

Nick was quiet for a moment.

"Tess isn't like any of the girls I've dated before," he said eventually. "Not that we really dated. It was just a drunken kiss and a couple of evenings in the pub."

Zak couldn't help it; just these words were enough to crucify him with jealousy.

"We had absolutely nothing in common – as you can imagine," Nick continued. "It was never going to work, but the thing is that I really respected her. She was in a whole different league."

Zak closed his eyes. "Yes. She is."

"When she told me it wasn't going to happen, she was really decent about it. She even let me make out that I finished with her." Nick flushed. "And yes, I'm such an idiot, that's exactly what I did and Tess never said a word. She let me save face with the lads because she understood that was important to me."

This sounded like Tess. She hadn't even told Zak the full story. She was honest and true and kind.

"That's why I flipped when I thought you were messing her about," Nick explained. "She doesn't deserve it and I'm not going to let anyone mess her about, not even family. But anyway, that was a misunderstanding. No hard feelings?"

Zak sighed. "None from me. I did deserve it anyway. Drunk or not, I should have never let a conversation like that go on around me. I should have had the decency to tell everyone to shut up and grow up."

"Easier said than done though," Nick said kindly. "So what are you going to do now?"

Zak thought for a moment. "Eat lots of humble pie? Grovel? Leave?"

"Run away? Who do you think you are? Dad? No, this is bad, but it can be fixed."

Zak wished he was as optimistic. "Can it? What do you suggest?"

"You're asking me for advice now? No idea, but you're going to have to prove to Tess you're not the total dickhead she thinks you are. Maybe start by going to her place and apologising? Yeah, that's the first thing to do. If in doubt, grovel."

Zak had never listened to Nick in his life, but this did make sense, so once the ice had melted and his face was throbbing a little less he walked up the hill to Tess's cottage and knocked on the door. Unsurprisingly, there was no answer.

"Tess, will you please talk to me?" He knocked again. "I'm not going anywhere until you speak to me!"

He knocked a few more times. The holidaymakers soaking up the sun in the next door garden glared at him, but Zak didn't care. He simply knocked harder.

"Tess! Please! Listen to me!"

The sash window rattled from the first floor and Tess looked down into the street. Her eyes were pink and her nose was red, but even so, she had never looked more beautiful. Zak so wanted to hold her in his arms and promise to never hurt her again so badly that it was a physical ache in his chest.

"What happened to your face?" Tess gasped.

"Somebody took exception to me behaving like an idiot."

"Just the one person? I'd have thought there was a queue."

Zak guessed he deserved this.

"I need to talk to you," he said.

"So talk," said Tess.

Zak glanced around. The holidaymakers next door were agog and Sheila Keverne who lived three doors along would have ears out on elastic.

"Can't I come in?"

"No," said Tess. She sounded just like a teacher, and Zak realised that if he was going to speak to her, then it would have to be right here and in public. He felt like a bad Romeo.

"Tess, I know what you think of me right now."

"You reckon?"

"I can guess. That conversation in the pub, which I don't really remember by the way, was unforgiveable."

"If you don't remember it, then how come you know it was unforgiveable?"

It was a fair point.

"I've had some of the gaps filled in for me," Zak ventured. He took a deep breath. "That's how I know it was unforgiveable, but you have to believe me when I tell you that I never had any part of it."

"Thank you for clearing that up," Tess said coldly. "You can go now."

"I can't leave things like this," Zak cried. "I need to make you understand and I need you to forgive me. Please, Tess!"

"Why?"

"Because I love you!"

There. It was out. The three words that he had never, ever said before to any girl. They were torn from his very soul and as he stared up at the window, Zak knew he'd never meant anything so much in all his life. He loved Tess with everything that he was and would ever be. Why hadn't he told her before?

"Well, you have a strange way of showing it," Tess said quietly. She didn't appear impressed. "Do you know what I think, Zak? I think you'll say and do anything if it suits you and gets you what you want. I think you saw me in the pub, you and your pathetic mates, and you thought it might be fun to see if you could make me fall for you. It couldn't have been about the money from the bet, we all know you don't need that, so it must have been about the challenge – let's see if we can have some fun with the frigid schoolteacher!"

"No, that's crap! I never thought that! In fact, you were the last person I was interested in. You'd already made it clear what you thought of me. I only got involved because of the festival, and then the more time we spent together and the more fun we had, the more I realised just how wonderful you are. I'm just so sorry that it's all got so confused. And I'm so sorry that I hurt you."

She closed her eyes wearily. "Hurt is one way of describing it. Well, I'm sorry too because we did have fun and I thought... I felt..." The words stuttered into silence and Tess shrugged.

"What does it matter what I felt? None of it was real."

"It was real and it matters because you feel the same way I do!" Zak cried. "Please, Tess! Give me another chance. I won't screw up, I promise."

She shook her head. "I can't, Zak. I just can't."

"Why not?" Zak couldn't let it end like this. "I know you're angry, Tess, but I promise this is a huge misunderstanding. Why can't you just let me explain and make it up to you?"

Tears spilled from her eyes, rolling down her cheeks and splashing onto the window sill.

"You know why!"

"Because of him and what he did?" Desperation clawed at him. "I'm not Vassilly, Tess! I'm not like him!"

Tess stared at him for a moment.

"Do you know what? I haven't given him a thought since I met you. I thought you were somebody special and for once this isn't something I'm going to blame on a stupid mistake I made years ago. This is because of you and nobody else! You've broken what we had, Zak, that's why. You're not who I thought you were and I can't trust you. That's why. You've ruined everything. If you ever cared about me at all, just leave me alone."

Tess lowered her window with a thud. There would be no talking her round. Zak knew that when Tess made up her mind, she didn't change it easily. Her musical career was testament to that. She was steadfast and loyal and true and it was bitterly ironic that these same qualities he loved would prove to be the very ones that shut him out, both literally and metaphorically.

But Zak wasn't going to give up. All he had to do was come up with a way to show Tess beyond all reasonable doubt that he loved her and would do anything for her, and as he retraced his steps, Zak suddenly realised the way to do this was obvious. It had been there all the time.

Music was the key. Of course! It unlocked everything and, if he could only find the right notes, maybe it could unlock Tess's heart too? Zak only knew he had to try. Nothing had ever mattered so much.

Ruth Saberton

CHAPTER THIRTY-THREE

Alice was very worried about Zak. Not only had he come in the day before with a swollen jaw, an injury she recognised only too well as the product of a fight, but he'd shut himself in his room again. He'd seemed so much happier lately, which Alice suspected had a great deal to do with his blossoming friendship with Tess, and to see him revert to the reclusive and haunted-eyed stranger who'd first arrived home was a blow indeed.

This morning, Alice was making wedding favours with Summer, something which ought to have been fun and which she'd been looking forward to, but she simply couldn't concentrate. The idea was a simple but personal one and had come to Alice while she was gardening, which was when she had most of her best ideas. Rather than the usual almonds or dried flowers, which she knew from experience would only be binned or shoved in a drawer, Alice wanted to give all her guests something that could make a difference and brighten up the village. As she'd sat back on her kneeler pad and watched the bees thrumming in the lavender, the perfect idea had come to her – she would make bee bombs!

She'd brushed the soil from her hands before hurrying indoors and rounding up all available family members to accompany her on a trip to the local garden centre. The promise of lunch had lured Jonny from his armchair, while dear Summer had insisted she wanted nothing more than to browse the garden centre gift shop. After cheese scones on the sunny terrace, they'd selected a variety of seeds that, when scattered onto a garden or meadow, would bloom into bee-attracting wildflowers. Alice loved the idea of the walled gardens, grassy banks and clifftops of Polwenna Bay being splashed with colour and alive with bees for years to come. She couldn't think of a nicer way to celebrate this twilight marriage of hers.

Seeds chosen, they had driven to a craft centre on the north coast which sold the most exquisite handmade paper. Each thick page was plump with petals and Alice knew these could be fashioned into perfect handmade envelopes. Summer had beautiful italic handwriting and would write a brief message onto each one before attaching a loop of rustic string in the fashion of a bespoke carrier bag. Thrilled with the notion, Alice had been looking forward to a quiet couple of days before the wedding where she could sit out on the terrace at Seaspray with her family and put these together. It was the last task they had left to do, and once this was completed all she had to do was sit back and enjoy her special day. There was nothing left to fret about. Symon and Ella had everything organised at Polwenna Manor, Jules was set with the church, Mo and Ashley had taken care of Isla's bridesmaid's dress and the flowers, while Tess and Zak had supposedly pulled the musical entertainment together. Even the villagers were behaving themselves and everything was perfect. Jonny was being very tight-lipped about the honeymoon destination and kept teasing Alice about digging out her bikini, while wedding presents had started to arrive, even though Alice had told everyone not to waste their money.

"There's nothing we want or need," she'd protested, but their friends and family simply wouldn't listen and, protests aside, Alice was beyond touched, especially when the London branch of the Tremaine clan, Henry's cousins, had sent her a beautiful hamper from Selfridges and a card telling Alice how dear she would always be to the family. Yes, that meant a lot, but if she had to pick the best wedding present of all, it had been the news that Danny and Jules weren't moving to London after all, but were staying in Cornwall. Alice would have missed them horribly and she knew Morgan would have been in pieces. Now they were staying, Morgan was thrilled and Alice was too because her family would be together. Everything was working out perfectly.

Or so she'd thought. Now Alice was worried sick again about Zak.

"Do you think it's because of that story they ran in the paper?" she asked Summer when they took a break from making envelopes to sit in the garden with mugs of coffee. "You know how upset he was about that whole... incident."

Alice couldn't bear to think about what had happened to that poor girl. It was simply heartbreaking. It also made her blood run cold to know that her grandson had been a part of a world where young people, valued in terms of their earning potential, easily became lost and unhappy.

Summer sighed. "Maybe, Alice. It must have been awful for him."

"But the whole business was nothing to do with Zak. It wasn't his fault."

Henry's cousin, Edward Tremaine, was a solicitor in London and Alice had asked his advice on the matter. Ed had been adamant there was no case against Zak whatsoever. He'd even gone as far as to say that any tabloid suggesting otherwise could be laying itself wide open to a very nasty lawsuit.

"Libel cases aren't cheap and I should imagine Zak's record label has deep pockets and would fight any suggestion of blame," he'd said. "Besides, from what you've told me and what I've found out, there are enough witnesses who've come forward to confirm that the poor child was well known for recreational drug taking. It's tragic, but there's no more to it than an unhappy accident."

'Recreational drug taking' sounded so innocuous, Alice thought. It brought to mind images of children's playgrounds with brightly coloured swings and squeaking sea-saws. But Edward was right; it was just a tragedy, but inevitably from this had come a plethora of benefits and fundraisers and drugs awareness campaigns. Alchemist's stars had even released a record to raise money for a rehab centre and were all over the press and the airwaves, something which the cynic in her found rather opportunistic.

"We know that," Summer said, "but it probably feels very different to Zak. It was really traumatic and it'll take time for him to get over it."

Alice nodded. "I know, love, but he's seemed happier recently. I hoped he was seeing Tess. Do you think they've had a falling out?"

"I think you should ask him about that, Alice."

So they had fallen out. Alice knew it. She also knew better than to press Summer for answers. Somebody had punched Zak, and the village rumour mill had it that it had been Nick. The old biddies in the village shop really needed to speak quietly when Alice came in for her milk and papers; she might be old, but she wasn't hard of hearing. Alice just wished she knew what the fallout was about. Was Nick still sweet on the schoolteacher? And had Zak stepped aside for him? Surely not. Nick had dated Tess for about five minutes and it was clear they would never work out. Nick was a butterfly darting from one pretty flower to another, whereas Zak, if she was to continue the nature metaphor, was a swan looking for his one true love.

Alice felt very tired all of a sudden. From worrying about her own son to fretting about the grandchildren and the great-grandchildren, it was exhausting. She was actually starting to hope Jonny really was whisking her away somewhere hot and sunny where she would have nothing more pressing to think about than what to eat for lunch and whether her sun hat made her look silly!

"I'll speak to him, love," she said to Summer. "In the meantime, we've got another fifty bee bombs to make. Are you ready for round two?"

Summer smiled and reached across to collect their coffee cups.

"Of the bee bomb-making or the interrogation?" she teased, and Alice laughed.

"Oh, just the bees now, love. The rest is just going to have to wait."

While Alice and Summer were filling homemade envelopes with wildflower seeds, Zak Tremaine was shut in his attic room with pages of music paper spread across the floorboards. His fingers were ink-splattered and sore from playing and his eyes felt gritty with lack of sleep since he'd yet to go to bed. To keep himself awake, Zak had thrown open the windows so that the fresh sea breeze could race in, lifting the curtains, stirring the papers and blowing away any traces of exhaustion. He didn't feel tired. If anything, he was wired, his every molecule buzzing with energy as music – trapped inside for so long – poured out.

He had created something special here. Something very special. If he was still caught up in the world of wanting fame and fortune, Zak would have been jumping up and down with excitement. It was the feeling that Robbie Williams and Guy Chambers surely had with Angels or Adele with Hello; a spine-tingling certainty that this was something rare. The music was haunting and the lyrics wove themselves into the heart and stayed there, playing on the heart strings long after the final notes had shivered away to stillness. There was beauty here and a truth which spoke of loss and love threaded with regret. The song trembled with an emotional charge that would strike a chord with all who heard it. It was a song which Zak knew the big cheeses at Alchemist would walk over fire to possess. It was, quite simply, the best thing he had ever written. It was a song that flowed from his very soul and the career changer all musicians dreamed of.

But this song wasn't for Alchemist. Or even for Zak.

It was for Tess.

Ricky, Zak's manager, had called earlier, full of excitement because, with the Kellee thing dealt with, as he so casually put it, Alchemist were keen to press ahead with Zak's new contract. Not only this, but they were offering him exactly what he'd wanted: the opportunity to play his own music his way. Two months ago, he would have been overjoyed. Now he wasn't even remotely interested.

"Shall we FedEx the contract over?" Ricky had asked excitedly. "The sooner we get the ball rolling, the better."

Zak had sat back against the bed, his guitar resting on his knees, and closed his eyes. He was drained and he had nothing more to give. Once, in what felt like another lifetime, he'd have been turning cartwheels with this news. Now it felt utterly meaningless. What did any of this matter when he'd lost Tess?

"There's no need," he said.

"Are you coming back to town? That's great, mate. Swing by the office and we'll get the paperwork done."

"I'm not coming back, Ricky. I don't want to sign the contract."

Zak hadn't known until the words had left his mouth that this was what he was going to say, but suddenly everything made perfect sense. Even an explosion of invective from his manager, followed by cajoling and eventually exasperation, couldn't change his mind; this part of Zak's life was finished. He'd found the gift of music again and this was something he couldn't risk losing a second time, no matter how much fame and fortune he was offered. He wasn't willing to sell his soul as part of the deal. And if he ended up spending the rest of his life digging vegetables for Perry and playing his guitar in pubs, Zak knew he would be happy with this.

It felt one hundred percent the right decision.

His manager rang off, after telling Zak he was well and truly off the client list, and Zak continued to write his song. He felt no regret about pressing the self-destruct button on the possibility of fame and fortune. He didn't want that life; he just wanted what he'd been blessed enough to have had twenty-four hours ago. Without Tess, all the fame and fortune in the world was rendered utterly meaningless.

The song was written. There was no more Zak could do. Writing it was the easy part. The tricky bit was making sure Tess heard the song exactly as it was intended to be played, and for this Zak needed help. He also needed the courage to reach out to the one person who could help him, but would he even take his call?

If the situation was reversed, Zak wasn't sure he would be inclined to feel generous. He'd probably just hang up.

His stomach swooped with nerves. It would be so easy to talk himself out of this. He could ask Alex or maybe record a backing track, but that wouldn't have the magic that his special song needed. It was Tess's song and she deserved nothing but the very best that he could give her.

Zak also felt he had to put things right and apologise for his past behaviour. He'd made so many dreadful mistakes and now he had hit rock bottom. It was time to reach for his shovel and get digging and to put an old wrong right.

Zak reached for his phone and scrolled through the contacts until he found the name he was looking for. Before he could wimp out, he pressed the call button, his mouth drier than Seaspray's rain-starved garden, as he waited for an answer.

"Hello?"

The voice at the end of the line was so familiar that Zak was almost drowned by a wave of nostalgia and loss. He swallowed.

"Ned? It's Zak."

He braced himself for a sharp rebuke or for his old bandmate to hang up. Zak wouldn't have blamed Ned for either response. It would be no more than he deserved.

"Mate! How are you? I'd heard you were back in town," Ned said. "I honestly meant to get in touch, but I've been absolutely flat out. Sarah and I have just bought a house and I'm her DIY slave now. You can imagine what it's like!"

Zak was speechless. Ned sounded absolutely delighted to hear from him and every bit his usual chirpy self. Where were the recriminations? Or the anger?

"My days of being able to pop out for a pint are over, at least until the hall is decorated," Ned continued. "But now I have the perfect excuse and we must meet up. Name the day, get a pint of Pol Brew in for me and I'll be there."

"I'm surprised you want to have a beer with me after what I did," Zak said quietly.

"What do you mean?" Ned sounded genuinely nonplussed.

"After I let you down by breaking up the band," Zak said, and suddenly the words he'd wanted to say for so long were pouring out of him. "I should never have done it, Ned, and I am so sorry. Not a day's gone by when I haven't wished I'd been a better person and a better friend and held out for a deal for all of us. I should have told Alchemist where to stick their contract and told them it was the three of us or nothing."

There. He'd said it. Zak waited for Ned to tell him that yes, he had totally screwed up and ruined their lives and that they hated him for it.

But Ned just laughed.

"Bloody hell, Zakky! You always were a drama queen. I think that's probably why you were the lead singer rather than me or Ollie. What the heck are you on about?"

"The way I split the band up," Zak said miserably. Shame still gnawed away at him whenever he recalled the episode. "I betrayed you both because I was weak and I thought I wanted fame and success more than anything else. I even put it above friendship and I am so, so sorry. I was a selfish bastard. I wasn't a mate to either of you."

"You didn't betray us!" Ned exclaimed. "No way. Ollie and I had the time of our lives when we were in The Tinners, but we always knew you were the real talent. Yeah, of course we were pissed off when it didn't work out, but we know we'd never have got that far without you and we had a blast in London while it lasted. How many Cornish lads can say they were pop stars for a while? Ollie still uses that line when he's on the pull! We had a right laugh, but I think we're both far happier doing what we do now. I'm pleased for you, honest, and Ollie is too. There's no hard feelings."

Zak was stunned. All this time he'd believed his friends hated him and felt betrayed, so to discover this wasn't the case was quite a shock.

"Really?"

"Really," said Ned firmly.

While the stunned Zak listened, Ned described his new house in Bodmin, his job at the bank and his recent engagement to Sarah, the childhood sweetheart who had been eyeing up diamond rings since Year Eleven. She'd finally got her man and they were now excitedly planning their wedding. In between DIY and gardening, Ned played the guitar in a covers band and seemed genuinely thrilled with life. There were certainly no wistful longings for fame on his part.

"And what about Ollie?" Zak asked when his friend finally paused for breath. "Is he happy in New Zealand?"

"You are out of touch! Ollie's living near Fowey. He's got a tree surgery business and doing really well judging by his posh Land Rover."

"Wow, good for him," said Zak, impressed. "Is he still playing the violin?"

"He plays in my band when he's not swinging from a rope or picking splinters out of his arse," Ned chuckled. "We'll have to meet up. How about a Tinners reunion back in Polwenna Bay? We could have a jam. It's long overdue."

Sometimes, Zak thought, the Universe placed things exactly where you needed them. He crossed his fingers and took a deep breath.

"Actually, since you've mentioned it…"

Ruth Saberton

CHAPTER THIRTY-FOUR

Alice woke up on the morning of her wedding day feeling calmer than she had for months. For a moment she lay still with the early morning sunshine playing over her face and allowed herself to just be. This was a slice of peace and solitude that was hers and hers alone; the day was going to be busy – wonderful, for certain – but busy too.

The old house shifted and whispered around her, as it had for over half a lifetime, and the familiar sounds soothed and comforted her, from the gulls waking up outside to the sweet ripples of wild bird song from her garden. Her reflection in the looking glass might have changed hugely over the past six decades, but when she closed her eyes and listened to those sounds, she could have been any age. The sounds of Seaspray and Polwenna Bay had been there long before there was an Alice Pendeen or an Alice Tremaine, or even an Alice St Milton, and they would be there long afterwards too. The sense of continuity was hugely comforting. What did it really matter if today's wedding went according to plan or not? The tides would still turn, the gulls would still call and life would go on.

This was all very philosophical, Alice thought, feeling amused at herself. When she'd married Henry Tremaine all those years ago, she certainly hadn't had time to laze about in bed contemplating her navel! Pa had been up before dawn's first light had kissed the horizon to light the fire and wash his car, while her mother had no doubt beaten him to it in order to feed the animals and have the chores out of the way before changing into her wedding outfit. Alice had been up early with them to help out for the last time and she recalled how nervous she had felt. She'd not slept a wink that night knowing how her entire life was about to change. A new husband, a new home and a demanding mother-in-law were all waiting for her, and a part of Alice Pendeen had longed to change her mind and stay at home. Only the thought of dear Henry who she'd loved so very much had stopped her nerves from overcoming her.

What would Elizabeth Tremaine make of her, lazing in bed like a teenager? Alice wondered. Her formidable mother-in-law would never have countenanced such behaviour and had always risen at dawn. Back in the early days of her marriage, when she was a young mother and permanently exhausted, Alice had been convinced Elizabeth was doing this deliberately and to make a point of how much more efficient she was than her son's idle wife, but now, and with the wisdom that came with eight decades, Alice understood that rising early, along with aches and pains and too many wrinkles, was one of the annoying things about getting old. Much as she envied Nick his ability to sleep until noon, Alice's eyes always pinged open at half past five and there was nothing she could do about it. Luckily for her, Jonny was just the same and they generally bumped into one another in the kitchen and the first one to reach the Aga made the tea. After their honeymoon, Alice was planning to quit her big master bedroom and sleep downstairs in Jonny's room, so they would have to make a rota and take it in turns. Maybe he could bring her tea in bed!

Goodness. She was moving downstairs and leaving the bedroom she'd slept in for almost fifty years. It was one small flight of steps for a woman but one monstrous journey for Alicekind, and at this thought her stomach did a slow forward roll. You're a daft old woman, Alice scolded herself; it's not such a big deal!

Symbolically though, this was far more than a move of just a few feet. The big dual-aspect room with its deep window seats and glowing beeswaxed floor was Seaspray's master bedroom and for Alice's first decade it had been very much her mother-in-law's domain. When Elizabeth died, Henry had automatically assumed the room would be his and Alice's and had moved them in as a matter of course, but it had taken a long time for Alice not to feel like an intruder, and for months she'd had to stop herself from knocking on the door every time she went to go inside. This was the room where the mistress of Seaspray slept, so to move out meant far more than a simple change of sleeping arrangement; it signified handing over the reins to the next generation. Alice hadn't said anything yet, but she was intending to ask Jake and Summer if they wanted to have the room after she was married. It felt like a natural progression, if a rather frightening one, and Alice had the sense that her whole life had been a climb up a ladder and she was growing closer to the final rung. So many others had made the climb before her and now it felt as though she and Jonny were the last ones left.

Alice exhaled slowly. This was the natural way of things and this was how it was supposed to be. Her time as a Tremaine was drawing to a close, and since she'd been Alice Tremaine far longer than she'd been Alice Pendeen and certainly for far longer than she'd be Alice St Milton, it was only to be expected that she would be feeling a little melancholy. It was time to put that sadness aside and be thankful for everything that she did have; a fiancé she adored, a wonderful family, her health, and a wedding that was only hours away. She was blessed beyond belief.

The sun was stealing into the room now and Alice could already feel the heat. The bite of the predawn had receded and the day was here in earnest. It was going to be a glorious one.

Her phone beeped from its perch on the bedside table. Alice didn't even need to look at it to know this was Jonny, up at the crack of dawn just like her and probably reflecting on past choices, paths followed and the dear faces that wouldn't be here today.

Good morning to my beautiful bride! I cannot wait to see you! J x

Alice smiled. Dear Jonny. He was so confused by texting that he must have been working on this for hours, scowling at the screen and stabbing the buttons with an impatient forefinger until some kind of message appeared. It was usually a hit-and-miss affair with some very amusing predictive text errors, but that he'd made the effort to get today's message right was proof of love indeed.

Alice texted back.

I can't wait to see you too. A x

She couldn't either, and so wished he was downstairs, sipping tea in his customary place by the Aga, so they could chat. But Ella had been horrified by this idea, insisting that it would be the very worst variety of bad luck if the bride and groom should see one another before the wedding.

"Oh please," Jonny had scoffed, waving away her fears with a languid hand. "What's going to happen? One of us pops our clogs on the way to St Wenn's? Or maybe both of us?"

"Don't even joke about it," Ella had gasped, turning pale. "We are not tempting fate and that's final! No arguments, Grandpa!"

"Don't even bother to try," Symon had advised when Jonny opened his mouth to protest. "Take it from me. Your life won't be worth living if you disagree with Ella."

"I thought I was going to be dead anyway," Jonny muttered belligerently, but Alice had given him a sharp look at this point and so he'd grudgingly complied and spent the night before their wedding at the Polwenna Bay Hotel. Tradition was all well and good, but Alice could have really done with a chat this morning with the one person who would really understand how she felt, even if it was just to tell her she was being daft.

There were sounds of movement now. Feet padding past her door. The creak of the floorboard on the landing, which had always given away any child on the move. The thud of the hotplate lid being moved. The family members were up and about and before long they'd come looking for her and the wedding day would swing into action, gathering momentum like a runaway cart until she found herself at the altar saying her vows. Not for the first time, Alice found herself wishing that she could slow time right down so that she could savour every moment like a fine wine.

This was the start of a new chapter of her life. A new name. A new husband. A new adventure. It was exciting and wonderful, and how blessed was she to be given this second chance in her golden years? Today was going to be a perfect day that she would look back on and treasure. Already the day was sunny and her nearest and dearest had gathered from all across the world, even Jimmy and darling Emerald making the trip over, as well as Issie and her boyfriend Luke. She would shake these melancholy musings off like the last wisps of morning mist clinging to the River Wenn and cherish every moment.

Alice sat up slowly and swung her legs out of the bed. She certainly moved rather differently these days to when she'd first arrived at Seaspray. Getting out of bed was now a careful process involving working out which parts of her felt a little creaky and stiff and how energetic she was feeling. There was certainly no racing to the window, not since the time she'd caught her foot on the rug and gone flying. Dear Jake, not long back from Australia, had almost passed out with terror when he'd found her on the floor and, one sprained ankle later, Alice had learned to be cautious. Moving downstairs to a room with a fitted carpet, newly installed en-suite bathroom and near to the kitchen wouldn't be the end of the world. Change wasn't all bad!

The opened curtains revealed a day still newly minted and bright with promise. New beginnings. Alice leaned her forehead against the cool glass and admired the view. It was the constantly changing living picture that she'd seen for nearly all her life in one way or another and it never ceased to fill her with joy. From the pleasure boats in the marina to their elephantine trawler cousins tethered to the harbour wall, to the glistening beach revealed bit by bit by the retreating sea like a marine dance of the seven veils to the windows of Mariners glinting in the sunshine, it was all beautiful. She loved this place and the people who lived here and Alice felt a sudden rush of excitement. She could hardly wait to share her day with them.

Her dress was hanging from the wardrobe on a padded hanger. A simple coat-style dress lovingly stitched by Summer and Susie, it made Alice feel elegant and beautiful. It was perfect. The whole day was going to be perfect, from the service to the simple family meal at the Manor to the festival in the evening. Alice's only worry was Zak, who had been so pale and sad for the last few days. She'd had such high hopes for him and Tess and it was clear to anyone that they were made for one another, but there were some things people just had to work out for themselves. Alice only hoped it wouldn't take them as long as it had taken her and Jonny! She'd tried to speak to him, but Zak had simply said that he was fine and just busy working on her wedding song. If Jake or Nick or any of the others knew what had happened, then they were keeping it to themselves. Jonny said maybe that was just as well, as Alice had quite enough on her plate and Zak was nearly thirty after all. One of the hardest things about being eighty was realising that people had to find their own path. Accepting this never grew easier with time.

Alice studied the faded photograph of her and Henry that had been taken on their silver wedding anniversary and which had pride of place on the dressing table. Losing her beloved husband was another thing that never grew easier. You learned to live with the loss and life expanded and moved on as it needed to, but even years on, the loss could still bite and leave you breathless. Henry had been a good husband and Alice had loved him dearly and missed him every day. Marrying Jonny didn't mean that she would miss him any less and Alice felt sure Henry would approve of her second marriage. He'd been a practical man and never one to sit about and brood.

"Onwards and upwards, girl," was what he'd always said whenever she was down. Remembering his words this morning made her smile.

So yes, onwards and upwards. She'd made her peace with marrying again and everything was exactly where it should be. The wedding was planned, all her loved ones were close by and even the weather was on her side. There was nothing else left to do now but show the world just how much Jonny St Milton meant to her. He'd been her first love and now he'd be her last.

Alice could hear voices downstairs. Morgan's was shrill and excited; Issie's similar. The firm tone telling them to shush was Jake. The smell of toast suggested somebody was already getting breakfast underway and if Alice wanted everyone to have a glass of champagne with the bagels, smoked salmon and cream cheese she'd placed in the fridge, she'd better get downstairs and fast. Before long, Ashley, Mo and Isla would arrive with the flowers, Summer and Susie would come up to help her dress, while Nick and Danny headed over to the church. With Jake giving her away, Symon in charge of the reception and Zak overseeing the afternoon and evening entertainment, everyone had their role.

And this included her. Before she went downstairs and jumped into the fast-flowing river of her wedding day, there was something Alice knew she had to do... a final gesture she could only make today.

She glanced down at her hands. Lined and traced with veins, they were hands that had seen a lifetime of actions; hands that had wiped tears, baked bread, made love and dug the soil. On the left hand she was wearing the beautiful diamond cluster that Jonny had given her, while on her right she still wore the worn gold band and simple family solitaire that Henry had placed onto her wedding finger all those years ago. These dear friends and treasures were worth far more than their material value but, like the bedroom, it was also time to hand these on. Maybe Jake might want them for Summer? Or, and Alice longed so much for this, even Zak might find the right girl one day, if he hadn't already found her?

In any case, their time with her, like her time as a Tremaine, was done. Onwards and upwards, girl. Onwards and upwards.

Alice slipped the rings from her finger and placed them on the dressing table beside Henry's photograph before tenderly tracing with her forefinger the beloved face beneath the glass.

"Thank you for everything, my love," she said softly. "Thank you. You're not forgotten. Nothing is ever forgotten."

And then, with a heart as light as the foam on the waves, Alice Tremaine stepped out of her bedroom and into her wedding day.

CHAPTER THIRTY-FIVE

Alice and Jonny St Milton's wedding had been perfect, Tess thought, just perfect. It wasn't the biggest or the most extravagant affair, but in terms of happiness, the couple had radiated as they stood at the altar to say their vows, Alice elegant in a cream silk coat-dress and jaunty pillbox hat with froth of veil and Jonny distinguished in his top hat and tails, and with the goodwill from the congregation crammed into St Wenn's, she couldn't recall a wedding to match it. Isla was adorable as the flower girl, Morgan was the most diligent wedding photographer ever (Fact!) and St Wenn's was the most stunning backdrop you could ever imagine. When Alice had walked down the aisle on Jake's arm and Jonny had turned around to see her, the look of utter joy and love on his face had almost broken Tess and she'd had to blink very hard indeed to keep her emotions under control. It was a love that had waited a lifetime and a love that said there was always hope for happiness, even when it might feel as though that could never be further away.

In Tess's case, this was exactly how she felt, so it was hard to sit in the church surrounded by flowers and the celebration of love when her own heart had been trampled into the ground, and harder again to be just feet away from the man who'd done this to her. Since the dreadful morning when Mandy revealed Zak's bet, Tess had worked very hard to avoid him. She'd made certain that any final work she had to do on the arrangements for the festival could be done from a distance and had deliberately stayed away from the Manor. Zak didn't need her to be there for the staging to arrive or for the sound checks or any of the other technical aspects, and even if he did, Tess couldn't have faced seeing him. She still couldn't fathom how he could have been so cruel. The pain of his betrayal was a sharp knife through her heart. How could something which had been so special to her, something which she'd truly believed to be incredible and so precious, have been little more than a game to Zak? She'd trusted him and he'd simply thrown that trust back at her. She was clearly a dreadful judge of men and from now on she was staying single. That was a promise.

Even so, as she sat in the church, Tess couldn't help her recalcitrant gaze slipping to Zak, no matter how hard she tried not to look his way. All the Tremaine brothers looked heart-stoppingly handsome today in their morning suits, but it was Zak who drew all eyes to him. He had that effortless beauty reserved for film stars, although they usually had filters and makeup artists to assist them and spent hours in beauty salons having treatments, unlike Zak who was generally digging Perry's garden or stomping across the cliffs. His high-cheekboned face was smooth save the glint of golden stubble on his jaw, and his eyes, which had sought hers several times, were a startling blue against his tanned skin. Tess stared intently at her order of service and tried hard to pretend that she couldn't sense his gaze. It appalled her just how much she still wanted him. Didn't her heart have any self-respect?

As hurt as she was, and as cynical as she might be feeling about romance, when the older couple exchanged their vows, Tess was forced to blink very hard. Somehow she managed to make it through the service, even holding it together during Jules's beautiful sermon about love and the final rendition of All Things Bright and Beautiful without dissolving into a sobbing mess and totally disgracing herself. She slipped away before the final blessing though, not only because she wanted to head over to Polwenna Manor and make sure that everything really was ready, but she really couldn't face bumping into Zak. Knowing he'd be occupied with the photos, family lunch and ushering duties, Tess had the perfect window of opportunity to make sure she was happy with the arrangements without having to see him, and by the time Zak was free, there would be enough of a crowd for her to avoid him. Could she get away with pleading a migraine?

As Tess drove to the Manor, nearly being taken out by the Pollards' quad bike hooning around the corner and on the wrong side of the road, she wrestled with the knowledge that it was logistically going to be very hard to avoid Zak. It was one of the hazards of living in a rural community, but it hadn't seemed such an issue before. She and Nick had parted on good terms and the couple of other dates she'd had were fairly casual.

But Tess knew she had fallen in love with Zak and this newly fledged emotion was proving very stubborn. Her head could tell her heart all day long that he was shallow and cruel and an utter bastard, but her heart didn't seem to care. It was her heart that was desperate to catch a glimpse of his blonde head and that skipped a beat when she thought she saw him walking along the quay. Tess was starting to think the only way she would ever get over Zak Tremaine was to leave Polwenna Bay forever.

So he had broken her heart and destroyed her career. If she hadn't loved him, Tess thought she would hate him. Perhaps she did hate him? It was all so confused; a horrible fishing twine tangle of emotions, and it was exhausting too. As soon as this reception was over, she was going to sleep for days. Maybe she would even take a day off sick in order to lower her stress levels? Everyone knew teachers were renowned for stress overload, although granted this were more usually caused by league tables and large classes.

She walked past the house and onto the lawn where the trestle tables borrowed from the school canteen were set up. The WI had been hard at work arranging wire arches above the tables and festooning them with ivy and roses and white ribbons, while each table had been covered with silver tablecloths and would later on be laden with platters piled high with scones and dishes filled with cream and jam. Opposite this area, a hog roast was slowly turning on the spit, filling the air with mouth-watering aromas. To accompany it were mounds of crusty baguettes, bowls filled with homemade apple sauce and dishes heaped with stuffing. Not to be outdone, Chris the Cod had set up his mobile fish and chip stand and was busy dipping fish into batter. Nobody would go hungry, that was for certain.

Yet as impressive as the catering arrangements were, and as proud as Tess was for having managed to pull it all together (her arms still ached from wrestling the WI's tea urn into the Pollards' van), Zak's stage made her jaw drop. Whatever Tess had been expecting, it wasn't anything as professional as this. Several strapping men in stonewashed jeans and leather gilets and with a Beano's worth of ink on their muscular forearms were each putting the final touches to rigging the stage which, with its lighting and huge speakers, wouldn't have looked out of place at a professional concert. A sudden blast of feedback made Tess jump as Morgawr, the popular local band Zak had booked, did a final sound check.

Keen villagers were already starting to arrive for the music, spreading rugs onto the best picnic spots, unpacking their food and settling down for the day. Adam and Rose from the pub had set up a temporary bar and beckoned Tess over to sample the Alice St M cocktail they'd created in the bride's honour.

"What have you done with Zak? I thought you'd be with him," Adam had said with a wink. "Like peas in a pod you two are these days. Should Rose buy a hat?"

Tess chose to ignore this. If Adam Harper had been in The Ship that night, more than likely since he was the landlord, he must surely have known about the bet. The very thought made her hot with humiliation. Feeling miserable, Tess had returned to her car for a quiet moment before the wedding party arrived and the event began in earnest. Once Big Rog got on stage, there would be no peace for anyone.

Tess took a deep breath, blotted her eyes with a tissue and fixed her makeup. In a few hours, all this would be over. She could get through today.

Forget violin concerts and Ofsted inspections. This was the biggest challenge of her life.

"I give you the bride and groom, Mr and Mrs St Milton!"

When Symon Tremaine made this announcement, there was a burst of applause and loud cheering. Alice and Jonny, hand in hand and beaming, stepped out of Polwenna Manor into the glorious late afternoon sunshine. Behind them were the rest of the wedding party: Teddy and Ella flanking their grandfather – and Teddy sober for once – and the huge Tremaine clan following Alice. The family event was over and Tess suspected that the villagers were actually cheering because now they could get on with the main event, namely Polwenna's Got Talent. Tess felt like cheering too because her afternoon had been hectic and she was thrilled to have survived it. She'd had to dress a scraped knee, take over at the bar while Adam Harper, who'd sampled too many of his own cocktails, did his best to sober up, and then she'd been called to break up the fight which broke out when Eddie Penhalligan took exception to Caspar putting cream first onto a scone. By the time the band were into their set, the strain of it all, and of avoiding Zak, was making Tess fray around the edges. Needing time out, she slipped away to the side of the stage where she could stand unobserved in the shadows and catch her breath.

Or so she thought.

"What are you doing hiding yourself away, Tess? You should be up and dancing after all your hard work. If it wasn't for you, none of this would have happened! This reception is a huge success!"

Tara Tremaine, two glasses of champagne in hand, was clearly in the mood to party.

"Thanks, Tara," Tess said, hoping she didn't look as disappointed as she felt at having her solitude disturbed. "I can't take all the credit, though. There were lots of other people who helped too."

"Like Zak, you mean?" Tara said, as if Tess could forget.

"Yes, like Zak," Tess replied through gritted teeth.

It was lucky Tara had already enjoyed a few glasses of fizz and didn't notice the catch in her voice when Tess spoke his name. She gulped back the lump in her throat, adding brightly, "So many people have helped today and somehow it's all come together. It's been a real village effort. I still can't believe the WI insisted on having their tea urn lugged all the way up here."

Tara, pressing a glass into Tess's hand, grinned.

"You don't think they'd let Alice's big day go by without offering her a decent cuppa, do you? And they've made sandwiches too and cheese straws and vol-au-vents. It's like a trip back to the seventies on a plate!"

Tess tried to smile, but she was finding this harder by the minute. The dull ache in her heart made her feel as though she was made of lead, and simple things like chatting to a friend were almost more effort than she could dredge up. How could she stop herself thinking about Zak when each time she closed her eyes she could almost be back here on that magical night when the stars had danced through the dark sky and his beautiful mouth had captured hers?

She ventured a smile, but her chin wobbled a little so she took a sip of her drink and hoped her friend hadn't noticed.

Yeah, right. There was no chance of that! Tara's bright eyes narrowed and instantly she looked exactly like Morgan did when puzzling over something in class.

"Is it Zak? Is it true that you guys have fallen out?"

"Sort of," Tess said. "It's not important."

She couldn't cry. She wouldn't cry. Not now. If she started, she would never stop.

Tara frowned. "Somehow I don't believe that. It looked to me like whatever was going on with you two was really important. I don't know the truth of what happened, but I can promise that I've never seen him like this with anyone. Trust me, Tess! I've know Zak a long time. You're special."

Tess's lip curled scornfully. She was so special that Zak had made a bet he could pull her as easily as any other girl daft enough to fall for his good looks and smooth talk. Special? Yeah, right. Tara could believe that if she wanted. Who was Tess to disillusion her?

"And if it's any consolation, Morgan tells me his uncle's been a right old misery lately. Fact!" Tara continued when there was no reply. "He's been hiding away in his room like a teenager and not talking to anyone, so whatever he's done to upset you, I think he's very sorry."

She waited for Tess to say something, but there was no way Tess was going to be drawn.

"I'm sorry too," was all she said.

And she was. Tess was sorrier about this than she had ever been about anything. Compared to this, the unhappiness she'd felt over Vass had paled into insignificance. That was a crush that had grown out of all proportion, Tess realised now. She'd behaved in the classic teenager way of sabotaging her own career in the mistaken belief it would upset him, but it was nonsense. She'd only hurt herself and for what? Vass had never made her heart sing the way Zak had and, in spite of all the hours she and Vass had spent playing together for exam preparation, they had never been as much in tune.

In Zak, Tess had truly believed she had found her soulmate, and he could be as sorry as he liked because there was nothing he could do that could persuade her to forgive him for destroying that certainty. Tess didn't think she could ever believe Zak Tremaine again. He'd said all those fine words when he'd stood outside her cottage and pleaded with her, but how could she trust him? Tess didn't think there was anything in the world that he could say or do that could make her change her mind and give him a second chance.

And this was what broke her heart the most.

Ruth Saberton

CHAPTER THIRTY-SIX

Things always worked out in the end, Alice St Milton reflected as she sat at one of the trestle tables beside her brand new husband and with serving plates piled high with scones and cucumber sandwiches in front of her. After months of fretting about the flowers and the reception and the guest list, everything had gone beautifully and she really couldn't have asked for more. The sense of excitement she'd felt when she'd first arisen that morning had stayed with her, hand in hand with a sense of peace when she'd stepped into St Wenn's and seen Jonny waiting at the altar. Everything after that felt a little hazy and dreamy, which could be utter bliss or a little too much champagne!

Alice glanced across the lawns of Polwenna Manor. Just as she had hoped, everyone she knew was here – and quite a few more besides – and nobody had been left out. Bee bombs had been scattered (Perry would be hearing a great deal of buzzing in the years to come), speeches made and toasts raised and now the serious business of partying was taking place. She sighed happily. This was the village wedding that she had hoped for and it was quite simply perfect.

It was almost ten o'clock and dusk was falling. Fairy lights and hurricane lanterns threw pools of light onto the cool green lawns which were still crowded with dancing guests, many of them now in costume for the talent show. It was an eclectic and levelling mix; Boy George was dancing with Madonna, Dolly Parton and the Phantom of the Opera where throwing shapes by the stage and even a couple of Spice Girls had dusted off their platform boots for the night. In terms of musical merit, some of the singing left a little to be desired, but what the contestants lacked in ability, they certainly made up for in enthusiasm.

The current act drew to a close and Alice clapped politely, even though privately she thought that Dr Kussell should really stick to medicine. He made a very tuneless Bing Crosby. The judges, who consisted of an ashen-faced Zak (oh dear, seeing her grandson looking so unhappy was the only cloud lurking on Alice's horizon), Sheila Keverne in her capacity as choir mistress and bell ringer and, the biggest coup of all, a TV-presenting couple who'd been huge in the nineties and had recently relocated to the area. They bickered a great deal, Alice had noticed, and looked rather as though they wanted to be on the stage themselves, but their presence had caused a huge amount of excitement and even the local paper had sent a photographer. Fame at last for me, Alice thought, even if by proxy!

"Why on earth are you clapping?" Jonny asked her, looking pained. "That was bloody awful. If his medical talents match his singing ability, then I'm registering with Richard Penwarren first thing tomorrow!"

"Shh!" laughed Alice. "He's tried so hard, dear of him."

"Not hard enough. I think I can hear Bing spinning in his grave." Alice's new husband rose creakily to his feet and rested a hand on her shoulder. "I'm going to have a chat with Teddy, love. He's looking very down and I know today wasn't easy for him with Emerald being here."

Alice followed his gaze to where her new step-grandson was leaning against a tree with his bow tie loosened and his head bowed. He did indeed look a picture of misery, but try as she might, Alice couldn't dredge up much sympathy. Emerald was lucky Teddy hadn't killed her when, drunk and speeding, he'd clipped her in the lane. Ted might well be nervous about his looming court appearance, but Alice thought it was no more than he deserved. He'd been wild and reckless for far too long and she was secretly pleased he was due to get his comeuppance, but Alice also knew how devoted Jonny was to his grandson. Alice understood what it was to love your family and worry about them. Love wasn't conditional on good behaviour.

"You do that, love," she told him, resting her hand over his briefly.

"Can I pinch Jonny's seat?"

It was Jules, changed out of her vestments and looking curvy and pretty in a floral wrap dress. She should dress up more, Alice thought. It suited her. She really was a lovely girl. No wonder Danny adored her.

She patted Jonny's space. "Of course, love. I've hardly seen you all day – except in the church, of course. Thank you so much for a beautiful service. It was very special and you did a lovely job."

Jules flushed. "Thank you. I'm over the moon to be a part of it all."

"You're a part of the family now. There's no escape."

"I wouldn't want one," said Jules. "I guess now you and Jonny are married, Danny and I are next, unless Symon or Jake decides to pop the question."

"Or Zak," added Alice.

"Zak? Really?"

"Stranger things have happened," was all Alice said. You didn't get to be eighty, or know a young man all his life, without learning a thing or two. Zak was head over heels in love with Tess Hamilton. It was as clear as the nose on his handsome face, and that he and Tess were also studiously avoiding each other was another dead giveaway. What could it be that had stopped their blossoming romance in its tracks? Surely nothing that couldn't be sorted? If only young people realised how brief a time they really had, then they wouldn't waste a single minute on misunderstandings and pride.

"I guess so," agreed Jules. "Like Dan and I both secretly wanting to stay in the village."

Alice smiled. "You're certainly a right pair, but I'm so glad you're not leaving, my love. I would have missed you both dreadfully and so would everyone else. You're a part of the Polwenna family too, you know."

On the stage, Big Rog was starting to gyrate to the opening bars of Sex Bomb. Poured into leather trousers and with his unbuttoned shirt revealing a hairy pot belly and several clanking medallions, he was certainly going for it.

"I'm starting to think that being a member of the Polwenna Bay family isn't such a good thing!" giggled Jules.

"Too late now," Alice said. "It's for better or worse, a bit like marriage!"

"Sex Bomb! Sex Bomb! You're my sex bomb!" sang Big Rog, his leather-clad groin thrusting towards the stunned audience in perfect time with each word. "Come on ladies! Throw your knickers at me! Don't be shy, Sheila Keverne! You know you want to!"

"This is definitely for worse. I may have to reconsider the London move," said Jules, peeking at the stage through splayed fingers and cringing. "Or even book in for therapy?"

Alice laughed but, bad karaoke aside, the villagers were her family and she loved them, at least most of the time, and being a part of their community meant everything. Pride filled her heart as she looked around and saw all her friends and family gathered together for her special day, exactly as she'd hoped. Nobody felt excluded and everyone was having fun, in Big Rog's case a little too much fun. Jake and Summer were deep in conversation with Jimmy, Issie was dancing with Isla, while Mo hobbled beside them and even Danny was joining in so Morgan could take more photos. Soon everyone was singing along. Zak had really excelled himself with the band and the talent show. All that remained was to see if he'd managed to compose her song. Alice so hoped he had because Zak not writing was simply wrong and against his very nature. Had she pushed him too hard? If she had, then it was only with the best of intentions.

Big Rog finished his song to huge applause and a giant pair of red and white spotty pants. As he bowed and waved, he had the look of a man who had found his true calling in life.

"I can do an encore if you like?" he said hopefully.

"Dad's Delilah is legendary! Isn't it, Pa?" called out Little Rog.

"That's right, my boy!" agreed Big Rog. "That's right!" He puffed out his chest and began to sing, "I saw the light on the night that I passed by her window!"

Without the help of a backing track, this attempt was slightly less tuneful, if no less enthusiastic, and the male TV personality was up on the stage in a flash to gently shepherd Big Rog into the wings.

"That's marvellous, but sadly we don't have time," he said.

Big Rog stopped in his tracks. "Don't have time? But I'm the last act! Save the best for last, we all agreed. Well, here I am!"

"You were the last," said the presenter, "until we had a wild-card entry at the eleventh hour."

Big Rog, who clearly thought he had it in the bag, was most put out. "But that's not on! It's not in the rules!"

"There aren't any rules," hollered Meatloaf, aka Eddie Penhalligan. "Get off the bleddy stage, you harris!"

Looking mutinous, Big Rog stomped off stage, or rather stomped as much as a very big man in very tight leather trousers could stomp anywhere. Alice shook her head at just how competitive this talent show had become. If a village music event was this cut-throat, just what had it been like for Zak in the world of million-pound contracts? No wonder he was so bruised.

"And last but by no means least, I give you our final and last-minute contestant!" said the TV host. "Mrs Karenza Pollard as Elaine Paige!"

"What?" Big Rog almost fell over in shock, although this could just have been restricted movement courtesy of the tight trousers.

Alice had known Karenza Pollard, WI member, holiday cottage cleaner and keen gardener, for nearly fifty years, but she had no idea Karenza could sing and neither, judging by the stunned expression on his face, did Big Rog. She certainly looked very different dressed in a long sparkly gown and heels rather than her usual attire of jeans, sweater and trainers. Her husband's chin was almost on the floor and her son was beaming.

"It's Ma!"

"That's right, my boy," gasped his father. "It bleddy well is!"

The music began to play over the PA system. Mrs Pollard took a deep breath, clasped hands and opened her mouth. When she started to sing, a stunned hush descended over the evening garden as Alice and Jonny's guests fell under the spell cast by the sweet and pure beauty of the voice speaking to them of memories and nostalgia and chances lost. The music rose and fell, haunting and lonely, and it was impossible not to feel moved. Alice swallowed back the loss of her youth and the years that had once stretched ahead. Across the lawn, Tess Hamilton was wiping a tear from her cheek, while Ashley Carstairs pulled Mo close. Even Ella and Symon stepped out of the restaurant, hand in hand, to listen and Jonny threaded his way back through the guests to clasp Alice's hand and raise it to his lips. Beside Alice, Jules's cheeks were wet, and glancing around at all the rapt faces, Alice thought this was what could only be called a Susan Boyle moment. She'd never imagined anything like this.

A local star was born!

The music shimmered to a close, the last note trembling in the air, and for a moment there was stunned silence before the entire place broke into rapturous applause. Then Big Rog was on the stage twirling his wife around and around and telling her over and over again how proud he was.

"I think we have a winner!" beamed the former TV personality and there was absolutely no disagreement from anyone else. "How did you keep that talent hidden?"

Mrs Pollard blushed. "I'm not talented! I just sing along to Pirate FM when I'm cleaning. It's my husband who's the real talent in the family."

"Not any more, right Dad?" said Little Rog.

"That's right, my boy," nodded his father. "Mum's not bad at all. Maybe we could do some duets at the campsite karaoke next week, love? Sonny and Cher could be good." He threw back his head and began to sing, "They say we're young and we don't know—"

At this point, there was a screech of feedback from the mic and Big Rog was drowned out. By the time sound was restored, the TV personalities had awarded the prizes and everyone had started to chat amongst themselves once again.

"I think we can call our reception a big success," Jonny said to Alice. "You included everyone in the village, scattered a football pitch worth of wildflowers, saved the Polwenna Festival and found Mrs Pollard a new career. I'd say your work here is done! Are you ready to head off on our next adventure? Shall we say our goodbyes and start the first leg of our honeymoon?"

Alice's eyes widened. "We're really going away?"

"Of course we are! Did you ever doubt me? Although we will stay at the hotel for the first night since we don't fly until the morning."

"Fly? Are we going to a tropical island after all?"

"Better than that, my love. We're going to a beautiful island, but without even needing to leave the county. I've booked us a suite in a boutique hotel on Tresco."

Alice was thrilled. She loved the Scillies and as much as the idea of jetting across the globe had appealed, she knew that a long-haul flight would be far too much for both of them. This way, they would still have icing sugar sands, crystal clear waters and deserted beaches without leaving her beloved Cornwall.

"I love you, Mr St Milton," she said.

"And I love you too, Mrs St Milton," Jonny replied. "Would it be selfish to say that I'd like my bride to myself now?"

"You just want your bed and a cup of tea," Alice teased, threading her fingers through his, loving the way their hands fitted as perfectly now as they had when they were teenage sweethearts another lifetime ago.

"You know me far too well," he laughed.

"Tea and bed sounds wonderful to me," Alice agreed. "But before we leave, there's one last thing I need to do – I need to ask Zak to play his song."

"Do you think he's written it?"

Alice wasn't sure. She certainly hoped so. Not only would it mean a great deal to have a special song composed by Zak, but to know he was writing again would be the best wedding present she could think of.

She rose to her feet and took a deep breath.

"There's only one way to find out," she said.

CHAPTER THIRTY-SEVEN

Tess was exhausted, the sort of exhaustion which bit to the bone and which came not just from the physical efforts of shepherding people onto the stage and running around to make sure that the right music was queued, or concentrating on making certain all the details were in place, but mostly from trying not to let her thoughts drift back to Zak. Like a recalcitrant child tugging on its mother's hand, Tess's mind kept doing its best to drag her attention back to him. Ignoring it, and pretending she didn't feel his eyes on her or know without even looking exactly where he was, was torture of the worst and most exquisite kind. No matter how many times her logical mind told her she hated Zak, Tess's heart was telling her something very different.

This evening had been so hard, harder than Tess had ever imagined it could be. The irony was that the event itself, which had been worrying her for weeks, had run so smoothly and everything, from the food stalls to the morris dancers to the bands, had fallen into place with incredible ease. Even better was the undoubted success of the talent show. Nobody had misbehaved, the celebrity couple had added a gloss and, in awe of them, even Big Rog and Eddie Penhalligan had followed instructions. But the highlight of the night had to be the surprise winner. Whoever knew that the quiet Mrs Pollard had a voice like that? Talk about hidden talents.

As the daughter of professional musicians, Tess had heard enough singing in her time to recognise a real talent and was thrilled that Karenza had been brave enough to enter. Now that the main event was over and the dance floor had filled again to the strains of a local string quartet, the diehard locals, who preferred a bit of Status Quo or Queen, had regrouped at the bar where Mrs Pollard was celebrating with her friends. Big Rog couldn't have been prouder if he'd won the talent show himself. He had his arm around his wife's shoulder and was singing her praises to anyone who would listen. They looked so happy and it brought a lump to Tess's throat to see it. Big Rog had his faults, most of them mainly to do with his building skills and quad bike riding, but he adored his wife and would do anything for her.

It must be wonderful to know that kind of love.

Tess smothered a yawn. She was so tired and it was growing late. The light had all but gone, stars domed the sky and the party was lit by the white fairy lights that she had spent ages helping to thread through the bushes and drape from the gazebo. The scene looked as romantic as she could ever had wished it to, and even in her melancholy mood Tess felt the thrill of pride that came from knowing she'd done a good job. Maybe this was why she felt a little flat? For weeks now, this evening had been the object of so much of her energy and now it was over she was bound to feel a little lost – just like she did at the end of term when even tired and glad of a rest, she found herself feeling empty. Yes, that must be it. It was the abrupt shift from giving all her focus to something to having that goal removed, no matter how successfully achieved.

That and the massive void left by Zak no longer being a part of her life. How was it that she had never felt the lack of his presence before, yet now he was gone everything felt empty and echoey? She still had her job and her friends and keeping fit. Nothing had really changed.

Nothing outwardly, anyway. The problem was that in her heart it felt as though everything had changed. Life was still good, she was still successful, she was still busy; the sparkle had just dulled, that was all. It was no bad thing. This was real life and she should have known better than to allow herself to believe it could be any other way. She was lucky that she had school to lose herself in and lots of work ahead, with end-of-term plays and summer fairs and reports to write. If only the long summer holidays weren't looming, and with them all the empty days. She must be the only teacher in the county who looked forward to September. She sighed.

"Isn't it romantic?" said Kat Evans. She was leaning against the staging and rubbing the small of her back with one hand. "They are so in love, even at that age. I'm sure I'll have throttled Alex by then."

Alice and Jonny had stepped onto the dance floor, swaying in perfect time to the music. Dancing cheek to cheek, they were holding one another close and as though they would never let go again. Tess knew they had been childhood sweethearts and that this late chance of love was one they would never take for granted. They had waited a lifetime for this and how lucky were they to find one another again? Brave too. Tess wasn't sure if she would ever dare risk her heart again.

"They look very happy," was all she said.

"And so will I when I'm not the size of a small planet," Kat said with a grimace.

"You look lovely," Tess told her firmly. Kat really did too. In her flowing floral dress, long red hair in loose curls and her ivory skin glowing, Kat Evans was simply stunning. No wonder Alex was never far from her side; he looked like a man who couldn't believe his good luck.

Actually, where was Alex? And Zak, whose presence Tess had been acutely aware of all night, had also vanished.

Kat was rolling her eyes at Tess's compliment.

"I look as though I've swallowed a space hopper and I need to pee every five minutes. It's a bloody nightmare. Thank goodness you hired enough Portaloos! That makes the night a big success in my book!"

This did make Tess smile.

"I wouldn't have spent all those hours fretting about the music if I'd known lots of loos were the key to success!"

"You mock all you want. When it's your turn to be up the duff you'll know exactly what I mean," Kat promised.

This was hardly likely to happen now she had all but decided to become a nun, Tess thought. Aloud, she said, "Well, until then I'll take your word for it. Anyway, I think I'm going to head home since my work here with talent shows and Portaloos is done."

"You can't go yet! It's only early and the party's still going!" Kat protested.

"I've been here most of the day. I'm partied out," Tess said.

The truth was she didn't think she could face much more. Avoiding Zak had been so painful and catching glimpses of him even more so. There were too many memories in the night-time gardens of Polwenna Manor. It was time to catch the Pollard shuttle home and be alone to reflect on it all.

"Just a bit longer," said Kat. Her gaze was drifting over Tess's shoulder, and since years in the classroom had given Tess a great instinct for when somebody was up to something, she was instantly on alert.

"What's going on?"

Kat's eyes were wide and innocent. "What do you mean?"

"Come on, Kat! I'm a teacher too. We always know when people are up to something. So what is it? Why are you desperate to keep me here? It's not as though you want to dance."

"Jeez! No, I'd probably go into labour!"

"So? Or do I have to close all the Portaloos until you confess?"

Kat held up her hands. "No! Anything but that! Okay, the thing is Alex has asked me to make sure you're here when Zak plays the song for Alice. He was adamant."

Ouch. Just hearing his name felt like a punch to her heart. How could she bear to hear the song that had been such a part of their short friendship? Tess had been there from the start, through the agonizing that he might never write again, and had been there that magical night when the music had started to play again for her. Her chest felt like the harbour wall on a high tide as a thousand emotions churned and broke against it. How could she bear to stand here and watch him play, listen to the words he had written and know what he had done? How could she stand the agony of knowing that the happiness she'd felt when he had held her close was now as out of reach as the stars that looked down from above?

It was unbearable. How could Kat and Alex be so cruel? They might be good friends of Zak, but she had thought Kat was her friend too and might have understood just how painful this was.

"I can't," she said quietly.

"Look, I don't know what's happened exactly, but I do know that whatever Zak's done, he's really sorry," Kat said frantically. "You're angry with him and he's been an idiot. You don't even have to see him again, but at least hear him play. Alex says you really must hear it. He made me promise to get you to stay."

Tess was really confused. "What's this got to do with Alex?"

"He's Zak's friend and he says it's only because of you that Zak started writing again. Writing properly too, the best songs of his life. Alex should know. He's worked with Zak before and I've known him a while too. You've changed him, Tess. He's been so different since he met you. He's himself. You made him happy."

"I don't think that's true," Tess said. "Quite the opposite, in fact. Anyway, it wasn't real."

Kat pressed her hand against her stomach and grimaced.

"It was! Even the baby agrees and says he won't stop kicking unless you listen! Please, Tess! Just stay for a few more minutes. Please! Or I swear I'll give birth right now to stop you leaving!"

Tess was on the brink of refusing point blank when the lights swirled upwards and Zak Tremaine appeared at the corner of the stage.

It was too late to run anywhere now. Like it or not, and as painful as it would be, Tess had no choice but to stay and listen. She didn't think she could have walked away now if she'd tried.

CHAPTER THIRTY-EIGHT

Tess might have been tucked alongside the far edge of the stage and hidden in the shadows, but even from here she was still close enough to reach out and touch Zak and smell the scent of his skin as he came out onto the stage. The longing to be closer still was as strong as it had ever been and the intensity appalled her, rooting Tess to the spot as the most dreadful realisation washed over her.

She still loved him. In spite of everything that had happened and all the stern lectures she'd given herself, Tess was still in love with Zak Tremaine. She certainly couldn't have moved an inch, let alone walk away. Her feelings for him were far stronger than she'd even realised and Tess's poor bruised heart despaired. What could she do? Would this feeling ever go away?

Two more men followed him onto the stage. One, short and plump, was wearing a guitar and the other, who was tall and wiry, was holding a violin loosely in his hand. When they appeared, the crowd went wild.

"It's The Tinners!" somebody screeched and immediately the whole place was alive with applause and crackling with anticipation. There were whistles and screams and suddenly Tess understood what it was that Zak could do; he had the magic to make a stage appearance electrifying.

"Zak's reformed his band," Kat said to Tess. "Please stay."

Tess nodded. She understood how hard this must have been for Zak. This must mean something significant, but she wasn't certain what.

Zak was still in his morning suit with his golden hair swept back from his face and his guitar held loosely in his right hand. The man who had played to stadiums looked terrified. He stepped up to the microphone and cleared his throat.

"Some of you here will know that I write music," he began, and there was a buzz of amusement at this since everyone in Polwenna Bay knew Zak was a big talent.

Zak picked up the guitar and strummed a chord. Notes shivered in the air.

"What you might not know is that lately I haven't been able to write or play a note," he continued. "If you read the papers, or...," Zak looked straight across the dance floor towards Kathy Polmartin, "use the village shop, you'll know why that is."

There was a burst of laughter. Tess imagined quite a few people had been the focus of gossip in Keyhole Kathy's shop.

But Zak wasn't smiling. He was serious and his beautiful eyes were midnight black with sincerity. He ran his free hand through his hair and sighed.

"So when my grandmother asked me to write her a special wedding day song, you can probably imagine how terrified I was. I was terrified of letting her down, terrified of not being able to write; basically, I was just terrified of the whole idea. I never wanted to write again and I certainly never wanted to find myself back on the stage. I'd decided that part of my life was over. I was finished with music. I thought I was finished with everything."

He looked across the stage and Tess realised he'd seen her standing in the shadows. When they locked eyes, she knew there was no way she could leave. She had to see this performance because no matter what Zak had done or how much he'd hurt her, she knew better than anyone else just how hard it was for him to stand on a stage once again and attempt to play. Tess's entire being was willing him on.

She could scarcely breathe.

"I tried to write a song," he said. "God knows I tried. I sat on the cliffs for hours and hours watching the waves and trying to capture the swell of emotion, and I walked for miles to outpace the restlessness in my mind and it didn't work. I thought I would never write again. I thought music was my past. I was finished. Washed up. Over."

A rapid pulse beat in Zak's neck, fragile as the flutter of a butterfly's wings and, despite being hurt by him and broken by what he'd done, Tess longed to press her lips against it, hold him close and tell him not to be afraid. Zak's gift, like hers, had never left. It had simply been waiting to be invited back into his life.

"Then someone came into my life and she turned it upside down. Suddenly the music was a torrent, a flood, a spring tide of harmonies and words that wouldn't stop," he continued. "I was writing and playing again and it was all because of her."

There was a collective sigh at this, but Zak shook his head.

"No, like an idiot I messed that up too, but no matter what the future holds, and if I never write or play again after tonight, I need her to know that this song couldn't have been written without her and that she is everything. She showed me the path home."

Tess could hardly breathe. Did Zak mean it? Did she want him to mean it? Could she trust a single word he said?

Zak cradled his guitar like a precious child. His hand strayed to the strings and a soft chord rippled in the air.

"Ollie and Ned know how much this song means to me," Zak said, turning and smiling nervously at the two musicians who were standing just slightly behind. "And they've been kind enough to join me tonight for a one-off Tinners reunion. They're the only people I trust with a song of the heart and the only people in the world who can do it justice."

There were more cheers at this, while Ned and Ollie beamed and waved at the crowd. Zak, though, was still looking nervous.

"Ladies and Gentleman, on Alice and Jonny's wedding day, I give you

Lifetime Love, the song for the woman I love."

As the lights swooped down, the tall man began to play his violin, teasing out a plaintive melody so bittersweet and beautiful that Tess's throat tightened. Her musician's ear recognised that perfect blend of notes in a shiver-inducing minor key that tugged the heart strings and wrenched aching strands of longing from the very depths of your soul. Then Zak and the shorter man started to play their guitars, the instruments harmonising so perfectly that it was impossible to say where each one began and ended. The hairs were already stirring on Tess's forearms, but when Zak began to sing she knew beyond all doubt that this song was something really special.

The lyrics were haunting and told a story of a love that was lost and never forgotten. It spoke of years gone by and the racing of the heart at a glimpse of a face in a crowded street or curve of a cheek which sent memories spooling and hope rising, only to be dashed on the rocks of mistaken identity. Faded photographs, once-treasured love letters, a lock of hair, fleeting dreams and first kisses, and promises from a long-forgotten friend. Memories that are always slightly out of reach and the heartbreaking knowledge of something precious that has been squandered.

"My midsummer faded to autumn
Leaves drifting like days
Slipping into the winter
And time just a haze,
I found her again
More beautiful than before
If the boy loved her once
The man loved her more…"

As Zak sang the chorus, there was a catch in his voice which made the song even more poignant. Tess had to look away because he was singing to her about loss and forgiveness and those wasted chances that might never come again. The message couldn't be clearer. Just as Alice had forgiven Jonny and fallen in love with him again after a lifetime had passed, so the narrator of the song searched for the woman he had wronged and lost and whom he had never forgotten.

Alice and Jonny, sitting at the front of the stage and holding hands, exchanged tender looks and Jonny raised Alice's hands to his lips so lovingly that it almost broke Tess. They had their second chance and they were blessed by it, but she wondered how many people spent their lives running away from love because they were afraid of being hurt and only knew bitterness? If Alice had never forgiven Jonny for the mistakes he'd made as a young man, an entire lifetime ago, then this wonderful day would never have happened and two people who were clearly so happy together would have missed the chance of happiness.

If Zak had written this song as a message to her, then it was working...

261

Unable to hide her feelings, Tess bit her lip and looked down at the tips of her pink satin ballet slippers. Then she studied the green embroidery on her pink prom dress for a moment or two until she felt ready to look up again. When she did, Tess saw she was not alone in feeling moved. Ashley and Mo were wrapped in each other's arms, Danny and Jules were holding hands and even the notoriously tough Ella was wiping her eyes. As Zak sang the bridge and returned to the chorus, Jake led Summer onto the dance floor where they held each other close and swayed to the music, lost in the melody and each other. Before long, they were joined by more couples and even the bride and groom took to the floor.

When the last note trembled in the air before fading away with the last glimmer of daylight, there was an awed hush. Then the gathered guests broke into rapturous applause.

"Now do you see why you had to stay?" Kat said gently to Tess. "I've heard that song over and over again for days and it's told me all I need to know. Whatever he did or didn't do, Tess, Zak truly loves you."

Tess could barely register her friend's words. Her pulse was racing, her thoughts were whirling and she had never felt so confused. Not even when she'd seen Vassilly with Marina.

"I have to talk to you, Tess. Please."

Zak was at her side and taking her hand to pull her through the crowds and away to the edge of the garden.

Tess didn't resist.

The night was velvet and the sky picked out with silver stars. They stood in silence, not far from the party, yet feeling as though they were the only two people in the whole world. Zak took Tess's hands in his, his forefinger tracing her palm and drawing out ripples of longing from deep down inside her. All her hard-made resolutions were turned on their head.

"Thank you, Tess," he said.

She looked up at him, thrown. "For what?"

"For helping me find music again. For teaching me what it really is to feel."

Tess shook her head. She couldn't take the credit for this.

"No, you did all that yourself, Zak. Your song tonight was just perfect. You're an incredibly talented man and you would have always found your way back to music. I'm happy for you, I truly am. Nobody should have to live without music. Not when they love it as much as you do."

"I can live without music," Zak said. He reached out and traced the curve of her cheek, "but I can't live without you, Tess. I wrote that song for you and it's the best I've ever written. It's a once in a lifetime song, like you are my once in a lifetime person."

Tess stepped back and broke the contact. She had to if she was to think clearly. When Zak Tremaine was this close to her, it was impossible to hold onto rational thought.

"Zak, I—"

"You don't have to say anything," he said quickly. "I don't expect you to say or feel anything in return. Christ knows I don't deserve it after the way I've behaved in the past." He reached into the inside of his jacket to pull out a thick brown envelope. "Here. This is for you."

"What's this?" Tess asked.

"It's not a begging letter if that's what you're worried about. I know I've blown it with you and I don't blame you for hating me."

"I don't hate you," Tess said quietly. "Of course I don't."

He shrugged his broad shoulders. "Well, you should. I'm an idiot and I've been an idiot most of my life. In the past, I've mistaken sex for a game, I've hurt people, I've let myself be involved in stupid pub behaviour, I've let friends down and a million other awful things too. I'd be here all night if I listed the lot. I'm no better than Vassilly. In fact, I'm worse because I know what he did but, unlike him, I really do love you."

"Zak, I—"

"No, please, Tess! Let me finish. What I'm trying to say, and saying really badly, is that I'm not proud of myself. I've blown everything that's good in my life at some time or another and I know I don't deserve your forgiveness. I just want you to know that I'm sorrier than I can ever say for hurting you. I wouldn't have had that happen for the world. You are everything to me. I would do anything to turn back time and take away that stupid night in the pub."

"Please, you don't need to say any more," Tess pleaded. It was too painful to go over old ground. "You don't need to explain."

"I bloody well do," Zak said angrily. "It was a stupid conversation and I have never been so ashamed of myself."

Tess had no fight left. "I'm not totally naïve, Zak. I know how men talk in pubs and, for what it's worth, I do believe it wasn't you who made the comments."

It was the best she could offer when it still hurt so much.

"That doesn't matter. I should have stopped them talking and I should have been man enough to walk away. I'm not proud of who I was that night and, as crap as it probably sounds, I was a different person. I never knew what it was to want someone else's happiness more than your own or to care about another person more than yourself. I never knew what it meant to think about someone else from the moment you wake up to the moment you close your eyes. I never knew what it was to love someone the way I love you."

Tess was lost for words. This was how he felt? Truly?

Zak pressed the envelope into her hands.

"I don't expect you to forgive me. I just need you to know that I am so grateful I met you. You've changed everything. You helped to heal the hurt I carried after Kellee died. The police might have told me I wasn't to blame and so might my family, but only you understood what it had done to me. You listened to me and you didn't judge me when I couldn't play. You're the best friend I ever had. Tess, before you I never knew what it was to love someone so much that you would do anything to make them happy, even if that meant breaking your own heart and walking away."

His eyes closed for a moment as he struggled to keep his composure. When he looked at her again they were dark with sadness, a sadness that Tess longed to take away. Yet how could she? How could she ever trust again?

"I'll walk away if that's what you want," Zak told her quietly. "I promise that I won't hassle you or make you uncomfortable. I'll step right away and hope that one day, maybe in many years to come, you'll forgive me and we can be friends again. I truly hope so because to come so close and lose everything, including your friendship, is the one thing I don't think I can bear."

Tess nodded. His friendship was something she really missed. Chatting to Zak and laughing with him was just as wonderful as their intense physical attraction.

"What's in here?" She held up the envelope.

"Open it and see when you're alone," Zak said. "It's yours to do what you want with and it's the only copy. Burn it or keep it, Tess. It's entirely up to you."

Then he walked away from her. His back was straight, but the slight tremor in his shoulders gave away the strength of emotion he held in check. Once the darkness swallowed him up, Tess was alone once again and with her head spinning.

Zak loved her and Tess knew she loved him. If she was honest, she knew she loved him from the moment they had first met up in the café and realised they had so much in common. Maybe even before when she'd seen him at Mariners and had to fight an attraction that had both elated and appalled her. Love had never been in question.

But how could she ever trust Zak again? Was he different from Vass? It was true that men like Zak could wrestle their creative demons into submission and produce wonderful music, but keeping your word or not letting someone down? These seemed far more difficult accomplishments to achieve.

Tess opened the envelope with shaking hands, gasping when she realised what Zak had given her. Rather than the letter she was expecting, a score lay within, reams of sheet music covered with notes and instructions and scribbled words, frantically penned as though they couldn't be written fast enough.

Lifetime Love

for Tess Hamilton

Tess was holding the only copy of Zak's incredible song. In her hands was the very music he had just played, the music that was undoubtedly the best thing he had ever composed and which had moved so many people to tears. It was powerful and poignant and it was in her hands both literally and metaphorically.

"It's yours to do what you want with and it's the only copy. Burn it or keep it, Tess. It's entirely up to you," Zak had said.

The responsibility was huge. Of course, a part of her, the part that was hurt and angry was tempted to hurl it into Perry's lake as a symbolic gesture, retaliation for how he'd hurled her feelings back at her. But what would this achieve? It was petty and cruel and, as she started to read the lyrics, absolutely the wrong thing to do because this song was beautiful and the words broke her heart all over again.

It was a composition about the seasons of a life: the journey from boy to man and from youth to old age. It was a reflection on mistakes and choices made, roads travelled and journeys taken, and the final arrival at the quiet harbour of old age where there was no more time left to put things right and make changes. Life was set and all that remained was to make peace with it. As the notes danced inside her mind, Tess read the music by sight and heard the melody once more, and this time the tears fell fast because it was truly the most beautiful thing she had ever read.

It was a love letter from the future. It was Zak telling Tess that if she could forgive him, he would spend the rest of his life loving her. The choice was hers to make; she could tear it up and walk away or, as in the song, turn back and start again with new eyes and a heart ready to love.

Zak loved her and he wanted to spend the rest of his life with her. The question wasn't whether or not she loved him – falling in love was the easy part – but whether or not she was brave enough to risk her heart and be with him.

A life without Zak felt like a life half lived. Just a week without him had been bleaker than any wasteland. If Tess had thought it had hurt when Vass left her, she knew now that the pain then was as nothing, a small scratch in comparison to the agony of severing an artery. In reality, he had been little more than a crush that had grown out of proportion inside the hothouse of secrecy.

But Zak?

What Tess felt for him was love. It was real and it hurt and it was the most wonderful, painful, powerful thing she had ever known. Yes, that was love and it terrified her.

Could she forgive Zak? Dare she forgive Zak? Was she brave enough to take a chance and see where this could lead?

Tess turned and retraced the path they had taken not so long ago. The score was clutched in her hand, but she didn't need to look at it to hear the music or read the lyrics; these were etched into her heart. Music was how Zak expressed himself and the song told her everything she needed to know about his feelings. The bigger question was what she was going to say to him. Could she ever get over her hurt?

The party was winding down. The guests had thinned out and the distant chugging of the quad suggested that the Pollards were starting to take people home. Tess looked around for Zak, but there was no sign of him with his family and he wasn't with the usual suspects at the bar.

"Are you all right, love?" Alice Tremaine said when, on her third circuit, Tess passed her seat. "Sit down for a moment. You've hardly stopped all day."

As fond of Alice as she was, Tess didn't want to waste a moment.

"I'm fine, thanks," she said. "I've just got a few things to sort out."

"If one of those is talking to my grandson, I saw him heading towards the orangery," Alice told her. "Zak's become very fond of gardening and seemed in a dreadful hurry to check the plants. Plants are good listeners, I find, and they never breathe a word. They never judge either. Maybe they see people make enough mistakes to know it's part of the human condition?"

The older woman's eyes met Tess's and there was sympathy in their faded blue depths.

"May I give you a word of advice on my wedding day?" Alice St Milton said gently. "And not as Zak's grandmother either, but simply as one woman to another? And one with a little hindsight, rather like in Zak's song?"

How could Tess refuse? "Of course."

Alice's gaze drifted towards the manor house, softly lit now with warm yellow light the exact hue of Cornish butter, and where Jonny was deep in conversation with Ella.

"With my eyesight, he still looks eighteen. That's the age he was when his mother told him I wasn't good enough to marry a St Milton. Of course, those were different times and we all respected our parents and generally did as we were told, but even so, I was so angry with him for caving in. Even years afterwards, and once my wonderful husband was long gone, I still refused to talk to him. I held a grudge and I wasn't letting it go."

"It was fair enough you were upset," said Tess. Zak had told her Alice's story and Tess didn't blame Alice at all for being mad at Jonny.

"Yes, love, when I was a teenager perhaps, but not after nearly fifty years! I was in my late sixties when Henry died and when I think about all the years between then and now that I wasted being cross with Jonny for a stupid mistake he made when he was young..." Alice's voice tailed off and she simply spread her hands in a gesture of hopelessness. "As you know, I forgave him in the end, but those missed years hurt so much and time is so precious. Shall I tell you what we regret most in life when we're old, Tess? It's not the mistakes we made, but rather the chances we didn't take and the things we didn't do. Taking risks and trusting people is hard, but believe me, holding back because you're afraid can be far more painful."

It was as though Alice could see all Tess's deepest fears.

Alice took Tess's hand. "Zak's a good man, my love. He feels things deeply and I always knew when he gave his heart it would be forever. I only hope you can find it in yours to forgive him. After all, who hasn't made mistakes or choices they regret?"

Tess was afraid that if she didn't act soon, she'd be making a mistake herself.

She leaned across and kissed Alice's soft powdered cheek.

"Thank you, Alice," she said. "I think it's time I went and looked at the plants myself. Who knows what they might have to say?"

The orangery was a rather smart name for the dilapidated glasshouse at the rear of the Manor. At one time, it would have been filled with exotic fruits grown as status symbols for the family to show off at banquets and balls, but now some of the big panes of glass were patched up with electrical tape and it was home to Perry's organic tomatoes and cucumber. Tess let herself in and as her eyes grew accustomed to the dark, she saw that Zak was slumped against a bench and looking more dejected than she'd ever seen him. Hearing her approach, he spun around and his eyes widened when he saw her.

"Tess? What are you doing here?"

In answer, she held up the score. "You said this was mine? To do what I wanted with?"

"Yes. Yes, it is."

"Good." She stepped forward and pressed it into his hands. "I want you to have it back because I don't want the score, Zak Tremaine."

"You don't?"

"No," said Tess. "I want the real thing."

She put her hands on his shoulders and moved closer, feeling the heat of his body through her cotton dress and her senses reeling with the delicious tang of his skin. She heard a sharp intake of breath as she pressed her lips against his.

"I want you to show me what that song was about, Zak. I want you to show me what that young man would have done if things had been different."

"If the woman he loved forgave him for being an idiot?" he said quietly.

"Yes," Tess whispered. "And if he forgave her for not listening to his side of the story and for letting her own fears get in the way."

"Then he would do this," Zak whispered as his mouth brushed hers, in a kiss so soft and so right, that it made her melt.

"And then what?" Tess asked.

"And then he would say that he loved her and that if she would only give him a second chance he would never, ever let her down again."

"And he'd really mean that?"

"Oh yes," whispered Zak. "He would mean it with everything he was and he would mean it for the rest of his life. He would know he was the luckiest man in the world to love a woman like her."

Tess adored hearing these words. They filled her heart and soul with a warmth she had never imagined possible, but even if Zak hadn't said them out loud, Tess would know what he felt just by looking into his eyes. When he pulled her closer, Tess's eyes filled with tears because being back in Zak's arms felt so right. It felt just like reaching the final bar of the most beautiful and intricate symphony.

"And she would be the luckiest girl," she told him.

Then Tess returned Zak's kiss, and this kiss told her beyond all doubt that he meant every word. There was nothing to fear; with Zak Tremaine, Tess was in perfect harmony. Her heart would sing as the music soared in endless and beautiful melodies, and just like the endless rhythm of the tide as it met the shore, they were perfectly matched and meant to be together. Being in Zak's arms felt safe and right and there was no place Tess would rather be. She knew she would be there forever and that just as in his song, the tides would turn, the seasons change and years whirl by, and she would never take him for granted but would make the most of every moment, every kiss and every touch.

Hand in hand, they walked through the garden and back to the wedding celebrations. Alice's bouquet had just been caught by a delighted Summer and the happy couple were saying their farewells. As they waved Alice and Jonny goodbye, blowing kisses and wishing them luck, Tess felt Zak's arms close around her and knew she was lucky and blessed beyond anything she had ever imagined.

"Shall we go home?" she asked him once Alice and Jonny's car had slipped away into the night. "Only somebody's written me an amazing song and I can't wait to play it on my violin. In fact, I know I'll be playing that music for a very long time."

And Zak's reply was to kiss her tenderly and Tess knew the years of being afraid and guarding her heart were over. The tide had turned, a new rhythm was beginning and the beautiful music of their life-long symphony was ready to be composed.

The End

SIGN UP FOR RUTH'S NEWSLETTER TO FIND OUT ABOUT FUTURE BOOKS AS SOON AS THEY'RE RELEASED!

I really hope you have enjoyed reading The Rhythm of the Tide. If you did I would really appreciate a review on Amazon and Goodreads. It makes all the difference for a writer.

YOU MIGHT ALSO ENJOY MY OTHER BOOKS:

Runaway Summer: Polwenna Bay 1
A Time for Living: Polwenna Bay 2
Winter Wishes: Polwenna Bay 3
Treasure of the Heart: Polwenna Bay 4

Recipe for Love: Polwenna Bay 5

Magic in the Mist: Polwenna Bay novella
Cornwall for Christmas: Polwenna Bay novella

Christmas on the Creek
The Letter
Rock My World
The Season for Second Chances
The Island Legacy
Escape for the Summer
Escape for Christmas
Hobb's Cottage
Weight Till Christmas

The Wedding Countdown
Dead Romantic

Katy Carter Wants a Hero
Katy Carter Keeps a Secret
Ellie Andrews Has Second Thoughts
Amber Scott is Starting Over

Writing as Jessica Fox
The One That Got Away
Eastern Promise
Hard to Get
Unlucky in Love
Always the Bride
Writing as Holly Cavendish
Looking for Fireworks
Writing as Georgie Carter
The Perfect Christmas

ABOUT THE AUTHOR

Ruth Saberton is the bestselling author of *Katy Carter Wants a Hero* and *Escape for the Summer*. She also writes upmarket commercial fiction under the pen names Jessica Fox, Georgie Carter and Holly Cavendish.

Born in London, Ruth now lives in beautiful Cornwall. She has travelled to many places, including living in the Caribbean, but nothing compares to the rugged beauty of the Cornish coast. Ruth loves to chat with readers so please visit her Facebook Author page and follow her on Twitter.

Twitter: @ruthsaberton

Facebook: Ruth Saberton Author

www.ruthsaberton.com

Printed in Great Britain
by Amazon

29017450R10158